It's Not a Cult

It's Not a Cult

◆ *A NOVEL* ◆

LAUREN DANHOF

alcove
press

Copyright © 2023 by Lauren Danhof

Published in the United States by Alcove Press, an imprint of The Quick Brown Fox & Company LLC.

Alcove Press and its logo are trademarks of The Quick Brown Fox & Company LLC.

Library of Congress Catalog-in-Publication data available upon request.

ISBN (trade paperback): 978-1-63910-438-3
ISBN (ebook): 978-1-63910-439-0

Cover design by Philip Pascuzzo

Printed in the United States.

www.alcovepress.com

Alcove Press
34 West 27th St., 10th Floor
New York, NY 10001

First Edition: August 2023

10 9 8 7 6 5 4 3 2 1

To my girls—Zoe and Wren—you inspire me and, honestly, scare me a little. Keep it up! (Also, you're not allowed to read this book until you're eighteen because mommy used some grown-up language and adult situations. Love you!)

In the ninth grade, I told myself I would dedicate my first book to my English teacher, Mrs. Pamela Banner. Mrs. Banner, thank you for instilling a love of literature in me and all your students!

◆ 1 ◆

PROFESSIONAL AND LAW-ABIDING

THIS WASN'T GOING TO go well.

I knew it. He knew it. The frowning lady with her arms crossed, glaring down at me from the anti-sexual-harassment-in-the-workplace poster, knew it.

"I'm sorry I'm late! Thank you for still seeing me!" I plunked down in the office chair, the plastic boning of my medieval corset digging into my armpits. Droplets of water fell from the ends of my hair onto my résumé. The smeared ink complemented the mustard stain nicely.

The man across the desk from me looked at my disheveled appearance with concern. "Are you okay, Ms. Glass?"

"Oh! Yeah, I—I'm sorry. My shift at Maypole ran late, and I didn't have time to change. I'm the wench."

"The wench?"

"Uh, yeah, I work the Drench-the-Wench booth at the Renaissance fair." I pulled the laces loose at the bottom of the corset so I could breathe. "So, like, people pay money to try and dunk me, but I get to shout insults at people all day, so it's okay, I guess." I glanced down and realized my massive skirt was leaving a dark ring of damp carpet around my chair. "It's just a temporary thing. I started a couple months back. You know, after I left my MA program there was, like, nothing. The job market isn't great, as I'm sure you already know—or maybe you don't, seeing as you have a job—but I'm this close to selling a kidney on the black market."

He let out a small laugh, but I couldn't tell if it was genuine or uncomfortable. He cleared his throat and reached for my résumé, pausing for a moment as he held it by the corner, trying to decide where to lay the damp document down on his desk.

"You, uh, have a master's degree in English?" he asked.

"Well, technically no. I was studying early medieval literature and did three semesters, but dropped—postponed completion for an undetermined amount of time." I leaned back a little, trying to slow my breathing from the frantic run through the parking garage, up two flights of stairs, and down a never-ending hallway to this guy's office. What was his name again? Mr. Wilson? Mr. Wheelhouse? "I kind of realized not many people are looking for someone to quote *Beowulf* nine to five." I laughed at my own quip, but Mr. Whatever was still distracted by my soggy résumé. Finally, he laid it on top of a menu from a Thai place, then steepled his hands and stared at me.

"You applied for the position of Internal Integration and Implementation Architect Assistant II. What skills do you have that would make you a good fit for this job?"

I reached for the bottle of water in my bag while I quickly glanced around the office for some clue as to what this company actually did. I had applied to so many jobs, at this point they were all starting to run together. The office was bare besides a floor plan stapled to the wall with all the emergency exits marked. The fluorescent light flickered and hummed. I took a sip of water while breathing in and immediately choked.

"Are you okay?"

"I'm—I'm fine!" I sputtered, dropping the half-empty bottle, spilling the remaining water straight onto my lap. "Shit!" I winced. "Sorry." His expression remained confused. Gah, what *was* this dude's name?

"Sorry about that . . . yes, so . . . specific skills. Yeah, I am very confident that as far as implementing and integrating, I would be a great asset, and as far as the internal assisting and architecting, I'm your girl . . . although, I don't know about the II part—is that like the sequel? Internal Integration and Implementation Architect Assistant II: The Revenge of the Copy Machine."

Seriously? Nothing? Stop making jokes, Glinda.

"The 'II' refers to the level of experience of the employee. A level II requires at least seven years' experience working within a related field," he said without batting an eye. "How many years' experience did you say you had in integrated systems?"

"Technically . . . zero." I bit my lower lip and glanced down.

"Ms. Glass, why do you think you would make a good fit in this position?" These corporate types were so good at signaling disapproval with only the slightest facial movement—a raised eyebrow, a slight crease around the corners of the eyes. It was really quite fascinating, watching him silently judge me.

"To be honest, Mr.—er—sir, I know I can communicate, despite the contrary evidence at this particular interview. I can talk and I can write, and I can do both things pretty damn well. I'm smart and I'm passionate and I want to learn. So, I enter this big, bright world full of possibilities, but I don't find a job listing that says, *"Smart, passionate communicator, apply here."* I find an endless list of tedious-sounding positions so vague in their description that I'm not sure I'm reading about a job or the ingredients list on a bottle of shampoo. So, I guess what I'm trying to say is . . . I probably should shut up now."

Mr. W glanced up at the evacuation poster and then turned to me. "I can appreciate your honesty."

Really? Maybe I could salvage this.

"Tell me, Ms. Glass, what would you describe as your greatest weakness?"

I should have been ready for it. It's a standard interview question. And maybe the lack of preparation for the question truly revealed my apathy toward this generic office job and my own propensity for self-sabotage. But in that moment, teeth chattering from the AC vent blowing directly onto my wet hair and clothes, the equally standard answers, strengths disguised as weaknesses—*"too honest," "works too hard,"* all of that—fell through the cracks in my brain.

"My greatest weakness? Can a person's entire personality be their greatest weakness?" I sighed and leaned back. "My mom would probably say that my greatest weakness is my sarcasm—or, no, wait, my skepticism. But she's in a cult, so I don't think her opinion on that counts."

His eyes widened. "A cult?"

Crap. I hadn't meant to bring that up.

But I could get out of this, just had to think on my feet, stop talking about the goddamn cult—

"Yeah, my mom's in a cult." *Stop talking.* "It's a whole thing. Robes, chants, magic visions." *Enough, he gets it.* "Their leader says that aliens or some shit visited him, and now he knows the secret to eternal happiness and peace."

A wave of uncomfortable silence swept the room. Mr. W shifted in his chair and pretended to study my résumé again. Finally, he cleared his throat and stood. I jumped to my feet, nearly knocking the chair back.

"Ms. Glass, I want you to know that I appreciate your coming to interview. But you know, we have a lot of interviews to do, so . . ." He shook his head and then rummaged through his desk drawer for a moment, eventually pulling out a business card. "If you . . . well, if you need to talk to someone, this is my psychiatrist. She's really good."

★　★　★

Out in the hallway, I leaned against the wall for a minute, trying to compose myself. It was still and quiet, apart from the murmur of voices and clicks from keyboards behind the cubicle walls. A woman in a freshly pressed suit strolled by and did a double take at my damp, disheveled, anachronistic appearance.

"I think I nailed it." I laughed louder than I had intended. The woman nodded her head quickly and hurried away.

This wasn't the first time I'd let my brain vomit all over someone I'd just met, though it was the first time I'd done it during a formal job interview. It was all the pent-up angst and neurosis that had been collecting over the last year. Poor Mr. Wombat—or whatever his name was—just happened to be the unlucky one that unplugged it.

I cringed, wishing I could sink into the floor and disappear.

Dorothy wouldn't have botched the interview. She was the better twin, always had been. She'd never admit that, of course. When I was thirteen, I told my parents they'd named the wrong kid Glinda, because Dorothy's middle name might as well have been "the good." She was prettier, smarter, and far less abrasive. She'd have sat there, perfect and pristine, and would probably have been hired on the spot.

What would Dorothy have said was my greatest weakness? I shuddered to think. My ego? My selfishness? My inability to trust anyone? Well, what did she know, anyway?

I checked my phone. Twelve missed calls and one unread text. It said: *Can you stop and get butter? Sincerely, Mom!*

I waited until I was walking through the parking garage before calling her back. "Hey, Mom, you called twelve times?"

"Oh, sorry—I needed butter for the cookies I'm baking, but since you didn't answer, I sent West to get some."

"I didn't answer because I was in an interview."

"Yes, I sent you a text when you didn't pick up your phone."

"Right . . . but if you'd texted me to begin with . . . never mind." I got in my car and let my head fall to the steering wheel as the car's stereo picked up the call, blasting my mom's voice around me in surround sound.

"You know I prefer calling to texting," she said.

"Yes, Mom. But the thing is, I'm not going to answer a call during an interview. Also, we've talked about this—you don't have to sign your name to every text. I know it's from you. The phone tells me it's from you."

"I just don't want any miscommunication."

"So . . ." I rolled my eyes. "Are you even going to ask how the interview went?"

There was a brief moment of silence before she sighed, causing a horrible rushing sound in my speakers. "I still don't understand why you need to go out and get tangled up in the corrupt web of the working world, my radiant sunbeam. Your inner light is just waiting to come forth, to experience a simpler life."

I slowly backed out of the space, silently mouthing all the terrible, ungrateful, unforgivable things I wanted to say to my

mother at that moment. It was one of my many unhealthy strate-
gies for dealing with her over the last year.

I gritted my teeth and took a breath. "Well, my inner light
would like to make loan payments and eventually move out of
her mother's house, no offense."

"My darling, Light and Wisdom, this is your home." She'd
started this new thing where she replaced my name with positive
attributes in some attempt to influence my subconscious, but it
was starting to really piss off my outer conscious. She paused a
beat and then spoke with a tone of obligation. "How was the
interview?"

"It went great." I rolled my eyes again and pulled out onto
the street.

"I'm sensing sarcasm. Sarcasm is a defense."

Yep, my favorite defense. I turned onto the access road.

"Well, you don't have to worry, Mom. I'm not getting the
job."

"Glinda, you sound disappointed." For a moment she seemed
concerned, surprised even.

I threw my hands in the air and mouthed a "what the hell?"
before forcing a smile and hoping my tone matched.

"I am, Mom. This job paid pretty well, and I haven't been
getting a lot of calls for interviews."

"I know, dear, but you're my little bird, and I just don't want
to see your wings clipped by something that won't bring you
self-satisfaction. You've just got to spread your wings and see all
those other fish in the sea."

Her metaphors made about as much sense as her recent life
choices. And now I was imagining a bird of prey swooping down
to impale a poor, innocent fish on its talons. Lots of blood.

"Look, I'm pretty exhausted right now. Can we talk about it
later?"

"What is 'later,' Glinda? 'Later' is a phantom."

"No, later is just not right now." I sighed. Getting off the
phone with my mom was like negotiating a hostage situation.

"Glinda, the present is all there is. The past is an illusion."

"I thought we were talking about the future, Mom?"

"We are. Your inner light is traveling backward from the future to the past. You have to learn to meet it at that moment of intersection with your consciousness and then harness it to guide you back up toward the future."

"Hey, Mom, I think . . . I think I'm getting another call," I lied.

"Oh! Maybe they're calling you to tell you that you got the job!"

"Maybe so—gotta go!"

"Glinda, I love—" I hit the hang-up button before she finished. Not intentionally.

I found myself alone, at a traffic standstill on a five-lane highway in the middle of rush hour. There was this tiny, annoying, gnawing feeling just on the edge of my mind that told me to call her back, to tell her what had happened, to ask how she was doing. But I was tired, and I was over hearing about my inner light.

I put my AC on full blast, untied the top of my chemise, and took a long sip from the massive Big Gulp soda I'd let melt in the car during my interview. It tasted like lukewarm tears and corn syrup.

I didn't want that job anyway, I told myself. I'd spent my life dreaming of traveling, writing, reading, basically existing in some kind of *Eat, Pray, Love* state of perpetual self-discovery, financed by a ceaseless (and unexplained) cash flow. Instead, I was broke and aimless, watching my friends from school get married, have kids, get promoted. I mean, I watched them from the comfort of my phone on social media. I hadn't talked to anybody from school in months.

And now I had to pee. Traffic was at a dead stop, and I was a quarter mile from the next exit. I took a long draw from the straw of my tepid soda and then shook my head. *Stop it, you idiot!*

I turned on my stereo. "Don't Go Chasing Waterfalls" came blasting out. Hell no. I tapped another app on my phone and settled into a true crime podcast.

Miranda was last seen leaving her boyfriend's house around 2 AM Sunday night.

"The boyfriend did it," I said aloud.

Once she left, he says he tried calling her several times, but she never picked up—

"Because he murdered her."

A lot of people described Miranda as stubborn and overconfident of her own abilities. That might be why she decided she should cut through the woods that fateful night.

"Okay, so we're blaming the victim?" I shut the stereo off and tapped the wheel impatiently. In what felt like thirty years, I had crept forward five inches.

It was bad enough I was still in my Renaissance costume, which was finally somewhat dry—I wasn't about to pee on myself. I flipped on my hazards and started blasting my horn like a crazy person. The sedan to the right of me stopped in confusion and I slid into the shoulder and pressed on the gas, much to the shock and anger of all the law-abiding citizens I left in my dust.

I made it to the exit ramp and then swerved into a gas station, parking diagonally across two disabled parking spaces. I know, I know . . . but if I held it one more minute, I was going to develop a kidney infection, end up on a transplant list, and probably qualify for a disability tag anyway.

I ran into the store and immediately knocked right into a display of sunglasses. The thin wire rack spilled its contents onto the floor.

"Shit! Sorry!" I called out, jumping over the scattered assortment of glasses toward the bathroom. The guy behind the counter raised his head in confusion. "Bathroom emergency!"

The women's restroom was in use. I stood there, dancing like a five-year-old and looking around desperately for a solution. The door to the men's room was wide open and empty as could be. I closed my eyes, steadied myself, and stepped in.

As I sat on a toilet that appeared to have been last cleaned sometime in the '90s, I stared up at the fluorescent light and counted the corpses of flies who had died trapped in the dirty plastic cover. Fourteen. *How do those little guys even get in there in the first place?*

My phone dinged and I saw I had a text from Dorothy. This was highly unusual because, well, Dorothy didn't text me . . .

or call me . . . or pretty much have anything to do with me anymore.

Her text said: *We need to talk.*

I shook my head and typed back: *Can I call you when I get home? Probably 30 minutes.*

I waited for what seemed like an eternity, but she didn't reply. I realized I'd spaced out when the knob started jiggling.

"Yeah, yeah!" I shouted.

Finally, a message lit up my screen.

Dorothy: *I will call you in one hour.*

I chewed my thumbnail. She wouldn't be texting me out of the blue just to chat, to tell me how she'd found a good sale on art supplies or how the guy at the library looked just like Santa Claus. We weren't like that anymore. Not since the thing.

I pulled my skirt back up, readjusted my corset, and opened the door to the StopNGo cashier in his stupid red vest, with his hands on his hips.

"Did you just use the men's room?"

"It was an emergency. Also, gender is a construct."

His eyes narrowed.

"All yours." I stepped past him and hurried out of the corridor.

I stopped in the middle of the store, rummaging through my purse for a bottle of hand sanitizer. What could Dorothy possibly have to say to me after not speaking to me for a year and a half?

I was still lost in my thoughts when I perceived a man stepping in front of me, blocking my exit to the parking lot.

I looked up and there was that same annoying cashier. I glanced at his name tag.

"Hey, *Robert.* There's a sign in the restroom that says to see an attendant if the bathroom needs cleaning." I made a grand, sweeping gesture back toward the restrooms and started to step forward, but Robert wasn't moving.

"You knocked down my display."

I tightened the grip on my purse and held my nose a little higher. "I do apologize. However, to be fair, it was an ill-placed display, right there in the doorway for people to trip over."

He glanced behind him at the door and then back at me. "And is that your car taking up two disabled spaces?"

"Yes, and I feel badly about that, so if you'll kindly step aside, I will move my car."

"Bathroom's for paying customers," he said, folding his arms across his chest.

"Well, this customer has had a less than stellar experience in your establishment."

He just stared at me. I didn't say another word. I stooped down and gathered up the sunglasses, stuffing them haphazardly onto the rack. One little bastard slipped back down and onto my foot. I picked it up and pushed past him to the counter. I slammed down the glasses and my phone while I dug through my purse for my wallet.

Robert came around to the register, adjusted his vest, and then smiled at me like nothing had happened. "So, you doing some kind of cosplay thing or something?" he asked, as though I'd come in here just to shoot the breeze.

"No, Robert, I traveled through time to save my long-lost Scottish lover." I feigned a look of distress. "Oh God! What year is it?!"

"That'll be three dollars and fifty cents," he said, completely ignoring my theatrics, and then proceeded to straighten a row of cellophane-wrapped pecan pralines lined up next to the register. I pulled out a credit card and tried to hand it to him. He pointed to a little index card taped to the card reader that said in red pen: "No credit charges under $5."

"Are you freaking kidding me right now?"

He raised an eyebrow and smirked.

I stood there, the veins in my head pulsing. Now, in general, I consider myself a good person. I tip waiters, I hold doors for old people, I release spiders back into the wild. But this guy was messing with the wrong woman on the wrong day. I pursed my lips, looked long and hard at Robert, and then, as my brain screamed *No, don't!*, I grabbed the glasses and my purse and ran out the door before Robert could say another word.

I slammed the car door closed and started the engine. The podcast came blasting out of my speakers:

Had Miranda double-crossed the wrong person this time? Had her past crimes finally caught up to her? There was blood, everywhere—

"Shut up!" I slammed my hand against the dial. "Shit! Shit! Shit!" I hit the gas and peeled out onto the access road. Not only was I unemployed, but now I was a criminal. I dared to glance in my rearview mirror, assuming I'd see the guy in the red vest chasing me on foot. He hadn't even come outside.

I seized my Big Gulp and took another swig of the melted Coke water.

"Dammit!" I screamed at no one and threw the Big Gulp out the window as I entered the freeway.

FORTITUDE AND POSITIVITY

I PULLED INTO THE driveway, which wound through post oaks to the house where I grew up. The tires crunched over the dried branches and dead leaves. My dad had always referred to the forty acres around the house as "the farm," no matter how many times I pointed out that we had no livestock and the barn was being used to store car parts and Christmas decorations.

When I was growing up, the house had seemed like something from a storybook, a brick house with white shutters, neat rows of bushes, and a cement bird bath standing in the center of the yard. Now the paint was peeling, the bird bath was filled with marbled glass orbs, and the whole yard was sectioned off with wooden borders into my mom's complex vegetable garden that spanned the front and back of the house. My tire swing still hung from the large elm on a frayed rope, but so did countless wind chimes, their dissonant tones grating on my nerves every time the wind blew.

The house always smelled like incense—sandalwood with a hint of eucalyptus. My mom said sandalwood calmed her chi, but truth be told, I think it was to cover up whatever scent of my father remained in the house, his spiced cologne, the worn leather smell of his office, the country fair–like aroma of the pancakes he'd make every Saturday morning. Mom was out back, collecting laundry from the clothesline. I set my purse in the dining room and looked up the stairs, debating whether or not I had it in me to interact with my little sister.

My parents had done a lot of unfortunate things in their lives, but nothing as unadvisable as getting drunk on peppermint schnapps one Christmas Eve when I was eight, and accidentally conceiving what could only be described as the very opposite of a Christmas miracle—my little sister, West. As in the Wicked Witch of the West. The musical *Wicked* had just come out, and my parents completely embraced the whole anti-hero thing.

West was seventeen and living the good life of being the baby of the family—and an only child for the last half a decade. Since moving home, I had felt this obligation to interact with her once every day or so. Maybe I thought I might rub off on her— you know, give her a little dose of normal every day to keep her grounded. Problem was, she didn't need me.

West was everything I hadn't been in high school: cool, smooth, popular. She wore her confidence every day like a thick perfume. She also wore a thick perfume. It smelled like funeral home potpourri with subtle notes of angst. Anyway, she was captain of the volleyball team, vice president of the improv club, and official eye roller of the Glass family.

When I knocked on her open door, she was draped across her bed, staring at her phone.

"How was school?"

"Gucci." She didn't even look up.

I interpreted her response as a positive and stepped over a pile of her clothes to sit on the bed next to her. Apparently, this was not "Gucci" because she rolled her eyes and hid her phone immediately.

"What's up, Sis? How was the interview?" she asked with what, I imagined, was the most interest she could feign.

"Not so great."

"Sucks."

"Yes, I suppose it does."

She sighed deeply and then actually looked at me. Her eyes widened and her mouth quivered like she was struggling to contain a laugh. "What the hell are you wearing?"

I hadn't told her or my mom the specifics of my new position. I'd told them I was the new chair of the hydrodynamics department at a nonprofit. They were so used to tuning me out when I started talking about academia that they hadn't questioned it.

West held her phone up, pointed it at me, and then lowered it, pressing buttons and apps faster than I could process.

"Did . . . did you just take my picture and send it to your friends?"

"Of course not."

Silence. I looked down at my sweet little sister, with her baby-smooth skin, her exhaustively overanalyzed wardrobe choices, and her bored expression.

"It's my Halloween costume," I attempted.

"It's July." She raised a skeptical eyebrow.

"Did you know Mom's going to another cult meeting tonight?" I asked, changing the subject.

"Yeah."

"Can you let me know next time? I could have come up with something to keep her from going for a second time this week."

"I *did* let you know." She sat up and looked right in my eyes. I shrank back a little. How could someone so young channel such power? "And this will be the *third* meeting this week. You don't pay attention when I tell you things."

"I think I would remember you telling me."

"Okay, Glinda, whatever you want to believe." She flipped her ponytail behind her shoulder and lay back down. "Don't worry about it. I've got Mom handled."

"You know that's why I moved back in, right? To keep tabs on her so you don't have to." I stood.

"Oh, okay," she said, her voice heavy with sarcasm. "All this time I thought you moved back because you cracked in grad school and couldn't find a job. But sure, you take care of Mom." She rolled her eyes and went back to her phone. "If that's the case, then you think you could concentrate on her for more than three seconds before worrying about yourself again?" She raised her eyebrows, and my cheeks grew hot. "Why don't you go pop a couple Adderalls and get back to me."

I pursed my lips. West was well aware of my Adderall dependency during grad school, though she didn't know the whole story. Those pills had quickly become my crutch for getting all my work done, teaching classes, and not completely melting down every semester. They also resulted in missed sleep, missed meals, and . . . well, more loss than it was worth.

"Never mind." I shook my head and retreated, wounded but determined not to show it.

My instincts had been correct: I shouldn't have engaged. I went to my room and changed clothes, shoving the damp costume into a ball and tossing it behind my door.

My mom was in the kitchen, pulling freshly baked oatmeal cookies out of the oven. As the smell of warm brown sugar and nutmeg hit my face, I forgot, for just a second, that I wasn't seven years old, waiting for a cookie and some milk, my mom a perfectly normal stay-at-home parent, and my dad a perfectly normal civil rights lawyer.

Not that my parents hadn't always been a little weird—they had. My mom used to walk us to school in hemp sandals and sew all our clothes. And my dad insisted we only eat vegetables from the little garden in the back because produce from the grocery store was poisoned by the government. Oh, and I'm pretty sure the herbal cigarettes they smoked every evening in the backyard were weed. Yeah, no, they were definitely weed. But all of that seemed normal because they were my parents. I accepted their eccentricities because it was all I knew.

When I looked at her now, she just seemed . . . small. Vulnerable. My mom was hunched over the open oven, and I could see the curvature of her spine through the fabric of her dress. Around her neck she had stopped wearing the little sapphire heart necklace my dad had given her on their tenth anniversary and instead was wearing the gold star pendant that every member of the Society wore. It swung back and forth as she bent down and peered into the oven. Her hands were wrinkled but steady, and I noticed her check twice that she'd laid down a trivet before she set the hot cookie sheet down on the counter.

She looked up at me and smiled. "My darling Peace and Purpose! You're home!" She rested her hand on my shoulder, staring into my eyes.

"Mom," I started, gingerly lifting a hot cookie from the pan, "I hate to say it, but I think West might be evil." The cookie was too hot and fell apart in my hand. Half of it landed on the counter. I picked it up and shoved the whole thing in my mouth. "Thee aunt paw cookehs, aw they?" I said with a full mouth.

"What?"

"These aren't pot cookies, are they?" I repeated after swallowing.

"Glinda!" My mother did her best to look shocked.

"I'm looking for a new job, Mom. Gotta be careful."

My mother knitted her brow and licked her lips. "You haven't reconsidered the position I told you about, at the center?"

"Mom! I am not going to work for your cult!"

She sighed and turned to the sink to start on the dishes. "Glinda, as I've told you numerous times, it's not a cult. The Starlight Pioneer Society is a *lifestyle community*. And Arlon said this position would be perfect for you—he said you'd do such a good job recording our meetings and writing our history. Sister Beverly's handwriting is atrocious."

"Are there benefits? Dental? Health? A two-thousand-dollar deductible, and then you get your own planet in the Vega Nebula?"

My mother spun around. Uh-oh. She was pissed.

"Glinda, I'm not going to talk to you if—" She stopped suddenly, her face drained of color.

"Mom? You okay?"

"Yeah, sorry." She rubbed her eyes and looked at me hard. "Sorry, it's just . . ."

"It's just what?"

"Oh, nothing. It's silly. Just, when I turned around, the look on your face—you looked so much like your dad that it surprised me."

"Oh." I hated it when she told me I reminded her of my dad, because it always made her look so sad. I was desperate to change the topic. "Hey, you talk to Dorothy recently?"

A shadow passed over my mom's face, and she cleared her throat. "No. Not since Mother's Day."

"Well, she texted me today and said she'd call, but she hasn't yet."

Oh, shit! Did I switch my phone off silent after the interview? Maybe she'd tried to call, and I hadn't heard it. I raced back into the dining room, where my purse was still sitting, and reached in for my phone. There was my wallet, the bottle of hand sanitizer, a loose tampon, but no phone. I dumped it out on the table. Wadded-up receipts and sticky pennies rolled across the table, but my phone was MIA.

Oh no.

I took the stairs two at time and burst into West's room, scanning the bed, the top of her dresser.

"Um, can I help you?" She lifted an eyebrow.

"My phone—did I leave my phone in here?"

"Nope," she said without removing her eyes from her own phone.

"Okay, listen, can you call it for me please?"

"Uh-huh," she muttered.

I waited. "You . . . you didn't call it did you?"

"Sure I did." She fought back the crack of a smile.

"Ugh!"

I raced back down the stairs and headed for the front door.

"Mom, can you please call my phone? I'm going to check in the car. Maybe it fell under the seat."

If Dorothy had tried to call me and I hadn't answered, that would be it. It would be six more months, at least, before I heard from her again.

Under the seat of my car, I found a rotting, half-eaten apple and a bottle of aspirin, but no phone. The backseat yielded negative results as well. Dejected, I went back into the house and laid my head and arms across the kitchen island. I reached over and took another cookie to console myself.

"I called it and I didn't hear it in the house," Mom said.

"Great." That meant I'd left it on silent and dropped it somewhere. My shitty paycheck barely covered my gas; I really could not afford a new phone right now. And I was *not* going to ask my mom to pay for one . . . again.

"It'll turn up." My mother patted the top of my head. I went to grab another cookie, but she swatted my hand away. "Glinda, if you eat any more, there won't be any left for the Starlight Pioneer Society meeting tonight."

A primeval groan overtook me as I lifted my face from the countertop and plopped onto a barstool. "You're going to the Society Hall again? That's like every night this week." I'd never actually been to the cult meeting hall, but I imagined a large square building with torches out front.

"Arlon needs me there."

"Arlon needs a lot of things, Mom, but you are not one of them."

Arlon Blight was the president of the Starlight Pioneer Society. At first, he'd seemed all right—charismatic, thoughtful. But as time had worn on, I'd developed bad taste for him, like a sugar-free cough drop.

He was traditionally handsome, this weird conglomerate of conventionally attractive features—tall, broad shoulders, the perfect amount of graying at the temples. But there was something off about him, something that I couldn't quite put my finger on. There was nothing striking about his appearance, nothing to break up the monotony of his perfectly symmetrical, smooth features. And that was part of the problem. When you first saw him, he was fairly unassuming, disarming even.

He was probably around fifty, maybe a few years younger than my mom. His voice was deep and smooth, and I could see how some might find it authoritative. He could be persuasive, obviously, but once I had seen through his tricks, his tactics, I couldn't unsee them. It was like having a magic show ruined because the magician keeps dropping the cards.

"You really make me sad when you talk about him like that," Mom said. "You know Arlon is a good friend." She placed the cookies in a large tin and finished cleaning up. "I'm dropping West off at swim practice and then picking her up afterward, so you'll be here all alone." Thank God. I could use a few moments of solitude. "But you know, Approachable and Open-Minded, you could come with me."

I sighed. "I have applications to fill out." I went and sat on the couch in the living room and stared at where the TV used to be.

At six thirty West came stomping down the stairs, eyes still glued to her phone. She had on a white swimsuit cover-up and her ponytail was pulled back so tight that the skin on her forehead strained.

"We're leaving now, Fortitude and Positivity." Mom was wearing her Society robe, a long green velvet thing with a hood. Around her neck she wore her star necklace and a long string of garlic cloves.

"Have a great time," I said dryly.

"There's leftovers in the fridge, that mushroom soup I made last night!" Mom called over her shoulder as they exited out the door to the garage.

"Psychedelic mushroom soup?"

She hadn't heard me. That was for the best.

I was alone in a house that should have felt familiar and comfortable, but instead seemed like a shell of a place I once knew. At least it was quiet now. I closed my eyes and exhaled. Every once in a while, especially when I was feeling overwhelmed, I would concentrate really hard and try to send a telepathic message to Dorothy. I watched a thing on TV once about how twins can supposedly feel when the other one is in trouble, and some claim to be able to send each other messages with their minds. In twenty-five years, it hadn't worked yet.

Dorothy, I thought to myself, *if you can hear me, I need you. I need you to come here and help me.* I let the silence surround me, imagining my message floating on the clouds, finding its way to my sister . . .

A sharp knock at the front door startled me so much I screamed and fell off the couch onto my butt.

"No way?" I hurried to the door and threw it open.

There, standing on the porch was my Renaissance fair coworker, Troy. He took money and handed out balls while customers attempted to dunk me. He was tolerable, a little younger than me, and he wasn't full of braggadocio like all the other guys that worked at Maypole. Plus, he let me rant about life—not that I had ever told him about the cult or my fractured family or the shit that had gone down my senior year of college or anything remotely personal at all.

He was still dressed up from work. A tunic and linen pants with a leather fanny pack to keep the cash in. On his head he proudly wore a velvet cap with a turkey feather. Troy was tall and lanky, like his bones kept growing and his muscles stretched lean to compensate. His hair was dark and shaggy, and his complexion was a golden olive that, unlike my pasty, freckly skin, tanned beautifully day after day standing around in the summer sun. He'd told me once he was half Afghan on his mother's side. Seeing him outside of work, much less on my front porch, was as unsettling and surprising as if an actual sixteenth-century peasant had fallen from a wormhole in front of me.

"What the hell are you doing at my house?" I said by way of hello.

"Weird, I don't think I've ever seen you in normal clothes," he said with a slight smile. I glanced down at my oversized T-shirt and baggy sweatpants.

"I'd be embarrassed, but you know . . ." I gestured to his attire, and he smirked, pulling his hat off and clutching it under his arm. "Is there a reason you're here?"

"Your phone. You left it at some gas station." He held up my phone.

Relief almost knocked me out. "What? How did you get it?"

"It's locked, but I called you to see how your interview went, and the guy at the StopNGo answered it and told me that some crazy lady had robbed his store and left her phone. So I went and got it, and now I'm here, bringing it to you."

I opened the door wider and held my hand out. He placed it in my palm, letting his fingers linger a half second too long.

"Thank you," I muttered, pulling my hand back and trying to ignore the anxiety that crept through me. I didn't make it a habit of touching men. Not since— "Wait a second. How did you know where I lived?"

"I texted Mike for your address."

"That's not legal."

"I mean, you could just say 'thank you.' "

"Thank you." I slipped the phone into my pocket.

"You're welcome." He smiled sheepishly and ran his fingers through his hair.

"You really didn't need to come all the way out here. You could have just given it to me tomorrow at work."

Troy's face fell, and he stepped back, looking at me like he didn't understand me. "Okay, I guess I'm sorry for bringing you your phone."

"I'm not complaining. I'm very happy to have it back. I can't believe I left it—shit! Now that guy probably has my name, and I robbed his freaking store. Did he say anything?"

"Yeah, he said you stole a pair of sunglasses."

"Shit."

"It's fine, though. I paid for it. He's cool."

"You paid for it? He didn't call the police?"

"Over a pair of cheap plastic sunglasses?" He laughed and rocked back on his heels.

Oh. I swallowed. I'd just given him the third degree, and he'd not only driven all this way to bring me my phone, but he'd also bailed me out of my little misdemeanor. "Well, thanks," was all I could think to say.

He shrugged, repositioned the hat on his head, put his hands in his pockets, and retreated down the front path to his car, a large, rusty van, probably thirty years old. I almost yelled, "Thank you" again and then decided against it. Why prolong the awkwardness?

I glanced down at my phone and saw two missed calls from Dorothy and one text. I glanced up to make sure Troy was back in his van before I read it.

Dorothy: *Yeah, that's about what I expected. Nice to know I still can't count on you.*

I let the screen door slam behind me and sank down on the porch steps as I dialed her back, knowing it was pointless.

The call went straight to voicemail. I stared into the setting sun, letting my eyes burn as I listened to her outgoing message.

"Hey, you've reached Dory Glass. Leave a message, and I'll get back to you at some point. Namaste."

I ended the call without leaving a message, and set the phone next to me. Wrapping my arms around my knees, I buried my face and began to cry. I hated crying. But somehow, while I wasn't paying attention, a single thread had snagged, and now the whole tapestry of my life was unweaving before my eyes. Growing up, I was the daughter who was going places. Dorothy was the responsible one, West was the baby, and I was the dreamer.

In fact, I used the very clichéd quote, "We are the music makers, and we are the dreamers of dreams . . ." as my quote in my high school yearbook.

Turns out that quote is from a poem by Arthur O'Shaughnessy, who only wrote poetry for four years and then gave up and died by getting caught in the rain and developing pneumonia when he was thirty-seven years old. So that's what dreaming gets you—a washed-up career and dead by thirty-seven.

I was trying to push down my sobs, pressing my eyes against my knees so hard I saw fireworks, when I realized I wasn't alone. I looked up and there was Troy, sitting next to me, hands on his knees, watching the lazy Texas sun set.

"I didn't mean to make you cry," he said softly, his expression both confused and guilty.

"You didn't. I'm crying because I'm having an existential crisis." I sniffled and rubbed my face.

"Oh." He snapped open an energy drink and took a swig.

"Yeah, sooo . . ." I waited for him to get back up and leave, but Troy seemed to be settling in, leaning back on his elbows, admiring the wind chimes above us. He picked up the can and took another drink before offering me some.

"Thanks, I'd rather drink battery acid."

"They taste about the same," he said with a shrug and took another sip. "It's nice out here. Peaceful. Maybe I should move to the country."

"Well, thanks for checking on me," I said impatiently, and grasped the railing to pull myself up.

"So, what's your deal?" The tone of his voice was innocent enough, but his expression reminded me of a naughty kid poking an anthill with a stick. I sat back down.

"My deal?"

"Yeah, your extended crisis?"

"Existential," I corrected.

"Hmm," he muttered and looked back to the sunset. "So why are you existential-ing?"

"If you must know, the interview didn't go well."

"Oh, gotcha. And you aren't happy at Maypole?"

"I mean, it's something, but the pay is shit, and like, I have a master's degree." I stopped. "Well, part of a master's degree." I sounded like such a prick—"part" of a master's degree wasn't exactly a thing. But Troy smiled eagerly.

"What in?"

"Oh, ha—early medieval literature and studies."

"For reals?!" His eyes widened.

"Yeah? Most people don't get that excited when I tell them that."

"No, I just think that's badass. I'd love to learn about stuff like that."

"Seriously?" I raised an eyebrow. He seemed so eager and sincere. "I had plans to go all the way in grad school, get my PhD, but I dropped out last spring and moved back home."

"That's incredible! I've never had a smart friend before."

"I'm not smart," I replied, although the word "friend" was what threw me.

"Oh please, don't even try that false modesty thing with me. You're smart and you know it." He smiled. He had a really nice smile, the kind of smile that made you smile back, whether you meant to or not. The sun had gone down, the porch light had come on, and we were being eaten alive by mosquitos, but neither of us moved—or suggested moving—from our spot on the front steps.

"Okay, yes, I'm smart." I laughed. Then he laughed and that made me laugh harder. It was weird how easy it was to talk to him about stuff like this.

My face flushed hot, and I looked at him. I mean, for the first time I actually took a moment to look at him. He was probably a year or two younger than me. He had the mere shadow of a beard because he probably couldn't grow an actual one, but then, his eyes were old, dark amber, framed with dark lashes.

"I'm just kinda bummed you'll be leaving the fair once you get a different job. I've liked hanging out with you this summer."

"You know, I have too," I realized out loud. Then I shook my head and focused on the van parked in my driveway. "But, you know, working at the Renaissance fair has always been kind of a temporary thing for me. I'm just waiting to get a real job."

"I get it. I've been working at Maypole for four years, and it still barely covers my rent." He sighed. "I sometimes take shifts at the laundromat."

"Yeah . . ." I cringed, thinking of all the bills my mom was currently paying while I looked for that perfect job. "I'm sorry."

"It's fine. I get by." He took another drink.

"I feel like such a whiny little brat. I need to just shut up sometimes."

"I like listening to you. It makes work bearable." He laughed.

"I just need to remember it could always be worse." I looked at him and sucked in my breath. "No offense."

"No offense taken. And see, you're working through your existence shit already."

I laughed. It felt good. Warm.

"Hey, it's better than my last job." I smirked.

"Oh yeah?"

"I worked the night shift at a bowling alley before this."

"That sounds fun," he mused.

"I got fired for being 'rude' to the customers." I put air quotes around "rude" and scoffed.

He laughed and nudged me a little with his elbow. "You? Rude? No way!"

"And before that I worked at Chili's."

"That didn't go well either?" Amusement played on his lips as he spoke.

I sighed. "Apparently when a customer asks you for a recommendation, they aren't looking for a ten-minute rant about our meaningless existence as a cog in the machine of modern society."

"Damn, Glin, you really know how to win people over." He chuckled and played with the tab on the can.

"You have no idea." I pushed a lock of hair out of my eyes.

"I've never noticed that." He pointed to the small tattoo, black letters scrawled along the side of my wrist. *Wander with purpose.* What's the story?"

I clamped a hand over it and changed the subject.

"I can't believe I stole gas station sunglasses. I mean, for my first robbery, that's really kind of pathetic." I let my forehead fall against my knees again in a dramatic display of embarrassment.

"Well I could tell from the first time I saw you that you were a hardened criminal."

"Please tell me you did not go into the StopNGo in your costume." I laughed. "That poor cashier is probably so confused."

"Of course I did," he confirmed. "Did you?"

"Yep. Corset and all."

I glanced up and he shot me a sly smile. I blushed and we both grew silent, a silence that lingered into the realm of awkward. He clicked his tongue.

"So, this is your place?"

"Yes, well, no, it's my parents' . . . my mom's place, I guess. My dad died a couple of years ago."

"Oh. I'm sorry."

"Thanks."

"My parents are dead too."

"Oh, damn. I'm sorry." I shifted my weight and watched the lightning bugs streaking their brilliant little light at the end of the gravel circle drive.

"Yeah, it's fine. They died ten years ago. That's when I moved out here to live with my uncle and aunt."

"You still live with them?"

"Oh hell no. I got myself a shitty apartment with an even shittier roommate as soon as I graduated high school. I live alone now."

We both grew quiet. It was like someone had poured cold water on the conversation. I picked at my thumbnail, and Troy crunched his empty can in his hand.

"Well, thanks again for returning my phone."

"Oh, no prob." He jumped to his feet while I pulled myself up by the railing.

He stepped down and started toward his van.

"Oh wait!" I said. "Just—just hang out for one sec!"

I dashed inside and grabbed the sunglasses off the table. When I got back outside, Troy was standing by the van waiting. I thrust the glasses into his hand.

"What's this?" He laughed.

"A thank-you gift." I stepped back, smiling.

"Nice." He slipped them on—plastic, neon orange, rimmed— and gave me a thumbs-up. Then he jumped into the driver's seat and started the engine.

"Please don't drive in those! It's night, Troy."

He straightened the glasses on his nose, gave me a smirk, and then pulled away from the house. I watched his taillights bob between the tree trunks as he drove back up the drive, toward the main road. I waited for the sound of a crash.

When none came, I went inside, locked the front door, and breathed deeply. Then I chuckled to myself and let out a groan for all the stupid things I'd said. I lay back down on the couch and started browsing job listings, when the house phone rang.

Dorothy! I jumped up and grabbed the cordless off the end table.

"Hello?"

"Is Arlon there?" a man asked.

"This isn't Arlon's house—why would he be here?"

"You must be the other daughter, the dropout, right?"

What the hell? "Who is this?"

"Listen, sweetie, if Arlon's not there, he will be soon. You tell him that Matthew Harrigan is looking for him."

"Are you a cult member?"

The man laughed, but it was dry and forced. "Not anymore. That son of a bitch con man ruined my life."

This was an interesting development. Whoever this Matthew guy was, he shared my distain for Mr. Blight. "Well, hey, same here." I returned the laugh. After all, the enemy of my enemy probably had some dirt to share or tea to spill.

"You listen to me, sweetie. He seems harmless, even inept, but you watch yourself. And get your mama away from him. He's dangerous." The receiver clicked and the line went dead.

Well, well, well. So there was trouble in paradise. I didn't know this Matthew Harrigan, but I could have kissed him at that moment . . . except not really. My mind drifted to that place I habitually strived to stay far away from, to the last time someone had kissed me. To Patrick and his marauding tongue, forcing itself into my mouth. The taste of blood as his tooth split my lower lip.

My brain snapped back to the present, and I shivered.

I returned to the couch and resumed scrolling until I heard the garage door go up.

A moment later, my mom appeared, holding an empty cookie tin. I held out my phone triumphantly.

"You'll never guess—" I stopped. My mom had the weirdest look on her face. My stomach dropped. West came in behind her, looking completely devastated. She was crying. I hadn't seen West cry in years.

Not since the afternoon I had to break the news to her about our dad. The sound of her torn scream was still etched in my memory.

You know that feeling you get when you know your whole world is about to change? That horrible, hollow feeling that fills up every place inside you. Numbness, dread, and an indescribable feeling of not understanding how life is supposed to continue. I'd had that feeling then, and I had the same feeling now.

I heard myself talking, but my brain was two seconds behind. "What's going on?"

"Glinda, everything is all right," my mom started.

"Yeah, right!" West burst out. "Just tell her! Tell her about Arlon!"

I looked at my mom, trying to make sense of what West was saying.

She sighed and unclasped her cloak, folding it in her hands. She looked at me, her eyes glassy. "Arlon has selected me . . ."

"Selected you for what?"

"I will be joined with Arlon and our inner lights will be braided together with the life force of the universe." My mom tried to put her arm around West, but she pulled away.

"What the hell does that mean?"

"He asked her to marry him, Glinda!"

He . . . what? "You're marrying a cult leader?" I heard myself say.

"Arlon is a wise man. He has shown me that my place is by his side as the pioneers prepare for the next chapter of our journey." I had never seen this look on my mom's face before. She'd always seemed happy when she talked about the cult, but this was something else. Her face was blank, save a smile that seemed painted on. She looked at me with the eagerness of a child waiting for her parents' approval.

I didn't know what to say. I didn't know what to ask. Only one thought popped into my head. "What do you mean 'the next chapter'?"

"Acceptance and Understanding, we—"

"My name's Glinda!" I interrupted her. "My name's Glinda, Mom. You should know—you named me. What is 'the next chapter'?"

She stared at me through a gaze of fog. "In the place beyond, a higher plane of existence."

Shit.

◆ 3 ◆

DARKNESS AND
NEGATIVITY

AFTER THE INITIAL SHOCK of my mother's announcement the evening before, I hadn't had much luck getting anything else out of her. She'd assured me we'd talk in the morning. I'd gone to West's door to try and get the story from her, but she'd refused to let me in.

I was hoping to get a chance to talk to both of them today. But when I came downstairs, it was Arlon's voice I heard coming from the breakfast table.

"Brother Matthew has never truly accepted my message, though," I heard him say as I hung back in the hall, waiting.

"I just know he wants to belong," Mom said. "Deep down."

"Julie, he's threatened to sue me!"

"But he hasn't actually done it yet. Remember what you tell us, Father, that doubt is the final step before reaching the higher plane. All the forces of darkness and negativity will fight against us until the moment we fully embrace the enlightenment."

"You are wise, Sister Julie."

I took a breath and came around the corner into the kitchen, like I hadn't been listening in. Arlon's bright eyes and wide grin greeted me. I took a step back and tightened the belt of my robe.

"Hey, everyone?" I muttered, trying to smooth down my tangled hair. "Didn't know we were having company."

"Sister Glinda, how nice to see you," Arlon said in way that seemed friendly on the surface but lacked any warmth.

"It's just Glinda, like I've said before."

"Glinda, Arlon is here to discuss our upcoming wedding." My mother's eyes were sparkling with excitement.

"Yeah, so that's still happening." I grabbed the carafe and poured black coffee into a mug.

"Glinda, you don't drink coffee—"

I put up a finger to silence my mother and raised the mug to my lips with two hands. I took a long, deep swallow, then set the cup down with a thud. Gah, that stuff was gross, but it was too late—I couldn't bat an eye now.

"Glinda, we want you to understand what's happening," she tried again.

"You, um, you've agreed to marry Arlon here."

"It's so much more than that, dear Sister Glinda," Arlon broke in, waving his hands as if to clear away my preposterous ideas. "We are braiding our inner lights—"

"Yeah, yeah, with the universe and the next plane of existence, I heard." I raised an eyebrow and took another sip of my coffee. It wasn't sitting well in my stomach, but I wasn't going to show any sign of weakness. My mother placed a bran muffin in front of me, on one of the little ceramic plates she never actually got out except when we had company.

"So, what? You get married, you have control of my mom's money, and then you guys build a giant rocket ship?" I sank back and crossed my arms. *Time to explain yourself, Mr. Arlon Blight.*

"Don't be ridiculous, Practical and Humble," Mom said as she watched me pour another cup of coffee, her face full of confusion.

"Not a spaceship, my dear," Arlon said to me. "No, we will build an entire community."

"Excuse me?"

Arlon straightened his shoulders and leaned forward like he was letting me in on some big secret. "We're building a commune. A place where we can practice our faith freely. With a swimming pool. A really big swimming pool." He held his hands out wide to show me the grandiose nature of this alleged structure.

"Huh?" I turned to my mom for some kind of clarification but was met with a big smile and no answers. "Why? Why would you need a place like that?"

"Sister Glinda, you are so young and so easily taken in by the lies of the modern world."

I'd woken up in crazy town. "*I'm* easily taken in? *Me?*"

Arlon wiped the corners of his mouth with one swipe and then looked at me like he felt sorry for me, like he *pitied* me. Then he replied in his smug tone of superiority, "The world is a prison, and I am creating a space of freedom."

"Uh-huh." I looked back at my mom, but her eyes were glued on Arlon with admiration. He rose and went and stood behind her chair, his hands possessively resting on her shoulders.

"Your mother, my dear Julie, is the heart of the pioneers. It is only right that the foundation of the Outpost is here."

"Here where?" Slowly, his meaning became clear. "Wait, *here*? Like, at this house?"

My mom nodded.

"So, you're moving in?" My stomach lurched. I took another sip of coffee to keep the headache that was forming at bay.

"Not just me. The entire Society."

The coffee caught in my throat as I tried to cry, "*What?*" Instead, I sputtered coffee through my nose, and my nostrils burned. "The whole cult is moving into our house?"

"We will have to build some cabins behind the main house for everyone to live comfortably," Arlon said, "but there's plenty of land. Plenty of land."

My mother took my hand and gestured around her with the other. "The three of us don't need this much space, and it's important to me."

"Dad renovated this house! You are not about to let a bunch of weirdos come in here and destroy our family!"

"A house is not a family, Glinda."

It was possibly the one true and lucid statement she'd made all morning.

"Mom! You're marrying a cult leader, you're turning our house into a commune, and you're giving up the farm that dad loved to strangers!"

"Do not speak so disrespectfully to your mother! We are not strangers—we are a family," Arlon said coolly, although I noted the top of his brow flushing a dark crimson. I was getting to him.

"I've heard enough from you, Jim Jones," I snapped.

"Glinda!" My mother shot daggers at me.

"I am not living with a bunch of brainwashed weirdos!"

Arlon looked at me with narrowed eyes. "Then maybe you won't live here."

"What the actual fuck?" I shouted, jumping to my feet.

"Language, Glinda." Mom was looking down, avoiding my eyes.

Arlon's nostrils flared. "You don't know anything, because you haven't opened your mind to the Society! I *am* the higher plane—I am the star prophet. I will lead those who will follow to a place of freedom and love and ecstasy!"

I stared at him, unblinking, and snorted.

I put my hands on the table and craned my neck toward Arlon, zeroing in on the object of my disdain. "You know what pisses me off the most, Arlon? You're not even a good cult leader."

"Glinda!" my mother cried.

"I mean, it'd be one thing if someone *smart* manipulated my mom with some diabolical plan. But you—you literally just spout off new age jargon without any regard to how little sense any of it makes! You're like a cult leader Ken doll, and your bogus ideas are as generic as you."

My mom tried to put her hand on mine, but I pulled away and straightened up.

"*Glinda Rainbow,*" she said, using my middle name. "Arlon is a guest, and it's not a cult."

Arlon dropped his hands from her shoulders, a vein in his neck throbbing. He took several deep breaths and then attempted to resume his placid demeanor.

"My beloved Sister Julie, we'll have to discuss the rest of our plans later. Your offspring has frazzled my inner light. I need to go resync." My mother jumped to her feet. He wrapped an arm around her waist and kissed her on the lips, keeping one eye open to look at me. A cruel smile cracked from the corner of the kiss. I looked away in disgust.

My mom saw Arlon out and then stood on the porch, the two of them talking in low voices. I was twelve again, waiting for my punishment for talking back to Grandma.

But when she came back in, it was even worse than I could have imagined. She had been crying and wouldn't look at me.

"Glinda, I don't even know what to say to you," she began.

"Mom, he's the worst!"

"He's a visionary."

"He's a con man and not a very good one."

"Glinda, enough." Suddenly her voice sounded very cold and distant.

I took a deep breath. "Okay, you know what? It's your life. But he obviously thinks you have money because you live in this big house with all this land. That's what he's after."

I had no idea how much my dad had left my mom, between his savings and his life insurance policy. I assumed it was a lot, but I didn't know. I just blindly took my allotted amount and didn't ask questions. Having a fixed amount felt too finite, like knowing how much time one had left on earth. And since jobs that actually paid a decent salary were apparently urban legends, I lived in perpetual avoidance of finding one, while remaining dependent like a damn child.

So the idea of this creep coming in and plundering my parents' money—money that I felt such tremendous guilt for using in the first place—sent my blood into a rapid boil.

"If you marry him, he'll have access to everything! What about West? What about her college fund?" I stooped my shoulders. "And not to be ungrateful, because I appreciate everything you've been doing to help me lately, but what about our shared bank account that you've been putting money into every month? I'm paying my student loans out of that account."

"Money is a chain holding you to your problems," she responded.

"Oh, okay. Well, defaulting on my loans is one sure way to make sure I never have money again."

"Glinda, Arlon is not a monster," my mom offered. "If you'd just join us, once we seal ourselves off from the world in the Outpost, these artificial financial bonds won't matter anymore."

"I—" I stopped. There was nothing more to say. I threw my hands up, ran upstairs, and banged on West's door. No response. I charged in.

She was on her bed, reading a book. When she saw me, she threw her book under a pillow and grabbed her phone. "Excuse you!"

"West, Arlon Blight was here!"

"I know. I heard you screaming."

"I wasn't—never mind. Look, you've got to tell me everything you know about the cult. Apparently they're all moving in?"

My sister's mouth tensed. "Oh, I know."

She does? "Well, what are we going to do?"

"Oh, blah, blah, blah. Do you know how old you sound?"

"I sound like an adult."

She dropped her phone to the bedspread and gave me her full attention, finally. "Okay, then. What *exactly* do you think you can do about it? Because I've played out every scenario, and there isn't one where Mom doesn't end up devastated, pissed at us, or both."

"May I remind you you're going to be sharing a room with twenty people who don't believe in deodorant?"

"Glinda, I'll be eighteen in September. I start college in the fall. I'll crash at Molly's if it gets too weird here. I've already planned my escape from this madhouse, and I suggest you do the same."

"West, what about Mom? What about your college fund? What about your future?"

She shrugged and then narrowed her eyes at me. "At least I won't get trapped being financially dependent on my mom when I'm almost thirty."

Then she lowered her head to her phone and waved me away.

"Ooh, low blow," I mocked. "I have five more years before I'm thirty. And that's a pretty bold prediction coming from someone who still sleeps with a stuffed animal."

Without a word, West pushed her well-worn teddy bear, Mr. Huggles, off the bed and kept scrolling on her phone.

I went to my room and decided to hide under the covers until I had figured out a way to fix this whole mess. I grabbed my phone and opened up a new text convo.

Dorothy, I know you don't want to talk to me. But we have to talk about Mom. It's important.

I deleted it before pressing "Send," and tossed my phone down. What was the point? I'd sent her plenty of desperate texts before, and she never responded. I was perfectly capable of solving this without dragging unwilling participants into it.

"Glinda?"

I pulled the blanket off my head and looked up to see West standing in the doorway, looking more intense than usual.

"Yes?" I snapped. I don't know why I snapped. It just seemed the natural thing to do.

"I just—I wondered . . ." She frowned. "Do you think there's anything left?"

"Left of what?"

"Mom."

I stared at her, puzzled. "West, she's not dead. Of course there's something left. She's still Mom."

There was a pause, and then she said, quietly, "Do you really think there's something we can do?"

"Yes!" The word came out on a cloud of frustration. Sometimes talking to the people in this house felt like talking to a wall. "I already said that! I'm going to figure something out."

She shook her head, and I watched as her walls went back up. "Never mind." She turned away.

Crap. I thought about jumping up and running after her. But something stopped me—a small, broken voice from deep within, somewhere buried under pounds of sarcasm and an odd assortment of other defense mechanisms. It was something I'd said once, long ago, a foolish sentiment, but one I couldn't take back now.

"I'll take care of everything."

TREACHEROUS AND UNWISE

Nineteen-ish months ago

Dorothy's always been ready to fall in love. When we were little girls, I wanted to be a writer, and she wanted to be a bride. It was so obnoxious. In ninth grade she had her first boyfriend, Finn. That lasted all of four months, but during those four months I was basically invisible to her. I mean, you have to understand—we were *twins*; we'd literally been best friends since conception. Anyway, after Finn there was Paul, then Aiden, and each time it was like she wasn't even there. It got old really fast.

And then something else changed. Dorothy started scoring higher and higher on tests, and eventually they moved her up a grade. At first it was devastating—*I'd* wanted to be the smart one. Now she was graduating a year before me. Now she was testing out of her freshman courses. Now she was going to law school, and our dad brought it up in every conversation. He was so damn proud of her. And here I was, writing poetry in notebooks and stacking up debt. I was proud of her too; I just wished someone could be proud of me. I wished *I* were proud of me.

But I lost a part of myself that final year and finished college feeling more worthless and aimless than ever.

After Dad died my senior year, Dorothy got even more serious with her studies, took summer courses, applied for internships. And although I was jealous of her success, I appreciated the fact she didn't seem to have time for boyfriends anymore. That was, until her final semester of law school.

Nineteen months ago, I'd been completing my first semester as a grad student. I was at this pricey little liberal arts school about two hours from town, and Dorothy was at home finishing up her final internship before graduation and the bar exam.

That's when she met James. He was a witness for a case, and she was assigned to take some statements from him. James had been two minutes late leaving his house, and because of that was passing the bank when the robber raced out and smacked right into him. One minute earlier and he wouldn't have witnessed a crime, and he and Dorothy would have never met.

Flash forward to Thanksgiving break. Thanksgiving break was the one time when Dorothy and I always got to hang out— go Black Friday shopping, watch movies, act like we used to.

It was Thanksgiving Day, in the morning, and Dorothy was sitting on her bed, sketching in a book. I came in, hoping to finally get some time alone with her.

"What about seeing a movie tonight?" I asked, trying to sound as casual as possible.

"Tonight? Tonight's Thanksgiving dinner. Besides, James is coming over."

"Ugh, he's coming here again?" This long-haired, plaid-wearing dude from Austin had been spending a lot of time at the house, sleeping on the couch and spending every single waking moment with my sister. Oh, and he was *obsessed* with the potential existence of Bigfoot. "Why?"

"Because I love him, and his parents are in Cancun all week."

"So, he's driven his own family away and now he wants to mess with ours?" I sat on her bed and watched her erase a line on the paper. Then she set the book down and looked at me.

"What is your problem with James? I really care about him."

"Oh my God, don't be so sensitive. Listen, I just think that maybe you're selling yourself a little short in this relationship."

"I'm not selling myself at all, Glinda. I am not a prostitute."

"Oh, ha ha, you know what I mean."

"Yes, I can read the subtext. You don't ever want me to be with anybody because you're too freaked out to find your own somebody, and you'd rather we all just stay in this house together until . . . what, Glinda? Until we're old and dead?"

I wasn't too "freaked out" to find someone. But in my experience, finding someone meant losing me. Finding someone meant saying things I didn't believe, just to make him happy; doing things I didn't want to just to make him stay; and even then, it ended with pain and heartbreak. Finding someone meant pretending, relenting, getting used, and then being discarded like a disposable commodity.

"Of course not." I shivered off the dark memories. "I'm going to get my PhD and be a professor and travel the world and find treasure and shit. I'm certainly not going to move back into my mother's house and never leave."

"Really? First of all, you just described Indiana Jones. Second, there's no way you don't come back here. You come home every chance you get."

"Counterpoint to your first point, I think melting faces off Nazis sounds like pretty fulfilling work. Counter to your second, I just worry about Mom being here all alone with West. I like to check on her."

"Hello? I live here too."

"Yeah, but you're always at James's place."

"Mom is fine. Besides, she has the Society now."

Mom had been a member of the Starlight Pioneer Society for a couple months at that point. That whole thing started early in the semester when I hadn't been able to get home as much as I would have liked.

"Ugh, don't get me started." I rolled my eyes.

"And Arlon has been over here supporting her so much lately."

I raised an eyebrow. "You know he's a cult leader, right?"

"It's not a *cult*; it's a lifestyle community."

"Dorothy, they wear those star pendant necklaces and think that they're actually domesticated pets of a superior alien race."

She appeared to consider that. "Yeah, that part's weird."

"And I don't like how fast this guy moved on Mom. Did I tell you the other day he came over and when they went to sit and talk in the dining room, he put his hand on the small of her back?

I actually vomited and gagged at the same time, so I choked on the vomit and almost died."

"And here we are again. You don't want anybody to be in love." She always thought she was so much wiser than me, even though we were literally the same age.

"Puh-lease. First, Mom and Arlon are not 'in love.' He's just a handsy creep. And I don't care if Mom starts dating. Just not that guy."

"*Nobody* is good enough for you, Glinda. It's like you're anti-relationship."

"I'm not anti-relationship!" I scowled. "I just think that falling in love leads to ruin and despair, and we'd all just be better off without it."

Dorothy sighed. "Is this because of the guy who broke up with you after you vomited on him?"

"I don't even know what you're talking about." She knew better than to mention Patrick. I mean, she didn't know all the gory details, but she knew I was sensitive about bringing him up. "Just because I can't get close to a guy without wanting to throw up doesn't mean I'm anti-relationship. I just happen to have this working theory that love doesn't exist and we're all just fooling ourselves into believing we're not each completely alone in an indifferent universe."

Dorothy rubbed her temples and groaned. "You're so stupid."

"*You're* stupid."

"No, you're not stupid—you're lonely. You're trying to hold on to a time when Dad was alive and you were a kid and emotions were simple. But, Glinda, even if Dad were still alive, we're adults now. It's time to make our own families with the people we choose."

I clapped slowly, with one eyebrow raised. "Yep, you got me all figured out."

"Yeah, or maybe you're jealous that I'm in a serious relationship and have my life figured out, and you're staying in school as long as possible to stall actual adulthood."

"Shut up! Just because you got through law school faster than anybody ever doesn't mean that you are an authority on higher education. Some of us like to take our time."

"Well, you're certainly doing that. What exactly are you going to do with that doctorate in medieval literature?"

I stuck my tongue out at her and stormed out of her room like we were freaking fifteen again.

I was pissed. James was driving a wedge between us worse than anything had before. I mean, she'd invited him over for Thanksgiving dinner. I was still brooding when I happened to glance into the bathroom—and noticed Dorothy's phone sitting on the counter.

So, I knew it was bad. But I couldn't stop myself. I picked up her phone, and sure enough, there was a text from James.

Can't wait for tonight.

You know what I think the tipping point was? Her stupid wallpaper. It was a selfie of her and James, in the woods, and she's kissing his cheek and he's smiling like an idiot. You know what my wallpaper was? Me and Dorothy and West, when West was like five, and we'd taken her to a carnival. Oh, and my mom and dad are standing behind us, smiling like idiots who have no idea that world actually sucks really hard.

Seeing this picture of her and James just kind of made me lose my mind.

I deleted his text.

As if that wasn't bad enough, I went a step further.

I typed: *I'm really sorry, but I'm going to have to cancel for tonight. Things have just not been feeling right with you for a while. I think I need some space.*

My finger hesitated over the "Send" button as I debated whether I was really willing to sabotage my sister's happiness for what I perceived as her own good.

I sent it. Then I deleted the evidence from her phone and went into her settings and blocked James. That way his texts wouldn't come through. Then I changed his number in her phone to mine.

I placed the phone right back where I'd found it and went about my business, feeling completely right that the ends justified the means.

At one PM, she texted him and it came to my phone.

Dorothy: *You can come whenever.*

Me (as James): *I'm not coming.*

Dorothy: *Why????*

Me (as James): *I'm sorry to do this over text, but I'm done. We aren't compatible. Don't text me, don't call me.*

Those three little dots bounced once, twice, and then she didn't reply.

It was about four in the afternoon when I walked in on Dorothy sobbing into a bowl of cookie dough. And the gravity of what I'd done became suddenly apparent.

"What's this?"

"Cookies. James loves butterscotch." She let the spoon fall into the bowl and then threw her arms around my neck, crying so hard I was worried she was going to pass out. Shit. "I think James broke up with me!"

"Oh?" I tried to sound innocent. But inside, I was regretting everything. I'd never seen Dorothy cry over a guy like this before.

My mind raced with how to fix it without her realizing what I'd done, when we were interrupted by the chime of the doorbell.

A wave of dread washed over me; it might be James, ready to confront Dorothy about the text. I was nothing if not short-sighted.

"I'll get it. You just stir that dough." I didn't wait for her to reply. I sprinted for the door and opened it only a crack.

It was James, all right. And it was bad. His eyes were red, his hands were trembling. He looked like he was waiting to receive a death sentence.

"I need to talk to Dorothy."

"Um, I don't think that's a good idea," I whispered, keeping my foot firmly planted in case he tried to open the door.

"Please, Glinda. Please."

"Listen, I need to talk to—"

"James?" Shit. Dorothy had come up behind me.

"Dor, I understand you want some space, but how could you not answer me like that?"

"Like what?" Dorothy croaked. She pushed past me and opened the door all the way.

"Can we talk?" he asked softly.

"Y-yes," she sobbed.

They went up to her bedroom to talk. It felt like they were up there forever.

I sat at the kitchen island, watching my mom start dinner, and rolling my right index finger around the left one over and over and hoping, praying, trying to will reality to my side and not have James and Dorothy realize what I'd done.

A chill settled over the house; it was like I could feel the shift when Dorothy realized the truth. About a minute later she came charging into the kitchen, her face completely white, with just the edges of her nostrils and the wrinkles of her furrowed brow a brilliant red.

"I need to talk to you."

We went into the dining room and she just glared at me for the longest time. Then her expression changed, and she studied me, like she was desperately trying to understand me, to reconcile what I'd done with the sister who loved her. When she finally spoke, her voice was strained, like she was trying to keep from crying again.

She made her accusations. And she had the facts correct, of course. James had showed her the message on his phone.

"Why would you do that, man?" James said, coming up behind Dorothy and putting his hands on her shoulders like he owned her or something. He glared at me and I glared right back.

"Don't call me 'man,' dude."

"James, stop, please," Dorothy said. "I need to talk to my sister alone."

"Fine, I'll be in the living room." Then he sauntered out like he had some right to be in my house.

"I'm sorry, Dorothy." My voice sounded small.

"You're *sorry*? I know you're jealous, but when did you become this vindictive, evil witch?"

I bit my lip as tears welled in my eyes. My mom's voice from the other room saved me from saying something I no doubt would have regretted. "Glinda, can I talk to you?"

I immediately jumped up.

"This isn't over," Dorothy remarked as a tear rolled down her cheek.

I came into the kitchen, where my mom was standing by the stove, stirring some dressing.

"I'm guessing you were eavesdropping?"

"Of course, hon." She kept her eyes on the bowl. "Now, I don't know exactly what you did, but it sounds like you really stepped in it this time."

"I'm sorry, okay? I wasn't thinking."

"Hey." My mom lowered her voice. "I don't think this is just another one of Dorothy's boyfriends."

"What the heck does that mean?" I played ignorant, but my stomach had dropped to my feet.

"They seem . . . happy. I'm just saying you might need to get used to him."

"What the hell, Mom?" I whispered back, waving my arms in place of screaming at the top of my lungs like I wanted to do.

"Glinda!"

I rolled my eyes. "Fine, what the *hey*, Mom? They barely know each other," I hissed through my teeth.

"Sometimes when you know, you know. They're good together and I know it's hard for you to have someone else in your sister's life, but someday it'll be you."

I doubted that. "Gross."

"I just wanted you to think about that because—well, my love, it's always good to remember that tomorrow isn't guaranteed, and the hurtful things we say in the heat of the moment might carry a hurt much longer than we intended."

She looked at me with that soul-piercing expression of wisdom and pain that only people who've gone through hell can pull off.

"Come on, seriously." I slapped my forehead and rubbed my palm across my face. I had to do something.

"Glinda, you remind me so much of your dad. His first instinct was always to protect his family—act and then ask questions later. I know that's what you're trying to do. But he also wasn't ashamed to admit when he'd screwed up."

"Okay, all right. Look, I'll fix this."

"Do you want me to come? Because I'm concerned about—"

"No, Mom, I got it. I'll take care of it."

My mom gave me a gentle pat on the shoulder, and I slunk into the living room, where James was sitting on a chair, staring gloomily at the game on the TV.

"If you want to feel better, you shouldn't torture yourself with the Cowboys," I offered, and then glanced behind me to make sure Dorothy hadn't come into the room.

James looked up at me and scowled. But behind the scowl was a guy in the throes of angst. The last thing I wanted to do was humanize this guy.

"So, look, man, I screwed up," I muttered, coming closer to him.

"Yeah, you did." Ah shit, now he was tearing up. Great.

"I realize that. I didn't understand how intense this thing had gotten."

"You know, it doesn't matter what your perception of the intensity of our relationship is. It's not your place. It's not your business."

"She's my sister. My *twin* sister."

"I don't care. You hurt her, and I'm not going to let you do that again."

I bit my tongue and shook my head. "So, it's Thanksgiving and I'd like to not give Dorothy any more reasons to hate me. So, please, if you'll put this behind you, I promise I won't do anything like that again. Okay?"

"I will follow her lead. If she wants to forgive you, fine. It's not my place to interfere with your relationship." He stood up and faced me. "But you and me, we're not okay. So don't think we are."

"Cool," I said dryly. So much for that.

I rejoined Dorothy in the dining room, where she was now sitting in a chair, sobbing into her arms on the table.

"Dorothy, listen, I screwed up."

She looked up at me with big eyes and tearstained cheeks.

I took a breath and steadied myself.

"I am really sorry. Obviously, I didn't realize what you two meant to each other." The words sounded like they were coming from somewhere else.

"Glinda, you tried to break us up." Her expression said that she wanted to be wrong. Her eyes were begging for some complicated excuse. Nothing as simple as that she had the worst sister ever.

I took a seat next her and tried to take her hands, but she pulled them away.

"I thought I was protecting you."

"Bullshit."

"I just wasn't sure about you guys, and—"

"You don't even know him!" She seemed surprised by how angry she sounded.

"I'm sorry! It was a terrible thing to do. Obviously, you guys are perfect for each other," I lied.

"Don't patronize me, Glinda. I'm not stupid. You didn't just screw up. It wasn't a quick moment where you made a mistake. There were multiple steps to this. You had multiple opportunities to stop, to tell me. You let me cry, you pretended to comfort me."

"I wasn't pretending!"

She continued as if she hadn't heard me. "This is, without a doubt, the worst thing you've ever done. I don't know how I am ever going to trust you again, even if I somehow figure out how to forgive you."

We both sat in silence for a moment.

James appeared in the doorway and cleared his throat. "Hey, Dorothy, you okay?"

Then she was out of her seat, with her arms around his neck, sobbing into his shoulder. He was stroking her hair and pulling her closer. I rolled my eyes, but they didn't see me.

"I think I'm going to get out of here," I heard myself saying. "You know, give everybody some space." My ears felt like they were filled with cotton, and my heart was all twisted up in between my ribs.

My mom was waiting at the front door for me.

"I wish you'd stay. James and Dorothy will calm down, and then we can have dinner."

I licked my lips and tried to understand how she could possibly still not get it. Nothing was okay. Nothing would be okay. Men were not to be trusted. Not a single one—except maybe our father, but he was gone. And now my sister was way too obsessed with this guy, and I'd pretty much just guaranteed she was never going to listen to me again.

♦ 5 ♦

CARELESS AND OBLIVIOUS

Present

"YOU'RE REALLY TAKING ME out of the story."

"What the hell are you talking about?" I tugged at the bottom of my corset. This thing was going to be the death of me.

"I have this whole narrative going in my head, to stay in character. I'm a lowly serf charged with guarding the damsel who has been accused of witchcraft. But when you keep talking about anti-chrony things like you just did, it really strains my suspension of disbelief."

"Anachronistic," I corrected. "And I'm sorry if you don't appreciate my feminist analysis of *The Bachelor*, but it might as well be set in the fifteenth century!"

"At least use a British accent. You have to use a British accent."

"Like hell I do." I crossed my arms and glared at Troy, who was standing there in his peasant's costume, counting dollar bills.

"It enhances the visitors' experience," he said with a cockney accent.

"Please, stop. You're embarrassing yourself."

"It's time for the lovely damsel to get up on her seat." This time he sounded like a drunk Sean Connery.

I rolled my eyes and climbed the rusty ladder up to the wooden plank and then scooched over until my legs were dangling over the tank of freezing water. Around me the Maypole

Renaissance Festival sprawled out, a million colors of banners and ribbons, costumes, tents, and little medieval storefronts, the smells of funnel cakes and fried meat and strong beer. Under a small, crudely built pavilion, a man was playing a lute while a woman in period clothing was singing "Greensleeves" softly to the passersby. Some of the visitors were dressed in costume, and some in street clothes. Kids had their faces painted, and women had ribbons woven into their hair.

"You gonna take the sweatshirt off?" Troy asked. "You know Mike is gonna give you shit about it again."

I shrugged. Just because I had to wear a corset and sheer white blouse didn't mean I couldn't accessorize with a loose-fitting hoodie, gray and printed with "Princeton" in fading blue letters. I was burning up in the July heat, but I pulled the strings of the hood tight and shoved my hands in my pockets. I could only take so much ogling from passersby before the security sweatshirt became necessary. At least every time I got dunked, the wet fabric cooled me off until it dried like thirty seconds later in the oppressive heat.

Troy had tightened the screws on the seat, so it only dropped if they hit the target really hard, which hardly ever happened. He claimed it was to get them to try again and spend more money. I didn't care as long as it kept me dry.

I gave Troy the signal and then selected my first victim, a douchey-looking guy in a muscle shirt with a backward ball cap.

"You there! Yes, you artless bull pizzle! I see you, you idle-headed lewdster!"

The guy waved me off and passed on by.

"Where do you even come up with these insults?" I asked Troy.

"Shakespeare."

"Ah."

A man walked by with his girlfriend and I smiled to myself. The way they clasped hands and she was leaning on his shoulder—too easy.

"Hello, there, you goatish, clay-brained codpiece!" I shouted.

The guy ignored me.

"Not man enough to defend your lady's honor?" I called after him, and sure enough he stopped. "That vain strumpet beside you!"

That did it.

Mr. Macho strolled over and stared up at me.

"Oh, now you hear me! But me fears you are too thin in the arm to hit the target."

He narrowed his eyes and called up to me. "I don't know what you're saying, but I'm gonna drench the witch!" He laughed, taking a baseball from Troy.

"It's *wench*!"

"What?"

"Geez Louise, it's *wench*!" The last word was on my lips when he suddenly threw the ball, the seat fell away, and I was plunged into the cold, murky water. The tank was only about four feet deep, and I always seemed to land wrong on my ankle, so I had started curling my legs up as soon as I realized I was falling and ended sitting on the floor of the tank before pushing off and surfacing again.

But this time, as I found myself submerged into the quiet, cool of the water, I wondered how long I could just sit at the bottom before Troy pulled me out.

Unfortunately, falling in was only the first part of the act. The second was to climb out and let the victor see me fully humiliated with my wet clothes clinging to my body. That's why we were really there after all. So, I gripped the ladder and pulled myself out, wiping the hair out of my face as I slung a leg over the side.

"Take that, witch!" the man yelled triumphantly as I squeezed the water from my skirt. Then his girlfriend held up her phone and motioned for us to stand together. I rolled my eyes and he put his arm around my shoulders, and she took her photos.

"Come on, babe, let's go get some beer." He dropped his arm and started walking away toward the concessions. The woman gave me a sheepish smile before handing me a ten and faintly muttering, "Thanks," before catching up with her man.

Troy handed me a towel and held out his hand for the ten.

"Make sure you're putting that in the right pocket," I said, rubbing my face and hair.

"I got it, I got it," he replied. "Payment on the right, tips on the left."

"Look, we're getting paid shit as it is, don't need to accidently give Mike our tips on top of it."

"I told you, I got it." Troy pulled an unwrapped Slim Jim out of his pocket and took a bite.

"All I've seen you eat all week is beef jerky. Please tell me you eat actual food when you go home."

Troy shrugged, pointed back at the seat above the tank, and then took another bite. I sighed and pulled myself up the ladder.

My legs dangled over the dunking booth once more, and I stared into the water, completely lost in thought.

"You okay up there?" Troy was looking at me, squinting in the sunlight.

"Yeah, I'm fine." I shook my head to clear it and looked out at the fair. It was dead. Probably because it was so damn hot.

"What do you think of Bigfoot?" I asked.

Troy's eyebrows raised. "Bigfoot?"

"Yeah, my sister's boyfriend is like a Bigfoot hunter or something."

"Seriously?"

"Yep."

"West's boyfriend?"

"No! No, my other sister."

"You have another sister?"

"Yeah, I've got a twin. Her boyfriend is the worst. God, Troy, do you ever just wish someone didn't exist?"

"Uh . . ."

Our conversation ceased when I caught a glimpse of a slender man staring directly at me from across the path. He was wearing a dark gray jacket despite the heat of summer, and his skin was a sickly yellowish hue. Wisps of dark still clung to his scalp, but just barely. And he wasn't moving. I took a breath of relief, thinking it must be a prop that someone had left out, but then he blinked once.

I slid down the ladder and stood next to Troy.

"What's with the crypt keeper over there?" I said softly, directing my eyes at the specter. Troy turned his entire head to look and I hit him in the arm.

"Don't be so obvious!" I hissed.

"You mean that skinny guy?"

"Yes."

"That's just Mark."

"Who the hell is Mark?"

"He owns the place."

"I thought Mike owned the place," I said.

"Nah, Mark owns it, Mike operates it. They're brothers. Or cousins or something."

"Why is he watching us?"

"Oh, well, rumor has it he's allergic to sunlight because he never ever comes out of his office, so the fact he came out to see the newest hit attraction means word has spread about how awesome you are."

"Dude, I sit on a seat and yell insults at people. That doesn't require a lot of talent." I glanced back to Mark, but the spot where he'd been standing was empty. I scanned in both directions, but there was no sign of him. "Holy shit, he, like, vanished."

"Yeah, he does that."

"Speak of the devil," I said under my breath as Mike came waddling around the corner. His cheeks were red and chapped, and he'd sweated right through his shirt.

"Hey, Mike!" Troy called out.

"Why are you two just standing around?" He narrowed his eyes at me. "Why are you wearing that damn sweatshirt?"

"I'm cold," I said dryly.

Mike scoffed. "This is why I can't put you at the bar."

"Sir, I never said I wanted to work the bar," I interjected.

"I only put C cups and bigger on bar duty." Mike was staring hard at my sweatshirt.

I stood there, stunned for a moment, trying to interpret what this Neanderthal was saying to me.

"I'm sorry, are you telling me that my breasts aren't big enough to do anything but let idiots dunk me?"

"I'm full up on beer wenches."

"I have no desire to have my ass grabbed and serve beer to man-boys who never outgrew playing pretend!" I spewed.

"What she means is we're both perfectly fine working Drench-the-Wench, right, Glinda?" Troy broke in, trying desperately to save the situation. "I mean, sir, she has a master's degree in medieval stuff. She's an asset."

"It's fine, Troy." I tried to sound completely unruffled, despite the deep pang of humiliation searing through my gut. "And my degree is irrelevant here—the only historically authentic aspect of this place is the level of misogyny—well, and the smell of body odor."

Finally, Mike looked up at my face, but his expression was not one of a man about to repent.

"You best watch it, Linda. Or I'll replace you. I'll put Troy up there and yank Dylan from the log game." He seemed to notice our confusion. "We used to do Dunk-the-Drunk, but then Kyle drowned."

"Oh my God!" I gasped.

"Oh, not here—in his backyard after a heroin binge."

Damn. "That's terrible."

"Yeah, it was one the favorite attractions. So"—he clapped his hands together and looked at me, his expression softened by the tragic tale of poor Kyle—"we gotta get you outta that shirt."

"No."

"—and tighten that corset, really make those laces work—"

"Nope."

"For Kyle." He looked at me long and hard.

"F–fine." I yanked the sweatshirt over my head and tossed it behind the chair.

"That's more like it!" Mike was smiling now. "And remember, when you're up on the seat and you shout insults at all the men that pass by—you know, be a real ballbuster."

The look in his eyes was like that of a child who had just been told he was receiving a large cupcake for dinner. In fact, I could have sworn he drooled a little.

"You're being really misogynistic."

"I really am a genius for pairing you two up. You know? 'Cause you're all 'rah rah rah,' and Troy's, like, got this innocent baby face, and it's like the domineering wife and her poor broken bastard husband—and then they dunk you!" He was roaring with laughter now, and his already red cheeks were turning a deep purple. I looked around to see if there was a defib anywhere in case he collapsed. I waited until his laughter had subsided into a delighted smile before I spoke.

"Thanks for the feedback, Mike."

"All I know is, I'm tired of catching you up there in that hoodie. You get up there without your little shirt and then at the end of the day, you tell me how much more you make in tips."

I narrowed my eyes. "You could just pay us more."

"This is a nonprofit, honey, not a charity."

"Just because you're not making any profit doesn't make you a nonprofit. That isn't what nonprofit means."

But Mike was done with his inspection. He patted Troy on the shoulder. "Just keep your girlfriend in line, okay, pal?"

"I'm not his girlfriend!" I exclaimed.

Troy shoved his hands into his pockets and rocked back on his heels. Mike either didn't hear me or didn't care, but in any case he continued his patrol of the fairgrounds and wandered away from us.

"It's a Renaissance fair in Texas!" I grumbled more to myself than to Troy. "If he wants authentic, maybe he should start by chasing the possums out of the employee bathrooms."

"Sorry about that, Glin." Troy looked at his shoes and bit his lip.

"He's a complete animal." I shuddered. "I gotta find another job."

Troy looked like his pet goldfish had just died as I climbed back up the ladder. Troy was not my boyfriend, nor would he be. He was nice enough, but the last thing I needed was to go and develop feelings for a guy with a high school education, whose career goals had been met at a freaking Renaissance festival . . . a guy who was sweet and funny and pure in a way I hadn't encountered before. I wasn't going to ruin my illusion of him by actually letting him in.

★ ★ ★

"Why is your hair wet?" was West's greeting as I walked in the front door after work.

"Forgot my umbrella?"

"We're in a drought." She stood at the top of the stairs, arms crossed, like she'd been waiting up for me or something.

I decided to try just being completely honest.

"I fell into a tank at work."

Her eyes narrowed. "What do you do again?"

"Hydrodynamic physics. You know what? It's really too complicated to explain to a high schooler."

West raised an eyebrow and pursed her lips. Then she came down the stairs, looking around the corner to see if the coast was clear.

"Listen, Mom's been acting really weird."

"Ha, yeah, I'm aware."

"No, like weirder than usual." She looked so serious; it was really throwing me off.

"Weirder than joining a cult?"

"Yes."

"Weirder than saying she's going to marry Arlon?"

"Glinda, I'm telling you, something is really wrong." Her voice had dropped to a whisper.

I rubbed my forehead, where a migraine was taking root. Could I not go one day without having to worry about the stupid cult? "Okay, like what?"

"You probably haven't noticed because you're working all day now, but she's been clearing out rooms."

"Yeah, she's been doing that since she joined the cult. All 'evil modern technologies' and stuff." I emphasized my annoyance with air quotes.

"No, not like with the TVs. She's getting rid of *everything*." West looked to make sure the coast was clear. "I found a box next to the garbage cans by the garage. It was full of our family photo albums and pictures of Dad."

I felt my insides deflating as I tried to make sense of my sister's words.

"I put them in my room, under my bed," West added.

"I just—" I shook my head. "I need to talk to her."

"No! Don't!"

"Then why'd you tell me, West? What did you think I was going to do?"

"I'm dealing with it. I just wanted you to know so you'd be sure to stay out of the way while I figure out what's going on with her."

"That's ridiculous. I'm an adult—I should be the one talking to her."

"Glinda, you didn't even notice anything was wrong. You're too wrapped up in yourself."

"*What?*" My jaw dropped. She was standing on the first step, making me look a few inches up to see her face. I wanted to scream at her—really let her have it—but instead I sized her up, running my tongue along my top teeth. Then I took a breath and forced myself to relax.

"Tell me, West, is 'hypocritical' an SAT word? Do ya know that one?"

"Whatever, Glinda. Just do me a favor and stay out of it before you eff it up like you eff everything up!" Then she flipped her hair over her shoulder and raced up the stairs.

"I'm not arguing with a girl who's still too scared to say 'fuck'!"

I was answered with a door slam.

I dropped my purse on the dining table and made my way out the back door as quickly as possible. I needed some air. It was strange—I hated almost everything about work, but at least there I had someone to talk to, someone to joke around with. I could relax and be myself. As soon as I set foot in my house, it felt like all the air had been sucked out of me. Moving, talking, even breathing seemed like a burdensome thing.

I stepped out on the back step and filled my lungs with the cool breezes of evening.

The land behind the house sloped toward a small river. At the bottom of the hill, beside a large oak, was a flat, clear space by the water. A large rock sat in the middle, like it had been placed there specifically for when one needed a seat to just stop and be.

My dad had named it Lothlórien after the Elf realm in *Lord of the Rings*, and after he died, I spent many hours sitting on that rock, crying or reading or just closing my eyes and listening to the birds and the running water. My mom and I used to go down there and sit back to back on this rock and read books or just talk about school and boys or whatever. Some of my best conversations with her had happened on that rock. She hadn't been down there since my dad died..

I hadn't been down there since the thing with Patrick happened.

Now I found myself standing there, next to the rock, looking up into the trees. The string lights my dad had hung were still woven around the limbs in a web above my head. I sank down on the rock and closed my eyes.

I opened my eyes just as the lights burst on, illuminating the spot like they did every evening when the sun went down. My dad had set them on some kind of sensor or timer or something. I knew better, but it had an ethereal effect, like he was bringing light from the other side.

I inhaled the cooler evening air and concentrated. *"I am the master of my fate; I am the captain of my soul."* Or, wait, was it captain of my fate and master of my soul? Shit! I couldn't even get the thing I'd spent years studying right anymore.

"Glinda!" My mom's silhouette stood out against the tress at the top of the hill. The last beams of sunlight dipped behind the horizon as I trudged back up the hill, pulling myself along by grabbing onto tree trunks. Scaling that hill quickly had been child's play when I was sixteen. Now I reached the top and had to lean against a lamppost for a minute to regain my breath.

"You called?" I panted, putting my hands on my knees.

"Helpfulness and Acceptance, I was hoping you'd join me for my sunset meditations."

"Oh. I thought you actually needed something."

Her face fell as she gripped a small bundle of dried flowers to her chest. She turned away and I called after her.

"Hey, Mom! Weirdest thing." She turned back to look at me. "So, West found a box out by the trash full of old family photos. Do you know how it got there?"

She looked at me long and hard before slowly shaking her head side to side. I wanted to believe her. I wanted it so bad that, in that moment, I did.

I smiled at her, but her face remained expressionless as she turned back to the circle in the garden and walked away.

There it was again, that annoying little gnawing at my brain, like whispers in a crowd I couldn't quite make out. But my head hurt, so I pushed them down and went inside.

★ ★ ★

A little over two and a half years ago

My senior year of college, I lived in the dorms with a community shower. I found every excuse to drive home and shower in my own bathroom, with my scented soaps and the white tile that my mom kept sparkling. The community showers were a dull green tile with cracked vinyl curtains, yellowed from age and hard water. Whenever I used them, I slipped on my shower flip-flops and carefully stacked my clothes on a towel right outside, so as little of me or my belongings as possible actually came into contact with the Petri dish floor.

That night I ran straight into the showers barefoot, slipped out of my T-shirt and pajama pants, and threw them in a pile beside the stall. I stepped in and turned the water on, pulling the curtain closed like it was some kind of barrier between me and the rest of the world. And in my tiny stall, I did feel alone, though not protected.

I opened my mouth and let the water run in and wash away the taste of vomit and his tongue. I hadn't grabbed my caddy with my shampoo or loofah. I just stood there, letting the luke-warm water wear away at me like a river-worn stone.

I had no idea how long I stood there before my silence was interrupted by the cackling of familiar voices. It was Mandy and Jordan from down the hall. We were in American Lit together and they came over to my room to study all the time, although I did end up writing a lot of their papers for them. But that didn't matter; they were my friends. They thought I was hilarious.

Relief washed over me at the sound of their voices. I needed help. I reached for the curtain to pull it open and call out to them, when Mandy's voice stopped my hand in motion.

"That's so fucking gross!" Mandy said. "She actually threw up in his mouth!" She stepped into the stall next to me and turned on the water.

"Right? I gave him my entire bottle of mouthwash!" Jordan shouted back.

My blood froze in my veins, and my stomach plummeted to the hospital green tiles of the shower floor.

"I'm surprised he didn't vomit when he finally saw her naked!" Mandy laughed. "He said she had a full bush!"

"Ugh! Stop! I don't want to think about her pubes clogging the drain while I'm literally in the shower!"

They didn't give a shit about me. They were using me, just like Patrick, and I was such a fucking idiot for not seeing it. I braced a hand against the wall as my stomach lurched again. I retched silently, but there was nothing left to come up.

"He said her boobs look like a cross-eyed Muppet!"

At that moment, I should have been filled with horror. Humiliation. But I felt nothing. It was like my heart had caved in on itself and left a hard knot in its place. Fuck them. Fuck Patrick and his ultimatums. His "If you love me," his "You're so hot, I can't stop."

He could say what he wanted. He could tell Jordan—hell, he could put a billboard up on the highway: "I was Glinda's first and last!"

More like: "I pressured her when she said she wasn't ready, threatened her, gaslit her by insisting this was what she wanted, that she was the one making this happen, forced myself on her even after she asked me to stop, and kept going until she vomited right in my face!"

But the truth didn't matter because there'd been no witnesses in that space between us, in that dark room, in that pressure cooker of a relationship that should have ended long ago.

I turned the water off and stepped out. Both Mandy and Jordan were hidden behind curtains, still shit-talking me. I spotted Jordan's purple towel with the little yellow daisies. I took it off the hook and dried my crotch before hanging it back up. Then I pulled my clothes back on and left, leaving wet footprints behind me.

When I got back to my room, all traces of Patrick were gone except a discarded, empty condom on the floor.

He'd been so charming when he introduced himself in the theater class I'd taken to fulfill an elective. He'd made my heart flutter. He gave me the warm fuzzies that Dorothy always talked about. He'd made my brain go places I'd never dared go before: me not going to grad school, living in downtown with him and a dog, a wedding dress, a kid maybe. He'd told me I was pretty. He'd tightened his grip. He'd grown cold with the weather. He'd told me I'd look better if I worked on my abs. He'd told me I was lucky to be with him.

There was a missed call on my phone from Dorothy. I lifted a finger to call her back and then lowered it. I couldn't. I couldn't talk to her right now. How could I possibly explain? I just wanted to curl up in my blanket and go to sleep. Problem was, when I looked over at my bed, the blanket was knotted up at the end, covered in vomit. And the space where I slept, the space that had always seemed the safest, now felt strange and unwelcoming.

I sank into my desk chair and turned on my laptop. My phone lit up again, and I saw my dad was calling. Again, I started to answer, but I couldn't. I let it go to voicemail.

I didn't listen to the message until the next morning.

"Hey, Glin, just sitting here at Lothlórien and missing my girl. I don't really have anything to say. Just hope you're not stressing about your Dickens essay. I know you have *Great Expectations* for yourself, but this is a *Bleak House* without you in it, and I hope these *Hard Times* come to an end and we'll see you soon. Okay, I'm out of Dickens puns. Love you, sweetheart . . . wait, the semester is almost over and then we can sing *A Christmas Carol*. Okay, I'm really done. Bye."

It was the last time he'd call me.

IRRITATED AND DISTANT

Present

I WAS LYING ACROSS the bed with my laptop open to the Peace Corps website. Four thousand words. They wanted a four-thousand-word "Motivation for Serving" statement. I'd been staring at the blinking cursor for so long that I could see it when I looked up at the blank wall.

I began typing.

Why do I want to join the Peace Corps? I want to join the Peace Corps because nobody else will hire me, and I have to get away from my crazy mother and her cult leader boyfriend.

I backspaced until the page was blank again and then rolled onto my back with a long groan. I hated roughing it, I was pretty selfish, and the only foreign language I spoke was Old English. The Peace Corps was out. I closed the laptop and hopped off the bed. Another wasted morning to add to my collection.

I came downstairs and heard the clicking of keys coming from my dad's office. For a split second I forgot. I forgot he was dead and I couldn't just open the door and see him sitting there, working on his cases, a big stack of books resting next to his computer. The moment lasted less than a second, but it was enough to shift my entire mood from bad to ruinous.

I knew who was in there before I cracked the door open a sliver. Arlon was planted behind my dad's desk, typing feverishly on the computer. I closed the door without him noticing me and stormed off to find my mom.

"What the hell is he doing in there?" I said through gritted teeth as she sat at the kitchen table surrounded by piles of green fabric, feeding pieces through her sewing machine. The familiar, comforting humming of the motor ceased, and my mom sighed and looked up at me with an expression of pure exhaustion.

"Glinda, you are going to have to accept that Arlon is a part of our lives now."

"Fuck that."

"Language!"

"He's here constantly!"

"My dear Courteous and Considerate, I am marrying Arlon. Soon he will live here." Her gaze drifted back to her sewing.

"Mom, look at me." My tone was less than courteous or considerate.

She sighed again and turned to face me, waiting patiently for me to speak.

"Mom, I hate to make ultimatums, but I need you to know that if you actually go through with this, if he actually moves into this house, I'm leaving."

"Where will you go?" She raised an eyebrow, and for a moment I felt like I was eight again, threatening to run away from home.

"I'll—I'll join the Peace Corps."

She cracked a smile. I hadn't seen her smile at me, like really, genuinely smile at me, in ages.

"Glinda, you hate camping and you're terrified of flying." She pressed the pedal with her foot and went back to her sewing with a tiny, amused smirk resting on her lips. Now it was my turn to sigh.

I grabbed a novel I'd already read and didn't like that much off the coffee table and marched to the back door.

"Sorry, Mom. I can't be in this house as long as he is."

She either didn't hear me over the machine or pretended not to.

I went down to the creek and tried to read, but I couldn't concentrate. Instead, I cried. It started out as a few tears falling onto the pages, and then I was heaving and sputtering and wishing I hadn't painted myself into a corner, because I really wanted to go back into the AC. However, I am nothing if not stubborn, so I crossed the creek and walked the old familiar paths through the trees and cried some more, and finally I sat down at the creek again until dark, ignoring my growling stomach, ignoring the mosquitos feasting away on my exposed arms and legs, ignoring the burning, achy feeling of my eyelids after too many tears.

She didn't call me in for dinner. She didn't come check on me after the sun went down. So I watched the water, moving like a glassy ribbon over the rocks and thought about Dad and Dorothy and how fucked up everything was, and how fucked I was. Fucked or fucked up, or both.

And when it became evident that Arlon was staying the night, I pulled out my phone and called the only person I could think of to call.

★   ★   ★

Eighteen-ish years ago

I almost drowned when I was seven. We'd gone to Wet 'n' Wild in Arlington for the Fourth of July. My mom slathered us up with sunscreen and put us in these matching purple swimsuits with a silver shell on the front. Dorothy and Mom had stayed in the wave pool, but I had gone with my dad to ride the slides. We did a little yellow one and then a bigger orange one with a steeper drop. It scared me and I begged him to take me back to the yellow slide.

I sat in a child-sized black inner tube and waited at the top, feeling the jets of water on either side of me until the lifeguard at the top signaled I could go. I pushed off with my hands and then flew down the slide, twisting and turning, squealing with delight. But when I reached the bottom, the tube flipped, and I sank down in the pool. The water was just over my head and the jets from the bottom of the slide that were supposed to push your tube away were pinning me down.

I don't know much about near-death experiences and certainly not about how children process them, but for me, I never panicked. I opened my eyes. All I could see was blue, lighter at one edge of my vision and darker at the other. I didn't struggle. I didn't try to push myself up for air. I sat there, floating beneath the surface of the water, completely still. I remember it was quiet. Quiet and blue. And then I thought, *Okay, this is how I die. I'm dying.* And it wasn't scary. It was just a fact. I was surrounded by the endless hazy blue, and I imagined it would last forever.

And then my dad pulled me up, and the moment my head broke the surface, I freaked out, crying and clinging to him. He was breathing fast, and he pressed my head against his chest. His heart was racing.

"You're okay, I got you; you're okay, I got you," he said over and over as he carried me out of the pool. We rested on a lounge chair in the sun. "Are you okay?"

"Yes. I got some water in my nose."

"That'll sting." He smiled so big and patted me on the back. Then he breathed hard some more and laughed. He laughed for a long time and that scared me.

"It's not funny," I finally said. "I almost died."

"You didn't almost die, but you did scare me. And sometimes when people are scared and then they're not scared, it makes them laugh."

"Why?"

"Because the feeling you get right after you've been scared is the best feeling. It's a laughing, happy crying, big hugs feeling." And then he hugged me tight.

★ ★ ★

Present

"Hey." Troy opened the door wider and gestured for me to come into his apartment.

"Thanks for letting me come over."

"Of course." He shut the door behind me and then noticed the duffel I had hanging off one shoulder. "You, uh, you staying awhile?"

"Oh, that? No." I clutched the strap and shook my head. "I just grabbed some things—I don't know. I don't know what I'm doing exactly. I just had to get out of there."

"It's cool." He ran his fingers through his hair and twisted one way and then the other, looking around his apartment, no doubt trying to figure out how to backtrack and get this crazy lunatic out of his place.

"You can sleep in my bed," he said finally.

"No!" I said with a little too much force.

"No, I mean, I'll sleep on the couch." He knitted his brow.

"No, it's okay. I'll take the couch."

"No, I insist. You're my guest—actually my first guest—so you get the bed."

"Troy, please don't take offense, but when's the last time you washed your sheets?"

"Uh . . . okay, so you can sleep on the couch."

"Thank you." The awkwardness was palpable. I should have just slept in my car like I'd thought about doing.

"Um, are you hungry?"

"No . . ." I shook my head to try and clear it. *"Say what you mean, and mean what you say,"* I could hear my mother telling me, another mantra of hers that predated the cult by decades. "Actually, yes. Very."

Troy smiled and the tension in my shoulders lessened. He went over to the tiny kitchen attached to the living room and started rummaging through the fridge. I started to set my bag down on the couch and noticed a small pile of laundry and several empty cans of MaXout. I put the bag on the floor and went to the small bar that separated the rooms, leaning across it on my elbows.

"I've got leftover pizza and a can of SpaghettiOs."

"How old is the pizza?"

"Um . . . it's Tuesday, right?"

"It's Friday."

"Sweet. It's still good."

I raised an eyebrow as he pulled an entire pizza box out of the fridge and set it in front of me. He lifted the lid and there were four slices of pepperoni pizza, the orange grease congealed on the top from sitting in the fridge.

"You, uh, want to microwave it?" Troy asked.

"No, that's okay." I reached for a piece. My stomach rattled inside me, the reality of not eating all day hitting me like a semi. I wolfed down a piece and then another. Troy pulled out a couple of beers from the fridge and gestured one toward me. I nodded enthusiastically, my mouth still chewing the stale crust.

He popped the tab and slid the can of beer across to me. I usually was more of a craft beer girl, but tonight cold pizza and cheap beer were all I needed. I took a swig and relished the bubbles dancing all the way down my throat.

When my hunger had been sated, I became self-conscious, being alone with Troy in his place. I wasn't sure what to do or say, so I settled on the obvious.

"Thank you, by the way."

"Sorry I didn't have anything better."

"No, I mean, thank you for letting me come over."

"Sure!" He smiled his pretty smile.

"Truth is, I left in a hurry, and I honestly didn't know where to go." I paused. "I don't have many friends. None, actually, at the moment."

"Well, you've got me." He smiled again, and I hated how much I liked it. I prayed my body hadn't betrayed me by blushing.

"So, um, you want to talk about it or—"

"Um, what about? Talk about what?" I fumbled over my words.

"Why you left."

"Oh!" I nearly laughed I was so relieved that that was all we were talking about. "Sure, yeah, let's talk about my life imploding."

He smirked.

"So where do I start? My mom's in a cult. Have I told you that?"

"No." His eyes grew wide. "So, are we talking doomsday cult, terrorist cult?" He gulped, then lowered his voice. "Sex cult?"

"Ew, gross! No!" I fidgeted with the pizza crust on the counter. "Like a higher plane of existence, cult of personality."

"That sounds pretty awesome." Troy laughed. I didn't.

We were both quiet for a minute, and then he tried again.

"I mean, dude, do they have like a cult house thing where I could live for free?"

"It's called a commune, and no, not yet. But the leader, Arlon, is planning on moving the entire group into my mom's house. That's part of why I left. He was there and I just . . . I just can't be around him."

Troy pursed his lips and knitted his brow. "That's not cool," he said, his words dripping with indignation.

"No." I sighed and dropped the pizza crust. "Oh, and he's marrying my mom."

"What?"

"Yep."

"How have you not told me any of this before?"

"Because it's not funny. It's basically my life falling to complete shit."

"So that's really what this is about then? Your mom getting remarried?" He looked slightly amused.

"You don't understand. At least your parents went together so neither of them could—" I slapped a hand across my mouth. For an instant he betrayed a look of hurt but then immediately regained composure and looked across the bar at me like nothing had happened. "Shit, I'm sorry, Troy. That was so stupid to say. I didn't mean it—I mean, I should be glad I still have—you know what? I'm going to shut up." My cheeks were burning from embarrassment. If I could have sunk down through the old carpet and disappeared forever, I would have.

But he reached across the counter and gave my hand a squeeze, letting his fingers linger across mine for a moment. The swallow of beer I'd just taken caught in my throat, and I let out an awkward cough.

"It's okay. We shouldn't compare; we've all got shit that's bad to us." He let go and I felt the weight of my own hand, alone on the laminate counter. What the hell was that? I took a deep breath and rubbed my eyes with the heels of my hands, trying to clear my head. Bury it, bury it back down.

Troy didn't seem to notice my slight distress.

"So, uh, you've never told me why your parents gave you and West such interesting names. Is there a story there?"

I straightened up a bit and smiled.

"So, I told you I have a twin sister. Dorothy and I were conceived at a drive-in double feature of *The Wizard of Oz* and *The Rocky Horror Picture Show*. So, it could have been a lot worse—my name, you know. Frank N. Furter or Magenta or something."

"You're joking."

"Nope."

He laughed. "That's crazy."

"It *is* crazy." I snickered.

"Dorothy, huh?"

"Yeah."

"You don't talk about her much."

"Uh, yeah, we are kinda sorta not speaking at the moment."

He waited, wide-eyed for an explanation. I sighed. Why not? I'd just unloaded the cult on him; an estranged sister was just the cherry on top.

"I sort of, maybe, tried to break her and her boyfriend up." I winced. Troy was watching me, not betraying any reaction. "It was really dumb, and I feel like shit about it. But yeah, shortly after that, she and her boyfriend, James, took off for some cabin in the woods to hunt Bigfoot, and I haven't spoken to her in about a year and a half." I didn't mention what happened that Christmas. How, after the Thanksgiving debacle, things had gone from bad to worse.

"Seriously?" Troy said.

Why was I spilling my guts to him like this? Now he was going to hate me too.

"Yeah, I know, I know. It's awful. But to be fair, James is the absolute worst. He basically took my sister from me."

Troy stared at me for a long while. He started to say something and then shook his head.

"I'm sorry." I groaned and rested my chin on my fist. "I know I sound super immature. It's just—how do I explain this? It's like no one else seems to care if our family drifts apart. I don't mean we need to all live together and be codependent and shit—I just mean, I always assumed we'd be close, we'd be in each other's lives. And now my sisters and my mom are each headed down paths in completely different directions, and I'm just so tired of stretching myself to try and hold onto them."

Troy looked thoughtful for a moment and then nodded. "You know, I probably don't know what I'm talking about, but one year, I was working the Balancing Log booth with some guys, Charlie and Nathan. They were idiots. Anyway, I knew how to run the ride, so I just did it. They'd offer to help, but I didn't really trust them, so I'd just tell them it was fine, I got it. I kept that booth running. Eventually they stopped offering and just hung around back all day, smoking weed and goofing off. Then one day, it was really busy, and I was trying to keep up and do everything myself, and I slipped up and got my hand caught in between the logs and crushed the bones."

"Oh my God!" I glanced at Troy's hand and noticed a faint scar for the first time. "Shit, that sounds really painful!"

"Oh, it hurt so fucking much." He laughed. "But then Mike had Nathan and Charlie come back and take over—and they had no idea what to do. Because I'd done everything, they hadn't had to learn how to do anything. And because I overextended myself, I got hurt. So, all three of us ended up on bathroom duty for the rest of that summer."

"Gross."

He grinned. "I can't even explain the scene in those stalls after BOGO turkey leg day."

"Hmm, that's a pretty convenient and transparent allegory, Troy."

"What? No. I was just trying to cheer you up with a stupid story." He smiled and then nodded toward the TV. "You wanna watch a movie?"

That sounded wonderful. Like really normal and comfortable and wonderful. And I was beyond grateful not to have to talk about Dorothy anymore.

He walked past me to the living room, where he pushed all the crap off the couch. We each sat at either end of it and then spent thirty minutes deciding what to watch on Netflix. A whole bunch of "Oh, have you seen this?" and "Oh no, wait, maybe you wouldn't like that," until finally we settled on *The Princess Bride* because we both agreed it was the absolute perfect comfort movie.

I grabbed a fleece blanket off the floor and curled up.

Troy went to his room and returned with a joint and a silver lighter. "Do you mind?"

"Of course not!" I said, trying to sound nonchalant, like I had any experience at all with this particular rite of passage, but it came out weird and high pitched.

He raised an eyebrow and sat on the couch, looking down at the joint. "We don't have to. I just thought it might take your mind off the shit at home."

I cleared my throat. "Uh, we? Oh yeah, totally."

He put the paper to his lips, lit the end, and took a long pull of smoke. The smell instantly brought me back to closed doors in college, parties I wasn't invited to, smoke breaks in stairwells that seemed to always end before I got there, leaving only the lingering scent of weed and the echoes of closing doors.

He took another drag and then held it out to me.

I took the joint gingerly between two fingers, put it to my lips, and inhaled. The hot smoke floated down into my lungs and I blew it out slowly, watching the wisps of white dissipate into the air. Immediately I dissolved into a coughing fit.

"First time?" Troy asked, doing a really bad job hiding his smirk.

"Why would you think that?" I cleared my throat, and refrained from mentioning that my drug of choice in graduate school had been more of the pill variety. I took another couple of draws and handed it back to him.

I leaned my head back and waited for the high, but I felt the same—the same worries, the same anxieties, the same dark thoughts all roaring around in my skull. "Huh."

"What?" he asked.

"I guess I'm just one of those people that weed doesn't work on."

Troy shot me a bemused smirk and then hopped up to turn the lights off.

The movie started and the comforting warmth of nostalgia washed over me. After twenty minutes I stretched my legs out a little, not touching him of course.

My mind began to wander, back to Troy's story about the Balancing Log booth. I had been trying so hard to fix my family, to bring us through this period of darkness, and all I'd done was drive everyone further apart.

I slept harder than I had in a long time and when I blinked my eyes open, bright morning light streamed through the blinds and a message on the TV read: *Are you still watching?*

Troy was asleep at the other end of the couch, his legs still in front of him, the rest of his body leaning on the arm of the sofa.

It was fine. We were friends. Friends fell asleep on couches watching movies all the time. No biggie.

My back popped as I swung my legs around and grabbed my phone from my purse. I'd forgotten to plug it in, and it was at thirteen percent. I had, like, forty-six messages from West. Geez. The kid probably couldn't find her hair straightener and assumed I'd taken it. I had, but she had no way of knowing that.

West (7:16 AM): *What asshole is making all that noise downstairs?!*

West (7:16 AM): *Glinda, if it's you, stop!*

West (7:17 AM): *Are you home? Where are you?*

West (7:20 AM): *Okay, so you're clearly not here. I hear some guy downstairs screaming. It's not Arlon. I hear Arlon too.*

West (7:23 AM): *Some guy is here in the office arguing with Arlon. They both sound super pissed. I think they're fighting about money.*

West (7:24 AM): *I wish you were here. I'm a little freaked out.*

West (7:25 AM): *Mom's being the ever dutiful hostess. She's baking muffins and serving coffee in the good china.*

I sighed and shoved the phone in my pocket. I didn't have time to read through her play-by-play of the very reason I wasn't at the house right now. She'd said it herself—we needed an escape route, and I'd found a momentary reprieve from the madness.

I looked down at Troy. His lips were hanging slightly apart, and his chest was rising and falling steadily. He was actually quite attractive when you weren't distracted by the ridiculous things coming out of his mouth. I wondered what it would feel like to curl up beside him. What would he do? Would he jump up and demand I get out? Would he try to kiss me? Try to go further?

I blinked hard, and the illusion was shattered. I was in a dark, dingy apartment with a guy whose diet consisted of beef jerky and energy drinks. And I had to pee.

Curiosity got the better of me as I passed his bedroom, the door slightly ajar. Glancing over my shoulder, I made sure Troy was still out. Then I peered in. His bed was unmade. Not surprising. His dirty clothes were in a pile in a chair in the corner. Interesting. I had a chair pile too. But then I noticed the framed photos on the dresser. There was one of what I could only assume were his parents, a light-skinned man and a darker-skinned woman, wearing '90s clothes, with '90s hair and glasses. They were standing side by side, with their arms draped around a small boy with an infectious smile and deep-set dimples.

Stop. Now that was too cute.

I pushed the door open a little wider and stepped into the room. Next to the first photo was one of the same boy, slightly older and at a skating rink, his arm slung around the shoulders of another boy, this one fair skinned with light brown hair and blue eyes and freckles. Troy was seriously an adorable child. I glanced at the other boy. There was something about him, something ever so slightly familiar. His eyes, the shape of his mouth . . .

My phone chimed and I dashed out of the room, pulling the door closed.

When I came out of the bathroom, my phone chimed again. Good God, West! I groaned and pulled the phone out.

West (7:38 AM): *Glinda! Come home, please! Please answer me!*

West (7:38 AM.): *He collapsed! He came out of the office with bloody foam coming out of his mouth. OMG, Glinda, I don't know what to do! Mom is crying! Please help!*

West (7:38 AM): *!!!*

West (7:59 AM): *I did CPR. I've never had to do it before, and I just know I messed it up, and he's going to die and it's all my fault!*

West (8:01 AM) *The paramedics took over. They're taking him now.*

I glanced at the current time. It was 8:07 AM. My heart was racing, and I took in a breath of air for the first time since I'd started reading. Who was she talking about? Was it Arlon? I stood there, rigid, until I felt a sudden hand on my shoulder. I yelped and spun around, gasping for breath.

Troy dropped his hand. He was trying to wake up completely, blinking hard and adjusting his jaw, running his tongue along his teeth to lubricate his mouth to speak. "Are you okay?"

"I . . . I don't—"

Another ding and my eyes shot down to the screen.

West (8:07 AM): *Not that you'd care, but he's dead. They took him to the hospital because I guess they have to work on him until a doctor can officially declare him dead, but I heard them say it was a DOA.*

West (8:07 AM): *He died on our freaking living room floor and Mom is a mess, and why don't you just do us all a favor and not come back if this is how helpful you're going to be!*

"Oh my God!" I said, louder than I meant to.

Troy looked at me, concerned. "What is it?"

"I think Arlon *died*."

"Arlon?"

"The cult leader. The dude who's trying to marry my mom."

Troy's eyes went wide. "Oh shit."

"At my *house.* " I was rereading the texts feverishly, trying to understand what had happened.

Troy brushed the front of his shirt like he was trying to rub the wrinkles out and then ran his hand through his hair before letting it rest on the back of his neck. "Is your mom okay?"

"Probably not. I, uh, I need to go home. I'm sorry. Thank you for the couch. I'm sorry, uh—" I said all this while fumbling for my duffel and sliding my shoes on. Then I opened the apartment door wide, letting the morning light baptize me in its white glow.

I stepped out and then turned back to Troy, not sure what to say.

"Thanks. I'm sorry to just bolt—I just—I gotta go!" I licked my chapped lips and pulled a bra strap up that had slipped while I slept.

"Do you want me to come with you?" he asked.

"It's okay. See ya at work." He gave me a shrug and then watched me until I pulled out of the parking spot in front of his apartment. I glanced in my rearview mirror to check for cars, and when I looked back he was gone and the door was shut.

· 7 ·

CURIOUS AND QUESTIONING

Tʜᴇʀᴇ ᴡᴀs ᴏɴᴇ ᴘᴏʟɪᴄᴇ car in front of the house when I arrived home. I ran up the steps and threw the door open. My mom was sitting in a chair by the hearth. Her face was tearstained, and she looked up at me with helplessness, like she was silently begging me to somehow make it better. Reverse time. Bring back the dead.

West stood behind her chair, rubbing her shoulder. She glared at me. "Where were you?" she mouthed.

"Arlon? He's, he's—"

West pointed toward my dad's office. "He's giving a statement to the police."

My stomach dropped as the situation suddenly came into clarity. Arlon was alive. It was the other man, the one West didn't know. Did my disappointment over Arlon being alive and not, in fact, out of our lives forever make me a bad person? Probably.

"What happened?" I came toward my mom. "Who was he?"

"Brother Matthew," my mom spoke so softly I could barely hear her. Brother Matthew?

"Matthew Harrigan," West said flatly. Immediately my mind shot back to the phone call on the night my mom told me she was marrying Arlon. This wasn't a cult member; this was an ex-member, a traitor.

West whispered something in my mom's ear, glared at me hard, and turned toward the kitchen. I followed her.

"Nice of you to finally show up," she said, grabbing a glass from a cabinet, not bothering to face me when she spoke.

"West, I'm sorry! I came as soon as I saw your texts."

She put the glass under the faucet and filled it with tap water. "His mouth tasted like cigarettes and coffee." She was staring out the window above the sink. Water was overflowing and running down the sides of the glass.

"That was very courageous, what you did."

"I can't get the taste out of my mouth." She shut the water off and raised the glass to her lips, steadying herself against the sink. She swished the water around in her mouth, then spit it out. "I brushed my teeth, I used mouth rinse, and it's still there." She took another mouthful of water and spit.

"West, did Arlon do this?"

"I'm never going to be able to drink coffee again."

"West?"

"Mom kept screaming for me to save him. I was trying. I knew he wasn't coming back, but I kept trying until they showed up."

"West? Did Arlon do this?"

"The medics arrived and it was like déjà vu." She finally looked me in the eye. She'd been there when Dad died. She was home sick from school and was the one to scream for our mom and dial 911. Now, there was a tremble in fingers as she held the glass. She was fourteen again. She was scared. She was in over her head.

"West, listen, if Arlon somehow—"

"What? If Arlon somehow murdered him, then it suddenly proves your innocence with the whole James thing? Proof that it's everyone else out there who's dangerous? Is that what you're worried about? Jesus, Glinda!" She drained the glass into the sink and let it fall over with a clink.

I winced. "No, I'm not thinking about myself. Or James. But Arlon is dangerous. And I'm trying to figure out how this happened."

"This happened because you weren't here. Just like you weren't here when Dad—" She narrowed her eyes. She was trying not to cry.

"I'm sorry, West." I sighed. "But I'm here now, and I'm going to fix this."

Before she could respond I turned around and went past my mom without stopping. I marched up to the office door, took a breath, and knocked.

A police officer opened the door. He was one of two, both in plainclothes. The other officer was relaxing in a chair. The first officer looked me up and down. "Who are you?"

"I'm Julie's daughter. I live here."

"Dear Glinda, this is Detective Crumble." Arlon nodded toward the officer in the chair, and then to the one standing. "And this is Detective Bryant."

"I think we've got enough, Mr. Blight." Detective Bryant turned to Arlon, who was sitting behind my dad's desk, arms folded confidently. "We just needed some notes for the ME. Like I said, this is standard procedure when a death occurs outside of a hospital."

"Of course, of course." Arlon uncrossed his arms. "It's just such a tragedy. Matthew was such a good friend."

"Sorry for your loss." Detective Crumble stood up and offered Arlon a handshake. "Thanks for your time."

Then the officers shuffled past me into the hallway. Detective Crumble turned back to me and lowered his voice.

"Here's my card." He pulled a card from his breast pocket and placed it in my hand. "If you have anything you need to tell us, please give me call." Then he gave me a knowing look, and relief washed over me. They knew. Maybe.

"Thanks," I muttered, glancing down at the card.

West walked the officers out. The door closed. Arlon came up behind me and plucked the card from my fingers.

"Hey!" I spun around to face him.

He pocketed the card. "No need for this. It's best we move on from this terrible tragedy."

My mom frowned at me but didn't say anything.

"Your mother tells me that Dorothy made contact with you."

I closed my eyes and stifled a curse. "Yep. Thanks, Mom."

"Interesting." He gave me a little smile. "Well, hopefully things work out with that."

How fucking dare he.

"Don't ever talk about my family like you know anything."

"Glinda, enough!" Mom had found her voice, but she was still trembling. "Do you have any idea what it's like to watch a man die in front of you? For the second time, in the same house. Do you even . . .?" She couldn't finish, but her anguished expression was enough to keep me from saying another word.

"Arlon, may I have a word with you, please?" I feigned my nicest voice.

"By all means. Let's step into my office."

My office. I could have sucker punched him. Instead, I followed him into the office and shut the door. He resumed his spot behind the desk. I stood in front of it, hands on my hips.

"Ar—"

"You know," he said, cutting me off. "I have a terrible suspicion that those officers might be under the impression that Matthew's death wasn't natural. Now, I know that sounds ridiculous."

"Not really." I crossed my arms.

"Well, I'd hate for them to continue down that road because I know where it ends up."

"I'll bet you do." What a transparent idiot.

"You see, dear Glinda, if, say, someone were to have added something to Brother Matthew's coffee—which, again, I know sounds ridiculous—the problem is this: your mother made that coffee. And your mother served Brother Matthew that coffee."

My blood turned to ice water. "My mother had nothing to do with this."

"Of course she didn't." He steepled his hands and rested his chin on them. "Because Matthew died of a heart attack."

I fell back a step. The enormity of what he was telling me had come like a freight train. She couldn't have. She was brainwashed, sure, but not so blindly that she would—no, she wouldn't.

"W-what if they do a toxicology report?"

"I wouldn't worry about that." Arlon smiled. "Sister Arianne works in the ME's office, and it's very disorganized—stuff gets lost all the time. Small town, ya know."

Shit.

Arlon pulled the officer's card back out and slid it across the desk.

"Here. He gave this to you. You should take it, in case you remember anything that might help their investigation along."

I didn't reach for the card.

"Very good." He clapped his hands down on the desk and rose. I sank back into a chair and watched him come around to face me. "You're a smart girl, Glinda. I know you'll make the right choice." Then he left.

I closed my eyes and let the silence in, let it cool the fires that had risen up in my brain and in my chest.

What if she'd done it?

What if she hadn't, but it looked like she did?

Even if she did, the argument could be made that Arlon had brainwashed her and Arlon had controlled her actions.

I needed a lawyer. My *mom* needed a lawyer. I wasn't about to let her go down for his crimes. I rubbed my temples. Dorothy was a lawyer . . .

No. She was done with me. She wouldn't listen. She'd react like West. She'd accuse me of making this whole thing about myself. Or that I was being paranoid.

A few minutes later I came out of the office and found my mom still sitting in her chair. Arlon's heavy stomping from upstairs told me I had at least a few minutes alone with her. I threw my arms around her neck and whispered in her ear. "You don't need to worry, Mom. I'm going to get you out of this."

"Out of what?" She pulled back and stared at me blankly.

"Out of all of it." I squeezed her tighter. "I'll take care of everything."

• 8 •

WATERLOGGED AND UNSURE

"YOU GOT THE GOODS?"

I nodded and quickly climbed up Bessie's leg to sit inside her gaping mouth beside Troy. Bessie was the large wooden dragon at the center of Maypole—and our usual lunch spot.

I handed him a ham sandwich wrapped in plastic cling, and he took it happily. But as I turned to my own sandwich, I caught him shooting me a nervous glance.

"What's wrong?"

"Nothing." He took a bite and said with his mouth full, "What's wrong with you?"

I took a bite and swallowed before answering. "Nothing. I mean, nothing besides a man dying in my house under suspicious circumstances." I sighed. "It's really messed my mom up more, and I didn't think that was possible. She will hardly come downstairs; she spends most of her time in her room reading or meditating."

"I'm sorry." He looked out over the fair and then turned back to me. "Depression is the worst. Makes you feel helpless when you see it happening to someone you care about."

"Yeah." I looked down at my sandwich and picked at the bread. "But hey, there's nothing I can about it here at work, so do that thing you do."

"What thing?"

"You know, where you distract me from all the shit at home."

He nodded and gave me a weak smile before taking a sip from the can of MaXout in his hand.

"Okay, but seriously. What's wrong with you?" I pushed my shoulder against his, and he let a sheepish grin slip out.

"Nothing."

"Troy, what the hell is going on?"

"This is a great sandwich." He took another bite and closed his eyes to relish it.

"Come on, seriously."

"I just . . . I figured some things out recently, and I . . . well, I've got a situation." He glanced down at the sandwich. "Thanks for bringing this for me."

"Dude, you were eating so many Slim Jims I was afraid your heart was going to stop." I stopped. Bad choice of words.

I straightened up and surveyed the fair. There was a group of girls walking together, laughing and sharing some cotton candy. At a picnic table under a large elm tree sat a family: a young mom and dad with a little boy in an adorable dragon costume, and two older adults—the grandparents, no doubt. The grandfather bent over and held a soda bottle up so the little boy could take a sip. A little dribbled down his chin, and the older man laughed as he wiped his grandson's chin with his thumb. It was sweet.

I looked away before that sweetness turned to envy.

"I told you about the cult. I told you I have a twin who doesn't speak to me. I told you about a man collapsing in my house, and you give me nothing. What is your situation?"

"It's really nothing." He cleared his throat, a shadow of guilt passing over his face.

"Troy, I trust you. Do you not trust me?"

"Hmm," he muttered, and studied his sandwich. "So I noticed you've made it all day without getting dunked?"

"True, I think this is the first time ever I've made it this far into the day without a wet corset chafing me." I closed my eyes and tilted my head up to feel the sun on my face. "Today, I am untouchable."

"Riiiight." He laughed and scarfed down the rest of the sandwich.

"Okay, how about this. If I can make it until seven without someone dunking me, you have to tell me what your situation is."

He studied me for a minute and then grinned. "Fine. And if you do get dunked, you go see a movie with me tomorrow night."

I winced and then hoped he hadn't noticed. Despite our brief acquaintance and social differences, Troy and I had quickly become friends. I liked spending time with him—which was saying a lot. Still, going on a date was too close to dating, which was too close to being in a relationship and all the shit that came with it.

However, the gods of the dunking booth were smiling on me today, and I decided it was harmless to go along.

"Fine. I will go to the movies—as your friend—*if* this blessed dry streak is somehow broken between now and the close of business."

He held out his hand enthusiastically and I shook it, then rubbed my palm on my skirt.

"Gross, why is your hand sticky?"

"Some of the mayo from the sandwich got on it." Troy shrugged.

I stared at him, eyebrow raised. "You are like a child. It's unbelievable that you are actually legally responsible for yourself."

He only smiled and then leapt down from Bessie's mouth, landing on his feet in the dirt below. I shook my head and carefully climbed back down the dragon to the ground.

We started walking back to the booth, when we passed the main offices, hidden behind a thin, plywood wall. The sound of Mike yelling at someone drifted through the facade, though I couldn't make out the words.

"Yikes." I threw my gaze at the wall.

"That does not sound good," Troy said. "Wonder what's up."

"Maybe we should check?" I offered.

"Ha, nope. You can't get dunked if you're not on your seat." So, we continued on, ignoring Mike's tirade at some poor soul.

★ ★ ★

Back on my perch above the water, I stretched my arms and popped my back. I'd survived another hour and forty-five minutes, and it looked like I was going to maintain my streak. I'm not going to lie—it was nice to have a job that didn't require a lot of thinking. And yelling insults at people was hardly a chore.

"Come, come, you froward and unable worms!" I called out to the thinning crowd. Most people were out of money as the day drew to a close. They ignored me and continued on to the gates.

"Hey, Glinda!" Troy called up. "I know you're, like, quoting Shakespeare and shit, but people aren't going to stop if they don't understand that what you're saying is actually an insult."

I rolled my eyes. "Fine!"

I scanned the crowd until I spotted a couple of guys holding their girlfriends' purses while the women got their faces painted.

"You two! You lumpish foot-lickers!"

"What the hell you call us?" One of the guys stepped forward with his bro right behind. Shoot, I hadn't noticed how big they were from a distance or how pronounced their arm muscles were. Nor had I noticed their college football shirts. I was definitely getting dunked. I looked over at Troy, who was smiling like he'd just won the lottery.

"You know, in the sixteenth century, 'lumpish foot-licker' was actually considered a compliment!" I tried. The first guy shoved his hand in his pocket and pulled out a wad of bills.

"That witch is going down!" His friend clapped him on the back in support.

"It's wench! Wench!"

The guy wound up his pitch. I braced myself for the drop. *Slam!* The rubber ball struck a wooden crate and fell to the ground. *Slam!* The next ball hit about two inches from the target. He looked up at me and spit on the ground. Then he pulled his arm back and released the ball. It flew straight at the target, bounced off, and landed in the dirt. The spring squeaked, but I didn't drop.

"This shit's rigged!"

I let out a sigh of relief as the guy gave us a wave of dismissal and sauntered off with his friend.

I unclenched my fingers from the plank and laughed. Only yesterday a little old lady had been able to dunk me. What had occurred today could only be described as a miracle.

"Where do you think you're going?" Troy asked as I scooted backward on the plank to get down.

"It's five till—everybody's leaving," I replied.

"The agreed upon time was seven, not 6:55."

"Oh, come on, man. Nobody else is going to stop." I gestured around at the empty paths and gave him a smug look. "I won. It's over."

"We have five minutes."

"Four minutes now."

He gave me a mischievous grin. "Whatever. There's still one chance to break your streak."

With that, he picked up a rubber ball and rolled it around his hand with his fingers.

"Wait, wait, wait!" I shouted. "What do you think you're doing?"

"I'm very clearly going to throw this ball, hit the target, and dunk you *before* seven o'clock."

A wave of panic washed over me and I shook my head. "That's not—nope, that's cheating."

"We didn't make any rule that I couldn't be the one to dunk you."

"You know what, Troy? Fine. You get *one* try—and you have to stand way back." I waved at him, and he took three steps back.

"No, farther than that."

He continued backward, about twice the distance that we made the customers stand to throw. He squinted at the target and wound up the ball, but then dropped his arm and just smiled at me.

"What now?" I asked.

"I forgot!" He released the rubber ball, letting it fall to the ground, and then retrieved a baseball from his pouch, holding it up so I could see it clearly in the fading light. "I brought my own!"

My stomach dropped as I watched him hold the ball out like he was mentally measuring the distance to the target and then get in position.

"What are you doing?!"

"One minute to go!" He grinned, and wound his arm back.

"That's fine! Because the thing is, today I am unstop—" The sound of the ball striking the target and the spring releasing from under me cut off my boasting. The next thing I knew I was under the water, bouncing off the bottom and coming up sputtering for air.

"How the hell?" I gasped.

The electric light above us sizzled on, casting dark shadows across the pool. Clumps of wet hair covered my eyes, and I pushed them aside, spitting out a mouthful of nasty water. I bobbed there in the center of the tank, shivering. Then there was an open hand in front of me. I took it and Troy pulled me up so we were face to face, him balancing on the ladder, and me perched on the top rung, weighed down by my wet clothes.

"You son of a bitch," I said through chattering teeth.

"I'm sorry." The bastard didn't look sorry at all. "Did I mention I was the pitcher on my high school's baseball team?"

"Asshole! You rigged it! You tightened the spring so the rubber balls wouldn't trigger the release."

He only shrugged.

I stared at him. "Why would you do that?"

"Hold on to me and I'll pull you out."

"I can climb out of the damn tank myself," I snarled back, but the next thing I knew I had put my arm around his neck, and he had his arm around my waist and was lifting me up over the lip of the tank. We both froze at the same moment, our faces so close I could feel his breath on my cheek. I looked up into his eyes, and all of a sudden my heart leapt into my throat, and my brain went kinda fuzzy. I expected his goofy grin, but instead he stared back at me, his jaw set, his brow knitted.

He seemed perplexed, conflicted, like he was trying to make up his mind.

I realized I'd stopped breathing. I was entirely too aware of the places my skin was touching his. I gasped and pushed away, losing my balance and falling backward into the water. The world went silent as I sat at the bottom for a moment, racking my brain

for how to address the moment that had just taken place. *Ignore it.*
Yep, ignoring strong emotional reactions was always a great idea.
Suppress the shit out of it. I broke the surface and blew the water
out of my nose.

"Linda! Stop mucking around and get outta there!" Mike was
shouting beside the tank.

Troy offered his hand again, but this time I ignored it and
pulled myself onto the ladder. He hopped down to get out of my
way, and I clumsily climbed down, water flooding the ground
under my feet. As I stood facing Mike, Troy's arm brushed mine;
I silently took a step to the side.

Mike looked pissed. Like really pissed. His nostrils were flaring and his shirt was drenched with sweat. He held out a chubby,
calloused hand to Troy.

"Oh, um, sorry." Troy stumbled as he quickly unzipped his
pouch and pulled out the cash on the right side.

Mike snatched it up and shoved it into his pocket. "All of it."
He held out his hand again.

"Oh, these are our tips, sir," Troy protested, but Mike narrowed one eye like he was mentally placing a crosshair at Troy's
face.

The air was heavy now, and above our heads the mosquitos
buzzed in the flickering greenish hue of the security light.

"But, those . . ." Troy trailed off and then reluctantly handed
over the rest of the cash. I heard him spit a *dammit* under his
breath. Mike shoved the rest in his pocket and then folded his
arms across his broad chest. I looked over at Troy, waiting to see
what he was going to do. He was chewing his lip, his eyes con-
centrating on Mike, trying to work up the nerve to confront the
thief. Nope, I couldn't let him do that.

"Hey, what's the big idea, Mike?" I demanded, not hiding
the anger in my voice.

"Glin, don't," Troy started softly.

"No! You don't freaking pay us, and now you're stealing our
tips? What the hell, man?" I took a step toward Mike and was
surprised by how much he shrank back. It only gave me more
confidence. "You know what? You can fire me—or whatever,

but Troy has worked here forever and been a good employee. You need to give him that money back right now and never pull this shit again!"

I leaned back, waiting for Mike to explode at me, scream at me that I was fired. Instead, he thrust his hand into his pocket and pulled out a couple of bills and tossed them at my feet. Nobody moved. After a moment Mike cleared his throat and dropped his arms.

"My jackass, backstabbing cousin sold the land."

I blinked. "I'm sorry, what?"

"Mark gave the land away to some jerk. In a week or two this whole place will be bulldozed." He sounded utterly defeated.

"What?" Troy cried.

"Guess that's what I get for trying to run a nonprofit. Anyway, you two need to get the hell outta here. You're done."

"Done? What do you mean done?"

"I mean, if you show up tomorrow, you're going to be greeted by an empty fair. It's over. Today's everybody's last day." Then he bent over, scooped up the bills he'd thrown, and marched off, his fist clenched tightly around the stolen dollars.

"Troy, I don't know what to say. I'm so sorry," I offered, trying to see inside his head. His expression was tense, but just as quickly it relaxed, and he turned to me.

He gestured with his thumb toward the direction Mike had gone. "Talk about a lumpish foot-licker." Then he unbuckled his pouch, laid it across a stool, and walked away, tossing his baseball in the air and catching it as he disappeared into the shadows.

◆ 9 ◆

UNPREPARED AND FORSAKEN

"You okay, Wellness and Prosperity?"

"Never better."

"You want something to eat?"

I sighed. "Not really hungry. Thanks though." I plopped onto a bar stool and held my head in my hands. This sucked. Troy loved the fair. And despite what a goof he was, hanging out with him had been the first time in a long time I'd felt like my old self, the person I'd been before the cult, before Dad died, before Patrick.

I needed to talk to Troy. Needed to make sure he was okay. I knew he was working at the laundromat all afternoon, so maybe I'd just casually drive up there and check on him.

"Hey, Mom, I'm going out for a bit."

"Uh . . ." She looked at me strangely.

"What now?" I asked, getting that ominous feeling in my bones.

"Our transportation needs are changing, Glinda. We don't each need our own car."

"What? No!" My stomach dropped as I leapt off the stool and bounded to the front door. I threw it open and surveyed the front drive. My car was gone.

"Where is my car?" I came storming back into the kitchen. My mom's brow was knit, and she swallowed hard.

"Arlon had me sell it this morning. A nice man a town over gave us a good amount for it, considering how old it was. Don't worry—the money will go to good use."

"Dad bought me that car." I was surprised I wasn't shouting. I didn't feel like shouting, though. The fight had just emptied out of me, leaving behind a brittle shell. "Dad taught me how to drive in that car," I said, deflated.

"Glinda, the only way to reach a higher plane of existence is to completely disconnect—"

"Not. Now. Mom." There had only been a handful of times in my life when I dared be rude to my mother. Most of those instances had occurred around the age of thirteen and had not ended well. However, as I stared at her now, I knew two things: One, I wasn't thirteen anymore. And two, it was time for rude. It was time for anything that would break whatever spell this Arlon dude had over my mom.

"I don't know a lot, Mom, but I do know that all of *this*"—I waved my hands around dramatically—"would break Dad's heart."

She continued mixing her batter in silence, avoiding eye contact with me. I threw my hands up and went back upstairs to think.

★ ★ ★

I needed to talk to Arlon. One on one. I needed to look him in the eye and appeal to his humanity. I knew it was a gamble, assuming he had a shred of humanity left, but there was nothing else to do.

I pumped myself up, put on some makeup, and announced my plan to West, who was holed up in her room, as usual.

"What exactly are you going to say to him?" she asked.

"I have a plan."

"Hooray," she said flatly. "All is saved." Then she went back to organizing her closet.

But I wasn't about to be derailed from my mission by Ms. Gucci. "I'm applying Glinda's three-prong approach to appealing to one's humanity."

She raised an eyebrow. "Okay, I have to hear this."

"You scoff, but it's very effective. First: flattery. Second: reason. Third . . . third—well, I can't remember the third, but it'll come to me."

"Yikes." West resumed folding a shirt. I sighed and went downstairs.

"Mom?" I said, coming around the corner of the kitchen. I stopped short. She was bent over, with her forehead resting on the counter, her hands on top of her head, and she was weeping. Before Arlon, I had caught her like this many a time, but it had been awhile, and it caught me off guard. I had forgotten how uncomfortable and downright devastating it is to see your mother break down and not be able to do anything about it.

She straightened up and wiped her face with the back of her hand. "Glinda. I'm sorry. I didn't want you to see me cry." She'd used my name. My actual name. Without any attributes or ridiculous metaphors.

"What's going on?" I asked gingerly.

"Oh, nothing. I was just remembering something funny your . . ." She trailed off, her chin trembling. Your what? Dad? Sister?

I walked up with deliberate steps and hugged her around the middle. She stiffened and then relaxed, pressing her forehead against mine for a moment.

"I don't know what I'd do without you here to keep me from falling apart sometimes." She pulled away and gave me a half smile. "Now." She cleared her throat and shook her head like she was dismissing her sadness. "I'm going to be late for the meeting."

Before I could say anything, she was grabbing a plastic tub of cookies off the counter and walking briskly to the back door.

"Hey, Mom, uh, what if I came with you tonight?" I asked.

She stopped and spun around, her eyes wide. "Really?"

"Yeah." I shrugged. "I want to see what it's like." I did. It wasn't a lie. I also wanted to dismantle it, from the inside if I had to, starting with one Arlon Blight.

"Oh, Good News and Renewer of Spirit! My inner light rejoices!" She nearly dropped the cookies as she raised her hands up in excitement.

"Great." I forced a smile. Then I went ahead of her to the car before I could change my mind.

★ ★ ★

We pulled up into a gravel circle behind the Arby's, where a trailer was parked beside a dumpster. About ten cars were parked in the tall grass. I surveyed the sketchy parking lot for my car, but it wasn't there.

"What's this?" I asked.

"This is the meeting hall," Mom replied, and turned the car off.

"This trailer? *This* is the meeting hall?"

"It's temporary," my mother explained as she pulled out her compact to check her makeup.

Well no wonder the dude wanted to marry my mom and live at our house—this place was a dump. I followed her to the steps, where a man in a green robe like the one my mom was wearing stood in the doorway, holding folded pieces of paper.

"Welcome, Sister Julie." He handed her a program. "Ah, and this must be Sister Glinda! We're so glad you came." The man patted my shoulder and shoved a program at me.

We stepped inside. Immediately my nostrils stung with the smell of damp carpet and moth balls. Eight rows of metal folding chairs, four seats deep, were lined up in the center of the cramped space. At the front were two wooden pallets pushed together to form a makeshift stage, with another folding chair on top.

The windows were covered with thick, black canvas. A florescent light flickered in the center of the low ceiling, casting a harsh, green-tinted light down on the people.

The members were milling around in their robes, talking about traffic and the weather and so on. I stood behind my mom, scanning the room for Arlon and trying to dissuade anyone from coming to meet me. It didn't work.

"Why, hello there!" said an elderly lady with bright red nails and three rows of pearls over her robe. At her side she clutched an expensive but worn purse.

"Hello," I replied, trying not to show my discontent at the entirety of this scene.

"I'm Beverly McCoy. And who are you, sweetie?"

Beverly McCoy? The real estate lady whose picture was on every bus stop in town? Damn, Arlon was recruiting some heavy hitters.

"I'm Glinda," I said, shaking her bony hand. It was freezing.

"Well, I am so glad you're here, dear. I was so lonely before I joined Mr. Blight's social club."

"Social club?"

"Lifestyle community," my mom corrected her with a smile.

I looked at Mom in shock. Where had she suddenly gotten the nerve to correct a lady like Beverly McCoy? But Beverly only smiled and shook her head in confusion.

"Oh, dear me, yes, I keep forgetting. Well, it doesn't matter what we call ourselves. The point is, my dear, these people have become my whole world."

"I'm going to find a seat—" I turned around and smacked right into a sickly thin man with his hood hanging low over his face. He seemed familiar.

"Excuse me," I said.

"Sorry," he muttered, and pushed his hood back a little.

Shit. He *was* familiar. Standing before me, clad like a skeleton draped in ivy, stood Mark Willard, the owner of the Medieval Fair. His eyes darkened with recognition, and he sneered at me.

"Good evening, pioneers!" A woman at the front of the trailer was calling the meeting to order. Mark took the opportunity to duck away from me, and my mother pulled my arm in the opposite direction. What the hell was he doing here?

The woman in the front was standing on the stage now, and the members quickly hushed and took a seat. I slid in next to my mom and looked around anxiously as the lights dimmed. Mark Willard was a cult member? The woman on the stage produced a small remote control, and with the press of a button, a dozen battery-operated candles lit up around her.

"My inner light welcomes you," she sang out.

"My inner light is pleased to be here," the whole congregation said in unison.

"A few announcements before we get started. First, a reminder that if you do add cannabis to your baked goods, please mark it on the container before placing it out for everyone to enjoy."

I shot my mother a look, but she was staring straight ahead, nodding at everything the woman was saying.

"And please remember that Father Arlon has forbidden gluten-free desserts at this time. Second, if you have not set up a meeting time this week with Father Arlon to discuss your financial contribution to the Society, please do so before you leave tonight."

She reached down and turned on a black light, then held up her hands. "It is time. Father, we call you forth!" The crowd began to chant in a tone so low I at first thought it was coming from outside.

"Arlon. Arlon," they repeated. I looked at my mom's face. She was watching the stage in anticipation and chanting along with the others. I thought I was going to throw up.

"And now," the woman shouted excitedly, "let us listen to the wisdom of our leader, our space captain, and our father, Arlon Blight!" She took her seat in the small crowd.

Arlon Blight strolled onto the stage, and the whole group stood and applauded. He motioned for everyone to sit, then planted himself in his folding chair. He was wearing a white robe that glowed under the black light, and he clutched a cordless microphone that was completely unnecessary for the size of the room.

"Fellow pioneers!" he began, holding the microphone too close and making his words pop. "The time is now. What's your dream?"

The crowd hushed, eyes all fixated on this man quoting *Pretty Woman* like it was something profound.

"That's what the Starlight Pioneer Society is: a society of dreamers."

Oh brother. Here we go with the dreaming bullshit.

"Even now, I look out on this crowd, and I see doubters, people who have given up on their dreams, and I ask you to walk with me." With this, Arlon remained in place. "When I was a young man and no one would invest in my ideas, did I stop dreaming?"

"No!" the crowd cried out in unison.

"And when I was forsaken by everyone who had ever cared for me, did I stop dreaming?"

"No!"

"No. I started taking classes, and I worked my ass off. I grew a business and then another one. And did I stop dreaming?"

"No!"

"Damn right, I didn't. Because, in the face of adversity, do we stop and roll over?"

"No!"

Arlon was radiating as he pronounced his testimony into the crackling microphone. "No! No, we do not." Here he stopped and bugged his eyes out real big. For a second I hoped he was having a stroke. Then he held out a hand to the crowd. "I kept on dreaming and I dreamed of this, a society of pioneers, ready to fulfill any dream we dare to dream." He lifted up his face and closed his eyes.

Thank goodness that was over. Oh no, wait, he was still going.

"And from a cramped corner of a coffee shop to this trailer, which has served us well, to our new outpost, have we ever stopped dreaming?"

"No!"

"No. Fellow pioneers, we are so close now. Tomorrow we will gather up at our new place on Huxby Lane, our last earthly home before we travel to the stars, where we will each ceremoniously sign over all of our earthly possessions to the cause! And then, a little over two weeks from tonight, you will all witness the marriage of myself to the beautiful Sister Julie!"

The two dozen members erupted into cheers and applause.

Wait—*what?* Tomorrow? No way. Mom hadn't said anything about the cult moving in tomorrow. And the wedding was in *two weeks?* Weddings took months to plan. I'd thought I had more time.

"On that night, Julie and I will be joined in eternal commitment, and as I am your father, she will become your mother."

More cheers; this time I noticed that some members were weeping.

"For you see, pioneers, every dream I've had has come true. There have been those who have said I was crazy—and to them I say, I will dream bigger! I will dream the biggest dream a man can dream!" He paused for dramatic effect. "We will build a commune and live together in harmony. Because we are a family!"

The members were on their feet now, whooping and jumping up and down.

No. No way. I slapped my cheek. Nope. It hurt and I was still sitting in this nightmare of a meeting.

"It'll happen, believe me." Then he lowered his mic and gestured for everyone to sit back down and be quiet. "Yes, yes, I have discovered the secrets to fulfilling your dreams. But, pioneers, am I a selfish leader?"

"No!"

"No. I have taught you about your guiding inner light, the force that draws you to the answers you seek. And I have taught you to shun the mass media. Who here still owns a TV?" He scanned the room. "Go on, anybody, speak up!"

A balding man in the back gingerly lifted his hand, keeping his head bent low in shame.

"Brother Jason." Arlon shook his head. "Tell me . . ."

"I—I gave my TV to my sister back in March, but a couple of weeks ago, I was in Target, and they were having a sale on these teeny tiny LCD screens. I mean, Father Arlon, I just got it to put in the garage to watch the game, you know. It's not even HD."

"I've heard enough." Arlon held up his hand toward Jason. "Come here, brother." There was a gasp that ran through the crowd as Jason stood up and slunk to the front of the room. He stood in front of the stage, facing the other members. Arlon placed his hand on Jason's head and began massaging it. I winced. Jason stood motionless, like a criminal waiting for his sentence.

"What's your dream, Jason? Say it—we've all heard it before—say it!"

"I dream my wife would come back and love me!" Jason exclaimed, and then his face fell.

Arlon stopped massaging his head and stepped down off the stage to stand beside Jason. He put the microphone on his chair and then placed both his hands on Jason's shoulders.

"Look at me, Jason. Jason, the floor can't help you. Look at me."

Jason looked up at Arlon sheepishly.

"Brother Jason, your dream is as valid and as attainable as any of mine. Your wife abandoned you!" Arlon's face turned redder, and he appeared completely enraged. "Is there a greater transgression, my brothers and sisters? Is there a greater transgression than to betray and abandon a person you've sworn to love?"

The crowd erupted into angry shouts of "No!" Arlon, whose face had very quickly returned to calm and placid, settled them down by patting the air with his free hand.

"Your dream is coming true, Brother Jason. Stick with me, every day. Do as I say. Listen to your father. And she will see the light, just as you have. Brother Jason, we're going to change the world. Are you with me?"

Jason nodded and tears began falling from his eyes.

Arlon grabbed the microphone again and put his arm around Jason's shoulders. He whispered into the mic. "Brother, will I ever leave you?"

"No, Father Arlon," Jason murmured.

"Will anyone in this room ever leave you?"

"No," Jason mouthed.

"And you would never leave us, right?" Arlon leaned closer to Jason's face. Jason shook his head. "Say it, brother, say it aloud."

"No, Father Arlon, I will never leave you," Jason said, his voice catching in his throat. Arlon fully embraced him, and Jason sobbed into Arlon's shoulder.

"Now, you bring that TV up to Sister Julie's house tomorrow, and we are going to sell it." Arlon patted Jason on the back.

"Yes, Father Arlon." Jason sobbed as he pulled away. Arlon looked out at his followers.

"That goes for all of you. You bring with you the last remnants of your old life that are holding your dream back, and we'll trade them to the brainless members of society and take what is owed us." Then he put his arms around Jason and hugged him again.

Jason wiped his eyes and smiled, then returned to his seat quickly. Beverly McCoy turned around in her seat and offered him a tissue from her purse, which he took gratefully.

"All our dreams are coming true, pioneers. But dreams aren't free. So now, let us spend some time in meditation. Let us think back, into the recesses of our minds, and see if we've forgotten some secret stash of money. Perhaps your subconscious is holding out on you. Think: *Did I tell Father Arlon about the secret vacation fund? Did I check the kids' piggy banks?* Let your inner light win out over your subconscious. Every penny counts."

Did I sell my grown daughter's car behind her back? I set my jaw and glared at him, wishing I could choke him with my mind like Darth Vader.

The members closed their eyes and hummed softly. Arlon looked around the room happily and then retreated through a door behind the stage. I looked at my mom. She had her eyes closed, and her hands were balled up into tight fists. She squeezed her eyes tight, and a tear rolled down her cheek.

"Mom, what is—" But my questioning was cut off by the woman, who now was standing center stage again. She bent down and turned on another black light at her feet. Now her teeth glowed white in the dim light. She switched the candles off so we were washed in blackness and neon.

"Please rise for the commencement of the Unity Ceremony."

There was a chorus of squeaky chairs as the crowd stood. Mark walked down the center aisle and stood at the front of the room, just off the stage, holding a small leather pouch in his hands.

"Come, brothers and sisters, bring your offerings and receive your inner light's nourishment," the woman said, her arms raised up. The congregants slowly made their way to the center aisle and formed a line. They stepped forward, dropping twenties and fifties into a small basket in the woman's hands and then went Mark, who would reach his slender hand into the pouch, pull out something I couldn't quite see and then place it on the member's tongue. The member would bow and then return to their seat, waiting silently for the rest to follow in this eerie communion ceremony. My mother and I were at the back of the line.

"What the hell are they eating?"

My mother lowered her head toward mine. "Silence and Reception, we must be quiet."

"Mom," I whispered back, "what are they eating?"

"A vitamin."

One by one the congregants gave their weekly contribution and then received their reward. When my mom and I reached the front, my mother dropped in a wad of twenties and then stood before Mark. The gray in her hair glowed under the black light in an unholy halo as she closed her eyes and stuck her tongue out. Mark placed a small tablet on her tongue. She closed her mouth, bowed her head, and walked away. I bypassed the basket and went straight to Mark.

"What is this?" I said through my teeth. He only glared at me, the whites of his eyes glowing hauntingly above me. So, I held out my hand. He frowned and shook his head. *Fine. I'll play along.* I stuck my tongue out and he sighed, reached into the bag, and pulled out a tablet. He dropped it onto my tongue, and I walked away quickly. As soon as I had my back to him, I spat the thing into my palm and examined it. It was an orange dissolvable tablet, stamped with a smiley face.

Ecstasy. Shit. I recognized it immediately. The guy I got my Adderall from in college used to always try to get me to buy it.

I stuffed the tab in my pocket and returned to my seat.

"Mom, did you swallow that pill?"

She turned to me and nodded, her face vacant of emotion. Clearly this was not her first time taking something at one of these meetings.

"Mom, it's X. It's a drug."

"Honey, everything is a drug," she whispered back.

"No, that's—what?" Two women in front of us shushed me. My mom had started to cry again, and she was muttering things under her breath I couldn't make out.

It was time to do what I'd come here to do. I stood quietly and followed Arlon through the door.

It took a minute for my eyes to adjust to the brighter light of the small office behind the stage. There was a desk along with a couple of chairs and several cardboard boxes filled with manila envelopes. An outdated computer sat on the desk. Arlon was facing away from the door, rifling through a stack of papers on his desk.

"Hello, Arlon."

He jumped. "Sister Glinda? What are you doing here?" His hand rested on his heart.

I closed the door. Every fiber of my being yearned to walk straight up to this con man and punch him in the nose. But then I remembered my mom and how far under his control she truly was. I had to be careful. I had to be delicate. I couldn't be side-tracked by how intensely I wanted him to fall over dead.

"I just wanted to come apologize for the other day," I forced out through a tense smile.

"Oh, oh that." He let his shoulders relax and went to sit behind the desk. The locks of his hair were wet with sweat and plastered to his scalp. My stomach turned. "That was a hard day for everyone. No need to apologize." He gestured toward a chair, but I continued standing.

"It was very upsetting," I agreed. "I just want to clarify something."

"What's that?"

"In my dad's office, you mentioned the coffee?"

Arlon studied me, then tapped his desk with his index finger.

"What?" I asked, not interpreting his signal.

"Your phone. I will not speak with you until you put your phone where we can both see it."

Dammit. So much for that idea. I pulled my phone from my back pocket and set it on the desk. Arlon lifted it toward my face so it unlocked and then immediately went to the recording app and stopped the recording.

"How can I trust you, when you do things like this, Sister Glinda?" he said with false disappointment.

"Can you blame me?" I said. "You implied that my mother helped you murder someone."

"That was wrong of me."

"No shit."

"No, I mean, saying that to you was wrong of me. Obviously poor Brother Matthew passed of natural causes." He smiled in way that most would have interpreted as kind and sympathetic, but I knew better. "I said it to antagonize you. But I am a bigger man than that."

"So my mom isn't involved with anything nefarious?" I asked, anxious.

"Of course not, dear sister. Of course not."

I breathed out. I wanted so badly to believe him, but I couldn't. I wanted to believe he'd made it up to press my buttons, to make me think I was losing it. But I'd seen too much, and nothing in me could trust anything he said. Worse still, I knew my only hope of making any progress was for *him* to trust *me*, something I was certain was just as impossible. Still, I had to try.

"Okay, look, you're about to marry my mom. I think we should be on better terms, yes?" I said.

He steepled his hands and watched me carefully. "The terms we are on were set by you. I have only ever tried to be welcoming and forgiving."

I choked down a sarcastic laugh. "Your speech out there was very inspiring," I offered instead, tasting the insincerity in my words.

"Not everyone is as bright as you, Sister Glinda. I've learned I have to be simplistic, explicit, pedestrian." He smiled. "Not everyone can understand at the level you can."

Flattery wouldn't work if he could see through it and shoot it right back at me. Fine, on to step two. I had to use logic.

I took a seat and scooted it up to his desk. He appeared slightly taken aback, but recovered quickly, relaxing with that smug look on his face.

"Arlon. Why my mom? You could have your pick of followers. There are richer members than my mom, there're more connected members than my mom. It just doesn't make sense to go after a grieving widow whose daughters are not going to make things easy for you." I straightened up, trying to look strong.

"And that's a promise. I will do everything in my power to stop her from marrying you, because I think it's the wrong decision for her. She's not in her right mind. Surely you can see that?"

"Are you finished?" he asked.

"What do you want from her?" I continued, desperate for something—anything I could get a hold of—in order to gain the upper hand.

"You think me so shallow that all I would care about are money and connections?" He sneered. "Believe it or not, Sister Glinda, there are things a person can offer that are far more valuable than the material. Now, let me ask you something. Is your mother happy?"

"Of course not!"

"No, I'm not asking for your opinion—or what you expect from her. I'm asking you, is Julie happy? With me?" he said. I stared at him, grappling with the thought that it might be possible. "When I met her, she was lost and broken, under the shadow of death and loneliness. You remember? Yes?"

"Yes," I admitted softly.

"She wasn't eating, she wasn't going out, she had no friends, she was drowning." He leaned forward. "Do you remember that, or were you too high to retain any of it?"

My blood pressure rose as I watched this man pretend to know anything about me.

"So, I ask you, is she happy? Is she better?"

"There's a difference between *seeming* happy and *being* happy," I said.

"Is there?"

"Of course!" I paused. Just because Mom seemed happy in the cult didn't mean it was what was best for her, right?

Was I making a mistake here? Could it really be better to let her live content in a lie than to bring her kicking and screaming to the surface?

I shook my head. He was doing it: he was getting in my head.

"Arlon, please . . ." I shuddered. Logic had failed me. It was time to tug at the old heart strings. I cringed but softened my voice and looked at him pleadingly. "She's already been through so much hurt. I don't care if she still wants to come here and sing 'Kumbaya' and dance around a bonfire or whatever. She's been in such a bad place the last few years after my dad . . . well, and then my sister . . . well you know, and you know how vulnerable she's become." Tears threatened to betray me, but I held them back. That was the line I would not cross. I did not want to cry in front of him. "I came here to see what it would take for you to leave her alone." The lump in my throat was turning into barbed wire.

Arlon was quiet while he seemed to ponder my words. He pursed his lips and appeared to study a stain on the ceiling. "I won't break her heart. Not because some strung-out, unemployed woman who won't grow up throws a temper tantrum."

I saw red. I wanted to leap across the desk and strangle him. Instead, I closed my eyes and breathed.

"You know," he began slowly, "you could always join us."

I laughed bitterly and turned away, taking in several more deep breaths.

"Sister Glinda," he continued, his voice an unnerving attempt at being soothing or sympathetic. "It pains me to see you like this, so alone. Despite what you might think, I am not taking your family away from you. *You* are leaving your family. But there is a way back to her. Accept that there is more than just your perception of the world, and open yourself up to learn to love."

I turned back around, reached into my pocket, pulled out the pill, and dropped it onto his desk. It bounced and then settled next to the computer.

"Love? You have to drug them to love you!"

The muscles around his mouth tightened, but he managed to pull out a smile. "That is just a vitamin, nourishment for the inner light. It's everything else—all the technology and the wicked world out there—that is the drug."

I shook my head. His ability to gaslight was effortless. After a long silence he spoke.

"I know you don't want me to marry your mother; you've made that very clear, but"—he stood up and positioned himself in front of me, half sitting on the edge of his desk so we were eye level, and way too close—"what if I made it easier for you to join your brothers and sisters in the Society? What if I could persuade you?" I could smell his spiced deodorant and the barbecue he'd had for dinner.

"There is nothing you could say that would make me consider joining your cult."

I started to back away, but he stood and took my wrists in his hands. I froze. Reluctantly, I looked up at him.

"Let's take away the ego, Sister Glinda, strip away the pride. What is left? You don't give me enough credit. I am sure I could find a way to make things easier for you *and* your sister. Or I could also make things much harder. For everyone."

I leaned back, but he held my wrists tight. My stomach lurched and my skin crawled, from my wrists all the way up to my scalp.

"You have lost your damn mind. Let go of me," I said through clenched teeth.

"Glinda, what are you doing?" he said, his voice low. "I see a girl wasting her potential. Deep down, you know I'm right."

"Stop." I glared up at him. I couldn't breathe. I looked at him, and suddenly all I could see was Patrick Nelson. He was holding my wrists together, above my head, pressing them hard against the vinyl mattress. I pulled and pulled, but he was stronger. His grip was locked tightly, and he didn't care if he was hurting me.

"Your mother is a wonderful, generous woman, Glinda. I'm not going to give her up."

"Stop," I growled. Sweat beaded up at my hairline, rolling down the sides of my face.

"There is nothing she wouldn't do for me. Nothing."

"Let me go."

"Come back to us, Glinda."

"Stop." It was only a whimper now.

He was too close, gripping me too tight. There was a faint buzzing in my ears, my head was swimming. I had to get away, I had to escape. I could knee him in the groin, or I could head butt him in the nose. But before I could decide, he leaned in and whispered in my ear, his horrific barbecue breath enveloping me.

"You're so muddled up, Glinda. Can't trust anything anyone says. But then again, maybe you shouldn't."

When he pulled away, he brushed his thick, wet lips across my cheek. Immediately instinct intervened, and it was Patrick Nelson all over again, and I vomited onto his shoes.

He cried out in disgust and immediately released my wrists. I staggered back and then raced to the door.

"Sister Glinda!"

I turned in the doorway, my whole body shaking. He was looking down at his shoes in revulsion. Then he met my eyes with a wicked smile.

"I'm the only one who can protect her now."

My eyes burned as I glowered at him. I wiped my mouth with the back of my hand. "I'll get a lawyer. I'll get a conservatorship for her, and I'll keep her away from you! You forget who my sister is."

He glared at me for a moment and then relaxed his face and let out a sarcastic laugh. "You mean the sister who dislikes you or the sister who downright hates you?"

"Fuck you." I turned away.

"And Glinda, one more thing."

This time, I didn't face him. "What?"

"You picked a good night to come. It's Julie's turn in the circle."

I slammed the door behind me and pressed my back against it, taking in breaths, trying to stop myself from hyperventilating. No one noticed me. All the congregants were still distracted with their "meditation."

I raced to my mother's side. She looked up at me, her eyes dilated wide. She smiled a drunk smile at me and held her arms out. The ecstasy had kicked in.

"Come on, Mom. We're getting out of here." I looked around. Several pioneers had their arms wrapped around each other and were swaying back and forth in their seats to music only they could hear.

"I can't. Father Arlon has not dismissed me yet."

"Mom! Now!"

I shook her shoulders, but she kept smiling dreamily at me. I looked up and saw Arlon and Mark were standing in the aisle looking at us. Arlon was laughing.

"Sweet Sister Julie, stay awhile; in fact, stay the night with me."

"Of course, Father Arlon." Her eyes were so vacant, her voice so hollow.

"Mom! Mom, listen to me. He's controlling you!"

My mother's eyes narrowed at me like she was trying to understand what I was saying. Maybe I was finally getting through to her.

"Liar," she hissed.

I gasped. "Mom?" I cried, sobs rising up in my throat.

The entire Society had now turned to watch us.

"I think it's time for the circle," Arlon called out. "Mark, is everything prepared?"

Mark nodded and gestured toward the door.

Like automatons, the cult members turned and began shuffling out the door. I was pushed farther and farther back until I was standing alone in the center of the trailer.

I reached into my pocket for my phone. It wasn't there. I rifled through my purse. Shit, not again.

"Can I help you with something?" I spun around to find Arlon standing there. He had traded his vomit-covered shoes for a pair of worn loafers that looked too big.

"My phone, I think I left it in your office—"

"Oh, of course, here you are." He held out my phone and smiled. "Join us when you're finished with your call." Then he strolled out after his followers, his robe sweeping the threadbare carpet.

The phone shook in my hands. Enough was enough. This had gone too far. I dialed and waited until someone picked up.

"Sheriff's office."

"Hi, I—uh—I need to speak to Detective Bryant or Crumble—just one of them, please," I said quietly.

"Hang on, I'll transfer you." I slunk against the wall; no one had come back in to get me.

There was a set of beeps and then a man answered. "This is Detective Bryant."

"Hey—hello, uh, one of you gave me a card, but I lost it. Uh, this is Glinda Glass—I need to talk to you. It's important."

"Oh yes, of course. How can I help you?"

"It's about Arlon Blight."

"You know what, sweetheart, I'm actually off duty presently, but if you'd rather speak in person, we can meet up." I was relieved, but also terrified. If my mother had had anything to do with Matthew Harrigan . . . well, I couldn't let my mind go there. There was just no way.

"O—okay, I just need to be discrete. This is extremely delicate."

"Sure thing. Why don't you step outside and we can talk."

"I'm sorry, what?"

"Step outside, Sister Glinda."

I dropped the phone. I could only manage quick, shallow breaths as I approached the door to the trailer and stepped out. There, on the ground, looking up at me, was Detective Bryant. He was wearing a green robe.

"You've got to be kidding me," I muttered through gritted teeth. "Son of a bitch."

"You need to file a report, Sister Glinda?" Detective Bryant smirked and shot Arlon a wink. My stomach dropped. I really was in this alone. There was no one to help.

Mark stood beside him, completely deadpan. On his feet, he was wearing only a pair of gray, holey socks. The rest of the group was standing around a small pile of rocks, with a large, rusty coffee can atop. There was a squeeze bottle of lighter fluid under a dingy lawn chair beside the pile and a propane lighter sitting on one of the stones, far too close to the can. Arlon stood near the center of the circle, holding onto my mother's arm. She was clutching her small brown purse to her side.

"Go ahead, Sister Julie, tell our visitor what to do." Arlon nudged her forward.

"Can you gather some sticks and place them in the can, Glinda?" Then she sat in the chair and closed her eyes. I watched her eyeballs move around erratically under the lids. My heart was beating so hard I thought it might burst from my chest.

"Do as she says, Glinda," Arlon warned. Reluctantly I walked away from the group, searching the ground for sticks in the dark. I found a few at the edge of the parking lot and broke them over my knee so they'd fit in the can.

"Okay, now what?" I heard myself say.

"Let them burn," she said, not opening her eyes.

With a sigh, I carefully opened the bottle, squirting a small amount of lighter fluid onto the sticks. I held the propane lighter's flame to the sticks, watching as the whole can lit up with orange tongues of fire. The light from the flames seemed to suck all the other light away from the world, and I shivered in the darkness.

"Mom?" I asked quietly, but she only shook her head. I waited, almost forgetting the dozens of eyes on us. For that moment, we were the only people there, in this space of darkness and the hellish glow of the fire. The sticks crackled and the lightning bugs began firing off in the field behind us. I swatted a big, engorged mosquito that had landed on my arm. The sound of the slap caused my mother to finally open her eyes, just in time to see me wipe a streak of bright red blood across the top of my forearm.

"What does your heart desire most?" she said, her voice tenuous.

"Um, besides for this to be over? I guess peace on earth? A million dollars?" I watched her. The dancing flames cast weird shadows across her face. It was weird to not recognize the woman who raised you. She opened her purse and pulled out a small bundle, wrapped in a yellowed cloth. She set the purse down and clutched the bundle to her chest.

"That is the beginning of your journey. You must first identify what you desire before you can pursue it."

"Okay, fine, Mom. What do you desire most?"

She stared into the fire, unblinking. When she spoke, her voice was strange and quiet. "I desire to be released from my grief."

A single tear rolled down her cheek and dropped to her lap. Her lip trembled, and for a moment I saw my mom like she was in the days right after my dad died, raw and broken, not the brave solider she had become in the years since.

"Mom . . ." I started, but I trailed off. I had no idea how to respond to that. "Is that why you threw away the photos of Dad?"

She turned to face me, and my breath caught in my throat. Her eyes looked almost wild and her face was ashen. She blinked and a wave of calm overtook her expression. When she spoke again, it wasn't really her. It was Arlon's iron mask, locked over her face.

"The only way to reach a higher plane of existence is to completely disconnect ourselves from the memories that pull us back down."

"I don't think that's what your grief counselor told you."

"Glinda, you are so much like your father. When you speak, sometimes it's like he's here."

But I'm not my father. I'm not. I am a poor imitation of what he'd always hoped I'd be. If I could have been more like him, we wouldn't be here right now. He would have known how to save her. He saved me from drowning when I was a kid. He could save everyone. All I was capable of doing was driving the people I loved away.

"Arlon has brought me closer to a place of peace than I have ever been. The answer is, you must let go of the bonds that tie you to your old life."

With that she laid the bundle in her lap and unwrapped it. Inside were three school photos. One of West from last year in her volleyball uniform; one of Dorothy from ninth grade when she got her braces off; and one of me, a scrawny little seventh grader, my hair in two braids. She fanned the photos out over her lap and traced over our faces, tears welling up in her eyes.

"One's heart cannot take orbit if it is tied to earthly anchors. Your father's death is a burden, and you remind me of him, every day. I have to let you go."

Then I realized what the cloth that she'd wrapped the photo in was. It was a handkerchief I'd given her when I was in the second grade. I had used a pink Sharpie and written a poem out on it and presented it to her on Mother's Day. She'd always kept it in her vanity with her other prized possessions.

No sooner had I realized the significance of the cloth than she scooped the photos back up into it and, before I could react, stuffed the entire bundle into the burning coffee can. I grew lightheaded as I watched her standing over the fire, like some kind of Shakespearean witch. Around her the congregants were swaying slowly and humming this eerie melody that was barely audible above the sound of blood rushing in my head.

"Mom! Mom!" I was frantic now, grabbing her face and forcing her to look at me. "Listen to me. I'm your daughter! You have to come back with me! You have to leave Arlon behind. You have to come with me!"

Her eyes finally focused on me, although her face was obscured in shadow, so all I could see were two tiny points of light.

"I know what you're trying to do. And I need you to understand, in case you didn't learn the last time you tried to come between two people, you won't have your way." She turned back toward the trailer. "I'm tethered to Arlon now." Then she returned to Arlon's side, and I sank down into the chair. My body was stone, my hands too heavy to lift off the arm rests.

The fire turned a sickish green as the photos were consumed.

"I am Arlon's. I am tethered to him for all eternity. All of me," she said and then, like a sleepwalker, she wrapped her arms around his waist.

He leaned down and kissed her, then looked up at me and winked. "These are her words, Glinda, not mine."

I was going to vomit again. I tried to jump up but ended up tripping over the chair and landing on my back in the gravel. Pain shot up my tailbone as I lay there for a moment stunned.

I'd never been stabbed, but I imagined the sensation was similar to how I was feeling now, like my chest was hot and icy all at the same time and a sort of numbness was crawling into my lungs, making it hard to breathe.

Arlon walked by and kicked something on the ground toward me. I didn't look, I couldn't move. He and my mother silently walked past me and into the trailer.

Slowly, I made my way to kneeling. I closed my eyes and rocked back and forth. It was only after the fire had died down and gone out that I realized I was the only one left outside. The smoke from the extinguished flames rose up like white ghosts from the can and faded into the night.

The object Arlon had so carelessly kicked beside me was my phone. I reached for it. There was a large spider web of cracks across the screen. With trembling fingers I opened it, the light causing me to squint. The first thing I saw was my photos app had been cleared. Every single photo of my family, every stupid selfie, the couple of goofy photos I'd taken of Troy in his Renaissance getup, and every single photo of my dad was gone. In their place was a single photo.

It showed Arlon sitting against his desk, offering up a mug of coffee and a sinister, knowing smile.

And I knew one thing for certain. Arlon was in control, and my mother was far enough under his spell to do almost anything he asked. Even kill.

♦ 10 ♦

DESPERATE AND DETERMINED

A little over two and a half years ago

I WAS LYING ON a bare mattress, staring at the dorm ceiling, when my mom called. It had been three days since the vomiting incident, three days since Patrick did what he had done to me, then dumped me and told everyone that he'd taken my virginity and I'd upchucked into his mouth. I couldn't think about it without getting full body shakes. I wanted to dig a hole in the middle of the quad and lie in it.

My Dickens essay was open on my laptop, half finished. I hadn't talked to my family. I couldn't. The last thing I wanted was sympathy. I was Glinda—I was the strong-willed and vivacious one. I couldn't let them see me broken.

She called again.

I'd been expecting this. It was only a matter of time before my mom noticed my lack of communication and there was no way in hell she'd stop until she'd heard from me. Either I answered now or she'd be knocking on my door within a couple of hours or however long it took her to drive the distance going ninety.

"Hey, Mom." I tried to sound as casual as possible.

She didn't speak. There was a sharp intake of breath. Silence.

"Mom?" I said, sitting up fast.

"Glinda?" Her voice was so tiny—not a whisper, just small and soft. My stomach dropped to my feet, and my heart thumped against my ribs. I held my breath, my lungs were glass, my heart was glass, my throat, my brain—all crystalized, hard, and thin.

"I need you to come home." She got it out and then sobbed.

"Mom? What's wrong?"

"He was in the office, working." She gasped out another sob.

Tiny fractures splintered throughout my body, pieces held together by some last shred of hope that my instincts were wrong, that she was overreacting, that my dad was fine, that he was hurt, that he was sick, but he was here, that he was alive.

"Glinda, he's gone. He—he died."

Everything inside me shattered. My body was full of shards of glass, slicing and severing.

I knew denial was the first and most common reaction to death. I didn't experience that. I wasn't in denial. I knew. I'd known as soon as she'd said my name. That's not to say I was processing it or that I even completely understood all the words she was saying. Nonresponsive. Aneurysm. Paramedics. These words were alien to me. But I knew he was dead.

"Glinda, your sisters don't know. West is at the house. She saw him, but she doesn't know he's . . . and Dorothy . . . I can't—I can't say it again!" She was barely understandable.

It was like someone had jolted me with a thousand volts of electricity. "I'll get them, Mom," I whispered. "I'll take care of everything."

"Glinda?"

"Yes, Mom?"

"I need you. Oh God. You're the most like him. You know I always say you have his dry sense of humor—you know that, right?" She actually chuckled a little, although it was hard to distinguish it from her crying.

"Yes, Mama."

"And his eyes . . ."

"I—I know." It was tough to speak, my mouth had gone so dry. My lips kept sticking together.

"Glinda, you're my fearless one. I don't know what to do. He's the one who would know what to do! I can't—" She trailed off into sobs again. I took a deep breath, my mind in a state of shock, although I didn't recognize it as such at the time.

I wasn't crying; I was just numb. But I knew one thing: If my father was gone, then it was up to me to take care of my family, to get us on the lifeboats and row as hard as I could.

"Mom, I'll take care of everything, okay? Please, just stay where you are. I'm coming. I'll take care of you, of them, no one else needs to worry. I'll take care of everything."

Why did she think I was strong enough? To tell my sisters, to bear our collective broken heart? I wasn't even strong enough to bear my own.

★ ★ ★

Present

It was going to take sixty-four minutes to walk home, according to my phone. Considering my flip-flops and overall level of fitness, I guessed I'd be home sometime the next day.

More time to think, I guess. I had collected myself, let my horror and distress convert to pure hatred for the man who controlled my mother. So I walked and I seethed.

I passed the last little store on the edge of town and stared down the long, dark country road that led to my home, whatever was left of it. I had to get there before . . .

I shook my head. I couldn't stand the thought of my home taken over by strangers.

I'd listened to enough true crime podcasts to know better than to walk down a lonesome, deserted road at night, but there was no way in hell I was turning back and riding home with my mom. A dead possum lay curled up on the shoulder, and I gingerly stepped around him, averting my eyes, which led me to stumble and snap the strap of my flip-flop.

"Dammit!" I screamed. I yanked the broken sandal off my foot and screamed again, throwing it as hard as I could into the field beside the road. But it wasn't enough. I wanted to rip my own heart out and hurl it away from me.

"Fuck!" I grabbed my other shoe and threw it hard, screaming again.

And as soon as the rage had ebbed, it dawned on me how stupid it was to throw one's good shoe into a dark pasture with no hope of retrieving it.

Using the light from my phone, I stepped forward slowly, wincing as the gravel poked the bottom of my feet. The last thing I needed was to step on a broken beer bottle and bleed out on the side of the road.

A vehicle rattled down the road from town and slowed behind me. I reached into my purse and gripped my now useless car keys, ready to plunge them into the neck of the serial killer who was about to grab me. A white van pulled up alongside me, and the window rolled down.

"Hey, little girl, you want some candy from the back of my van?" a deep voice shouted at me. I rolled my eyes and lifted my light to look at Troy's dumb, amused face peering down at me.

"What the hell are you doing here? Are you stalking me?" I stepped forward and leaned against the open window.

"Nah, I was on my way to your house!"

"Why?"

"For our date!" He grinned.

"Date?" And then I remembered the stupid bet we'd made. And then I remembered how Troy and I weren't going to work together anymore, and swallowed the twinge in my throat.

Troy glanced down and back up at my face in confusion.

"Where are your shoes?"

"In the field."

"Okay?" He pursed his lips. "So, I take it you forgot about our date?"

"Sorry," I said dryly. "Some shit came up."

He glanced down the road and tapped his fingers on the steering wheel before looking back at me. "Well, do you want me to take you home?"

"No, I'm good." I crossed my arms. As soon as I said it I was kicking myself. Why was I being an asshole to him? He hadn't brainwashed my mom. He hadn't burned my childhood photo or basically disowned me. No, the only offense he'd committed was to exist in a place untouched by my tragedy. He had the audacity to think about going on dates and having fun.

He furrowed his brow and opened his mouth to respond, but I ignored him and pulled the driver's side door open. I'd considered walking around to the other side like a normal person, but decided against tetanus. I climbed up and pushed across him, briefly finding myself in his lap. I ignored the flutters, the bated breath, and slid across the bench to the other side of the cabin.

"All right." He cleared his throat and adjusted his rear mirror, which I'd knocked off kilter. Once seated beside him, I realized he really had prepared for a full-on date with me. He'd doused himself in some kind of body spray I hadn't smelled since high school, and he'd combed his hair. For a brief moment I felt excited, carefree almost. I felt like I had before—before I learned that cologne and nice clothes were lures to bring you in, to trap you. He caught me looking at him and I turned away, trying to hide my face by staring out the passenger window.

"Uh, Glin?" He cleared his throat again. "Is something wrong?"

"No."

"I just found you walking barefoot down the road at night."

"Just needed some air."

"Yeah, well." He tapped the steering wheel with his finger like he was thinking. "You look like you've been crying . . . maybe?"

"Nope." I could only imagine what I looked like right now.

He turned onto another street and stopped the car. He flipped the cabin light on and turned to me. I sighed and looked at him, casting a very sarcastic smile.

"See?" I said, stretching the smile wider. "I'm fine."

He looked at me hard, then reached over and very gently lifted a piece of hair out of my face and tucked it behind my ear. My eyes burned and I reached up to turn the light off.

"Troy, listen, I just don't think I can talk about it, okay?"

"Okay, fair enough." He resumed driving and we sat in awkward silence. The look on his face, brushing my hair back, his eyes full of concern, seeing me, actually seeing me . . . it terrified me.

I shook my head. It was all a distraction from what really mattered. Troy was barely a friend, and friends are fickle: they drop you fast and hard and don't look back to see if you made it up or not.

We turned down my driveway and came to a stop in front of the house. All the lights were on, and it appeared as inviting as it ever had.

Troy braced the steering wheel and then turned to me, his expression softened.

"You know you can talk to me, right? I mean, when we talked before, I hope that helped." He ran his hand through his hair and looked up at the house.

He was being so sweet, so supportive, saying all the right things. Boys always said the right things before they did the wrong things.

"Thanks for the ride." I jumped out and started toward the house, but he got out and came up behind me. I spun around and did what I do best. I knew exactly what I was doing, and I knew I didn't want to, but the part of me that wanted to burn everything was in control right now.

"Stop being so pushy," I said coldly.

"I'm not trying to come off as pushy." He took a step back— strike one—and he looked hurt. Diminished.

The regret hit me instantly. I rubbed the back of my neck. "Listen, I'm sorry. This has just been a really bad day."

He smiled and nodded.

"You wouldn't get it," I continued, then winced.

The smile faded, and he seemed to be studying me. Strike two.

"No, of course I wouldn't know about bad days," he said. "I wouldn't know about getting laid off from the only job that brought joy to my life or anything."

"Are you seriously bringing up the stupid fucking Medieval festival at a time like this?"

"At a time like what, Glinda?" he threw back at me. "How am I supposed to understand you if you won't talk to me?" I started walking toward the house; he didn't follow. Strike three. Now he'd turn and leave. Now he'd never speak to me again. Now it was done.

Except he didn't turn. He just looked frustrated and confused.

"I didn't ask you to understand me," I spit out. There, that would do it. I jogged up the steps, my chest full of fire. I'd just put my hand to the handle when I heard him sigh behind me.

"Believe it or not, I understand what it's like to think you aren't deserving of anybody caring about you," he said quietly. A shiver ran through me, but I kept my gaze forward.

"You don't even know me, Troy."

"Maybe I don't know you, but I can tell when someone doesn't like themselves very much."

I turned around. "First I'm accused of thinking too highly of myself. Now, I'm too hard on myself. Jesus, I'm just trying to save my mom."

He gave me a sad smile. "More cult stuff, I'm guessing?"

I told myself to ignore him and go inside, but I just couldn't let it go.

"Yes, Troy, more cult stuff."

"Let me help you." He ran a hand through his hair and looked up at me with big, pleading eyes. He wanted to help so much it was causing him distress.

"There's literally nothing you can do." I was done dragging this out. "And since your impression of me is that I'm some sad, pathetic loser—"

"Not what I said," he interrupted me. "Glin, you're my friend, and I think you're funny and smart and amazing and—"

"Ha!" My laugh was full of shards of glass. "If you wanted to fuck me, just say so. You don't have to give me some ridiculous soliloquy."

He let out a low sigh. "I just wanted to get to know you better. But I get it. Sorry to bother you. I guess I'll see y—" He stopped, clicked his tongue, and pointed to his head. He'd remembered we weren't working together anymore. "Goodbye, Glinda."

And then Troy turned on his heel, skipped down the steps, and walked away, never to return.

The sensation of falling into that damn dunking booth came over me as he walked away. My mom's vacant eyes, the photos curling up and turning black in the fire—it all swirled around me like a suffocating tornado that was sucking all the air out of my lungs and crushing me into a vague shadow of who I was.

"Please don't go!" I cried out. "I didn't mean it!"

He turned around, this man so pure of heart that I instantly knew I was forgiven, despite knowing full well I didn't deserve to be. He opened his mouth to say something, when West flung open the front door and stepped out.

"Where's Mom?" she asked, looking at me accusingly.

"She's still with Arlon."

"What happened?"

"Arlon Blight is an evil man," I said, trying desperately not to cry again.

West gave me a skeptical look. "You're not going to tell me what happened? Did you confront him? Did you yell at him?"

"I went and asked him—*begged* him—to leave Mom alone."

"And?"

"God, I can't even with what just happened."

"Tell me."

I wanted to. I wanted to tell her how our mother had just severed herself from us, how she'd burned our photos, how she'd left me sniveling in the darkness. But I couldn't. Not yet. The thought of it just made me feel hollow and cold.

"Who the hell are you?" West had just noticed Troy, standing by the van, hands in his pockets, pretending not to listen.

"This is Troy. We work together."

"Is he in the cult or something?" She eyed him suspiciously.

"No. He's just being a friend."

"You have those?"

I folded my arms across my chest and glared at her. "West, you need to grow up."

She scoffed. "*I* need to grow up?"

"He's drugging her, West."

"What are you talking about?"

"He gives them *drugs*. It's this whole ceremony thing."

She wrinkled her nose. "I don't believe you. Mom wouldn't take drugs."

"West!" I cried. "They're moving in tomorrow!"

She took a step back. "What?"

"You didn't know?" I pressed.

"How would I know?"

"You spend more time with her than I do. She picks you up from swim practice right after those meetings, and you're telling me you've never noticed anything off about her? Jesus, if I had known earlier how bad it was, maybe we could have had a chance to get her out!"

She responded with a bitter "Seriously?"

"Yes, seriously."

"I effing tried to tell you something was up!" There was a throbbing vein in the center of her forehead; I had to make a conscious effort not to get distracted by it. "The photos! When she threw out the photos! Glinda, you are the most egocentric, narcissistic person I have ever met!"

"Way to use those SAT words!" I spat. "Dammit, West, I think about other people. I 'effing' worry about *you* all the time! Did you know I actually make it a point to come talk to you every day, even though you act like a little brat?"

"Yeah, thanks for that. That definitely makes up for not making any attempt to form an actual relationship with me over the years." She slung her hair over her shoulder.

"Everything I do is for this family, and not one of you can see that! Instead, you shit on me and blame me, and I'm sick of it!"

I couldn't read her expression. We stood there in uncomfortable silence. I hated that I could almost see the air between us like a physical barrier. And I regretted most of what I had just said. But when I opened my mouth to apologize, something else came out.

"West, I gotta go get Dorothy."

She swallowed—gulped, even. The meanness had been shocked out of her temporarily. "You can't."

"I have to."

"You don't have a car."

"I'll figure something out."

"Absolutely not."

"West, I have to!" I leaned close and whispered in her ear, "I think Mom may have been involved with Matthew Harrigan's death."

"What?" West looked at me, wide-eyed.

"I think Arlon made Mom poison Matthew's coffee and that's how he died," I mouthed, shielding my lips from Troy.

She gasped. "You *think*?"

"Yes."

"Do you have proof?"

I pulled out my phone and showed her the picture of Arlon.

"What's this?" She looked confused.

"He's got a coffee mug!"

"Are you serious? This isn't proof! That's just a dude drinking coffee." She pushed the phone away. "And why is your screen all jacked up?"

"Arlon."

"Arlon broke your screen?"

"Yes."

"You saw him do it with your own eyes?"

"Well, no, but—"

She rolled her eyes. "You sound so freaking paranoid."

"Listen, if I'm right, we need Dorothy. Dorothy is a lawyer. She can figure out how to declare Mom mentally unsound so we can help her and get her away from Arlon."

"No." She turned back toward the open threshold.

"West, I can't be here when they take over this house. I can't see it! It'll destroy me."

"So Dorothy's an excuse to leave?"

I hesitated. "No."

"Mom didn't *kill* anyone, Glinda. *You're* the 'mentally unsound' one." She paused and then put one hand on her hip. "If you're going to Dorothy then I'm coming with you."

"Absolutely not." I set my jaw and stared her down.

"Why not?"

"Because you're a child. I need to handle this myself."

"You think you're so much more mature than me." Her eyes flashed with a cold resentment. "You always say you're going to handle things and then, guess what? You screw them up even more. I may be seventeen, but I've got time to grow up. You?" She narrowed her eyes. "You're just a screwup. And you'll always be a screwup." She went inside and raced up the stairs.

I wanted nothing more than to chase after her and pour out the things I'd witnessed at the meeting. She didn't know—not the full extent of it. But I couldn't tell her. I needed to protect at least one of us from the complete, soul-sucking truth. And she was right, after all, about me.

I looked back at Troy, who was pretending to inspect the bark on a tree.

"Well, there you go. You wanted to know what was going on." I sank down on the steps. I was out of tears at this point. I was just really, really tired.

He approached cautiously. "Is it okay if I sit with you?" he asked.

I nodded.

He sat beside me and it reminded me of the night he'd first come out to bring me my phone. How the hell did that seem like a simpler time?

"I promise I was trying not to listen."

"It's okay."

"I mean, I did hear the part about this cult guy giving your mom drugs, but I promise that was it."

I laughed weakly. I was almost annoyed with how effortlessly cheerful he was, without a hint of minimizing my pain.

Without really thinking or caring what would happen, I let my head rest on his shoulder. I was just so drained.

I felt him tense up and then relax.

"You're wearing a lot of cologne," I muttered. "Like a lot a lot."

He laughed softly.

I bit my lip. "I'm really sorry about earlier. I didn't mean to accuse you—"

"Hey, no, I'm sorry. I *was* being pushy," he said quietly.

"I just haven't had the best luck with friends," I said softly, more to myself than to him. "Or with sisters."

"You just have to let people in, Glin. Sometimes they'll surprise you."

I sat up and faced him. Our proximity to one another had suddenly become very visceral. He was going to kiss me. I could see it in his eyes, deep and dark and scared shitless. Or maybe that was me.

I took a sharp inhale and backed away.

"Hey, so—" I gave him my most sheepish, pleading smile. "You want to take me to see my sister?"

♦ 11 ♦

MANIPULATIVE AND RESOURCEFUL

"I MEAN, WHEN I left my apartment tonight, I was thinking a movie or something, but yeah, sure, we can go visit your sister." Troy was trying really hard not to smile like an idiot.

"Okay, cool, um . . . it's a ways . . ."

"I do have a shift tomorrow, but . . . meh, who cares—seize the carpe and shit, right?"

"Yeah, sure, something like that." What the hell was I doing? Surprising my estranged sister in the dead of night with some guy I was letting in far, far too quickly. "Let me grab some stuff, like shoes." I stood up, feeling somewhat revived—exhilarated actually.

"Hey, can I help you with anything?" Troy had followed me inside.

"Nope, just need to leave a note." I stepped into the kitchen and pulled a sheet from the pad on the fridge.

Dear Mom,

And then I stopped. I mean, it wasn't like she'd care. In fact, Arlon would probably read it, and then he'd know what I was up to. I crushed it in my fist and tossed it in the garbage. Troy was waiting in the living room, hands behind his back, looking at family photos on the mantle.

"Where's your TV?"

"It was lost during the purge of modern evils."

I went upstairs, threw on a different pair of flip-flops, and tossed a change of clothes into a pillowcase. My gray hoodie was wadded up on the floor beside my bed. As I tied it around my waist, I looked around my childhood room, my stuffed animals still lining the windowsill, the quilt my grandma made me before she died, the little statue of Cthulhu my dad got me my first semester of college.

This was the last time I'd ever see this room untouched. I knew that. This sanctuary had always been here. Even in the worst of times, I could retreat here, and nothing had changed. And now I was leaving it to the vultures.

The only thing worse than the thought of those freaks taking over my room was being here to witness it. I turned and retreated down the hall, pausing in front of West's closed door. A twinge of guilt made me raise my fist to knock, but I stopped. It was better this way. She didn't need to be involved. This was my problem to fix. I dropped my hand and headed downstairs.

Troy was already back in the van, waiting for me.

"Okay, so where are we going?" he asked excitedly as I climbed into the front seat with him.

"Yeah, um, just head northeast."

"So, like, take the interstate?"

"Yeah." I was looking at directions on my phone. *Eesh, four hours.* "Yeah, that'll work."

Troy shifted into gear, and we slowly pulled away from my house . . . my mom's house . . . the cult's house. I looked back. It was still lit up; just one window was dark, where West was no doubt texting or reading one of the thick books she kept hidden under her bed so we wouldn't know she actually liked "lame things" like classic literature.

"You like music?" Troy asked.

"Sure."

He turned the radio on, and I turned to the window before he could ask me another question.

Then an awkward silence settled between us, and I stared out at the familiar businesses; the high school I'd gone to; and then, farther on, to where suburbia began to spread out and thin.

"You're gonna tell me when to exit, right?" Troy said after about twenty minutes.

"Yep."

"Okay, cool."

I had to tell him. But maybe a few more miles.

"The cult is moving into my house tomorrow. And then my mom's marrying Arlon in two weeks."

"I heard."

"Yep."

"Oh shit. And you're, like, unemployed now. Right. So that's gonna suck. What are you going to do?"

"I'm going to stop her, obviously."

"How?"

"That's why I have to get to my sister. She's a lawyer. She can come down here and help me get power of attorney for my mom."

"You really think it's that bad?"

"I hope I'm wrong. I hope that if I can get Dorothy to just come home and talk to her . . . well, she's probably the last person on earth left that my mom will listen to, but she's my last chance. And if not, then we go the legal route, even if that means dragging our mom away from Arlon kicking and screaming."

"You think Dorothy and you are ready to make up and shit?"

"Honestly, I don't know." I sighed. "But I don't know what else to do."

And she *had* texted me, the day of the interview. I still didn't know what she'd wanted to talk about, but still. I had to have hope.

"Well then, let's go get Dorothy!" Troy smiled. "But you're buying me dinner."

I raised an eyebrow. "I am?"

"I'm not driving straight through to Oklahoma without eating."

"Wait—how did you know she lived in Oklahoma?"

He paused. "You told me."

"I did?"

"Yep."

I shook my head. "Why would you agree to drive me all the way to Oklahoma?"

"Because you're completely insane." He laughed. "If I don't take you, then you'll try to go by yourself, and that would be irresponsible on my part because honestly, you'd probably end up in a ditch or as some hillbilly's slave or something."

"Hold up—you're taking me because you think I'm *insane*?"

He smirked. "Not like in a bad way."

"I'm not some broken person that needs fixing, ya know. And I don't *need* a man to drive me—I just don't happen to have a car is all."

"Believe me, I have no intention of fixing anybody."

"Great." I bit my lip. I just needed to take this win and not question it. I settled into my seat and closed my eyes. Maybe thirty seconds passed before I couldn't stand it anymore. "So why did you wear so much cologne tonight?"

"I didn't. This is my natural musk."

"Oh yeah, it's about as natural as my hair color."

"That's not your real hair color?"

"No, Troy, Ruby Fusion is not a color found in nature."

"Well, it's pretty."

"Thank you . . . and I like your cologne," I admitted despite my better judgment. "I just wish you used it a little more sparingly."

The current song ended, and something new and poppy came on. "Oh! I love this song!" He started twisting in his seat, throwing his arms up and doing a little dance.

"Dude, that's an ad."

"Huh?" He smiled and continued tapping the steering wheel. "It's catchy!"

We drove on, not talking, not bringing up the sexual tension between us that I was becoming far too comfortable with. I read on my phone until I started feeling carsick and needed a distraction.

"What's the worst thing you've ever done?" I asked, leaning my head against the cool windowpane. I looked up at the night sky, with its brilliant stars peeking out from behind white, wispy clouds.

"What, like stealing a pair of sunglasses?"

"Worse than that!"

"Uh . . . yeah, I'm not answering that." He laughed.

"I stole a banana from a kid in first grade," I told him. "Took it right out of his backpack."

"I mean, you were a kid."

"Yeah, but then I put it in the teacher's desk and it rotted and ruined a bunch of her paperwork. I never 'fessed up to it."

"Damn." He raised his eyebrows and chuckled. "I can't believe I'm laughing. That is truly horrible, Glinda."

"Yeah." I sighed. "Let's see, what else? I was addicted to Adderall."

"Shit, really?"

"Yep. Started out legit, but I realized pretty quickly that more of it made me feel like I could do anything. I thought I couldn't process life without it. Sometimes I'd take Desoxyn too, if I could get my hands on it. As long as it was a prescription med, I didn't feel like I was doing anything bad to myself. Anyway."

"You, uh . . . you still . . .?"

"Oh no. No, no, no. I quit that. I'm lucky that I stopped before I couldn't stop, you know? I barely take Tylenol now." It grew uncomfortably quiet. I coughed. "Okay, I told you three things. You have to tell me something."

"Shit, I dunno, Glinda. I can't think of anything."

"Oh my God, you liar." I laughed.

"Look, I'm not going to confess the worst thing I've ever done. We're not that close yet."

"Wow." I blinked hard.

"I didn't mean—"

"No, I get it. We're close enough for you to drive me across state lines, but not for soul-baring conversations. Got it."

"Glinda, that's not what I meant."

It got quiet again. I wanted to wring the awkwardness by the neck. It was my fault. I decided to change the subject.

"Okay, tell me this. Do you believe in an afterlife?"

"That's a big question."

"I've never been sure of anything—not anything big like that." I glanced at him and caught him looking at me with interest. Finally he responded.

"I guess I believe there's something bigger than us, and there are things we can't see. I don't believe your consciousness is some random accident, and I don't believe something as simplistic as death can snuff out something as incredible as existence."

"That's beautiful, Troy." I settled in again and sighed. "My mom believes in some goofy cult leader, and my sister believes in Bigfoot. I don't know . . . I guess I've just always found it safest to not believe in anything."

"You believe in stuff, but you probably don't even realize it."

I sat with that for a moment. "What are your feelings about Bigfoot?" I asked.

"Bullshit," he said.

I laughed. "You answered so quickly. You don't have some beautiful, romancing view of the universe for the existence of Bigfoot? Like he encapsulates our desire for there to still be mystery in the world?"

"Nah, Bigfoot is bullshit."

"Bigfoot *is* bullshit."

Why did I feel like we were moving so fast that if I spread my arms out, I'd take off into the sky? A giddiness swept through me. I glanced at his long fingers on the steering wheel, his relaxed smile, his broad shoulders. Damn. I was doing it again. I was losing myself in a feeling. I had to stay sober. It was important. I had to push down whatever urges he was causing and remain focused. I concentrated on the cold air blasting my face from the vent.

I wanted to keep talking about Troy's dismissal of Bigfoot, but when I turned to him, I realized he'd grown very quiet. He sat rigidly, his knuckles white on the steering wheel, his eyes darting back and forth to the rearview mirror.

"What's wrong?" I asked.

"Listen, Glinda—I need you to listen to me carefully and do exactly as I say," he whispered. I could barely hear him over the AC.

"What in the world?" This was what I got for agreeing to get into the van of a guy I'd only known a couple of months. What was happening?

"Glinda, listen to me. We have a situation. I am going to pull over, and I need you to get out as fast as you can."

"Troy, you're making me really nervous."

"I'll explain in a minute. Just as soon as I stop the van, jump out and close the door."

"I swear, if you drive off and leave me in the middle of nowhere, I will hunt you down—"

"Now!" He swerved the van to the shoulder and in one swift motion, pulled a handgun from underneath his seat, jumped out of the van, and slammed the door behind him.

"Holy shit!" I cried and fumbled with my seatbelt. I opened the door and fell out onto the pavement. "Holy shit!" I cried again, closing the door and stepping back from the van.

Troy came running around the front, watching the back, holding the gun up and narrowing his eyes.

"Holy shit, Troy! You have a gun!"

"Yeah, and it's a good thing. Somebody's hiding in the back of the van."

"What?"

"I thought I heard a sneeze a few minutes ago, and then I noticed some movement in the rearview mirror. Stay back—I'll handle this." He held the gun parallel to his face and marched to the back of the van.

"Shit!" I ran after him. He thought he was being all John McClane, but he looked like a scrawny idiot holding a firearm precariously close to his head.

What if Arlon had sent someone to off me? What if it was some kind of Starlight Pioneer assassin?

We reached the back of the van, and Troy motioned for me to get behind him. He pulled the handle, and the right door opened, revealing a dark interior. I saw some boxes and blankets, my backpack, but it was hard to make anything else out.

Troy pointed the gun toward the open door. "I've got a gun. Come out with your hands where I can see them!"

He repositioned his feet on the dusty asphalt and took a breath. I turned on the flashlight on my phone and pointed it at him. Little droplets of sweat were forming around his hairline, and I could see the veins in his temples pulsing. Then I moved the light to the open door and waited, holding my breath.

"Don't shoot—I'm coming out," a weak, shaky voice came calling out from the darkness. Two outstretched hands appeared, and then a tall, slender girl stepped into the light and sat down in the open doorway, with her legs dangling.

"West!" I screamed, and ran forward, embracing her and putting myself between her and the gun. "It's my sister—put that gun away *now*!" She looked up at me with large, scared eyes. I squeezed my own eyes closed and held her close.

Troy had lowered the gun and was standing with his hands on his knees, taking in deep breaths of relief.

"Just a sec." I marched over to Troy and grabbed him by the arm. "What the hell, Troy? Why do you have a gun? And why do you think it's okay to randomly aim it at people? You could have killed my sister!"

Troy sighed and held the gun out for me to see. "It's a paint-ball gun."

"What?"

"I mean, real guns aren't safe."

My jaw dropped, and I looked him up and down, trying to reconcile my friend with this . . . this moron. "Are you crazy? Somebody could shoot you! And you're telling me that you were going to protect me from a murderer in the back of the van with a *paintball* gun?"

"It's loaded, at least," Troy said sheepishly, and aimed the gun down at the road. He pulled the trigger, and a blob of neon green splattered into a rough two-inch circle on the pavement.

West had come up beside me and was clearly over her initial distress. "You work with this guy, Glinda?"

"I did," I replied, crossing my arms over my chest and glaring at Lieutenant Paintball.

"How about the fact that your sister stowed away in my van?" As he spoke, he used the gun to gesture in West's direction.

"You could take somebody's eye out with that," she snapped. Troy sighed even louder and then went and set the paintball gun in the back of the van and slammed the door closed.

"West, what are you doing here?" I asked. "How'd you even get back there?"

"I wasn't going to let you go screw everything up with Dorothy. And you weren't going to take me with you. So I waited until you two went into the house, and got in the back."

"I don't understand. You said you didn't care."

"Of course I care." She glared at me, tears welling up in her gray eyes. "All you think about is yourself, Glinda. You don't realize that other people might have feelings too, feelings they don't trust you with."

I couldn't believe it; I *wouldn't* believe it. This was some kind of weird trick. She was messing with my head for who knows what purpose.

She brushed her hair back and stretched her arms and legs.

"Well, now I'm going to have to call Mom and tell her where you are before she calls the police." It was the last thing I felt like doing.

"Nah, I told her I was staying at Lisa's house for the week."

I sighed. "West, you can't come with me."

"Why?"

"Well, for one thing, you're underage. You have to have Mom's permission or else you're a runaway."

"I'm almost eighteen."

We stood there, facing off, on the shoulder of the highway in the middle of Nowhere, Texas. I pulled out my phone.

"What are you doing?" West cried, her eyes big.

"I'm ordering you an Uber to take your ass back home." I looked down and saw a dollar sign followed by a three-digit number pop up on my screen. "I am *not* ordering you an Uber. Holy shit."

"Why can't she just come?" Troy asked from behind me.

"Don't get involved," I said, never taking my eyes off my sister.

"Sorry to break up your alone time with your new boyfriend, but if we're going to get Dorothy to come home, it's gotta come from me."

"Why you?"

"Because I'm not *you*."

I turned on my heel and went back to the front seat of the van. She had no idea what she was talking about. She was a kid.

She didn't know Dorothy like I did; how could she? For one sweet second I had the cabin to myself. I imagined jumping in the driver's seat and speeding off, leaving those two idiots in my dust.

West climbed in the driver's side and plopped herself next to me in the middle seat.

"He's not my boyfriend," I muttered.

"You guys sure flirt a lot for friends. I was barely able to sleep."

"So, you climbed into the back of a strange van and went to sleep?"

"Just a quick nap."

And for the first time, I realized West and I shared something in common: a complete lack of common sense.

Well, fine, so West had inserted herself into my thing, but that didn't mean I had to pretend to like it. I sat as close to the door as possible, arms crossed, staring angrily into the darkness.

Troy climbed back into the driver's seat. And so, we continued our drive across the flat prairie land until it began to bow and bend, and small trees dotted the roadside.

Troy politely asked West about herself and she responded, and it sounded like the answers of an actual human being. I tried to ignore their conversation, but I couldn't. I'd had no idea West had quit the cheerleading team last semester or that she was interested in chemistry. To be honest, I'd never heard West talk this much before. Her phone remained in her purse, and not once did I hear the word *Gucci*. So which side of West was the act? No, it didn't matter. Either way this almost adult sister of mine had shut me out every time I'd tried to engage her, and that in itself was unforgivable.

After about an hour, I knew that no amount of sitting silently and pouting would stave off the inevitable.

"I have to pee," I blurted out.

"Cool, I'm starving," Troy said.

"Okay, just pull off at the next McDonald's."

"Gross," West murmured.

"Sorry, Your Majesty, but I've got limited funds in my account that I've got to make last this whole trip."

West wasn't listening. She had pulled out her phone and was perusing Yelp reviews.

"There are no vegetarian restaurants out here."

"Since when are you vegetarian?" I asked.

"Since three years ago when we dissected a cat in anatomy class."

"Well, I don't have the money for a diner, so . . ."

"I've got Mom's credit card."

"Sweet," Troy broke in.

"No, West, we're not mooching off Mom."

"Technically, she's giving all her money to Arlon, so we're actually mooching off Arlon." She smiled at me, and I noticed the deep circles under her eyes. I nodded slowly in agreement and couldn't help but smile back a little.

"Hey, do you think Arlon would like to buy us gas?" Troy asked.

"Yes, yes he would!" I exclaimed.

"Cool, because this thing is expensive to fill up."

"Oh, Arlon won't mind." West laughed, tossing her hair and batting her eyes at Troy. I knew it wasn't on purpose. I mean, I assumed it wasn't on purpose, but the sight of her being flirty with him made me mad all over again. I took a deep breath and slouched down in my seat.

· 12 ·

HORNY AND HOPELESS

T ROY DIDN'T SAY ANYTHING as he pulled into a gas station
parking lot, and before he'd come to a complete stop, I leapt
out to use the restroom. When I was done, I came out and found
Troy pumping gas.

"Steal any sunglasses?" he asked as I climbed in. I rolled my
eyes and slammed the door.

West turned her face away from me, pretending to look back
at Troy pumping gas. Normally, at this point, I would have gone
to my room and avoided her for several hours, but currently we
had no way to get away from each other.

"You trust him?" West broke the silence.

I stopped. I did trust him. I didn't know when it had happened, but I really did. Hell, I'd spent the night in his apartment
and didn't worry for a moment about my safety. It was hitting me
all at once. Was I just being careless? Letting my guard down?
Perhaps, but that didn't do anything to diminish the fact that,
when I wasn't paying attention, Troy had become my friend, a
real friend. A friend that I felt safe with. "Yeah?"

"You've told him everything?"

"Yes. He's cool, West."

"You told him *everything*?"

Well, no. I haven't told anyone *everything*.

The cabin door opened, and Troy hopped in with a white bag.
He handed the card back to West and then dropped the bag in my lap.

"What's this?"

"When you're poor, you learn how to get the most bang for your buck."

I opened it to discover a dozen hot StopNGo taquitos wrapped in foil.

"And hey, West, there's a bunch of black bean ones in there, no meat."

West smiled and sniffed. "They smell really good." Troy looked relieved. West gingerly lifted one out and took a big bite. "Troy, you're the best!"

I took a bite of mine too. "Thanks," I said to him, finally relaxing a bit.

"See, there she is." He winked at me. "I knew you were just hangry."

"Troy gets me," I said with a full mouth to West. She couldn't help it and gave me a tiny smile.

"Troy, I like you," she said between bites. "I like him, Glinda." I rolled my eyes.

After the three of us crammed down the entire bag of taquitos, Troy started up the van and yawned. He shook his head and slapped his face. It was after midnight now.

"You okay?" I asked.

"Yes." He grabbed a MaXout from under his seat and popped the tab.

"I'm going to use the restroom before we leave." West climbed over me and out and headed to the convenience store. I watched her to make sure she made it in okay.

"She couldn't have gone when I went?" I said with annoyance, but Troy didn't respond. I looked over and realized he was looking down at our knees, which were now touching each other's after I slid over to give West room to get out.

He set the can down in the cup holder. The air was hot and heavy, and for the first time in my life I felt true tension, the kind that has its own gravity and pulls you closer and closer. I tried to think of something to say to break the silence, but my mouth had gone dry.

He swallowed and then softly placed his hand on my leg, right above my knee, just resting it there.

I flinched and he drew back immediately.

"Sorry," he murmured, furrowing his brow and frowning slightly. I sighed, ashamed of myself and my brain and how conflicted I was inside. How his touch made me panic and feel alive at the same time.

"I didn't—it's just—" I couldn't say it. Instead, I took a breath, reached out my hand, and ever so gently brushed a strand of his hair away from his eye. My hand came to rest on his knee.

I darted a glance up at him again, and he was looking at me, straight into my eyes. That was all it took.

Without saying a word, he lifted a hand and caressed my jaw, right below my ear.

This time, to my own surprise, I leaned into his touch, and he took that as permission to lean forward and kiss me softly. I'm not going to lie—it felt good. Like, really good.

I traced my fingers up his forearm, feeling the goose bumps pucker up under my fingers. I deepened the kiss and slipped both my hands behind his head, combing them through his hair. I'd never kissed someone and not felt nausea. I'd never kissed someone and felt . . . well, anything like what I was feeling now. And what I was feeling now was too much.

When I pushed away, he immediately stopped.

"What's wrong?" he breathed.

I looked down. "I'm sorry."

His eyes were bright. "For what? That was . . . that was—"

"Listen, Troy, I'm not—I don't . . . ." I stopped, trying to catch my breath.

"We kissed." He seemed so relaxed. How was he so relaxed? "It's not like we got married, bought a bungalow, and adopted a blind beagle."

"That . . . that was oddly specific," I murmured back.

He shrugged. I looked at him, his wavy dark hair that needed a trim, his tawny skin and aquiline nose, the dimple on his right cheek that appeared when he smiled big. I didn't have a type—I *purposely* did not have a type—but somehow, everything about him—his eyes, his smile, his energy—all culminated into a force that wrecked me when I looked at him. And now those eyes, dark and kind, were looking at me, inviting me back in. *Shit.* I knew where this road led, and it ended with a fiery crash and charred bodies. I had to hit the brakes.

"Look, I want to be your friend," I started. "Not even your close friend—just a friend. I haven't had the best luck with relationships. And if you agreed to take me to Oklahoma because you thought we'd hook up, then I should have been clearer. And if that means you're out, then okay, I will accept that. West and I can figure something out."

He looked offended and backed away from me. "You think I'm that shallow?"

I ignored the question, and only said, "We can't do that again."

"Sure thing." He frowned and tapped the wheel impatiently.

West opened the door. Troy took a long swig of his energy drink and swished it around like he was trying to get the taste of me out of his mouth.

"We ready?" West asked eagerly.

"Yep. I'm certainly awake now." Troy shifted into drive and peeled out before I could respond.

We rode in silence for a bit, and then West cleared her throat. "You two okay?"

I responded by unbuckling my seatbelt and twisting around in the seat.

"What the hell are you doing?" Troy asked.

"I'm going to take a nap." I climbed over the back of the seat. "Wake me when we get to Broken Bow." I grasped the heavy curtains in each hand and slammed them closed.

So stupid. Why was I so stupid? Why had that felt so good? Patrick had never kissed me like that. The rando I'd made out with at a Walk the Moon concert hadn't kissed me like that, although we were both drunk. I stretched out and rolled up my hoodie as a pillow. I lay my head down on it and gently brushed my fingers across my lips.

Dammit.

When I woke up, I knew some time had passed, but I wasn't sure how much. I'd forgotten to plug my phone in before I'd collapsed in the back. As I moved toward the curtain to grab my charger from the front, West said something that made my blood freeze.

"She didn't tell you about James, huh?"

I leaned closer, and although the curtain and road noise muffled their words, I could make out the conversation.

"She told me she tried to break them up. That was it."

"Oh my god, she didn't even tell you the worst part."

I could have opened the curtains and West would have shut up. I could have pretended I hadn't heard what she'd said, and we would continue on like almost nothing had happened. But I didn't move. I couldn't. It was like a force outside my body was holding me frozen in place. Like the universe had decided, *No, Glinda, that's enough of your bullshit; he gets to know the truth now.* Except, I couldn't blame it on the universe. It was me.

★   ★   ★

Eighteen-ish months ago

It was about a month after the texting incident with James and Dorothy. She hadn't invited me to her graduation, and it hurt. It was a big deal, and I'd been cut out like some kind of pariah.

I had hung around my grad school campus, under the guise of working on my dissertation, after everyone else had gone home for the winter break, but really, I was none too eager to face my sister and her boyfriend.

But Christmas Eve had come, and I couldn't put it off any longer. I swung by my box in the mailroom to make sure I hadn't forgotten anything before I headed home. There, sitting in the cubby, was a silver box with a white tag. It read: *To Glinda, from your academic admirer. I hope to be as smart as you someday. Merry Christmas!*

Secret admirers were few and far between for me, so I ripped the lid off the box to discover nine chocolate truffles, dusted with cocoa powder. They looked delicious. I glanced around the empty mailroom, wondering who in the world would have left this for me. One of my students? Nah. A fellow grad student? Maybe, but ever since I went off on the psychological unraveling of "Piers Plowman" in seminar, most of them had put a bit of professional distance between us.

I lifted one out to try it but stopped myself. I'd been carb loading since the texting thing, and I needed to rein it in. So I put the truffle back, placed the box in my backpack, and left.

When I got home, James and Dorothy weren't around. I trudged upstairs to put my stuff down in my bedroom when West came out of her room with a red gift bag stuffed with gold tissue paper.

"What's that?" I asked.

"It's a present." She rolled her eyes.

"I know, but who's it for?"

"It's for the gift exchange tonight, remember?"

The gift exchange. Crap. I'd forgotten all about it.

West continued, "Mom's been cooking all day, and James and Dorothy are out getting some firewood, so it'll feel all Hallmark Channel up in here."

"Shit," I muttered.

West raised a knowing eyebrow. "You drew James, didn't you?"

"Of course I did! Because the universe hates me. Shit!"

"You've got"—she glanced down at her phone—"twenty-two minutes to find a gift for the boyfriend of the sister that you royally pissed off at Thanksgiving." She laughed and tossed her hair over her shoulder. "God, I love Christmas!" She winked at me and then descended the stairs, her cloven hooves clinking on the steps as she went.

I raced to my room and threw my backpack on the bed, looking around frantically. I could wrap my old iPod. No, I'd lost the charging cord. What else?

And then, as if by divine intervention, my backpack shifted, and the silver box slipped out onto the quilt.

I ripped the tag off. It would have to do. I couldn't show up empty-handed. Not after what had happened.

I went downstairs and found myself face to face with Dorothy. Her eyes were stern, but she managed a weak smile and gave me a tiny hug.

"I'm glad you were able to make it," she said. Make it. Like I was a guest. But she seemed to be trying, and I hoped all the unpleasantness was behind us.

As we all sat around the fire, the smell of some kind of Ethiopian-inspired casserole wafting in from the oven, the gift exchange began. West gave Mom some new wind chimes—she loved them, of course. Next, my twin sister turned to me and held out a small brown paper bag with no tissue paper. I swallowed and took it from her.

"Thanks." I tried to hide my surprise. Surely, she was mostly over it if she had bought me a gift. Right? I reached in and pulled out a book. It was old and worn, with a green cloth cover and yellowed pages. The front was embossed with a small, gold axe. I turned it over. On the spine, in gold letters, it read: *Sir Gawain and the Green Knight*. Beneath that: *Tolkien and Gordon*.

"Do you like it?" She seemed nervous. "I know you probably have a million copies, but I found this one at this little used book shop by our—my place and anyway, I know it's in pretty rough shape. That's why I could afford it. The owner said if it was in better condition, it would be worth a lot more."

I gaped at her. "Dorothy, this is a first edition of Tolkien's translation of *Sir Gawain*. It could be completely destroyed and would still be literally the best gift I've ever received!"

She smiled and I sat back, completely bewildered by the book, tracing my fingers over its cover.

"My turn!" James interjected and reached across the circle for the only gift left, the silver box. I held my breath. "So, who's this from?"

"Me! It's from me!" I cried. Dorothy turned to the gift, watching it all with precision.

James lifted the lid and smiled. "Ah, sweet! I love chocolate!" He grinned at me. I shot a sly glance at Dorothy to gauge her approval of my gift to her boyfriend. She seemed pleased.

"I made them just for you," I lied. *So there, Dorothy! See? I've accepted your stupid boyfriend. You can't possibly hate me now.* At last, things were at peace.

He popped one whole truffle into his mouth.

"Not bad!" He ate another. Then he closed the box and set it on the couch next to him. "Thanks, Glinda." Our eyes met and I relaxed. Even though I was not super crazy about this dude, I was happy that the healing had begun. Now we could move on.

My mom looked so happy, like she'd been living under this dark cloud and was finally stepping out into the sunshine and stretching her tired muscles. She went to the piano and started playing "In the Bleak Midwinter." I stayed seated, even as Dorothy and West went to stand beside her and sing.

I glanced over at James, wondering if he was the kind of guy to think he was too cool to sing. His face had gone white and he was sitting very rigidly in place. His eyes were darting around wildly, and I noticed trails of sweat rolling down his neck.

Weird. I looked back to my mom and sisters and tried to join in with the song, but I was distracted. What was going on with this guy?

James was on his feet now, pacing the room like a madman. Mom stopped playing and Dorothy rushed to him.

"What's the matter?" she asked, her brow knitted.

"I can't breathe," he gasped. "I can't breathe. Oh my God, I can't . . ." His face was turning red, his eyes bulging out.

"James!" Dorothy was guiding him now back down to a chair.

"What did you put in those?" he sputtered out, looking right at me, fire bolts shooting from his eyes.

"In what?" I asked, dumbfounded. "The truffles?"

"Oh my God, my heart! My heart is beating too fast." He gripped Dorothy's hand, his knuckles turning white. "Yes, the truffles!"

Fuck. "Nothing! I mean, I don't know. I lied—I didn't make them."

"What? Where did you get them?" Dorothy looked at me aghast.

"I . . . I got them from school. Gah, is he allergic to anything? Maybe peanuts?"

James shook his head.

"Maybe it's a panic attack!" I offered. "I mean, it fits the symptoms. And obviously he can still breathe or he wouldn't be able to talk."

"It's . . . not . . . a . . . panic attack!" He spat out, heaving as he spoke. "I told you . . . my instinct about her . . ."

Her? Me?

"Take some deep breaths!" Dorothy cried.

"I . . . can't."

"James, we have to call 911." Dorothy was trying to get him to let go of her hand.

"No!"

"I'm already on it," West cried, holding the phone to her ear. "Yeah, my sister's boyfriend is having a heart attack or something!" She walked into the other room to finish the call.

"No . . . too . . . expensive!" James was calling after her.

"James, we have to. This is serious! What the hell was in the truffles, Glinda?" Dorothy was angry, but more than that, she was the most frightened I'd ever seen her.

"I told you, I didn't make them! I regifted them."

Now James looked up at her, his eyes wide and frightened. She put her arm around him and helped him sit on the floor, where he heaved.

Meanwhile, my mother had already picked up her phone and was dialing Arlon.

"They're on their way." West was back in the room, googling symptoms on her phone.

And I was still standing there, watching this guy dying in front of me, completely unable to move. "I've had panic attacks before, and sometimes it feels like you're having a heart attack."

"Glinda, you need to stop talking," my mother said in a low and blood-chilling tone.

I went to sit on the porch and wait for the ambulance. The cold night air felt good on my face, and I looked up at the stars, praying to God that he'd hear an agnostic's prayer and not let James die.

When the paramedics got there, they rushed in as the rest of the air in the house rushed out. Blue uniforms, red bags, plastic packages being torn open, and then the low murmur of voices, questions, checklists.

"Sir?"

James was lying on the floor as they checked his vitals. "Yeah?"

"Okay, sir, you gotta tell me what you've taken," one of the paramedics said.

"Um . . . nothing. I had a sandwich for lunch and then just water . . . and some chocolates just before I started feeling like my heart was going to burst."

"Any energy drinks?"

"No."

"Did you take any pills?"

"No, nothing."

"No stimulants, like caffeine pills? No Adderall or any other kind of amphetamine, legal or illegal?"

"No." He turned his head and stared directly at me, unblinking. Dorothy followed his gaze and her eyes grew wide.

"You aren't going to be in trouble," the medic continued, "but I need to know if you've taken any methamphetamines."

"No way!"

"It's important you're honest with us; you are suffering from extreme tachycardia."

"W-what does that mean?" He looked up to Dorothy and reached for her hand. She reached through the paramedics' arms and held it.

"Your heart is beating at a dangerously high rate."

"Oh my God!" Dorothy wailed, and West ran to sit beside her. "So, Adderall could have done this?" She sniffed, her eyes jerking between me and James.

"Yes, ma'am. An overdose of Adderall could cause these symptoms," the second paramedic replied quickly. The paramedics looked at each other knowingly. "Sir, did you consume Adderall?"

"I might have," he whispered hoarsely, glancing at me. He looked scared. A single tear rolled from the corner of his eye and landed on the carpet. He might have? I stared down at him, realization dawning on me. He thought I put my Adderall in the truffles. How could he possibly think that? I opened my mouth to protest, but the medics were moving fast now.

"We're going to get you in the bus and administer phentolamine."

"I'm going with him!" Dorothy cried, and in an instant all the commotion had been swept outside, leaving those of us behind reeling.

"Maybe I should follow in my car?" I suggested.

"No," my mother said softly.

"I just . . . I need to help."

"No," she repeated.

"Mom, I feel like this is my fault somehow and I need to explain—"

"Stop!" My mother's tone tore through me like shards of glass. "This isn't about you."

"I just—"

"For once in your life, Glinda Rainbow Glass, don't make this about *you!*"

★ ★ ★

Present

"Damn," Troy muttered.

"Yeah, I know, right?" West agreed.

"They didn't, like, test the chocolates for poison?"

"No." West sighed. "I'm not sure what happened with that. Nobody would tell me."

My chest was tight, like I'd been crying for hours, but my face was dry.

"So, I'm assuming Dorothy confronted Glinda?" Troy asked.

"Oh, big time. She had it out with Glinda and my mom. Dorothy accused her of outright trying to kill James with poison or something, and Glinda claimed that was insane. My mom wouldn't accept Glinda would do something that malicious on purpose, so Dorothy packed up a couple duffel bags and left, and that was it. She never came back home."

"Wow. That's awful," Troy muttered.

"I miss her. She calls me sometimes, but it's just not the same, you know." She sighed and popped her neck. "I know I shouldn't think like this, but sometimes I wish she'd stayed, and Glinda . . ."

She trailed off. Troy may have said something in my defense, but I had stopped listening. I slunk back down and curled up on the metal floor, letting my head rest on the cold. The vibrations of the road made my teeth chatter. The memory of it felt as real and raw as it had eighteen months ago.

After that night, I hadn't seen Dorothy again. She and James moved to Broken Bow and kept radio silence for six months. Finally, she reestablished communication with my mom, calling occasionally. My mom told me Dorothy and James had moved out into the woods and established what James called a Bigfoot observatory. Apparently Broken Bow, Oklahoma, was a Bigfoot hotspot. Who knew? My mom was always so happy when she'd call.

Dorothy texted me on our birthday. When I replied, she didn't. Same thing happened at Christmas, and then a couple times she'd just randomly drop a single line: *Still processing, need more time.*

It was stupid, but it was enough to keep this little, tiny flame of hope alive that someday we'd be able to talk it out. But this whole car ride, the closer I'd physically gotten to her, the tinier that flame had grown. And now, with the whole story laid out bare, my hope was gone.

I hugged my knees and let the motion of the van jerk me from side to side. This way, that way, and always forward, toward a doorstep on which I wasn't welcome.

♦ 13 ♦

LOST AND FRIGHTENED

AFTER A WHILE WEST pushed the curtain back and looked down at me.

"You awake?"

"No." I mumbled from underneath the hood of my sweatshirt, which I'd pulled on and retreated into.

"Get up here, weirdo. Stop hiding in the back."

Reluctantly, I climbed back through and plopped down between them. As we crossed the Red River, West chattered on about college and why she was going to major in sports medicine.

I relaxed. A few drops of rain hit the windshield, and then the dark sky opened, pouring sheets of water down to the earth.

Finally, we drove through Broken Bow and farther north toward Dorothy's address, into the pines, toward the lake.

Troy remained quiet. He kept his jaw set, his eyes forward. My knee tapped his by accident, and he jerked it away. I sighed. Great. See, this was actually what happened when you started kissing someone—it ruined everything.

It had been a good kiss, though. I could still taste it on my lips, still feel little sparks pricking my ribs when I looked at him. So I didn't look at him.

The van shuddered and we came to a rolling stop on the side of the road.

"Shit," Troy muttered under his breath. "Hang on." He climbed out while West and I looked anxiously out the window.

The wipers were still streaking across the glass, pushing the water around.

"We're not going anywhere for a while. Engine overheated." Troy climbed back into the van, soaking wet, his hair dripping onto the seat. "But we're not far. I know we're not far."

"How did the engine overheat?" I asked, glowering at him.

"It just does that sometimes." He shrugged. "This van's not used to hobbling along this far."

I looked out at the sheets of rain falling onto the dense, dark forest. It wasn't hard to imagine we were the last humans alive on earth.

"We really need to know where we are." I grabbed West's phone and went to look at the map. The page came up blank. "Weird, no service."

"It's really hilly here." Troy looked tense.

"How will we know how to go if we have no service?" West asked.

Troy glanced at his flip phone and cocked his head. "I have two bars."

"Can you look up the directions?" West asked.

Troy shook his head. "This thing barely sends text messages." He rubbed his face and gazed out into the night.

"My phone's dead." Perfect. I looked out into the rain. So, this was how it ended. Three weeks from now they'd find our emaciated corpses still sitting in this van. Well, Troy would probably survive on beef jerky and energy drinks, but West and I were doomed. I wondered if I'd be capable of resorting to cannibalism if it came to that.

"All right, all right, gather your stuff. We're going for it," Troy said, startling both West and me. He grabbed a flashlight from where it had fallen on the seat next to him.

"Going for it? I've never been here before, Troy. We can't just go hiking into the forest."

"Look, stay in the van if you like, but I'm going." And with that, he opened his door, letting the wind blow a torrent of cold rain into the cabin, and jumped out.

West gasped. "What do we do?"

Ahead of us we could make out the beam from the flashlight entering the tree line.

"Ugh, we should probably stay put." Even as I spoke the words, West was climbing out of the van.

"Troy! Wait! I'm coming!"

I sat there for a minute, arms crossed, with only the sound of the rain pounding on the roof and my own heartbeat in my ears.

Nobody ever listened to me. Especially not those two. I didn't know how much time I had left to get back to my mom and stop her from marrying Arlon, but at this pace we'd never make it.

Out of the corner of my eye, I thought I saw a shadow pass by the driver's side door. Something big and fast. I looked closely, but I couldn't make out anything. I could still see the light from Troy's flashlight about a hundred feet in front of me. The rain-cooled air hit my neck, and I shuddered. Something was not right. I thought I heard a twig snap, but I couldn't be certain above the noise of the rain.

Shit. I was not staying here alone all night. I opened the passenger door and leapt out, leaving it open to the elements. And I took off sprinting toward my sister and Troy. I'd made it halfway when my foot hooked under a raised root, and I face-planted into the mud. For a moment I lay there, waiting for something or someone to grab me, but nothing happened.

Stop being an idiot, Glinda. There was nothing in these woods except squirrels and deer . . . and maybe a serial killer, but probably not. I stood up, my face, my shirt, my pants, all caked with a thick, black mud. My knees stung from the fall, but I trudged on until I caught up with West and Troy.

Once we'd gone a little way into the forest, the branches blocked the worst of the rain, and we could actually hear each other.

Troy shone his light on me and shook his head. "You look like a swamp monster."

"You know, how about 'Are you okay, Glinda?' or 'What happened to you, Glinda?'" Troy pointed the light through the trees, and I saw we were actually following a little dirt path.

"We should go back to the road and try to follow it back to the highway," I said.

"It's this way." He gestured ahead of him.

"How do you know?" I asked, fighting the panic in my voice. He kept walking. West looked at me, and then she took my hand. I looked down in surprise and then squeezed it for reassurance as we followed our guide into certain death.

I wondered how long it would take our mom to realize we weren't coming back. Would she call in a missing person's report? Arlon would tell her not to worry, that we had transcended into another dimension or some bullshit.

Branches scraped at my exposed arms and caught at the ends of my hair. I knew Bigfoot was bullshit, but being here, in the deep, dark woods, it did make one pause and consider what might be lurking in the shadows.

We walked for a bit without saying a word, my sister's hand and Troy's light the only reminders I was not alone.

Ten more steps and I'm going back.

But ten steps later, I was still following him.

Okay, after this next turn, if I still don't see civilization, I'm going back.

But Troy turned and I turned too.

And then, all at once, the rain stopped, the moon came out from behind a cloud, and I could see a clearing up ahead—and a light from a window.

"Maybe they have a phone!" I whispered excitedly, but Troy didn't reply.

In the center of the clearing stood a large cabin with a chimney, like something out of a fairy tale. It had wooden shingles and white shutters. Smoke was rising out of the chimney, and I could smell something delicious cooking, even though it was well after midnight. In the yard was an empty clothesline and a wheelbarrow filled with firewood. Beside the cabin were two four-wheelers and a rusted out old Jeep.

We neared the front door and a security light flashed on, blinding us. Everything seemed so surreal in the harsh light. We were wet and dirty, faces pale and eyes wide. And then I saw it, hanging from a branch on a tree near the house, wind chimes with little hollow ceramic birds that whistled softly when the wind blew through them. My mom had the same one hanging in her front yard.

Troy knocked briskly on the door.

"Wait!" I hissed. Too late.

From inside came the *thud thud* of heavy boots on a wooden floor.

I wasn't ready.

"How did you know how to find their cabin?" I shot at Troy, my heart racing. He looked at me guiltily and opened his mouth to say something but turned back as the door creaked open.

Before us stood a man in dirty jeans and a flannel shirt, with a dark, shaggy beard. "Yes?"

Troy cleared his throat. "Hey, James."

James's hesitant expression rearranged into one of recognition. "What the hell, Troy?"

◆ 14 ◆

BETRAYED AND DISENCHANTED

"W HAT THE HELL, TROY?" I echoed. Did they *know* each other? How . . .?

Troy looked back at me and shrugged sheepishly. He wasn't angry anymore. He actually looked scared. "So, I may have forgotten to mention that James is kinda my cousin."

"Are you shitting me? What are you saying?" I was hearing my voice from far away. My head was spinning. I grabbed West's arm for support.

"What the hell did you do, man?" James said, staring at Troy in horror.

"I swear, I didn't know—I mean, not initially," Troy croaked.

"No. No, you would have realized it when I told you about my sister and James, and you would have told me."

Troy wouldn't look me in the eye. "I told you I had a situation."

"*This* is how you knew they lived in Oklahoma," I realized aloud. "I *knew* I hadn't told you that."

My heart dropped. Not him. Not Troy. He really was just like the rest of them—nothing but a liar. Not just a liar—he was James's cousin, the same James that had inserted himself between my sister and me. It was like I had this terrible taste in my mouth I couldn't get out. My eyes stung, but I wasn't going to cry, not for him.

I stepped forward. "James, I need to see my sister."

James looked down at me, eyebrow raised, lips pursed. "Glinda? Is . . . is that you? It's hard to recognize you."

I sighed and tried to rub more of the mud off my face. "Better?" Not waiting for a response, I pushed past him; he smelled like elderberry syrup and smoke. The cabin's interior consisted of one main room: a den with a fireplace at one end and a kitchen at the other. A large, rustic dining table separated the space. Stairs led up to some kind of loft area, and near the door, where one sofa was pushed up against a wall, was a hallway. I noticed a fire going in the hearth, a vase of wildflowers sitting on the table, a rocking chair. A couple of paintings I immediately recognized as my sister's work hung on the walls. There was no sign of Dorothy.

James had followed me in, with Troy and West behind him.

"Dorothy!" I called out. I was going to puke.

"She's in the cellar," James said.

"The cellar!" I crossed my arms and looked at him sharply. "You got her tied up down there or something?"

"Are you insane?" James shook his head.

I wandered to the table and traced my fingers over an open book beside an empty mug and a wet teabag. I lifted the book and read the spine: *The Pioneer Cookbook.* Yeah, that's what we needed, more pioneers. I set it back down.

On the counter, a large mound of apple skins and cores was piled up. The fleshy white slices of the apples were soaking in a bowl of water. Beside that was a small fruit knife with a wooden handle. I felt like I was surrounded by clues, hints, but no clear answers. Besides the obvious *Where is my sister?* there was something else. What was this life she'd built out here without me?

I peered into the bowl of apples as though I would discover some deeper meaning, but all I saw was my dirty reflection on the surface of the water.

"Where's Dorothy?" I asked.

"She won't want to see you." James crossed his arms over his chest.

My blood pressure was mounting. I had to stay level. I forced my frustration back down. "James, look, I'm very tired—exhausted really—and I don't have time for your bullshit."

"*My* bullshit?" He gawked at me. "Do you even understand how insane it is that you're here? It's the fucking middle of the night!"

"Sorry I didn't call first," I said sharply. "Oh wait—that wouldn't do any good since Dorothy doesn't answer her phone!"

"She doesn't want to talk to you." He said it slowly, overenunciating the words. There was nothing that made me more irrationally angry than someone else remaining calm when I was pissed.

"You haven't changed at all!" Yep, no chill. "You think she belongs to you!"

"She doesn't belong to anyone, least of all you!"

I wanted to smash my fist against the wall, and scream until I was hoarse. *No, push it down. Don't let him get to you. Stay rational, stay calm.*

"Please put the knife down," James said.

"What?" I looked down and saw the fruit knife in my hand. My knuckles were white, my grip on the handle tight. I didn't remember picking it up.

"Glinda, stop. Put the knife down." Troy sounded annoyed. *Annoyed.* That liar had the nerve to be annoyed with me. So I pointed the knife at him, like I would a finger.

"You've lost the right to speak to me at present."

"Whatever." He waved me off and went and flopped down on the couch.

"Glinda, put it down," James said, slowly again, like he was talking down a crazy terrorist.

"Right, because you think I'm crazy and tried to kill you?" I raised my eyebrows and pointed the knife toward him.

He held up his hands from ten feet away. I rolled my eyes.

West just stood there, watching us.

I lowered the knife to my side and glared at James. "You don't trust me? Well, I don't trust you. Where is my fucking sister?"

"Right fucking here. I needed more apples."

Dorothy was standing in the threshold, holding a basket of apples. She slipped out of a pair of rain boots and went to set the apples on the counter beside me. Without another word she took the knife out of my hand and began slicing her latest haul. James and Troy let out audible sighs of relief and West whimpered softly. And all the while, my twin sister continued cutting apples like nothing weird was happening at all, like her sisters she hadn't seen in eighteen months hadn't just mysteriously appeared, holding her boyfriend at knifepoint.

West, who had until now remained quiet and was still in the corner, gasped a couple of times and began sobbing. "Oh, Dorothy!"

"Oh my goodness!" Dorothy set the knife down and rushed to West and embraced her. West was doubling over now, and Dorothy held her up. West looked up into her eyes, her lips trembling.

"I've missed you so much!" she sobbed, and Dorothy hugged her tight and gave me a look—an actual authentic look. It was an *Oh shit, since when does West have real feelings?* look of confusion.

"Hey, I've missed you too, Westy." She pulled West away so she could look in our younger sister's face. "You look like you've been through some stuff." West only nodded and then buried her head against my sister and continued to sob.

"Van broke down about a mile from here near Trent's place," Troy muttered.

Dorothy looked at each of us with surprise. Her brow furrowed and she closed her eyes to think. Finally, her face relaxed, and she opened her eyes. "How about some dry clothes?" She said this directly to West, who nodded. Dorothy put her arm around West and led her into the adjacent room, where I heard a shower turn on.

She marched back into the room alone and went to the sink to cut apples, keeping her back to me.

She looked older than I'd remembered. Her mousy brown hair was swept up in a messy bun, and she was wearing glasses instead of contacts like she used to wear. But she looked good. One of the first things I realized was that while I had maintained my awkward, gawky physique, she had filled out. She looked like a grown woman.

"Wait . . . I thought you said you were twins." Troy broke the silence.

Dorothy spun around, put a hand on her hip, and stared at this intruder.

"We are." I sighed. *Idiot.* "We're fraternal twins." His expression remained uncertain. "We aren't identical."

"James, who is this?" Dorothy gestured toward Troy with the knife.

"Ah, yeah, this is Troy, my cousin, the one who lived with my family a while back."

Dorothy nodded as though it all made sense. She scooped the apple pieces into the bowl.

"You okay, babe?" James asked.

Gag me.

"I'm fine, dear," she replied.

Gag me harder.

"You want a beer?" James asked Troy.

"Yes," I interjected. I may have been the pariah, but this pariah needed a drink. James looked at me in surprise and then sighed. He retreated to the little yellowed fridge in the kitchen while Troy and I sat at either end of the sofa.

"Sooo . . ." I trailed off, looking at Troy with narrowed eyes.

"Um, so this is my family's cabin. We used to come here every summer growing up. That's how—"

"That's how you knew where you were going and got us here," I finished for him. He nodded. I just stared at him in disbelief. He seemed relieved when James interrupted the silence with a cold bottle for each of us.

James sat in the rocking chair and took a swig, studying his younger cousin carefully. "It's not that I'm not glad to see you, man. I just can't quite get over you showing up unannounced, at this time of night—with *her.*" He gestured to me, and I rolled my eyes.

"Hey. Glinda is . . . a nice . . . an interesting and funny person, and she's my friend."

"Was," I corrected him.

"Sure." Troy exhaled and took a long draw from the bottle.

"Did you know she was Dory's sister?" James asked.

"I figured it out."

Yeah, I'm sure he did. Probably during one of the many times I'd badmouthed his cousin and he chose to say *nothing.*

He took a long slow breath and then let it out. "I figured it out recently, and I was going to tell you, Glinda—honest, I just could never get up the nerve."

"I mean, I can understand being scared of this one." James gestured toward me.

I had to say something, had to try to fill in the hole I had so eagerly and feverishly dug.

"James, listen, I know we parted on less than ideal terms, but I need Dorothy's help, and if you will give me a chance to—"

James held up a hand, and I shut up. "Dory's the one you need to apologize to."

I cringed when he called her that. Dory. I occasionally called her Dor, but mostly we used our full names. We had wholeheartedly embraced our kitschy names with a sense of pride.

Dorothy finished up in the kitchen and then marched back across the room, stopping for a second to motion me to follow her down the hall. She never made eye contact. I stood, dusting off the sofa from where the dried mud had flaked off my clothes, and crossed the room to meet my fate.

"Listen, I know this might be a little overwhelming—" I started.

"Not at all." She turned and walked down a short hallway and into a bedroom. I followed slowly.

"I'm sorry to show up here so late. I mean, what time is it anyway?"

"It's a quarter to two."

"Really? Why are you still up?"

"Needed pie."

The room was small and cozy, with simple furniture and a quilt on the bed that looked about a hundred years old. I could tell who slept on which side of the bed based on what rested on the tops of their small white nightstands. On the left, James had a camo-patterned thermos, a pair of binoculars, and a large thick book with a picture of Bigfoot on the cover. On the nightstand on the right, I noticed a half-eaten granola bar and a familiar book with a woman and—but just as quickly as I had spied it, Dorothy was standing in front of me, ushering my attention to the T-shirt and black yoga pants she'd laid out across an old rocking chair in the corner.

"You'll have to wait for West to get out of the bathroom." She bent down and smoothed the shirt, avoiding looking at me.

"Dorothy, please."

"I go by Dory, if you don't mind." She rose and went over to a window. Folding her arms across her chest, she looked out into the night. "I see lightning in the distance. Looks like more storms are headed this way."

"You know what? No. I do mind. Mom and Dad named you Dorothy, and that's what I've always called you."

She spun around, and for just a moment she betrayed the anger and sadness burning behind her carefully maintained facade. But she regained her composure and even smirked a little. "Whatever you like, I suppose."

"Listen, I know we have a lot to talk about, a mountain of issues to work through, and I know I didn't exactly make a good faith entrance."

"Oh, you think holding a knife at my hus—at James . . . oh, shit." Her face fell and she dropped her gaze. Her cheeks flushed a dark shade of pink as I tried processing what she had just revealed. I grabbed her hand, and there it was—a simple gold band on the third finger.

I tore out of the room even as she called me to come back, desperation resounding in every word.

When I entered the main room, James and Troy were standing in alarm.

"What's going on?" James called to the other room, "Dor, you okay?"

I went straight to him and grabbed his hand, holding it up level with my eyes. The companion to my sister's ring, a cold, metal statement of complete and utter betrayal, was wrapped right below his hairy knuckle. He dropped his hand.

Dorothy had walked in quietly behind me, looking down and fiddling with her ring.

"When?" I managed to get out.

"About a year ago."

I spun around. "You've been married a *year* and didn't tell me?" I wasn't yelling. That surprised me. I was too tired and defeated for yelling. I was a coroner, clinically gathering information now.

"I wanted to! I just didn't know how after everything that's happened, and . . . I don't know, Glinda."

We stood facing each other like two strangers who'd just roughly bumped into each other and didn't know what to do next.

"So, wait, that means you're my family now?" Troy was looking at Dorothy with a big smile.

"Butt out, Troy," I snapped. The smile faded, and he quietly retreated to a spot on the couch and picked up his beer.

My sister rubbed her eyes with her thumb and index finger. "Okay, I think you need to tell me why you're here, because if it's to tell me again how much you don't like James, then you've just wasted a lot of time and a lot of gas." For Pete's sake, she was five minutes older than me. Why did she always have to act like she was so much more mature?

"Do you really think I'm so pathetic that I'd do that? You left and cut off ties, point taken."

"Fine, then why are you here?"

"It's Mom."

Dorothy's face went pale. "What's wrong with her?"

"She's healthy—it's not anything like that."

"Oh thank God!" She held her hand to her heart and took a deep breath.

"It's Arlon."

"What about Arlon?"

"It's the cult."

"You mean the Society?"

I rubbed my eyes with my thumb and index finger. *Here we go.* "No, I mean *the cult*. He's convinced Mom to marry him. *Marry* him, Dorothy! Not only that, but he's moving the whole cult there, into our house, and she's given him all her money and possessions.

And I think I would prefer to talk about this in private." I glanced at James. Dorothy held her gaze and shook her head. *Fine.* "Dorothy, he's got Mom into some really deep shit. I think—I think he murdered someone, and she might take the blame!"

Silence. Dorothy looked at me and then Troy, and then James, before returning her gaze to me. "Are you high?"

"No!"

"You sound high."

"I'm not high or drunk or anything. This is real—ask West." I went to the little hallway and rapped on the bathroom door. "Hey, West! Tell them about the commune and Mom!"

"What?" Came her muffled call from under the running water.

"Well, she'll tell you when she gets out."

"Arlon seems to make Mom happy, Glinda. I'm sure whatever this is, it all makes a lot more sense than whatever you're ranting about." Dorothy gave me one of those mother-knows-best looks she used to give me when we were growing up, the kind of look that usually ended up with me on top, pummeling her.

"He's crazy!" I cried in frustration.

"This person you think was murdered—they didn't eat any of your baked goods, did they?" James said under his breath.

"I didn't mean to almost kill you!" God, it made me want to claw my brains out at this point. "How many times and how many ways can I say it until you'll believe me?"

Troy sat silently, watching all of us in amazement.

I took a breath and tried to regain some composure, looking at my sister. "You have to come home and talk to her. She'll listen to you. She always listens to you. And think about how even more receptive she'll be after not seeing you in so long."

Dorothy did a double take. "Are you trying to make me feel guilty?"

"No."

"Because it's been almost two years, and it's not like any of you rushed out here to see us."

"I just freaking drove four hours in the middle of the night to see you."

"Yeah, because you want something from me."

"Dorothy, it's our mother. She's about to make a huge mistake. We need a lawyer."

"We do not need a lawyer. Our mother is old enough to make her own choices."

How was she not getting this? "She's been manipulated, brainwashed!"

"You think everyone's been brainwashed. You think James brainwashed me."

I scoffed. "Well, you're living in a cabin in the woods, looking for Bigfoot, so you tell me what other explanation makes sense."

"God, why are you so, so—you?" She threw her hands up in frustration and then walked back to the kitchen and began pulling things from the fridge: a stick of butter, an egg, a pitcher of milk.

I came and stood behind a chair at the table, grasping it with both hands. "I didn't come out here to fight," I said.

"Really? Because it seems like you aren't capable of anything but." She didn't turn around. She pulled out a canister of flour from a cabinet.

"Look, some really bad shit has happened." I took a steadying breath. "Arlon is not who you think he is."

"Says the anti-love apologist herself." Dorothy struggled with the lid of the canister. It didn't budge. Instinctively, I came around and took it from her. She looked at me, one hand on her hip.

"I'm so happy for you that you found your perfect partner, and it's been sunshine and rainbows for you both. But sometimes, Dorothy, sometimes the person we're with—even the person we think we love—isn't good for us. Sometimes they're bad people. Sometimes they're monsters." I struggled with the lid. It wouldn't come off. I pulled harder. *Dammit!*

"Give it here." She reached for the flour.

"No," I muttered, pulling on the lid as hard as I could, with zero results. I was going to say that badass thing about monsters and then pull the lid off and win this stupid argument. Dorothy sighed and rolled her eyes. I slammed the canister down on the counter and folded my arms in front of me. We both stared at each other.

"You are such a child. You still walk around thinking you're the main character, that you're somehow in possession of more knowledge, more instincts, and more wit than the rest of us."

"Shit, Dorothy, this isn't about me!"

"Exactly." Dorothy furrowed her brow and spoke sternly. "It's not about you. It's about Mom and what will make her happy. And I'm so sorry that you somehow missed the chapter of life called 'empathy,' but I'm here to tell you, once and for all, I'm done with your negativity, done with your prejudice, done with your self-importance, and done with your anti-relationship bullshit. I freaking moved to a different state, and even then you didn't get it. I'm done with *you*."

Her words cut me to the quick, but I wasn't about to blink now. Her admission wasn't a surprise. I'd figured it out by the time she'd ignored my hundredth text. So even though my eyes stung, and even though I could taste the prickling of tears in the back of my throat, I kept on with as much stoicism as I could muster.

"I understand you're upset, but I'm just here to talk, like two mature adults."

She reached over and pulled the lid off the flour canister. A little puff of white floated between us.

I gasped. "Bitch! You stole my badass lid move!"

"Dorothy?" West was standing in the doorway, in clean clothes with wet, tangled hair.

"Hey, Westy." Dorothy's glare dropped as she turned to West. How could her demeanor change so quickly from enraged to peaceable?

"Why are you guys yelling?"

"We're just talking about Mom."

West's face crumpled again as she worked to hold back a fresh crop of tears. "Oh my gosh, Dory, it's so bad."

"Don't call her Dory." I sighed. They both ignored me.

"Is it?" Dorothy's expression softened more, and she looked like she might tear up as well. What was happening?

"Yes, Arlon's gone off the deep end."

"Oh no." Dorothy glanced at me for a moment, like she was trying to decipher something. Maybe we were finally getting through to her. I mean, maybe West was getting through to her, since apparently anything I said was going straight in one ear and out the other.

"Tell her about Matthew Harrigan!" I interjected.

"Oh, Glinda thinks Arlon's murdering people," West said, shrugging slightly.

"She still listening to all those murder podcasts?" Dorothy asked, and West nodded.

So much for making progress. I slapped both palms to my head in frustration. I needed a break from this. "Fine. West, just tell her about the other stuff. I'm going to take a shower."

I stomped down the hallway and grabbed the clothes off the rocking chair and then locked myself in the little bathroom. The mirror was fogged up from West's shower, so I wiped away some condensation to see my reflection. Most of the mud had either run off in the rain or been wiped away, leaving a gray film over my face that made me look dead.

I peeled off my clothes, untied my hoodie, and left it all in a heap by the door.

All of Dorothy's shampoos and soaps had words like *all natural*, *chemical free*, and *hemp* on the front, and it pissed me off.

I showered and got dressed, but when I went to open the door to leave, I froze. She was married. Dorothy was married.

I turned and looked at myself in the mirror again. There was a woman with caramel eyes, a bridge of freckles across her nose, dark burgundy hair, and horrible light brown roots. All the pieces were correct, but it wasn't me. Dorothy was married. And I hadn't been there at her side. I hadn't been there.

She really was done with me.

· 15 ·

ANXIOUS AND HUNGRY

W HEN I STEPPED OUT of the bathroom, wearing Dorothy's clothes, the whole cabin smelled like Christmas.

"Dory's pie is almost ready!" West sang happily. To be honest, pie sounded amazing at that moment, but just like everything else in this strange little cabin in the woods, something felt off about it.

"Why are you baking pie at two in the morning, anyway?"

"I'm sorry, why are you showing up at people's doors covered in mud at one in the morning and then judging them for staying up to bake pie?"

"This place is awesome!" West sat down in a chair, rubbing her hands in anticipation for the pie. I stood behind a chair at the opposite end of the worn wooden table from my twin sister.

Dorothy reached into a cabinet and pulled out a stack of heavy ceramic plates. They clanged as she set them on the table. She began carving out slices of piping hot apple pie and passing them down the table to James, Troy, and West.

I gripped the back of the chair with both hands, letting it support my weight. Dorothy was carefully slicing another piece of pie. She set it onto the little ceramic plate, with a petite clink, and looked up at me.

"Seriously," I persisted, "why are you baking pie instead of sleeping?"

"I'm a grown woman in my own home, and if I want to bake pie in the middle of the night, I will."

"Is it, though? Your home, I mean."

"Excuse me?"

"As far as I can see, you're hiding up here in James's parents' cabin, like some kind of Doomsday Prepper Martha Stewart."

Dorothy slammed the end of the serving fork down on the table, causing everyone seated to jump.

I set my face, trying desperately not even to bat an eyelid. We stared at one another, dry eyed and pushing down all the things that were right there, just below the surface, just waiting for a tiny point of weakness to break through and devour us both.

"We're doing fine, Glinda," James finally jumped in, no doubt to keep his wife from jumping over the table and stabbing me in the neck with the serving fork. I could see that scenario playing out behind her eyes. Or maybe that was just in my head. "We're bringing in a nice little income with the website."

"Website?"

James rolled his eyes. Dorothy relaxed her grip on the fork and sat down, avoiding looking at me.

"The Southern Sasquatch Observatory and Research Center, or the SS-ORC, as our online community refers to us. We upload weekly content and make money from ads and fan contributions."

Meanwhile, Dorothy scooped out the center of the pie and plopped it onto a plate, then clutched the plate to her chest, devouring the pie like she hadn't eaten in days. Maybe she hadn't.

I sank down into a chair while the four of them continued shoveling pie into their mouths in silence. Well, not total silence. There was a lot of fork clinking and chewing noises that made me want to barf.

"Just so we're clear, you haven't actually found Bigfoot yet?" Everyone stopped chewing and turned to look at me, each with a varying degree of exasperation.

"Physically? No, but we're close." James laid his fork down and folded his arms across his chest.

"I'm sorry, but how else does one find Bigfoot if not physically?"

"Well, for starters—"

"James, babe, she's just being an asshole." Dorothy cut him off and then glared at me.

"I swear, I'm just curious how you two are making it in the middle of the woods with no internet and no success finding the big guy?" I cocked my head and shot James a sarcastic smile.

"He told you, ad revenue and contributions," Dorothy shot back. "We spend all week creating content for the website, including editing our various wilderness camera footage and writing up theories and observations, and then we drive into town on Saturdays and upload it at the coffee shop."

I stared at my sister in disbelief. How had she settled for this . . . for him? How had she left *me* for this complete absurdist horseshit?

"Dorothy, you've spent the last half a decade or so in school! You need a real job." I leaned back in my chair and rubbed my eyes.

"Ahem." Troy coughed.

"Shut up, Troy. Don't you dare."

"Glinda's been working all summer with me at the Maypole Renaissance Festival in the Drench the Wench booth!"

"The hell, Troy?" I slammed my hands down on the table as West covered her mouth in shock and devilish delight.

"What? Sorry, but she's right—you're being a little bit of an asshole." He said this softly, his head turned so I alone could hear. "Sorry, Glin."

"Drench the Wench?" James asked.

"It's a dunking booth." Troy just couldn't stop himself. "She's the wench."

"And you're criticizing *us*?" Dorothy's eyes were wide with amazement and just a touch of amusement.

West burst out laughing, little bits of apple spraying onto the table.

I just glared at Troy, shaking my head in slow disapproval.

"It all makes sense!" West looked like she was about to burst.

"Okay, okay, listen. It's late. Y'all are tired. I think maybe we should just plan to talk in the morning," Dorothy said as she snuck another spoonful of pie from the pan.

"That sounds like a good idea." James turned to me. "You know, before we start saying things we'll regret."

I shook my head. "I didn't drive four hours in the middle of the night to not talk about this."

"You didn't drive—Troy did," West muttered under her breath.

"I can't tonight." Dorothy gave me a stern look. "I need to sleep. We'll talk tomorrow."

"But—"

"Enough." That was it. I wasn't going to make any headway with her tonight.

Troy took the couch, and West and I were given a broken-down twin mattress to share in the loft. When Dorothy handed me a folded sheet and blanket at the bottom of the stairs, I took the bundle and then stopped her.

"I'm sorry. I haven't changed, I guess. Still always ready to put the old foot in the mouth."

"You're sorry for showing up unannounced? Or you're sorry for insulting me and my husband in our own home?" She raised an eyebrow. "Or you're sorry for the other thing?"

I opened my mouth but just stood there, gaping like an idiot.

She sighed and shook her head. "It's late." Then she spun around and retreated to her bedroom.

West and I climbed into bed, and she promptly rolled over, taking the blanket with her. Dorothy turned out the light downstairs, and I heard her bedroom door close. The couch creaked as Troy lay down on it. In an instant, the whole place went from lively to completely still and dark. I stared at the ceiling, illuminated by the faint moonlight that snuck through the windows.

"I'm getting a drink of water," I said quietly to West a little while later, but she didn't reply. I stood and stretched. The brief nap in the van had made my body stiff and achy. I crept across the boards and down the stairs, trying not to disturb the stillness of the cabin. I could just make out the living room furniture and what looked like a Troy-sized lump on the couch. The kitchen sink was at the far end of the front room, and I moved slowly so as not to run into anything. I made it to the sink and started fumbling around in cabinets for glasses, when I heard a board creak. I spun around to see a tall figure directly behind me.

"Glinda?" Troy whispered too loudly.

"Yes," I hissed back. "What are you doing up? I was just getting a glass of water."

He passed in front of me, opened a cabinet, and pulled out a cup. Placing it in my hands, he took a step back and cleared his throat.

"You know where everything is because you've been here before."

"Yes." His voice was tired, and it sent a shiver down my spine. I could sense him in front of me, his smell, sweet and piney.

You idiot, Glinda. This isn't some fairy tale where two eccentric people fall into each other and become soulmates. Soulmates? Where had that come from? He was a liar. A fake.

Jesus, why did this freaking hurt so much? More than it should. I wasn't even that attracted to him. He was just some loser with a van who'd agreed to drive me here.

"Listen, I want to talk to you about that—" he started.

"No need," I cut him off. We stood there for a moment in silence.

"Your sister said some pretty mean shit to you," he finally whispered.

"Yeah, well, I said some pretty mean shit to her too." I put the glass under the faucet and filled it, then leaned back against the counter and took a sip.

"Right, but, uh, I mean, I didn't want to say anything because it seemed like it was best to stay out of it."

"Your instincts were correct," I spat. "And thanks for throwing me under the bus. Really appreciate it."

"Are you talking about the dunking booth?"

"Yes, genius. I am."

"I didn't know it would bother you that much. I just didn't think you were being fair, and I wanted you to stop being a jerk, because I know you're better than that."

"First of all, I get to decide if I want to be a jerk or stop being a jerk. Not you." I set the glass down hard. Too hard. "Second, don't patronize me like that. You don't know shit about me, okay?"

"I'm sorry!" He shrank back. I heard him drum his long, slim fingers against the counter. Then he cleared his throat.

I picked the glass back up and took a long drink, hoping he'd be the first to speak.

"What's so embarrassing about working at the dunking booth until you find a better job?" he said, softer than before. "We've had fun."

"Look, Troy, I know you're freaking in love with that shithole, but I'm sorry—it's lame and pathetic." My heart was cracking in half, even as the words came rushing out of my mouth.

I couldn't see his expression, but I could feel the cold radiating off him.

"Troy?"

He didn't respond. For a minute I wondered if he'd snuck back to the couch without me realizing it.

"Troy? I didn't mean—"

"No, it's fine." His voice was distant now, aloof. "You're not hurting my feelings. It is lame."

"No, no, it's important to you. I know how much you loved that job."

"Yeah, well, it's gone now. And anyway, it was just a place to work until something better came along. Right?" Without another word he brushed past me and returned to the couch. I heard the groan of the legs as he plopped down on it and curled up under an afghan.

I was so tired. My brain. My body. Everything. And I was still thirsty. I downed the rest of the water and then refilled the glass.

To hell with it. I stumbled to the fridge. A soft, comforting yellow light poured out as I peered in. There was still a third of the pie in the pan, loosely covered in cling wrap, sitting on the middle rack. I scooped it up, grabbed my glass of water, and then marched back to the stairs, banging my shin against a side table in the process.

"Dammit!" I tried not to yell.

"What are you doing?" Troy whispered loudly from across the room.

"Getting a piece of pie," I hissed back, and then clambered up the rickety steps to eat my feelings and replay every stupid, regretful thing I'd said since we'd arrived.

◆ 16 ◆

SORE AND STUPID

THE NEXT MORNING WE all slept in. I didn't mean to, but when I opened my eyes, it was almost noon. West had kicked me in her sleep, and I had apparently rolled off the mattress and curled up in some kind of canvas tarp that smelled like fish. When I finally came stumbling down the stairs, my face sticky with pie and my back un-crinkling from the night, West and Dorothy were both up and dressed and sitting at the table, drinking coffee.

West looked up at me and snorted while Dorothy stared on in concern. "Are you okay?"

"Uh-huh." I went to the coffeepot and poured myself a mug.

"But you don't—" Dorothy started. I pulled back a chair, turned it around, and straddled it. "You look like you didn't sleep well."

"Yeah, well, West still kicks in her sleep." I raised the mug to my lips, and West wrinkled her nose. The blueish daylight, filtering through the plaid curtains of the cabin, had thrown a bucket of cold water on our argument. In the daylight, everything was more defined, less fiery, and much, much more awkward.

"You smell awful!" West scooted her chair away. "Like garbage."

"You stole the blanket, Your Majesty." I took another sip. "I had to use that canvas tarp up there."

"Oh!" Dorothy covered her mouth with her hand, and I couldn't tell if she was laughing or trying not to throw up.

"That's what they use to clean the fish on that they catch out on the lake."

"Of course it is." I looked around. "How far are we from the lake?"

"Oh, less than a quarter of a mile."

"Oh, okay." The awkwardness only intensified. I preferred the screaming from the night before. What was happening?

"Maybe we could go down there later. It's beautiful," Dorothy said with a little smile.

"Why didn't y'all wake me?" I asked.

"We've only been up for a little bit. James and Troy went to get the van." Dorothy was talking like everything was normal, but I noticed her face was puffy, and I knew she'd been crying, probably after we all went to bed.

"Hey, um, Dory, could I possibly borrow your makeup?" West leaned forward on her arms.

"Dorothy, we need to talk about Mom," I interjected.

Dorothy patted West's hand. "Sure thing, just go in my bathroom and you'll see it there on the counter."

"Dorothy!" I shouted.

They both looked up at me in surprise. I saw a flash in Dorothy's eyes before she blinked and her placid expression returned.

"I will tell you when I'm ready to talk." Her tone was firm. I hated how small and stupid her voice made me feel, like I was being scolded by an elderly relative.

I threw my hands up and left the cabin to go see what was keeping Troy and James. The forest was quiet, and I liked it. I settled down in a rusted metal lawn chair on the little porch and put my bare feet up on the railing.

I could see the charm of the place, although living here was still crazy. I closed my eyes and took in a deep breath of the fresh air.

"I see you're making yourself at home."

I started and dropped my feet down. Dorothy was standing in the doorway, watching me, her expression neither pleased nor angry, just kind of hard to read.

"Sorry, I needed some air."

"It's cool." She came and leaned against the railing, facing me. She pursed her lips and looked at me hard for a second. There was something, right on the tip of her tongue, but no sooner had I realized it than she swallowed it and smiled at me, this calm and collected bullshit smile.

"What?"

"Nothing."

"Dorothy," I said, leaning forward. "Please tell me, are you really okay? You're so isolated out here."

Dorothy let out a light little laugh and swatted away my concern. "I promise, I'm good." She paused again and wrinkled her nose. "I do want to apologize."

"For what?"

"For my behavior last night. I was not acting like a good person or a good hostess."

"Geez, Dor, I don't expect you to act like a good hostess! And honestly, I couldn't care less right now if you're a good person. I just want you to act like my sister, the one I know. Dorothy, be real with me. I'd rather you yell at me than continue with this creepy survivalist Stepford wife thing you have going on."

She shot me a side glance, and underneath the edge of her eye I could see the flicker of the anger that she was doing such a good job suppressing. Then it was gone. Fake Dorothy was back.

"Ah, here they are!" she said happily as the van sputtered its way around the curve in the dirt road and pulled up with a low groan in front of the house.

"Fixed her up!" James called, jumping down and wiping his hands on a red rag.

"I see that!" Dorothy gave him a kiss on the cheek as he passed into the house.

Troy was slower, collecting the bags out of the van that we'd left the night before. I stood up, cracked my back, and then ventured out in the yard to help him. We shared an awkward greeting, and I pulled my backpack onto my shoulder and took my purse from his hand.

"Thanks."

"Yeah, no prob."

"I, um—you had coffee yet?"

"Nah. I had a MaXout."

"Your heart is going to explode one of these days."

"Nooo!" West's scream cut through the quiet morning. Troy and I exchanged a quick glance and raced into the house. West was standing in the living room, looking down at her phone in complete shock and disbelief.

"What's wrong?" I cried, out of breath. Immediately I could picture my mother's face, lifeless. I could see her lying in a coffin, white and still.

"He cut our service!" She looked up at me and held out her phone so I could see.

"What?" I let the relief surge through me like an elixir.

"I still didn't have service, so I asked Dorothy if they get service out here, and she said they do, and then I checked everyone's phones, and it's just yours and mine. Arlon turned our service off!"

"Holy shit, West, I thought someone had died!" I grabbed my phone off the end table and checked it. Beneath the multitude of cracks was a *no service* signal. "I am literally going to kill you."

James cleared his throat.

"What do we do?" West was gasping, and I was afraid she was about to hyperventilate. I looked over at Dorothy and gestured toward our overly dramatic sister. "She's all yours."

Dorothy pursed her lips and then put her arm around West. "Hey, it's okay. We'll call Mom. We'll figure it out."

"Yes!" I exclaimed. "Call Mom! Dorothy, call Mom—she'll pick up for you."

"I will . . . I'm just not ready." She dropped her eyes to the floor.

"Not ready?" I looked at her in disbelief. When had she become so cowardly? "Then Dorothy, may I borrow your phone to call Mom?"

Dorothy shook her head. "Later."

Later. Why take care of something when you could push it off to deal with later? My adrenaline was up again. This whole thing was dragging out like some kind of excruciating melodrama while my Mom was at home with a fucking murderer.

"I made oatmeal," Dorothy said, patting West's back. "You'll feel better after we eat."

"Dorothy, I really need to talk to you." My gaze flitted to James and then back to my sister.

"Doesn't it smell delicious? You like cinnamon in your oatmeal, right?"

West nodded weakly, still looking longingly at her phone. Dorothy took her own phone out of her pocket and laid it on the hearth. "Come on, Westy, put it down with mine. We're going to be technology free for a moment, and that's okay!" She smiled. West reluctantly set her phone down next to Dorothy's and nodded.

"Dorothy."

She didn't respond.

"Dorothy, please, I need to tell you everything, but I thought maybe we could go in another room and—"

"You want some diced apples in yours, West?" Dorothy called out over me. I groaned in frustration.

James pulled out bowls and Dorothy stirred the pot of oatmeal on the stove. James leaned over and gave her arm a slight squeeze; she turned to him and they kissed. I winced.

"They're so cute," West whispered wistfully.

"Yeah, sure."

"I mean, this place and the two of them. Gah, it's so wonderful here."

"Is it?" I muttered back. "I mean, it doesn't seem just a little *Invasion of the Body Snatchers* to you?"

"What?"

"Nothing."

"Come on, y'all!" Dorothy called.

I stood there and watched as everyone came and sat at the table. Troy walked right past me without a word, and I shivered. He pulled out a chair and its legs screeched along the wooden floor. The horrible sound reverberated in my head, making it hard to think.

Spoons clinked against the ceramic bowls as the strange company ate in silence, which might have been mistaken for companionable by somebody who'd missed last night's shit show.

After a few minutes West got up to get more. "This is great, Dory! I don't remember you cooking this much."

"You get lots of practice when there's no fast food on the corner." Dorothy looked over at me. "Are you going to sit and eat, Glinda?"

"I don't really have an appetite."

"I'm sorry to hear that." She looked down and traced her spoon through the gray, sticky residue in the empty bowl. Everything about this was just prolonging the whole reason I was here.

"We have to talk, Dorothy," I said firmly.

"Not now." She twirled the spoon wistfully.

"Dorothy, I am asking you to please come talk to me."

"We are talking." Dorothy took a sip of milk. "We've been talking since you got here."

"You know what I mean."

"And I told you, it's not the time."

The awkward silence continued. I closed my eyes and took two long, deep breaths before pounding a fist on the table. The bowls clanked and the spoons rattled.

Everyone stopped what they were doing, and four pairs of eyes immediately shot to me.

"Goddammit, Dorothy! You are a lawyer. I need you. I don't have any money to hire someone else. I need you to come home with me and get Mom a conservatorship or power of attorney or whatever it is that legally allows us to make decisions for her while she's in the state she's in."

Dorothy kept her eyes on her bowl and set the spoon down. "You have no idea what the hell you're even talking about."

"For fuck's sake! She's taking ecstasy! They all are! Probably more than that!" I was practically shrieking, letting every last tool in my arsenal fall out onto the table. "And this one guy, Matthew Harrigan, he came to our house and fought with Arlon, and then fell over dead after drinking coffee that our mother made him—a point that Arlon seems keenly aware of. *So why haven't you gone to the police?* you might ask. Well, I'll tell you! It's because the fucking police are in on it! They're in the cult too!"

I gasped for air and fell back a step, unnerved by the anger seething out of me as I blurted it all out. When I opened my mouth to speak, Dorothy held up a palm and shook her head.

But I wasn't done. "You don't—"

"Stop, Glinda."

"I won't stop! I'm not going to stop until you listen to me!"

"Glinda." She spoke quietly, with a tone as grave as a judge's reading a death sentence. "You're back on pills, aren't you?"

I blinked at her hard, completely speechless. Son. Of. A. Bitch. All the rage and frustration I'd been feeling, all the ways I'd tried to convince her, and it was never enough. I would never be enough for her. And now this pent-up exasperation had no place to go.

I grabbed the one empty chair by the top and hurled it over on its side. Everyone winced at the clanging of the chair hitting the floor. I stood there, looking down at the chair and then back up to the faces of four people who genuinely looked frightened of me. I cleared my throat. "Well, I'm done."

"Glinda?" Dorothy said, for once with a genuine concern.

"I'm done pretending that everything's normal or whatever the hell it is you're doing. I'm going for a walk." I backed up from the table, toward the living room, and grabbed my flip-flops, which were sitting beside the fireplace. I glanced back to see all of them looking down at their bowls or at each other.

I took Dorothy's phone off the hearth and shoved it in my back pocket. No one noticed.

"So, by all means, y'all stay here and chat about how good Dorothy's gotten at making oatmeal. Forget about the group of strangers that's moving into our childhood home and our mother, who is being manipulated into marrying a con artist and signing over everything she owns to him." I shook my head. "And no, Dorothy, I am not on pills again—thanks for asking." I shot my twin sister a sarcastic smile. "Strange as it sounds, since you've been gone, I haven't felt the need to self-medicate."

I didn't stick around to see if my words caused any reaction. But I did stop at the sight of my hoodie, freshly washed and laid on the porch railing to dry. She'd washed it; she remembered how much it meant to me.

I looked back at the door. Hesitated. But no. She might have shown me a bit of kindness; it didn't mean she was ready to listen. I tied the hoodie around my waist and skipped down the steps before my sister noticed I'd taken her phone.

★ ★ ★

"Mom?" I said as soon as the other line engaged. I had followed a little path through the trees and found the lake; a small, white fiberglass rowboat was tethered to a rickety dock. Beside the dock there was a short wooden pole with a rusted old fuse box about halfway up and a security light at the top.

"No, this is Sister Arianne."

"Why do you have my mom's phone?"

"Sister Julie is not to be disturbed."

"I need to talk to her—it's important." I was losing patience.

"I'm sorry. Father Arlon and Sister Julie are in seclusion."

"Seclusion? I thought all you weirdos were moving in today."

"We are—we have." Arianne paused. She was breathing hard into the phone now and lowered her voice to a whisper. "Sister Beverly has passed on from this dimension. We just found out."

"Beverly? Beverly McCoy?" My pulse quickened. "At my house?" Dread was bubbling up from the pit of my stomach, and I was pacing the dock like a crazy person.

"No, she died at home, in her sleep. That's all I know." Then she hung up.

I looked down at Dorothy's phone. What the fuck? I remembered Beverly, so eager to welcome me at the pioneer meeting, her eyes sparkling as much as her gold necklace. That was just last night. This was real. Another person dead. Another tally mark next to Arlon's name. And I couldn't prove a damn thing.

I shoved Dorothy's phone into my pocket and sat on the edge of the dock. I set my shoes beside me and took a deep breath. My toes just skimmed the top of the water. Farther out, the midday sun caught the tops of tiny waves, and birds landed on the water, then took off again. I leaned back on my hands and closed my eyes. The sun burned bright on my face and made my vision go orangey-red beneath my lids.

Beverly was old. She'd died at home. I was losing it. I was making up conspiracy theories before I had all the facts. Occam's razor and all that shit—more than likely, Matthew Harrigan had died of a heart attack, Beverly McCoy had died in her sleep of old age, and James had had a panic attack. I slid down all the way so I was lying on the dock. It was hot. Really hot.

I had to get home. I had to find out what was happening.

Dorothy was never going to talk to me—

"You're going to burn."

I sat up with a start. Dorothy was wearing a white tank top with a plaid button-down tied around her waist, and a pair of worn jeans tucked into a pair of lace-up boots. She'd pulled her hair back and had tied a pink bandana around her mousy brown locks.

"I want to take you on a hike." She threw a pair of her brown boots at me.

"A hike? Why the hell would I do that?" I rubbed my face.

"So we can talk."

"You didn't want to talk."

"I said it wasn't time. It's time now."

She always did this, manipulating things so she could somehow control them. I was sure she would deny it. Maybe she didn't even realize she was doing it.

"You're not pissed at me for throwing a chair?"

"No. I'm not," she said simply. "You wanted to talk. Let's talk."

"You wear a half size smaller than me," I said, picking up a boot and examining it with suspicion.

"Yeah, well, that sucks for you I guess."

"Also, why do you have more than one pair of hiking boots?"

"That pair gives me blisters." She gestured toward the shoes in my hands.

"Wonderful." I kicked off my flip-flops and shoved the boots onto my feet, tying the laces haphazardly. She didn't say anything, just shifted a small backpack on her shoulder. Then she turned and starting walking away from me.

"So, you spend one year out in the wilderness, and all of a sudden you're like Off-the-Grid Barbie or something." I caught up with her as she marched through the trees, away from the lake.

"Are you done?" She held a large branch out of the way, for me to pass under. "Maybe we should go ahead and get the rest out of your system before we continue."

Inwardly, I relaxed, accepting her olive branch, even if it was an olive branch of passive aggression.

"I'm done."

She raised an eyebrow.

"Okay, fine. *Better Homes and Gardens* Bear Grylls. The low-budget Pioneer Woman." I sighed and lowered my voice. "Basic white girl Daniel Boone."

She shook her head. "Unbelievable."

We walked on, Dorothy ahead with some kind of destination in mind, and me trailing, wondering if this was all a ruse to push me off a cliff.

The pine trees grew taller and closer together the farther we walked. Peeking above their canopies was a cerulean sky that dared you to reach out and touch it. I would try, forgetting myself, and then a branch would snap underfoot, and I'd look up to see Dorothy in front of me, her gait sure and quick, and I would return to my thoughts and start wondering where this was all leading.

She'd said we were going to talk. This was it then, my chance to finally make things right. I had to craft the perfect sentences, say the exact right words, and then hope and pray she'd accept them. Anxieties swirled in my brain. Maybe her silence was a tactic. Maybe she wanted to freak me out so she'd have the upper hand.

Get out of your head. I could almost hear Troy's voice, like a subliminal warning that whispered through the trees.

Dorothy held up a hand and we stopped in front of a small clearing where the branches hung so close together that, standing in the center, you couldn't see the sky. She went to a large trunk and examined a small black camera that was screwed into the bark.

"What's that?"

"Our first stop." She opened a little door on the side of the device and pulled out a memory card. Then she set her backpack on the ground and retrieved a little metal case from inside. She swapped out the cards, clicked the case closed, and dropped it back in the pack.

"So, all this time I thought you had snacks in your bag, and it was camera equipment for your Bigfoot surveillance?"

Dorothy rolled her eyes at me, reached into the pack again, and tossed me a Ziploc of almonds.

"Thank you." I crammed a few almonds in my mouth. "Okay, but seriously, I thought we were hiking to talk, not to check your crazy boyfriend's—excuse me, *husband's*—crazy husband's paranormal traps." The word *husband* felt heavy and awkward in my mouth. I wanted to spit it out.

"We're hiking to change out memory cards, but yes, also to talk." She repositioned her backpack and started walking again.

"Okay, so let's talk," I called out, trying to catch up with her. "Let's talk about the whole Bigfoot thing. You *know* Bigfoot is bullshit, right?"

"Bigfoot is not bullshit." She stopped in her tracks and looked at me hard. I held up my hands.

"Okay, sorry, geez."

"Seriously, Glinda. Bigfoot is real."

"Whatever you say." Good lord, she'd lost it in the woods. She looked up at the trees and bit her lip. Then she turned back, lips pursed.

"Come with me." She took off, walking quickly away from the clearing. I nearly ran into her when she stopped suddenly. We'd reached a break in the trees; before us was a steep drop-off and the massive lake, with all its cuts and coves that spread out over the hills like a centipede. Dorothy sat down on a fallen log, set her backpack beside her, and pulled a water bottle out of her bag, tossing one to me first. I took a long drink and then sat crisscross in front of her in the dirt.

"Why are you acting so weird?"

"I just wanted to get away from the camera. It picks up sound and I don't want this conversation recorded."

Oh shit, this *was* the part where she shoved me off a cliff, and I had stupidly positioned myself between her and the drop-off.

Instead, she took another drink of water and then held the bottle between her knees.

"Okay, so Bigfoot . . . I, personally, do not believe that there is an eight-foot ape-man that lives in these woods. But James does. And I believe in James. So, I help him. I don't discount the search. Because you know what, Glinda? I might be going through this footage one random day and spot the big guy himself. And if I do, great. And if I don't, well, at least my husband knows that I believe in him."

"That's sweet or whatever, but the bottom line is, you don't believe in Bigfoot."

"I said I don't believe in an eight-foot ape-man. That doesn't mean I don't believe in Bigfoot."

"Huh?"

"I think everybody has their own Bigfoot that they're searching for, wanting desperately to believe in. Bigfoot is the thing that you're afraid of actually seeing but hoping urgently to find. So, in that respect, yes, I believe in James's Bigfoot, and he believes in mine."

I shook my head. "That's insane."

"Yeah, well . . . maybe so." She straightened up. "So, uh, you still addicted to Adderall?"

I bit my tongue and pushed down the first thing I wanted to say to her. I found my smile. "No, Dorothy. I haven't touched the stuff since that night."

She studied me, her brow scrunched as she contemplated. "Really?"

"Yeah."

"I'm glad." She took a long, slow, deep breath. "I'm sorry about what I said back there in the cabin. West filled me in on Matthew Harrigan, poor kid. As for the drugs, you're the only one who's seen this evidence, and you're not exactly the most reliable witness."

I looked up at the sky, crinkled my nose, and fought back the urge to respond.

Dorothy glanced out at the valley like she was searching for something. When she turned back, she seemed resigned. "So, I need you to know that I forgive you."

"For what exactly are you forgiving me?"

"Everything."

"Um, okay. Great. Good."

"Good."

"So, we're good?"

"I mean, understandably, James and I still need to keep our distance from you. But, if you came here for absolution, I want you to know you can go live your life and not carry this with you."

"Excuse me?"

"It can't be the same as it was between us, Glinda. But we can move on now."

"Move on?"

"This has been good." She paused. "Yeah, this was good." As though all our business together was now neatly boxed up and tied with a bow. As though she was satisfied that this had been a productive meeting, and she was ready to turn the page on it, on me.

I looked out over the trees and sighed. I had to make her listen.

I pressed my lips together and then swooped forward and snatched her backpack up. She looked up at me in confusion as I jumped up and walked toward the edge.

"First of all, I didn't come out here for absolution. I came out here because our mom is marrying a freaking cult leader." I held the backpack over the drop-off, trying not to look down.

Dorothy sighed and shook her head. "Seriously?"

"Yes. Now you're going to listen, or all your precious Bigfoot footage goes off the cliff."

Dorothy rolled her eyes. She didn't look nearly as anxious as I'd hoped this would make her.

"Do you remember the last time you tried this?" She gave me the most impatient, irritated, sarcastic smile. "We were twelve and you threatened to throw my stuffed bunny in the creek if I didn't go camping in the backyard with you and Dad."

I hesitated at the implication that I was acting like a child.

"Fine." I pulled the bag to my chest. "So like a week or so ago, this guy, Matthew Harrigan, called the house, and I picked up. He was looking for Arlon, and he was pissed. Really pissed. He was a former member, and he warned me that Arlon was dangerous. The next time I heard about Matthew Harrigan, he was dead on our living room floor."

Dorothy didn't respond, but she actually seemed to be listening.

"And then the police. You think I'm being crazy that they're in on it—"

"Paranoid," Dorothy corrected me.

"Fine—whatever." I continued on. "But these two cops showed up and gave me their card. After they left, Arlon heavily implied that Mom put something in Matthew's coffee. So, last night—Jesus, was that just last night?—I went to the cult meeting with Mom, and Arlon was legit passing out ecstasy tablets to everyone like some kind of twisted communion."

"How do you know what ecstasy tablets look like?" Dorothy raised an eyebrow.

"I used to—it doesn't matter. Anyway, I confronted Arlon and he threatened me."

"Okay?" Dorothy looked skeptical. I bit my lip and tried to fight the rising panic at the recollection of Arlon grabbing me, holding me by the wrists. Wait—I did have something that might convince her.

I took three long strides forward, dropped her backpack at her feet, and crouched down in front of her. I held up my wrists in front of her face.

"Oh my God!" She let out an involuntary gasp. Around the underside of each wrist were dark bruises that had come up in the night, blue and purple shadows of fingers, large, like a man's.

"I called the cops, the ones who gave me the card. Dorothy, the one who answered, he was already *there*. At the meeting. He's in the cult." I paused to let her respond, but she was just watching me now, wide-eyed. "And then there's this." I took my phone from my pocket and held up the photo of Arlon, with his sinister smile. "He deleted all my photos and left me this. I know it's not evidence per se, but geez, Dorothy, look at his face."

Dorothy stared at the photo. I could see the wheels in brain turning as she processed it. "I want to believe you," she finally said, her voice thin and low.

My heart sank.

She pursed her lips and looked straight ahead, like she was working something out in her head. Finally she spoke without looking at me.

"I'll be honest—I don't love it, but legally, Mom is a grown woman, and there's very little one could actually do to change what's happening down there."

"What are you saying?" My pulse quickened.

"Look, Glinda, you have to understand how hard this is. I get things are bad, but your perspective is skewed. I honestly don't know what to believe."

"Me! You believe *me*!"

"I talked to Mom," she said.

"What?"

"I called her this morning before you got up."

"What?" I repeated.

"I was concerned, so I called her, and she told me a slightly different story. She's worried about you, Glin. You're paranoid and you act recklessly without thinking."

"What are you saying?"

"I'm saying that, according to Mom, you're just upset she's getting remarried and because of what happened before, the thing at Christmas, she is honestly a little afraid of you." Dorothy looked down, and I saw a tear fall to her knee. "I'm not afraid *of* you, but I am afraid *for* you."

The truth hit me hard and fast. She was too far gone in her distrust of me to ever accept my word over our mother's. It felt like a tidal wave was bearing down on us, and I was standing there, arms outstretched, in some futile attempt to stop it from crashing against the shore.

"You know I didn't try to kill James," I said in one last desperate attempt to regain her trust.

"Nope, we don't need to talk about this." She frowned. "I just told you I forgive you for everything."

"I really, I really didn't make those chocolates and I really, really didn't poison them."

Dorothy was quiet for a long time. She still wouldn't make eye contact with me, so she reached down and started tracing circles in the dirt with a long stick. "I've run that evening over and over in my head, and each time I'm looking for an out for you, and I just can't see one."

"What if it was just a panic attack?"

Her eyes narrowed. "It wasn't a panic attack."

Okay, then there was one other possibility. "Dorothy, I can't prove it, but Arlon knew about my Adderall prob—"

"No! *Stop!*" She seemed startled by how she'd raised her voice.

"Dorothy, I swear, I didn't try to hurt him!" I cried frantically.

"You hated him," she gasped out as large tears started rolling down her cheeks.

"I didn't! I don't!"

"You tried to break us up!"

"I *did* do that." I came and sat beside her on the log and tried to take her hand, but she pulled away.

"How could you do that, Glinda?!"

"I don't know, okay? I was scared I was losing you!"

"Yeah, well"—Dorothy gestured around her—"You made sure you did."

"I know. I made everything a thousand times worse." I looked up at the sky, searching for some kind of answer. "I swear on my life—I swear on Dad's grave—I did not try to kill James."

At the invocation of my father's grave, Dorothy looked at me in surprise—no, disbelief.

"Please, Dorothy, say something."

"I can't . . . I can't even look at you right now." She stood quickly and grabbed her backpack. "I need some space to think." She started to walk off. Shit. Her phone.

"Wait! Dorothy!"

"What?" She spun around, tears streaming down her cheeks.

"I forgot." I reached into my pocket and pulled out her phone. "I took your phone to call Mom."

She marched back and ripped the phone out of my hand. She jammed it in her pocket and looked at me, all pretense gone. She was completely enraged now. Her face had drained white, and the tip of her nose was bright red. She opened her mouth to say something and then closed it.

"I'm sorry. I didn't know what else to do," I choked out.

"You haven't changed at all." She spoke slowly, trying very hard to control the modulation of her voice.

"I haven't changed?" *Shut up, Glinda. Just stop! Don't.* "What about you? You still think you're so much better than me, but you're still just a pathetic, controlling manipulator who mistakes being in a relationship for actually having a personality!"

I regretted every word the moment it left my lips.

Dorothy just stared at me until finally she narrowed her eyes and spoke, quietly and succinctly. "Fuck you, Glinda."

Then she turned and walked away again.

"Dorothy, wait!"

She disappeared in the trees.

"I don't know how to get back to the cabin!"

But she was already gone.

RECKLESS AND REGRETFUL

WHEN I WAS TWELVE, my dad decided to take Dorothy and me camping in the forest behind our house. I initially refused to participate, on account of it being outdoors, but was later lured out by the promise of s'mores. It wasn't super authentic—I mean, hell, we just ran inside to use the bathroom. But there was a tent and sleeping bags, and he made us a little fire.

"I'm teaching you to survive," he told me.

Survive. Ha.

Dorothy had evaporated into the foliage, and I had no idea where I was. The sun was getting lower now, and I'd been walking the trail back in the direction I thought the cabin was for a couple of hours. It was strange how the same forest, which had been so mesmerizingly beautiful just hours earlier, had taken on an unnerving, almost sinister nature with the casting of shadows.

It figured that, after everything, I'd end up dying alone in a forest, eaten by a freaking bear or something. Were there bears in Oklahoma?

West's predictions had come true. I'd made things worse . . . again. But my goal was pure, selfless, no matter what anybody else believed. Yes, vindication or even absolution would be a wonderful side effect of this trip, but my main objective was, and remained, saving my mother. And Dorothy wasn't going to be a part of it. I'd had her ear for a moment, I'd had my chance, and I'd blown it. I mean, really and truly blown it into smithereens.

She *had* to know I didn't mean it, right? All that shit about her being a manipulator and pathetic. I was upset. I said awful shit when I was upset.

"I didn't mean it!" I screamed into the forest. "Fuck! FUCK!" I screamed again and again until I was out of breath and gasping, holding myself up against a tree. I took several deep breaths and continued on.

I'd turned a corner when I heard a branch snap. The sound ripped through the quiet and echoed around me, so I had no idea from which direction it had come. I spun around and around, scanning the trees and the fallen logs, searching for the source of the noise. Nothing.

I walked faster now, my heart thumping against my ribs. The hairs on my neck and arms grew stiff, and an icy chill shot down my sternum and into my gut.

I sensed a presence. I didn't see anything, but I felt it. A threatening force watching me, stalking me, holding back and waiting for a moment of vulnerability.

Screw it. I ran. I picked up my feet and tore down the path. And somewhere nearby, I swear I heard footfalls and snapping twigs on the forest floor. The sound echoed off the trees, making it impossible to tell which direction they were coming from. I'd never really been chased before. Once, as a teenager, I'd run into the house after a neighbor's dog had approached me and growled in the front yard. But running with that primal fear taking over, turning you from a rationally thinking person into fleeing prey . . . yeah, this was a first.

I wasn't thinking now. I was only running, only surviving.

I leapt over a dead log in the path, turned a corner, and smacked right into Troy. We both fell backward to the ground, sprawled out and stunned.

"Shit, Troy!" I cried, sitting up and checking my limbs for injury. My palms were scraped, but otherwise I was unscathed. The sense of dread that had been stalking me dissipated as soon as I saw his face.

"Are you okay?" He offered a hand and I ignored it. I picked myself up off the ground, brushing dirt and dead leaves off my pants. The forest was docile again. The shadows were fading into the twilight, and a gentle breeze was gliding through the trees.

"Dorothy completely abandoned me in the woods."

"Why?"

"Oh, I don't know. Possibly because I wouldn't stop talking about James's near-death experience. Possibly because I invoked our dead father's grave to win an argument." I shrugged and looked over his shoulder the way he'd come. "At least tell me we're close to the cabin because I seriously thought I was going to die out here."

"Yeah, it's less than a half mile. I came out to find you after Dorothy got back."

"She made it back to the cabin?"

"Oh yeah, like two hours ago."

"Well, that's good, I guess." I rubbed my eyes. "But wait, she didn't think, *'Oh, maybe I should make sure Glinda isn't wandering in circles or being chased by Bigfoot or something'*?"

"She said she needed a nap and sent me to check on you." He looked at me critically. "Wait. Bigfoot? Glinda, you weren't running from Bigfoot, were you?" He had an insatiable grin smeared across his face now.

"Of course not. Bigfoot is bullshit." I didn't sound convincing, even to my own ears.

He let out a hearty laugh. "Seriously?"

"Shut up. It's spooky out here. Your eyes play tricks on you." And with that, I pushed past him and marched forward along the path. At least now Bigfoot would eat Troy before he got me.

He caught up, and even though I didn't turn around to look at his face, I knew he was still smiling.

"Troy, are we close to the lake?"

"Yep. The dock is actually just through the trees there."

"Perfect. I need some space to think. Okay?"

"But it's getting dark."

"Yeah, but I know how to get back to the cabin from the lake. I'll be fine."

"Dorothy wanted me to bring you back."

"You can tell Dorothy if she's so concerned with my well-being, then maybe she shouldn't have abandoned me in the middle of the wilderness." I came out of the tree line onto the shores of the lake. The water was lapping at the rocks with tiny waves while the whole of the lake was reflecting the orange sky like shards of a giant mirror dropped into the dark trees.

Troy stood beside me. He was gazing at the boat with a contemplative expression, but then he shook it away and turned to me. "You really should come back to the house. I'll take you out on the water tomorrow if you want."

"Please go. I just need some time to think."

"Fine. But if you're not back soon, Dorothy is going to kill me, and then she'll probably kill you too, assuming, you know, Bigfoot hasn't killed you first." He stuck his hands in his pockets and turned back to the path, stopping once to look back nervously.

The first thing I did was to untie and then kick my way out of those damn boots. When I pulled my feet out, the pinky toe on each foot was bleeding around the nail.

I took a deep breath and stepped out onto the dock. A burst of wind caught my hair up and blew it away from my face. It was invigorating. I walked over to the end of the dock and peered down into the boat, bobbing up and down in the water.

Before I knew what I was doing, I had grabbed the pole at the end of the dock and lowered myself down into the boat. It rocked violently and I knelt down, immediately regretting my decision. Eventually the rocking subsided, and I dared to sit up a little. The water was so close, I could just reach down and dip my fingers in it.

The rope was still wrapped securely around the pole, and the oars were tucked neatly along the bottom of the boat. This was peaceful. I pulled myself up onto one of the two benches and leaned my head back to look at the enormous sky. I could understand why Dorothy would like it here. Despite my best efforts, I was falling in love with it by the minute.

And now, finally, I could clear my head. Just sit here, floating at the dock, watching the sky grow dark.

"Glinda!"

Dammit.

Troy was standing along the shore about twenty feet off.

"I thought you left!"

"I did but I don't trust you!"

Same to you, buddy. "I'm just sitting in the boat. I'm not stupid enough to try and sail it!"

"It's a rowboat!"

"Yeah, so?"

"So, it doesn't sail!"

"Whatever, I'm just sitting here!"

"I don't think that's a good idea!" He was walking toward the dock now.

"I *told* you, I need some space to think!"

"Yes, but you also know nothing about boats or lakes!"

"I need to be alone!" I yelled at him, but he didn't stop. He walked to the end of the dock and then leapt forward onto the boat, one foot landing safely on the bow and the other dangling precariously over the water. He tottered for a moment before grabbing the tiller and steadying himself.

"Troy! What the hell?"

"Sorry. You were going to get yourself stranded out in the middle of the lake and die or something," he managed to say as he took a seat across from me and caught his breath.

I glared at him. "It's a rowboat, not a rocket ship. I think I can handle it."

"Prove it."

"Prove it?"

"Yeah." He stood and grabbed the edge of the dock with one hand, then used the other to untie the rope from the mooring. Then he used both hands to push off and sent the bow lurching forward, away from the shore.

"Troy, *what* are you doing?"

"Prove it." He smiled and gestured to the oars.

"Are you crazy?" I cried. "I was just sitting in it. You know, thinking and being alone."

"Yes, but this is better than thinking." He reached down to retrieve the oars, almost hitting me upside the head with one in the process. He set them into the metal hooks along the side and gestured to me to row.

"I am not rowing, Troy."

He smiled again and crossed his arms. "Guess we'll just float on forever, then."

I sighed and looked back over my shoulder at the western sky. The sun had gone below the horizon now, and the sky was a pale purple.

Finally, he grabbed the oars himself. "Glin," he said, beginning to row, "I need to talk to you."

"See! I knew it!" I grumbled.

"If you'll just let me explain some things to you, then I promise I'll row us back and leave you alone to drift out and get stranded on one of the little islands full of water moccasins." We were moving along at a steady clip toward the middle of the lake.

"Are you seriously going to hold me hostage until I listen to you?"

His smile faded. "I mean, when you say it like that . . ."

The water was still, and the shore didn't look too far away. I'd probably be able to swim to the dock. But even if I couldn't, at least I wouldn't be stuck for one more minute with this lying liar.

"You're thinking about jumping out of the boat, aren't you?" He stopped rowing and pulled the oars up out of the water. The boat rocked gently, and the lake and forest around it were silent. Troy watched me with consternation as I folded my arms in my lap and sighed.

"Fine. Let's talk, Troy."

"Great!" He sat up straighter and smiled.

"You and I were friends. You lied to me—about something really big. Your cousin is married to my sister!"

"I didn't know my cousin was married to your sister until we got here, same as you."

"Yeah, but you knew they were together."

He shrugged. "I realized it that night you stayed over. Do you remember? You told me about your sister and James and the cabin. That's the first time I put it all together. I wasn't sure, but after you left, I looked back through Facebook and confirmed that your Dorothy and James were the same as my James and his girlfriend, Dorothy, who, again, I had not met!"

"Why the hell would you not tell me immediately?"

"Hello, Glinda! I'm not sure if you realize how goddamn judgmental you can be. Your aversion to my cousin made me afraid that if you knew the truth, you'd be done with me too."

I shook my head. "That shouldn't matter! As soon as you realized it, you should have said something."

"Agreed!" he shouted, and seemed surprised by his realization. We both rocked in silence for a moment—then he rubbed his face in both his hands and looked up into my eyes, his own eyes pleading for my understanding. He took my hands in his, and although I thought about pulling away, I let them stay, feeling the warmth of his fingers against my skin.

He lowered his voice. "Look, when you asked me to drive you up here, I just did it. I didn't even stop to think about it because all I wanted was to be with you. Here, in Texas, at Maypole—wherever. I know I screwed up. I know you're pissed at me. I'm really sorry."

My pulse quickened. Damn. It was hard to remember why I was mad at him. "You lied," I breathed, more to myself.

Troy nodded. "Yes. I'm sorry."

Our voices were so low now that we had to come closer to hear one another.

"I've never lied to you, Troy . . . wait, yeah . . . okay, maybe I have, but nothing this big."

"We'll just leave that one alone, okay?" He smiled. That stupid, intoxicating smile that was making me fucking swoon. And now his face was just inches from mine, and I was losing my mind.

And when he leaned in closer, I didn't back away in anger or disgust. Instead, I closed my eyes and let him press his lips against mine. It was a short kiss, simple and soft. But it made my insides light up like a roman candle. He pulled away and looked at me longingly, his lips slightly apart, like he couldn't quite believe what had just happened. And that *innocence* was what did it. All my defenses, my excuses, my reasons were gone.

I leapt at him, knocking him back onto the bottom of the boat. His eyes were wide with surprise, and I could tell he was trying to ask me something, when I kissed him hard. His lips tasted so damn good. I wanted to devour him.

The boat rocked wildly, but I didn't care. His hands were in my hair, his tongue was wrapping around mine, and I was melting into him. I ran my hands along his chest, and he moved one hand down to the small of my back, where my T-shirt was riding up a little. The feeling of his fingers lit my skin on fire.

"Sit up!" I ordered, rising.

"What's wrong?" he panted, pushing up on his elbows.

"Sit. Up."

He rose to a sitting position, eyebrow raised. I grabbed the bottom of his shirt and swiftly pulled it up over his head. The hair on his chest was short and dark. The realization of what my actions meant seemed to dawn on him slowly as I pressed my hands against his chest and kissed him again.

"Oh," he whispered, his breathing jagged, and let his hands drift higher up my back now. I didn't break our kissing as I reached down and started unbuttoning his jeans. He rose up a little, slid out of them, and tossed them onto the side of the boat.

"You're going to get your pants wet," I said out of the corner of my mouth, not pulling away from his lips. He shrugged and grabbed me around the waist, pushing me gently onto the floor and then positioning himself a few inches above me. I could feel the stiffness through his boxers, pressing against my thigh. I looked up into his face and shuddered.

"What's wrong? Am I doing something wrong?" he asked anxiously.

"No," I whispered. "It's just . . . I just told myself I wasn't going to let this . . ." I trailed off as I raised my head up to kiss him again. He kissed my neck and my collarbone as I ran my fingers along his back. Dammit. I wanted him. No, worse than that—I needed him.

"Glinda, I need to know this is what you want."

"Yes, Jesus, Troy!" I sat up, crossed my arms, grabbed the hem of my shirt, and pulled it over my head. He sat back and looked at me in silence, his face unreadable.

"Sorry if it's not what you were hoping for."

"Glinda, sometimes you just need to shut up." He grabbed one of the sleeves of the hoodie around my waist, untied it, and placed it on top of his jeans. He pulled me up against him and we sank back down. The boat rocked with our movements. He gripped the side, white knuckled, and then lowered his head down and ran his lips down my sternum. My skin broke out in goose bumps, and I let out a soft moan. He stopped and then pushed up so there was about a foot of sweetened night air between us.

"What's wrong?" I gasped, shocked by how out of breath I'd become.

He smiled at me, almost reverently. "Nothing. I just want to look at you."

At that moment I heard a small splash. The place where our clothes had been piled on the side of the small vessel now sat empty.

"Shit! My hoodie!" I grabbed the side of the boat and looked over. Our clothes were floating away. I reached out but couldn't touch them.

"Glinda, it's okay. We can borrow more of their clothes."

I ignored him and leaned farther out. The hoodie was water-logged and bobbed once before sinking beneath the surface.

"Glinda, let me row to them, you're going to fall in!"

"Shit! Shit! This was a mistake!"

"A mistake?" Troy echoed.

I'd reached too far. The boat rocked hard and then I was fall-ing, but before I touched the water, I felt Troy's arms around my waist, pulling me back.

Unfortunately, our combined weight on the side of the poor little boat was too much and up it tipped, capsizing. I found myself plunging down into the icy black water.

I looked around wildly, trying to figure out where the sur-face was, but at night it was hard to tell. I steadied myself. To panic now was to drown. I straightened my body and rose slowly up. I kicked my legs hard and broke the surface, coughing. This was way worse than the stupid dunking booth.

Shit! Troy!

"Troy!" I called out, and tried to look around, but I was completely disoriented. The only points of reference were the moon above my head and the small point of light from the dock.

"Troy!" I called again, taking in a gulp of lake water. I sputtered and reached around me, hoping to feel his hand in the inky water.

"Glinda!" I heard him, but I couldn't see him. In front of me was the hulking underbelly of the boat, floating like a giant turtle in the black water. He must have been on the other side of it.

"Go to shore!" I called out.

"Are you okay?"

"Yes! Go to shore!" And without another word I started swimming toward the lamppost on the dock without looking back to see if he was following or not.

I had been on the swim team in high school. Okay, I'd been a backup on the swim team in high school, but still. Nothing cools your head like a splash of cold water.

By the time I reached the shore and climbed up onto the rocky embankment, I was ready to dig a very big hole and jump into it. I slipped on my flip-flops, which were still there on the dock and then sat on the edge, waiting for Troy to make it. I watched him lie on his back and frog swim to the bank.

"Are you okay?" I called out as he climbed out of the water, still in just his boxers. He came up to me, and I made sure to keep my eyes level with his face and not dare look any lower.

"I'm sorry about the boat," I mumbled, clutching my arms around myself and shivering. My hoodie was at the bottom of the lake by now.

"Yeah, it's all right. It's not the first time I've capsized it. It'll wash up to shore by morning. I'm just glad you're okay." Then he started to wrap his arms around me, but I ducked out of the way. "What's wrong?"

"Nothing. I just—I told you not to put our clothes on the side like that," I grumbled, trying to keep my growing frustration at bay.

"I'm sorry." He gave me a sheepish grin. "I was distracted."

I held my arms tighter and looked out at the blankness of the water. "Shit," I muttered.

"I'll go buy you another hoodie," he raised an eyebrow, "if you really think you need one in this heat, crazy person." At the mention of crazy, I narrowed my eyes and clenched my fists to my side. It was gone. It was really and truly gone. One stupid little mistake and poof!

"Shit!" I cried loudly this time, and in one swift movement, scooped up a stone and flung it into the lake. "Dammit!"

"Glin, I *really* am sorry. I'll take you to a store tomorrow, and you can pick out whichever sweatshirt you want—"

"It was my dad's." I turned sharply to face him, my wet hair whipping around and sticking to my cheek.

He shrank back, realization hitting him. "Glin, I didn't know—" He rubbed the back of his neck and kept his eyes on me, full of concern.

"Right. I know." I hated the hollow feeling ballooning up in my chest, pushing out room for anything else, anything good. "You didn't know because you don't actually know me, like I've said before."

A shadow fell over his face. "I know you're upset, but you know that's not true."

"It is, Troy!" I let out a small, sarcastic laugh. "And that, that out there . . . that was, that was—"

"What? A mistake?" The words fell like rocks at our feet.

"I'm sorry, okay? I can see how repeatedly making out with you might give you a certain idea about how I feel, but the truth is . . . the truth is I'm psychotic, all right?!"

"You're not psychotic." His tone was calm, and it pissed me off. "Glinda. I—I really like you. I really like you, and I'm just trying to understand what you want."

"Not this!" I threw my hands up and started to march away, but no, wait, we weren't finished, so I spun back around. "I know you have a crush on me, Troy. I mean, even before the dry humping in the boat, you were still pretty obvious. And yes, I took advantage of that to get you to drive me up here. But you haven't been very honest either, with your whole secret cousin thing."

"I've already apologized for that. I told you, I didn't realize it until we were already friends, and by then, it just seemed like a bad idea to bring it up."

"So, the best time to bring it up was the moment I laid eyes on the man who took my sister away almost two years ago?"

"He didn't take her away. She wanted space from you."

It grew considerably darker as thick, ominous clouds slid across the sky, covering the moon. I could barely see him now except for where the weak security light washed his side in orange.

"This whole thing is none of your business," I muttered.

"That's a pretty selfish thing to say, considering you've entangled me in every aspect of it."

"I'm done talking about this. This is between Dorothy and me."

"And I'm not trying to get between you and Dorothy." He paused and looked at me longingly, with a tinge of exhaustion. "I just want to know, Glinda. I like you, and I need to know if you like me too or if I'm wrong about all of it."

"You're wrong." And although it was intended for him, the words echoed back in my head like a sledgehammer. *You're wrong, Glinda. You're wrong.* I did like him. A lot. In fact, the things I felt for him were more intense than anything I had ever felt for anyone before. It was fucking terrifying. I couldn't go there. I had to protect my heart. "You're wrong," I mouthed.

"Because when you kiss me, it feels like—"

"Stop!" I looked defiantly at him. I had to stop this, kill it now, before I hurt him any more. Before he hurt me. "Listen to me, Troy. I blow shit up. That's what I do. And all that's left for me is to try and fix as much of the damage I've caused as I can. You're a good person, and I can't pull you into the dumpster fire that is my life."

He scoffed. "You already fucking did."

A big raindrop landed on my shoulder. "Yeah? And look what happened. You're standing here pining for me, and I'm breaking your heart." I glanced back at the tree line and then back to him standing there, motionless, expressionless, with streams of water trailing down his face and then down his chest and falling into a puddle around his feet. "I'm sorry, Troy. I used you, just like I use everybody else in my life. I used you up, and now I'm done. So just hate me like I know you want to."

"I could never—"

"Hate me? Yeah, okay. Just give it time."

A small groan escaped his lips. It was something from deep inside, something primal. I turned back and ran ahead through the trees, pushing aside the branches I saw and letting the others slap me across the face. A burning sting ignited across my cheek as a branch whacked me good, bringing tears to my eyes. I let them out. I ran and I cried—sobbed. I didn't care that I was stubbing my toes on rocks and sticks or that my pants and bra were soaked or that it was starting to rain.

I'd done it now.

The trees thinned slightly as I came upon the clearing with the cabin, lit up like a Thomas Kinkade painting. Through the windows, I could see Dorothy cooking in the kitchen and West sitting on the counter talking to her. James was probably in their room.

A streak of lightning ripped across the sky, and in that moment I saw the van. Behind me, the house was warm and dry and full of everything I didn't have and didn't deserve.

The rain was coming down harder now, cutting against me like tiny, icy splinters. Without a hesitation, I threw open the van door, climbed up, and slid into the driver's seat. The keys dangled from the ignition. I took a deep breath. The cabin smelled like Troy.

"God!" I cried out in agony, and then slammed my fists against the steering wheel. The glove compartment popped open, and I laid my head back against the headrest, eyes closed. "What are you doing?" I whispered to myself. Because the truth was, when he kissed me, it felt like fireworks and music and exhilaration, but there was a subtlety that swept through it too, like the peace of a quiet lake covered in mist or the exact moment the sun breaks over the horizon.

This was so stupid. I wasn't supposed to feel like this. This wasn't right. Feelings like this made people into idiots. Feelings like this ruined everything.

I glanced over at the open glove compartment and saw a joint poking out. Before I could think about it, I'd grabbed it and stuck it between my lips. Another bolt of lightning lit up the sky, and I saw Troy's silver lighter had fallen onto the floorboard.

The lighter was cold as I clutched it in my shaking hand. I flipped the lid back and struck the spark wheel, causing a tiny yellow flame to dance in front of my eyes.

I thought back to last night—was it really just last night?— when I pressed a button and lit the propane torch for the coffee can at the cult ceremony. I remembered the way the fire ate the handkerchief and the photos like a greedy monster with no satisfaction. I remembered the way the fire sucked away all the light and how the shadows danced across my mother's face.

With that, I held the flame to the joint and inhaled.

◆ 18 ◆

IRRESPONSIBLE AND INJURIOUS

Eighteen-ish months ago

"I DON'T KNOW WHAT to do."

Christmas Eve was waning into Christmas morning, and Dorothy and James were at the hospital. My mom was passed out in a chair, and West was upstairs, presumably asleep. I was sitting on the hearth, staring at the flames, too tired to make sense of much. Arlon was sitting beside me, his arms crossed over his chest, a serious look plastered on his face, his eyes watching the door without cease. He'd come over as soon as my mom had called, much to my chagrin. But in the weak hours of predawn, I turned to him, my cheeks stained with tears, and my voice broken.

"I don't know what to do."

It had been so long since I'd been able to go to my dad, wait for his reassuring advice, his strong hand squeezing my shoulder. It had been so long, and I was plunging. When I looked up at Arlon, all my heart wanted was that void filled; I so badly wanted someone to save me.

Inspire me, I wanted to say. *Build me up like you build up your followers. Make me believe in something bigger than my miserable, pathetic self.*

But his eyes, though twinkling, weren't familiar. They brought me nothing but the cold reminder that he wasn't my dad.

Arlon licked his lips. "Sweet Glinda, we're going to fix this, okay?"

"How?" I wiped my nose on my sleeve.

Arlon reached down and picked the box of truffles up off the floor. Tissue paper crinkled as he moved it to his lap.

I looked down at the box warily. Then, without warning, Arlon shoved the box into the fire. The flames crackled and hissed.

I held out my hands and then covered my mouth. "Why would you do that?"

"I'm protecting you. If there are drugs in those—"

"I thought you believed me!" I cried, jumping to my feet. My mom awoke and looked confused and frightened.

"Glinda, I'm trying to help you." His voice was calm and patronizing.

"Bullshit!" I gasped, backing away from him.

"Glinda, you need to listen to me. I can save you!"

"*Save* me?"

The sound of the front door creaking open stopped my heart. Dorothy slunk through, her coat draped around her shoulders, her face white and worn. She closed the door with her back to us and then slowly turned around.

"How is he?" Mom went to her.

"He's okay," she said hoarsely. "They gave him dopamine or something. They're observing him." She sank down onto the arm of the couch.

"What caused it?" I asked, anxious for the truth to be revealed. Dorothy examined the floor for an uncomfortable amount of time before she finally looked up at me, tears blurring her green irises. She cleared her throat and turned to my mom.

"He lied and told them he stole pills from his parents."

"*What?*" I cried.

"He'll get a lecture. *You'd* go to prison," she finally said to me.

"Now, wait—" My mom broke in.

"Do not defend her right now, Mom."

"But didn't they say it might have been a panic attack?"

"Dammit, Glinda! Why are you not getting this?! He could have *died*."

"But I didn't—"

In one fluid motion, Dorothy shot up, ripped my purse off an end table, and dumped its contents onto the floor. An avalanche of receipts and gel pens and loose keys all spilled out, along with two bottles of pills. They rattled as they rolled to a stop. She stooped down, picked one up, and emptied the contents into her hand. She stared down at them, seemingly lost in thought.

"What were you thinking?" she hissed, not looking up.

"I didn't—I wasn't—"

"I knew you were immature. I knew you were jealous. Hell, I was even starting to worry you were becoming a freaking addict. But what I still can't wrap my brain around is that you would purposely hurt someone."

Arlon had risen behind me. He placed his hands on my shoulders, and I jumped. "There is a dark force over this house."

I shrugged him off me. "We weren't talking to you, Darth Vader."

"Glinda, please!" My mother sobbed. I looked over and saw West sitting on the stairs, watching.

"If we could stop for a moment and realign our energies, I think—" Arlon began.

"Enough!" I yelled. Everyone grew quiet. I turned to my sister, and I threw my heart at her. "I'm your sister. I'm your best friend. This comes down to something very simple. Do you believe me or do you trust your boyfriend's 'instincts'?" I swallowed. "It's me or him. Dor, is it me or him?"

Dorothy's eyes grew wide for a moment, and then she spoke. "Him."

I couldn't breathe. My stomach was filled with lead. I blinked hard, expecting tears, but instead my eyes just burned.

"I didn't poison him, Dorothy—I promise you that. Because if I had, he'd be fucking dead."

She turned her cupped hand and the pills rained down, making little *tat tat tat* sounds as they struck the floor. And that was it.

She didn't say another word to me. She was gone by the time the sun was up.

★   ★   ★

Present

"Oh shit, I think it worked this time," I said aloud. Why was I talking to myself?

A flash of lightning lit up the inside of the van like an X-ray, followed by the loudest crash of thunder I'd ever heard. I froze. Maybe if I didn't move, the sound wouldn't see me. *Wait, thunder can't see . . . ooh, what if it can?*

The joint was now just a little stub in my fingers. I rolled down the window a crack and tossed it out into the rain. Water droplets poured in through the three-inch gap, and I shielded my face. The rain smelled so good; it smelled like the best smell I'd ever smelled.

Reluctantly I rolled the window back up. Now what? I looked longingly out at the lighted house and sighed.

"Those people don't want me." I gulped. "Those people don't need me." Argh, it was hard to hold onto a thought. I was on the verge of remembering something important, just to feel it slip away again into the fog of my brain. "I don't need them!" I yelled at the windshield.

It didn't respond. *Rude.*

Leaning my forehead against the cold glass of the window, I watched the raindrops slide down, trying to guess which little guy would win. A big fat one caught my eye, and I cheered him on as it tumbled down the glass like a big wet diamond.

I should go. I didn't need the people in that cabin. What I needed was to save my mom. Since I was apparently the only person who understood the gravity of the situation.

I knew no good would come of me running away, but it was unimaginable to stay. My sister thought I was a murderer, and my best friend . . . wait . . . was he? Yeah, I guess he was. So, my best friend liked me, and I'd ripped out his little heart and stomped on it.

I was done with Dorothy and James, I was done with Troy, and I was super done with Oklahoma. All I could do now was get back home as quickly as possible and somehow convince my brainwashed mother not to marry a con man. And I had to do it all by myself.

I took another breath and started the engine. Was this stealing? For some reason the thought made me laugh out loud. The
sound of my laughter made me laugh harder.

I pulled out onto the dirt road and into the deluge. The wipers just moved the water around on the glass and I had to squint
to make out where the road actually was. Great. The trees passed
by like bony clawed hands, reaching across the road to grab me.
I felt like I was going one hundred miles per hour. My knuckles
were white on the steering wheel as I glanced down at the speed-
ometer. Five miles per hour. I was going five miles per hour.
Damn, I was really high.

When I glanced back up at the road, my heart ripped through
the walls of my chest, and all the air left my lungs at once. The
lightning illuminated the trees and the road, and there, right in
front of my car, was a large, shaggy creature. It was Bigfoot! It
was fucking Bigfoot!

It all happened in slow motion. His head was turned, staring
right at me. Our eyes locked. My foot hit the brake pedal, and my
hands flew off the steering wheel as I screamed. The van came to
a sudden stop, but not before it clipped Bigfoot and threw him up
and onto the hood of the van. Green and black sludge covered the
glass. Were those his guts?

I'd *killed* Bigfoot.

Panicked, I unbuckled my belt and quickly opened the door.
A low moan came from the creature on my hood. Shit! I could
run. I could run back to the cabin and get help. I could find a big
stick and push Bigfoot off and keep driving.

I crept toward the front of the van, where the crumpled figure lay. "Uh . . . Bigfoot?"

"What the hell?" he moaned softly.

"You speak English?"

"Glinda?"

"You know my name?!"

"It's James," he muttered.

"Oh, that makes more sense." Wait—*James?* James!

Up close, he didn't quite look like Bigfoot anymore, but he
was covered in dark, muddy slime, with twigs and leaves stuck

to him in random places. I'd freaking hit James with the van! I reached up and touched his slimy arm.

"Are you hurt?" I asked.

"You hit me with a fucking van! Yes, I'm hurt!" His voice was louder now.

Slowly, he pulled his head up and looked down at me. Another flash of lightning gave me a good look at him. Blood was pouring from his nose.

"Oh my god! I don't understand how this happened!" I cried.

"Goddamn it, Glinda—this is like the third time you've tried to kill me!"

"I didn't mean to! Any of the times!"

"Help me down," he ordered, and I offered him an arm. He put a hand on my shoulder and slid down off the hood, falling to the ground. I reached out and caught him around the waist, keeping him from completely collapsing.

We huddled together for a moment in the pouring rain, both catching our breath.

"Why aren't you wearing a shirt?" he managed to wheeze.

"Huh? Oh yeah, that's a story . . ."

"Your headlights are out," he muttered.

"What?" I looked down at my bra in concern.

"The headlights. On the van. You were driving without headlights."

"Oh shit, you're right." I started laughing, so much so that I nearly fell backward.

James gaped at me. "Are you seriously laughing right now?"

"S-sorry." I steadied myself. "Can you stand?"

"I think so. See if you can help me to the back?" He braced himself with one arm thrown around my shoulders, and together we slowly rose up from the mud. He groaned and held his side. Taking excruciatingly slow, hobbled steps, we made our way back to the rear of the van, and I threw open a door. The interior light came on, and I could see blood on his shirt.

I'd done it. I'd really run down my sister's husband. There was no denying it now—some part of me, somewhere hidden down in a deep dark place, had homicidal tendencies for this plaid-wearing hipster mountain man.

He grabbed onto the frame, pulled himself up into the van, and collapsed on the floor with a scream of pain. I scrambled up behind him and crouched down to examine the extent of his injuries. But, okay, I was not a doctor and the sight of his bloody face was making me kind of queasy.

He winced and rolled onto this back and then lay still. Was he dead? Oh lord, what if he had a postmortem muscle spasm? I watched him intently, waiting for a sudden jerk of his leg or arm. Finally, I couldn't take it, and I gingerly poked his cheek.

His head snapped toward me and he scowled. "What is *wrong* with you?"

"I'm sorry! I was seeing if you were alive!"

"Yes, you managed to not successfully kill me *again*." He took in several sharp breaths.

"I thought you were Bigfoot!" I delicately patted his shoulder, and he narrowed his eyes at me.

"Are you freaking high?"

I rocked back on my heels and twisted my lips.

"Holy shit, you're completely lit." He started to smirk, but it quickly transformed into another wince.

"I smoked one of Troy's joints. I was sad, okay?"

"Why the hell were you driving while you're baked?"

"Last time I smoked, I didn't even feel it. I thought I was okay."

"Wow. You really are an idiot."

I raised an eyebrow. "Um, I'm not the one covered in bramble, standing in a dark road in the rain."

"I went down to the lake to find you both, and I saw the boat had capsized. I went to pull it back to shore, and I got caught in a giant algae patch." He wiped his face and flicked the slime and blood against the van wall.

"Oh yeah . . . that was my fault," I said, laughing again. Why was that funny?

"I figured. I was heading to the cabin to make sure you made it back. I really didn't want to have to tell Dory her sister stole the boat and drowned herself in the lake. But, no, you stole the van instead."

"I thought I'd go back to Texas and save my mom," I admitted quietly.

"Glinda, you can't drive back by yourself. That's crazy."

I snorted. "Like you care."

"Hey." He grabbed my arm and I looked down at his face. "I do care. Now stop throwing yourself a pity party."

After a beat, I said, "I didn't mean to almost kill you."

"This time? Or the time before?" He dropped his hand and winced.

"Either time!"

"I know." It was faint, but I heard it clearly. At once delirious relief rose up in my chest. I looked down at him in shock.

"You *do*?"

"Yeah, listen, Glinda. I'm sorry for how things have been." He cleared his throat. "For how I've been. It's just, when I see Dory upset, I want to protect her, you know? She's my family . . . but you are too."

"James! I hope you believe me when I say this—I'm really glad you didn't die. Either time." I threw my arms around his neck, and he moaned in pain.

"Hey, Glinda, first of all, I think you need to sleep your high off before we have any more serious, family-related discussions. Second, I may be bleeding internally, and I really think I'd better get back to the cabin before I do die."

"Oh right. Okay, hang on." I jumped out of the van and slammed the door. Halfway to the driver's door I stopped, spun around, and went back to James. I threw open the door.

He looked over at me, his face pale and grimacing. "What are you doing?"

"I . . . yeah . . . so I'm still really high. I probably shouldn't drive."

"Glinda, the cabin is less than a quarter mile behind us. You just keep driving five miles an hour, and we'll be fine. I need you to do this, okay?"

"Okay."

"Glinda?"

"Yeah?"

"I believe in you, okay?"

"You do?"

"Yes. I believe you can do this."

I stood there at the open door, letting the rain pound the top of my head while my feet sank deeper into the mud, but inside I was soaring. James believed in me.

"Glinda?"

"Yeah?"

"Turn the headlights on first."

"Right." I slammed the door closed and ran around to the cabin, practically skipping. He believed in me. I turned the van around, only backing into one tree in the process. The whole slow drive back to the cabin I couldn't wipe the stupid grin off my face.

When we reached the cabin, the rain had tapered off, and Dorothy was standing in the open doorway, watching. I turned the engine off and twisted around, pushing the curtain back. It was dark, but I could hear James muttering curse words under his breath. Good. He was still alive.

"Hey, Dorothy, so we have a situation!" I called as I hopped down. Dorothy came running out, followed by West and Troy, who had thankfully changed into some of his cousin's clothes. The sight of him sent flames to my face and chest. I wanted everyone else to just disappear so I could fall at his feet and beg him to forget all the stupid things I'd said.

"What were you thinking?!" Dorothy came right up to me, nostrils flaring. "Why would you take Troy's van? Where did you think you were going? And why in the world are you not wearing a shirt?"

"Shh. Listen, off-brand Barefoot Contessa." I held a finger up to her lips, and her eyes grew wide. "Stop. I can only process so many things at once right now, and there's a really important thing I can't forget about."

"What is wrong with you?" Dorothy slapped my hand away from her mouth.

"She's super high." Troy came up behind Dorothy with an amused smile. "Like, she's gone."

Dorothy's eyes narrowed. "Are you seriously *high* right now, Glinda Rainbow Glass?"

"Um . . . no?" Shit, no I was forgetting the thing . . . what was the thing? Shit! James! "Shit! James!"

"What?" The anger in my sister's eyes was immediately replaced by fear. "Where is he? What's wrong?"

"He's in the back. I sorta thought he was Bigfoot and hit him with the van."

"You *what?*" Dorothy flew to the back and threw open both doors. We all followed behind her. She was at his side in an instant, cradling his head in the crook of her arm.

"James, James, can you hear me?"

"I'm okay, I think," he muttered through gritted teeth. "She wasn't going that fast."

"What did you do?" Troy looked at me like he didn't know me, seemingly horrified by the overwhelming evidence that I had, yet again, attempted to kill his cousin. I shrank back, trying desperately to clear my head, to line up all the floating thoughts, to make everything make sense.

Troy and Dorothy got on either side of James and helped him into the house while West and I followed behind.

"What happened?" West hissed at me.

"Dammit, West. I was just trying to get back to Mom. I shouldn't have come. I shouldn't have come." And then something really weird happened—I was suddenly so tired and so overcome with it all that I just collapsed in West's arms, sobbing uncontrollably. She stumbled back a couple steps but caught me and held me. "I'm sorry!" I wailed.

She shushed me and led me inside the cabin, where we both fell side by side against the living room wall by the door. I laid my head against her shoulder and sniffed. It was stupid. I was stronger than this. I was the grown-up, and here I was blubbering like a baby to my seventeen-year-old sister. She didn't say anything; she just stroked my hair and leaned her cheek against my head.

"West?" I whispered.

"Yeah?"

"Your shoulder's really bony."

West just sighed, and we sat together there on the floor.

James groaned as he collapsed onto the couch. Dorothy knelt beside him while Troy filled a bag with ice and applied it to his cousin's ribs. They were all speaking to each other in low voices. I tried to listen, but I was still too far gone to pay close attention. My lids were heavy, and so I closed them and laid my head in West's lap.

It all faded away.

• 19 •

RESIGNED AND
BROKEN-HEARTED

WHEN I WOKE, WEST was gone, and I was lying on the hard floor. Someone had thrown a T-shirt over me. The muscles in my neck ached as I sat up and looked around. The room was quiet and dark except for a small light above the sink.

My eyelids were puffy from crying, and my mouth tasted like death. I slid the shirt over my head, cringing at how dry and crunchy my hair was. Standing, I peeked through the window. It was early morning. The sun wasn't up, but the darkness was lightening into a gray, dense fog that spread out from the cabin.

The door to Dorothy's room was open a crack, and as I neared it, the sound of voices and shuffling around trickled out. Pressing two fingers against it, I pushed it open a few more inches and peeked in. It creaked loudly, and everyone immediately turned to look at me.

"Glinda, are you okay now?" Dorothy's voice was wooden, like she felt obligated to check on me.

"I'm fine," I tried to say, but my throat was really dry. I just nodded and looked over at James, who was sitting on the side of the bed, without a shirt on. There was a large purple and red bruise on his side and a few scrapes on his face and arm.

"That's gnarly looking," I muttered in a hoarse whisper.

"We've been icing it, but Dory thinks he needs to go to the hospital," West said from the corner.

"It's just bruised." James looked exasperated. "I told you, I'm feeling better. It's fine."

"You should go to the hospital," I said.

Dorothy looked at me in surprise.

"Listen, you don't want to drop dead from internal bleeding."

"Then maybe you shouldn't have hit him with my van." Troy spoke with a sharpness in his voice that cut me to the quick. His face was completely drained of color, and his eyes were pointed at the floor, staring at something no one else could see. *At least look at me, man.*

But then something remarkable happened. James struggled to his feet and took a pained step toward me. "It was an accident." He gave me a weak smile and gripped the bedpost for support.

"James?" Dorothy came around him and looked into his eyes.

"Yeah, Glinda's fine. It was just a stupid mistake. She helped me. She brought me back here. God knows I've made plenty of stupid mistakes."

Troy kept his gaze on the floor, although his expression softened a bit. He blinked hard a couple of times. It knocked my heart back against my spine.

"If everyone else wants me to go to hospital, then I will." He kissed Dorothy lightly on the cheek, and I didn't feel like throwing up. "Okay, babe?" *Babe* was still a little much.

"I'm going to go," I said, finding my voice.

"I think you've done enough, Glinda." Dorothy shot me a warning glance.

"No. I mean, I'm leaving." I cleared my throat. "I need to get back to Mom."

No one said anything. Fine. If I had to ask, I'd ask.

"Dorothy, will you come with me?"

Dorothy's eyes widened and she gestured to James.

"I will drive you to the bus stop after I take my husband to the hospital." She folded her arms.

I pushed down the tears and turned to West. "West? You ready to go?" West looked down and shook her head.

"I'm staying with Dorothy."

"But—what about Mom?"

"I'm going to help Mom; I just can't do it with you any-more." She twisted her lips and looked up at me with sadness and a tinge of guilt.

It was numbing, being rejected like that by everyone you cared about. In this room, James, of all people, was the closest thing I had to a friend.

"All right, let's go then." Dorothy was so matter-of-fact about it now. She shoved her phone in her pocket, grabbed the car keys from the nightstand, and then was practically pulling James out the door. West wouldn't turn around. I looked helplessly across the room to Troy. Surely Troy would stop me, insist that he drive me home. He still had his arms crossed, but at least he was look-ing at me now, somewhat wistfully.

"Troy," I started.

"Hey, you should go," he said simply.

My heart sank. "You heard James; he knows it was just an accident."

"Yeah, I know." His tone wasn't angry, just disinterested.

I went over to him and lowered my voice so West wouldn't overhear. Troy bent his head down to listen. I took in a deep breath of him and then whispered. "Troy, what I said last night, on the dock . . ."

"It's fine, Glinda," he said in a quiet voice.

"I don't want to leave things like this."

"But you are leaving?"

"Yes, my mom—"

"So go then."

I looked into his eyes. For a split second his resolve seemed to waver, like he was going to drop his shield and be real with me, but just as quickly he blinked, and his defenses were back up. I sighed deeply, then turned and walked out of the room on the people I'd taken for granted. Two months ago I wouldn't have cared. I would have pushed it down and hardened myself against feeling anything. But now? Now my heart was ripping from my chest as I walked out the door and climbed into Doro-thy's car. What was I expecting, after all? In the end, everybody dumped me.

It took about thirty minutes to get to the county hospital. Dorothy drove while James sat dozing, his head resting against the window. I had about thirty dollars left in my bank account. That wasn't going to be enough. I gazed out at the small-town storefronts, the empty parking lot at the Pruett's, the sleepy town still struggling to wake up.

As though she were reading my mind, Dorothy glanced at me in the rearview mirror. "Do you have enough money to get home?"

"I'll be fine."

She raised an eyebrow and kept on driving.

I opened my phone and noticed the photos app had a notification. I opened the app and gasped.

"All my photos are back!" I wiped my eyes and began scrolling through; they were all there. Every last one. My dad smiled back at me from the stands at West's volleyball game in one; Dorothy and I made stupid faces in another.

"Oh yeah, Troy said he was fixing your photos or something," James said. "I think they'd been deleted, but not *deleted* deleted."

"Troy did this?"

"Yeah, yesterday, while you and Dory were on your hike." James tried to turn around to look at me, but winced in pain and continued facing forward. "He was working on it for a while, I think trying to keep himself distracted."

I couldn't say anything. My chin trembled and I nodded silently. I continued scrolling until I came to the last one. Troy had taken a selfie. He was crouching down in the forest beside the lake, a big goofy grin on his face, his head tilted, his tongue pointing out to the side and his right eye winking. He looked ridiculous. He looked wonderful. He looked completely different from the guy I'd seen this morning, the one with the sad, tired eyes.

I closed the phone and pressed it to my chest.

I insisted Dorothy take James to the hospital first, where he insisted she drop him off and come back after she'd dropped me off. As he climbed out of the car, he turned back and looked at me.

"Bye, Glinda." He gave me a half smile.

"Bye, James. I hope you aren't bleeding internally."

"Thanks, you too."

Then he shut the door and limped to the entrance of the ER.

Dorothy didn't ask me if I wanted to move to the front seat; she watched until James was inside, and then she sped off, ready to dump me and be done with it.

We drove in silence. It was another thirty minutes to the bus terminal, two towns over.

"So, hey," I said. "Um, would you let me know how he's doing? You know, email me or something?"

"Yeah, sure." She kept looking straight ahead but nodded.

"And um . . . yeah, I might not have enough to get home."

"I thought so." She reached over to her purse and pulled her wallet out. She tossed it back to me. I held the little pink wallet and examined it—worn corners, little unicorns on the front. I'd given her this when we were, like, thirteen and she was still using it.

"Take whatever cash is in there."

I unsnapped it and gasped. "There's three hundred bucks in here!"

"Yeah, take it. You don't know what things will be like at home."

"Okay, honestly, how are y'all making this much money with a blog?"

"Glinda, don't be so naive." She glanced back at me again. "That's, like, all the money I have left."

"Wait—what?" I leaned forward. "I can't take this."

"It's fine." She shrugged. "James works odd jobs in town, and I'll sell some more pies at the farmer's market. We'll be fine."

"Dorothy, honestly. Why aren't you practicing law? You'd be rich right now."

"I never took the bar, Glinda." She pulled up to the drop-off.

What? "Why not?"

"I was scared, okay?" She looked back at me, her eyes glassy, ready to spill over.

"Why?"

"You'd better get out; it looks like the bus is loading."

Reluctantly I took the money and stuffed it in my pocket, handed her back her wallet, and opened the door. Then I turned back to my sister, tears welling up in my eyes.

"Dorothy, I'm sorry. I promise you I never meant to hurt James or you, but the fact of the matter is, I did anyway. And I'm ready to take responsibility for that, to live with the consequences. Just promise me . . ."

"What?" She wiped away a tear.

"Promise me you'll take care of West."

"I'll get her home. Don't worry about it."

"And Troy."

She tilted her head. "What about Troy?"

"Tell him I'm sorry . . . for everything."

I shut the door and started to walk away, but then spun back around and knocked on the passenger window. She cranked it down slowly and peered out at me.

"Yes?"

"I think I've figured out what my Bigfoot is." I pushed a strand of hair out of my face. "You know, that thing you want to believe in, and think maybe, someday, somewhere you'll find it?"

"Yeah."

"I know what mine is now. But I've lost it." My Bigfoot was trusting someone enough to give them my whole heart and believing they wouldn't hurt me. My Bigfoot was a version of myself that could let somebody in, somebody like Troy. And just like Bigfoot, that version of myself was a myth.

"Glinda, I don't know what to tell you."

"It's fine. It's my problem to figure out." I pushed away from the window and swallowed.

Dorothy was staring straight ahead, still not looking at me as another tear spilled over her lid. She gripped the steering wheel and cleared her throat. Finally, she spoke, and her words were broken and hard to hear. "It's you, Glinda. By the way."

"What?"

"You're *my* fucking Bigfoot." Then she checked her mirror and pulled out onto the road, leaving me on the sidewalk. I lowered my head and stifled a sob.

I heard a sound beside me and glanced up. There was an older woman standing a few feet away, looking at me strangely.

"Yeah, you heard right." I shifted the backpack onto my shoulder and stared the eavesdropper down. "I'm fucking Bigfoot."

★ ★ ★

"Hi, sorry. My phone's dead—could I possibly borrow yours to call my mom to let her know what time I'm getting in?" The man peered over his glasses at me and looked me over. "Dude, we're in a bus. I'm not going to steal your phone. Where exactly would I go with it?" He sighed and handed it over. "Thank you!"

There were two numbers I knew by heart: Dorothy's and my mom's. I punched in the familiar numbers, held the phone to my ear, and prayed. I also turned around so the grumpy man would stop staring me down.

It rang twice.

"Hello?"

"Mom! Thank God you picked up!"

"Glinda?" Her voice sounded so far away.

"Yes, listen—Mom, are you okay?"

"Of course I am. Are you okay? West?"

"We're fine, Mom. We're good! Listen, I have so much to tell you, but I borrowed a phone from a guy on a bus—"

"A bus? Where are you?" Then she must have put her hand over the speaker because I heard muffled voices in the background.

"Mom?"

"Y-yes, I'm here, Glinda."

"My bus is scheduled to get in around five PM at the Denton station. Can you please come pick me up?"

"Five?"

"Yes. Denton."

There was a long pause. I held my breath. This was my mother. Surely, she wasn't debating leaving me stranded at the bus stop, was she?

"Mom?"

"Yes, dear. I'll be there." The line went dead. I pulled the phone away and stared at it in surprise. My stomach was all twisted up, like the time Dorothy convinced me to get on this roller coaster that I did not want to ride at Six Flags.

"Ahem?" The man sitting behind me extended his hand for his phone. I placed it in his palm and stared out the window without another word. *Yeah, yeah, whatever, I'm a bitch.* The thing was, I was over niceties. I was over anything that didn't help me get to my mother as quickly as possible. I should never have left her.

★ ★ ★

There, standing together at the curb, arm in arm, were a man and a woman dressed in long emerald robes, searching the small crowd eagerly. I walked right up to them and dropped my backpack at my feet.

"I'm Glinda." I sighed. Both their faces lit up instantly, and they each reached out an arm and pulled me in for a hug. My nose smashed into the guy's shoulder, the stiff velvet of his robe pressed into my cheek. I pulled away and dusted off the crazy.

"Sister Glinda, I am Brother Jason and this is Sister Laura," he said as Sister Laura nodded her head enthusiastically. "We were afraid you wouldn't be able to find us without a sign."

"Yeah, guess we lucked out." I shot them a fake smile that they did not pick up on.

"Well, I'm glad we found you!" Sister Laura cheered.

"Yes. We are supposed to bring you to Father Arlon. He's waiting for you."

◆ 20 ◆

ACCEPTING AND UNDERSTANDING

"I'M SORRY, WHERE'S MY mother?"

"She's at the outpost making preparations for the ceremony," said Sister Laura, as though her words needed no explanation.

"The outpost?"

"Yes, the dwelling on Huxby Lane, the home of the Starlight Pioneer Society."

My heart sank.

"Well, come on then—let's go." Brother Jason led us to a small white sedan on the curb, with another cult member at the wheel, idling.

He opened the back door and I crawled in, followed by Sister Laura, who, instead of sitting on the passenger's side like a normal person, scooted to the middle seat so that our hips were touching. Brother Jason jumped into the front and Brother Whoever pulled away from the curb.

The car smelled like cigarettes and chewing gum. Sister Laura sat happily beside me, her hands resting on her knees and a glazed-over expression of contentment plastered on her face.

"You don't have to sit so close to me." I tried to use my nice voice. I really did.

"Since Mother Julie could not be here in person, I am acting as her surrogate. I embody her light and good nature toward her wayward daughter." Damn, they were definitely trying to turn me into a handmaid or some shit. I had to get out of this car.

"So, you're my substitute mother?"

"Child of the stars, we are all your mother now." She smiled sweetly and squeezed my hand a little too hard. I pulled away and folded my arms.

"What about you, Brother Jason? You my mom now?"

"I embody the spirit of guidance and nurturing," he replied, not turning around.

"So, I'm assuming you all took your space vitamins today," I murmured under my breath and turned to look out the window. Laura seemed to snuggle closer to me, and I pushed myself as close to the door as possible.

We were on the freeway now, passing billboards and shopping centers. Everything was flat and brown compared to the hills and trees of the Ouachita Mountains. It was an hour's drive from the bus stop to my mom's house, and I felt every freaking second of it, Laura's elbow in my ribcage and Jason uttering random bouts of wisdom to me.

"You know, Sister Glinda, the apple may fall from the tree, but from its rotten and broken flesh may sprout new life."

"Mm-hmm." I had to get away from these freaks and talk to my mom. "So, what happened to Beverly McCoy?"

Laura lowered her gaze and frowned. "Poor Sister Beverly. The stress of the move, we think. She died in her sleep."

"It's funny," Brother Jason said from the front seat. "She was wavering on whether she wanted to move into the Outpost. Her daughter was apparently trying to convince her to move into her place in Florida. As it turns out, she was spared the choice. She transcended us all."

"Indeed." Laura nodded as if that settled it.

"How'd she die, though? Was Arlon there?"

"Sadly no. She died alone. We found her in bed, serene and restful. I did, actually. And Brother Jason." Laura wiped a tiny tear away with the back of her hand. "Arlon sent us to check on her when she didn't show up in the morning. But don't be saddened too much, Sister Glinda. She has become what we all will become: a great ball of light energy, floating around the center of the universe forever."

"That sounds great," I said dryly.

When we finally pulled in, I was horrified to see strangers' cars—and my old car, now the possession of someone else—lining the front drive all the way to the front circle, where another half-dozen cars were sandwiched in together. When Dad died, Mom had insisted on having a reception after the funeral. There had been this many cars then, all lining the drive. Brother Whoever pulled up to the front to drop us off.

As soon as the car came to a stop, I was out, practically falling onto the cement. I turned to face the house and let out an audible gasp.

All the windows were now shuttered with these dark gray boards. Several women were sitting on the front steps, sorting large baskets of laundry. Two men stood at the front door, one on each side, like guards or something. I raced past the women, up to the door, and placed my hand on the handle before one of the men held out a hand to stop me.

"Sister Glinda. I am supposed to take you straight to Father Arlon."

"Like hell you are!" I gripped the handle and pushed inside before he could stop me. The house was dark, lit only by real and battery-operated candles on side tables and shelves. Any sign of us, the family—any personal trinket or memento—was gone. Above the fireplace now hung a large wooden sign painted with big, black letters: "The Starlight Pioneer Outpost."

And the people. There were people everywhere. Some in green robes, others in everyday clothes, sitting or wandering through my house like zombie invaders.

At the reception after my dad's funeral, I remembered all the old ladies in dark dresses, standing around, glancing at me with these sympathetic looks. *The poor dear.* All I had wanted was to scream, "Get out! Leave us alone!" But I'd resisted for the sake of my mother.

Now the house was overrun again—only this time, they wouldn't leave after wiping out a couple fruit trays and telling my mom how sorry they were. These people were settling in.

I took the stairs two at a time until I reached the landing. All the doors were closed. I threw open the door to my room and sank down to my knees in disbelief.

My bed had been shoved into the corner. Two men were sitting cross-legged on it, facing each other, holding hands and moaning softly. Five more members were seated on small pallets on the floor, doing the same. No one opened their eyes to see what the commotion was. They hummed softly and swayed to a melody I couldn't hear.

The pictures on my walls were gone, the nightstand was empty. The closet was open and my clothes were missing. Instead, there were a dozen green robes hanging together. The room reeked of incense.

I gasped out, just trying to breathe, when two pairs of hands grabbed me by the arms and pulled me to my feet. I tried to shrug them off, but they held on tight.

"Get the fuck off me!" I screamed. The meditators didn't respond, but dragged me backward. I struggled and fought, but their grip was secure. They marched me back down the stairs.

"I'm calling the police!" I tried.

Nothing.

I went limp, fighting with dead weight. That didn't work either. They dragged me into the dining room. The room was filled with twenty folding chairs, all lined up in rows. The table had the leaf taken out and was pushed up to the end of the room and turned sideways. Behind it, in my dad's leather chair, sat Arlon Blight, hands tented together, lips pressed against his fingers. A slow smile spread across his face.

"Let go of me!" I shrieked again as the two men held me fast.

Arlon gestured to the men, and they let me fall to the floor. I jumped to my feet and put my hand on the back of a folding chair to steady myself. Slowly I raised my eyes to stare at this intruder.

"Welcome, Sister Glinda!" he said, his words bright and crisp.

"Fuck you!" I gripped the back of the chair until my knuckles turned white.

"Now, now, let's not start off that way. I am your soon-to-be father after all."

With that I seized the back of the chair tighter and then flung it against another, causing both to clang over in a pile of metal legs. Arlon waited for the sound to cease and then cocked his head.

"Sister Glinda, please don't come into my home and abuse my things."

"Your things?" I coughed in anger. "And what the hell did you do with *my* things? With my mother's things?"

"Your mother and I are soon to be married. Her things are my things. My things are her things. Besides, has dear Mother Julie never pressed you on the importance of not holding onto the material?"

"Where is my mother, Arlon?"

"She's in isolation. She requested the time to meditate before the ceremony."

That didn't sound good. "How long has she been in isolation?"

"Since about two minutes after you called her. You have no idea how much that phone call upset her. She felt she needed to reset her mind before the ceremony."

"Where is she? I'm not playing around. I'm calling the police, Arlon!"

"With what phone, exactly?" He smiled again, and I sneered back.

"So you did cancel my service. Mine and West's."

"Your mother gave me access to all her earthly accounts and finances," he said. "She trusted me to make the decisions about what should be held on to and what should be dropped."

"I can borrow a stupid phone. I'm still calling the police."

"Go right ahead. There's nothing illegal going on here. Your mother is in her room, and she specifically does not want to be disturbed by you." He snapped his fingers. "You know, you're welcome to use my phone. I do believe Detective Bryant is on duty. You remember Brother Bryant, yes?"

I shook my head at him, grimacing. Bryant was compromised, and Crumble probably was too. I had no way of knowing who was a fucking cult member and who wasn't, and I was so tired.

"I'm talking to my mother," I insisted. "And then all of you are going to leave my house!"

Arlon rose and the two men were holding me by the shoulders again. Arlon walked slowly around the chairs, meandering, until he was right in front of me, looking down at me with that smug little smirk. "You've always been so prideful, after all I've done for you."

I gaped at him. "Are you shitting me right now?"

"Of course not." He bent closer, sniffing my hair. I lunged forward, but the men held me back. "I did promise your mom I'd offer you a place to sleep here. It's a shame you refused so rudely." Then he signaled to the two guards, and they lifted me off my feet. I struggled against them, but it was no use. "And just to be clear, Sister Glinda, this isn't your house anymore."

"Fuck you. I will die before I let you win."

He shrugged and turned away. The two men pulled me back. "Keep at it, Glinda, and you might get your wish."

Then he was gone, into the kitchen, and I was being escorted back through the living room, out the front door, and down the steps, where I was promptly thrown onto the grass.

So much for all of them being my mother in spirit or whatever the shit they'd been talking about earlier. I looked up at my mom's window, all boarded up now. Was she even in there? She could be dead for all I knew.

I jumped to my feet and charged the front door. The two men had resumed their places and knocked me back. I stumbled backward down the steps and landed hard on my ass.

I kept my eyes on the house. I could try the back door, but I was pretty sure that was guarded too. How was Arlon outmaneuvering me? I was smarter than him—right?

Sister Laura was standing on the lawn, near where the old tire swing used to be, holding my backpack in front of her. I marched over and grabbed it out of her hands.

"Sister Glinda? Are you hungry? Thirsty? Your mother asked me to prepare something for you. She said to leave it at 'Lothlórien'? She said you'd know what I was talking about."

I didn't wait for her to finish. I sprinted around the house. A couple members were in the back, hanging green robes up on the clothesline. I raced past the garden with the circle of chairs. There was an extra ring around the first now, to accommodate more congregates. I ran down the hill, catching tree trunks as I went to keep myself from falling.

Completely out of breath, I came to a stop at Lothlórien and fell against a tree. Laid across the rock was a lace kerchief that had belonged to my mom's mom. Resting on the kerchief was a little basket and a bouquet of wildflowers—black-eyed Susans, my mom's favorite. I took cautious steps toward the basket, not trusting anything, least of all myself.

I traced my fingers along the wicker and peered inside. There were two sandwiches wrapped in wax paper, an apple, and a rinsed-out Gatorade bottle filled with water. Beads of condensation clung to the plastic. It was cold, fresh water from the fridge. My stomach growled at the sight of food, and I tried to think about the last time I'd eaten. Some toast and coffee before we'd left in the early morning. I looked around me, and satisfied that I was seemingly alone, I snatched up a sandwich and quickly unwrapped it. I was chewing the first massive bite when I noticed something in the bottom of the basket, hidden under the sandwiches.

I gingerly lifted out the book with the frayed green cover and the gold lettering. It was the first edition *Sir Gawain* Dorothy had given me for Christmas. I studied the book and took another bite. My mom had saved it . . . for me. She hadn't thrown it out with all the other things deemed unimportant in the Outpost.

She was telling me something. I pressed the book against my chest with my hand and looked up at the house. *Mom, what are you thinking? Talk to me.*

I placed the book back in the basket and lifted it onto my arm. I took a deep breath and started the long march back to the house. With each step my resolve grew, and I knew what I had to do.

When I reached the back door, I hesitated. Every part of my being was repulsed by this man and what he'd done to my family.

But this wasn't about him. It never really had been. This went deeper. It was time to stop fighting.

I rapped on the glass and waited. One of my friends from the front was there to greet me. He opened the door but blocked the way in.

"Hey, bro. So, I feel like we got off on the wrong foot, what with you physically assaulting me and everything. Anyhow, is Arlon around? I really need to talk to him."

The man looked at me skeptically, one eyebrow raised, but then he turned his head and muttered something to another dude, and then suddenly they had parted and gestured for me to enter.

Arlon was sitting at the table again, his feet up and crossed at the ankles. "Sister Glinda, you have had a change of heart?" he bellowed in his self-important way.

"Actually, yes."

He just looked at me, his face frozen, not a muscle betraying anything. Slowly he lowered his legs and leaned forward. "Come here."

I walked past the guards and swung a chair up to the other side of the table, like I was sitting across from him at a desk.

He cracked his knuckles and pondered me for a moment. When he spoke, it was careful and stilted. "Sister Glinda, I am hopeful. Please, tell me what you've decided."

"Well, Arlon, er—Father Arlon, I went down to the river behind the house to think, and one of your pioneers brought me some food, and—well, it just really touched me. That I, after being so rude and hostile, coming in here making demands and stuff, would still be treated so well by one of your followers."

"Which pioneer was that?" he asked, suspicion sweating off him.

"Oh, I couldn't say. Everybody looks the same in those stu— in those green robes."

Arlon cleared his throat and settled back down in his seat. "No matter, all of our pioneers are generous, charitable folks to the degenerates and the disgraced."

"Exactly!" I said, making sure to widen my eyes like a born-again pioneer.

He pursed his lips and narrowed his gaze. "I can see right through you, Glinda." He frowned. "And if you think you're going to somehow trick me, you have another thing coming."

"Think."

"What?"

"You have another *think* coming. That's how the phrase goes."

"Get her out of here," he snapped at the men behind me.

"No, no, no! Wait! I'm sorry! I can't help it!" And then I lifted my hand up and held my wrist out, showing him the tattoo. *Wander with purpose.*

He'd never seen my tattoo before; I'd made sure of that. It was an embarrassing reminder of my own naivety, but it was my secret weapon now. And Arlon knew why.

He stared at the words and then, sure enough, waved off his men. But I knew I would have to get even more real if he was going to buy my act.

"Arlon, look, you know I'm bad at being sincere, and I'm much more comfortable being in control. But let's say I gave it a chance—a real chance. Would you let me see my mother?" Mentally, I had one foot firmly grounded in my resolve to undo this man, to stay above the absurdity of his stupid cult, but now I felt the other foot hovering out, above empty air. What was I doing?

He studied me and then moved his eyes to the clock still hanging on the wall. Finally he looked back.

"You aren't going to talk to Julie until after the ceremony."

Until she was high on X, he meant. "No, I need to see her now, to make sure she's okay."

"Glinda." He leaned forward, locking eyes with me. "The first step is trust. You cannot join us if you don't hand over the control you're so desperate to keep. Don't you see it's strangling you?"

I licked my lips and looked around, first at the men behind me, then to the empty spaces on the striped wallpaper where our family photos used to hang, and finally back at Arlon.

"Fine."

Arlon straightened up and rolled his neck around, popping his spine. I winced. Finally, he looked at me hard and then smiled his devilish smile. "Very well, Sister Glinda. I am a leader who believes in giving everyone a second chance. Though this epiphany of yours seems a little sudden, I am not one to question the speed or the intensity with which the inner light speaks to each of us." He stood and held out his hand. "You are welcome to stay, provided you do your part and don't cause any problems. I know it will make Mother Julie very happy."

"Of course," I said cheerfully, standing and grasping his hand in a firm handshake. He gripped my hand tight and pulled me in, his lips brushing my ear.

"If you screw with me, there will be consequences. This is your very last chance." He let me go, and I stumbled back.

We locked eyes for a moment, and then I smiled. "Wouldn't dream of it."

Arlon motioned to his men, and suddenly there were rough grips on my elbows again.

"Wait, I thought we were cool?"

Arlon smiled. "My dear, sweet new sister. There is a process. All new members must be completely stripped of their former selves. You must be purified. Then, at the appointed time, we will baptize you into the society."

"Wow, you're just ripping off all kinds of religions, aren't you?" The words were out before I could stop them.

"Search her."

"Hey!" The men pulled my pockets inside out, grabbed my phone, and handed it to Arlon.

Then they dragged me backward. I stumbled, trying to get my feet under me, but they were jerking me around, disorienting me. They pulled me into the living room. The bastard was going to throw me out again.

"Stop!" I shouted. "I'm joining! I want to join!"

"Let her go!" Arlon stood by the stairs. They let me go, and I stumbled forward. Then I saw it—the little closet under the stairs, the place where Dorothy and I used to play tea parties, or cave explorers. The door stood wide open.

"What's happening?"

"You tell me, Sister Glinda," Arlon said.

"I don't understand."

"You want to join us?"

"I told you I did."

"Then as your first step, I need for you to go into the closet."

"What the hell?" I reared back.

"Glinda, I need for you to get in the closet," he repeated levelly.

"You're going to lock me in a closet?" I couldn't believe the words coming out of my mouth.

"Of course not. You have a choice. You always have a choice. Either step into the closet and begin your transition into the Society, or you may step out the front door and not come back."

I crossed my arms and blinked hard. "I'm not willingly getting into a closet."

"That's disappointing." He turned to the pioneers that had gathered around us. "It's so disappointing."

Their voices echoed around me. "So disappointing."

Okay, think Glinda, think. You've got this. He was trying to mess with my head, but I was smarter. I just had to maintain control.

"Fine," I said sharply.

The pioneers let out audible cheers as though I had just done something worthy of praise. I took a breath, crouched down, and stepped into the closet. Brother Jim came up behind me and pushed me.

My shoulder hit the wall hard and when I tried to stand, I slammed my head into a corner of the stair boards. Bright stars exploded in front of my eyes.

I heard Arlon's voice from somewhere above me. "Just in case you weren't taking this seriously, Sister, prepare yourself. Rebirth is never easy."

The door closed and the click of a key in the latch chilled me to the bone. The darkness was impenetrable.

"Shit." I touched the place on my head. It was slick with blood, right below my hairline. I felt around blindly. The space was completely empty. Just cobwebs and sharp places for me to bump against.

This was another one of Arlon's mind games. He'd let me out soon. He'd laugh it off. There was no way he'd actually keep me prisoner in my own house.

This was my choice. *My* choice. I was in control. Not him. He was an idiot.

I opened my mouth to call out, to tell them to open the damn door, but then I stopped myself. No. I had to rise above it. That's what he wanted. He wanted me to beg. He wanted me to panic and leave.

An hour or two passed—I wasn't sure. I couldn't hear anything on the other side of the wall. Occasionally footfalls sounded on the stairs above my head.

Did he do this to everyone, or was this bizarre torture just for me? Had he done this to my mom? If not, what *had* he done to Mom? How had he broken her? The thought of my mother suffering made it hard to breathe, hard to think.

I had to stay centered. I pushed the grief down.

He wouldn't break me. I was strong. I would sit tight. I would prevail.

More hours passed.

And then, just as I was about to fall asleep, the door creaked open, and a dark silhouette pushed in a tray with a cup of orange juice and a bowl of white rice. The door closed. I picked up the orange juice and sniffed it. Immediately my mouth salivated. I put the cup to my lips and sipped it. The sweet fluid washed over my dry tongue. I sucked it down, ate the rice with my fingers, and threw the empty dishes at the door to show my gratitude.

A moment later, the door opened again, and a hand found me and pulled me up and out of the crawl space. Darkness had overtaken the living room except for a few battery-operated candles, and I could sense many people sitting on the couches and floor, not speaking. Laura, who had pulled me out, gripped my arm with one hand, the other holding a flashlight. She shone it down at the discarded dishes and then pointed the beam right in my face, blinding me.

"What's going on?" My lips were sticking together.

"I'm going to take you to the restroom," she said matter-of-factly.

I didn't argue. My bladder was a growing kink in my resolve to stay under the stairs. I'd pee, get a drink from the sink, and then get the hell out of there.

She took me to the bathroom beside my dad's office, stepped in with me, and closed the door before turning the light on. The brightness made my eyes sting. I rubbed them and then squinted into the mirror. I was a sight to behold.

Dried blood was caked in my hair and down the side of my face. Dark circles were under my eyes. But it was my eyes themselves that unnerved me. I'd never seen my eyes look hollow before.

Laura crossed the room and turned the shower on.

"What are you doing?"

"Father Arlon wants you to shower."

"Are you going to watch me pee?"

"Yes."

I didn't even care. I sank down on the toilet and relieved myself. "I don't want a shower. I just want to talk to Arlon," I said after I'd pulled my pants back up. "I'm done playing games."

She went and stood in front of the door, her arms crossed. I sighed. I did need to wash the blood off, and a shower actually sounded amazing. So I'd take the damn shower and then . . . and then I . . . I . . .

My mom. I had to get to my mom.

I slipped out of my clothes, trying to ignore Laura's eyes fixed on me. I stepped in. "Fuck!" I jumped back out. "It's freezing!"

"We disconnected the hot water."

"Why? Why would you do that?"

"We believe in the purest form of living, free of the trappings of the modern world."

Of course. A sharp knock at the door stopped me from arguing.

"Sister Laura, do you need assistance?"

Laura looked at me, eyebrow raised. The last thing I wanted were my two friends to come in and force my naked body into the shower.

"I'm getting in." I gripped the shower curtain and then slipped into the cold stream.

The sting of the icy water took my breath away, but I bit down on my lip and used my hands to start rubbing the blood off my head. The cut stung, and I bit down harder to keep from crying out. There was no soap, no washcloth, nothing, so I used my hands and just scrubbed my skin, under my arms, everywhere, until I realized the cold was beginning to feel like heat. Probably a bad sign. After a minute, I stopped and just hugged my arms around myself and cried. My tears were boiling hot on my frigid skin.

I stared at the far wall and noticed the missing tile. It had come loose and fallen off years before. My dad had placed it under the sink, said he'd glue it back. He never had. He never would.

I still felt dirty, like there was this film all over me, but no matter how hard I scrubbed, it wouldn't come off. I tried to think of Troy kissing me, his hands, his lips, but then I could feel Arlon's hands holding my wrists in his office, bending forward, his sour breath so close to my face. I rubbed my face, my nose, my lips. I rubbed until my arms were turning red. I couldn't stop. I needed to feel clean.

I couldn't breathe. I was shaking uncontrollably. I was back in that dorm room, Patrick Nelson telling me I was pretty, but he was leaving if I wouldn't sleep with him. I didn't love him. But he was so good at making me feel like shit until I just really didn't care what we did or, rather, what he made me do. God, why was I so stupid?

Push it down, Glinda, push it down into the depths where it belongs.

I got out and Laura was standing there with a towel. She didn't hand it to me; instead, she held it up to wrap it around me. I stumbled forward and she hugged me. She pressed her body tight against mine, and as much as I wanted to stop crying, I just sobbed more.

"You've taken your first step, and I am so happy to be here for it," she breathed.

I collected myself and pulled away from her. "Where are my clothes?"

"We'll give you new clothes."

"I need *my* clothes."

"Your clothes are filthy." That was the end of the argument. She turned the light off and opened the door. I secured the towel around myself and stepped out.

The hallway was lined with pioneers now, each holding a candle, heads bowed slightly. I searched their faces for my mom, but she wasn't there.

Arlon was waiting at the end, arms outstretched to me.

I was exhausted, I was hurt, I was starving, and I was scared. More scared than I'd been in a long time. But the sight of him, reaching for me, made me want to hurl. I pushed past him and stumbled into the living room, where more pioneers waited for me. Large bodies stood at the doors, blocking me in.

Laura came and offered me a chair. My legs felt like they were about to crumple beneath me, so I sat, just until I could build up the strength to bust out of there.

I'd yell and scream, I'd kick groins and gouge eyes, I'd be a wild animal until they let me out. They encircled me, watching me sitting in nothing but a towel in the dim light.

"Why is everyone looking at me? What time is it even?"

"It's our midnight ceremony." Arlon's voice was near me.

"Give me my fucking clothes, Arlon."

"You have joined us, Sister. This is part of the process."

"Locking me in a closet for hours is part of the process?"

"In your case, yes. Your nature is corrupt. We must break through to your inner light."

They rushed me, a dozen hands on my head, my shoulders, my arms.

"Get the—" I stopped. The faces and lights were spinning, swirling, in and out of focus. I blinked, woozy. Was I fighting them off? I couldn't tell. My arms were so heavy.

I'd been high plenty of times, as recently as last night. This was something more.

"Wh—whatda what didya—" My tongue was too big for my mouth. My brain was quickly failing me. I tried to lunge forward, but the hands kept me in place, a hundred hands now—a thousand—and then Arlon's face, the only thing in my line of sight, speaking to me, stroking my cheek.

"Glinda, stop fighting this and be who you were meant to be. Let go . . . let go . . ."

Everything went white. Arlon's voice was coming from far away, saying words that made no sense.

I was standing in a field. A bright light, like a miniature sun, floated a few feet in front of me. A warmth more powerful and more intense than anything I'd ever felt was rising in my chest. It was so big, so strong that I was sure I was about to burst open. The orb glowed brighter, the warmth in my chest pierced through my skin, and then I was in the light and it was all around me, and I was floating and I was calm and for a moment I tried to remember what had happened before I came here, but I was coming up blank.

There were things, things holding me down outside of the light, but they were like faint shadows now, drifting away from me. And Arlon's voice was still there, as quiet as the breeze, directing me, guiding me.

Maybe I was safe here. Maybe I was dead.

And then everything just went black.

★ ★ ★

I cracked open an eye and saw sunlight straining through the boards on the window. I sat up too fast, my head still swimming.

I was in my mother's room, and she was sitting in a rocking chair, watching me. I glanced down. The clothes I was wearing weren't mine. I didn't remember how I'd gotten into them.

"Mom?" I tried, but no sound came out. The room was dim except for a single candle burning on my mother's dresser. I was surprised and yet heartened to see that the room looked much the same as it always had, save for the boarded-up windows and the missing photographs from her nightstand.

My mom was wearing a long white gown, and her graying auburn hair was braided and wrapped in a bun. She looked thinner than I'd remembered; her shoulder blades tented the fabric of her dress, and the material swallowed her frame as she sat, hands clasped together in her lap.

"Mom?" I heard my voice like it was coming out of some-body else's mouth. She didn't move. I pushed myself up off the bed and shakily came and knelt in front of her. Peering up into her face, I had to bite my tongue to keep myself from gasping. Her skin was pale, and her face looked about ten years older than it had just a few days ago.

"Mom?" I whispered. Her pupils dilated as she stared at me, like she was trying to recognize someone she used to know, maybe in high school or something, but couldn't quite place. Tears came rolling down my cheeks as I took several deep breaths, trying to find my voice again.

I heard the heavy steps running up the stairs and I knew our time was almost up. I grasped her hands in mine. She looked at me harder.

"Mom? Listen to me. I'm here. I'm here."

"Glinda?" Her voice sounded strange and hollow.

"Mom, please. You gotta snap out of it. We need to get out of here."

"This is my house," she said, knitting her brows.

"Yes, but right now I need to get you someplace safe. Some-place away from Arlon."

Hard pounding on the door made us both jump.

Arlon threw the door open and stepped in, his henchmen behind him. "Good morning, Sister Glinda!"

"I need to go to him," my mom said in a low voice and started to rise from the chair. I held onto her hands, causing her to sink back down.

"Mom, don't. Look at me, please," I sobbed. Her eyes drifted lazily toward me, but it was like there was a screen between us. She peered at me like she could just make out my outline but was missing the details. She was on more than X.

Slowly she pulled her hands out of my clutch and stood. I sprang up and stood in front of her. "Mom. *Julie.* It's your daugh-ter, Glinda!"

"I know you, Sister Glinda."

"No, just Glinda. Remember? Glinda Rainbow. How could you forget a name like that?" I said laughing through my tears.

She frowned and glanced at Arlon, who was standing with his arms crossed, a tiny smile playing on his lips.

I went and stood in front of him, holding my arms out to block her, but she stepped to the side and reached for him.

"Mom, please, listen to me! You told Laura to leave me a basket with sandwiches, made just the way you used to make them for our lunches, with a smiley face drawn in mustard!" She paused, looked back at me. "You gave her the book that you saved! The book Dorothy gave me—you kept it. Mom, you saved it. And then you gave it to Laura to show me because you wanted me to know. You wanted me to know that you're still in there, and you're trying to find me!"

And then those familiar hands lifted me up by the arms. I struggled against them, but it was pointless. Arlon stepped in front of my mother, blocking my view of her. "Still feeling spunky, even after the gift I gave you last night."

"Arlon, I just want to talk to her!"

Arlon smiled at me and then stepped aside. "And now you have. What did she say to you, hmm, Glinda?"

"Please, I'm sorry," I begged, desperate to keep my mother in my sight. "Please let me stay. I'll do whatever you want. I'll be good!"

My mother stared at me blankly. Arlon smirked. Then he gestured to his henchmen, and they dragged me from the room. I glared at Arlon, standing there watching me with a sick, amused look on his face.

The men dragged me down the stairs, shoved me into the closet, and locked it. I threw myself against the door, pounding on it, screaming until I was hoarse. No one came. No one would come. I was alone.

★   ★   ★

Not quite two years ago

"Yet a year runs full swiftly, and yields never the same; the beginning full seldom matches the end."

"What?" Dorothy asked from the other end of the phone line.

"It's from *Sir Gawain and the Green Knight*." I adjusted my phone and dodged a freshman on a skateboard.

"Okay? You realize I'm trying to study for my constitutional law class, not Old English literature?"

"Middle English," I corrected her.

"Okay, whatever. Listen, I really need to get back to this, so . . ."

I turned the corner and sat on a bench opposite from the library. I was only a few weeks into grad school, and between teaching and reading, I was drowning. And despite that, I was distracted.

"It's been eleven months, Dor."

"I'm aware," she said, and then softened her tone. "Are you okay?"

"I'm great. That's the point. A year ago sucked. A year ago was the worst time of my life. But I've had this epiphany."

"Oh, what kind of epiphany?"

"Okay, well, it's like the poem: just because a year starts out horribly, doesn't mean it has to end that way." I lowered my voice as a man passing out flyers for some event walked past me. "I've grieved for eleven months and I think I'm finally coming out of it—you know what I mean? I think a year is enough. So I've made it my goal to be fine by the anniversary."

"Glinda, we lost our dad. Grief doesn't have a time limit. My therapist—"

"I'm not saying I'm not sad he's gone," I cut her off. "But I really think I'm okay now."

"What does that even mean?"

"I look at you and West, and especially Mom, and I just— she's so sad all the time. Dor, she sleeps all the time, she's stopped hanging out with her friends . . . it's not great."

"Losing your husband is not great." Dorothy sounded like she was losing patience with me again. "It's okay to not be okay."

"See, statements like that kind of piss me off. This latest phase of so-called 'self-care' where you just double down on your depression and your flaws and say shit like 'It's okay to not be okay.' And I'm, like, since when? The whole fucking point of living is to be okay."

Dorothy was silent for a moment. "Glinda, how much Adderall are you taking, because you sound a little manic."

"I take what I'm prescribed," I lied. "Adderall is the only way I'm surviving grad school." That was the truth.

"Really? And how much sleep are you getting? I get texts from you at all hours of the night."

"Are you my mother?" I rolled my eyes.

"No, but you tell me you're not overdoing it with the pills and then go on tirades about things that don't make sense. I'm pretty sure you're not sleeping, and I'm also pretty sure you're not eating."

"I'm eating! Look, I'm eating right now!" I pulled a granola bar from my backpack and took a quick selfie with it, sticking my tongue out. "I'm sending you a pic."

"A granola bar isn't dinner."

"M'kay, I gotta go. Bye, Mom." I hung up before she could say another word. I looked down at the phone, sighed, and then tossed the unopened granola bar toward a trash can about five feet away. I missed.

"Dammit."

"Hey, you mean to throw this away?" The man passing out flyers had reached down and picked up the granola bar.

"Oh, thanks," I mumbled as he inspected it.

"You don't want this?" he asked.

"Nah, not really hungry at the moment," I said, looking back down at my phone. The man sat down next to me and unwrapped the bar. Great, just what I needed. He was middle-aged and dressed like a dad from a '90s sitcom. He might have been a nontraditional student or maybe even a professor. Professors often had no sense of style or understanding of how to appropriately interact with students.

He took a bite of the granola bar and munched on it loudly. I adjusted the strap on my backpack and decided I'd hit the library before going back home. But before I could stand up, the man turned to me and said something that gave me pause.

"You're right," he said, swallowing a bite. "Grief is a fucking racket."

"Excuse me?" I let the strap of my backpack slide back down.

"Sorry, didn't mean to eavesdrop, but your conversation caught my attention because I'm actually a part of a group—"

"Oh," I cut him off. "No, sorry, I don't want to join a grief support group. Thanks though." I stood up.

"No, no, no." He laughed—snorted, really. "We're not a grief support group. Actually, we're like the complete opposite of a grief support group—we're an anti-grief support group."

I spun back toward him and raised an eyebrow.

"I promise, we're not a support group, we're just a small group of people who meet and talk over coffee about life and philosophy and how to harness your brain's natural ability to create the energy to define yourself—who *you* want to be as a person, not what *they* tell you you should be."

I sank back down next to him. "What does that mean, your brain's energy?"

"I mean, here's the thing: everything is made of stardust, right?"

"Sure."

"So, that means your brain is also made of stardust."

"Right?"

"So, I know it might sound a little out there—"

"Oh, don't worry." I laughed. "My parents—my mom is a full blown hippie, so I've heard 'out-there' theories before."

The man laughed and scooted closer, lowering his voice. "You seem like a person of above-average intelligence."

I nodded.

"So have you ever wondered why some people are naturally smarter than others?"

"I mean, I chalk it up to genetics and lead paint, but yeah, I guess it is kind of weird."

"You're funny." He smiled. I smiled back. "What if, just imagine for a moment, that the reason you're so much smarter than all the people around you isn't because you won the genetic lottery. What if it was because you instinctually and subconsciously know how to access the energy from those eons and eons of the cosmos that make up your mind?"

I looked at him sideways. "I'd say I hope you're talking figuratively, because otherwise—"

"Of course figuratively! Metaphorically! I'm sorry if my analogies are too difficult to understand. I assumed you would be able to interpret them, but then I often overestimate my ability to explain such complex ideas."

"Oh no, I understand!" I said quickly. "I just wanted to make sure we weren't on a train headed to crazy town. No offense."

"No offense taken." He smiled. "If there's one thing you should know about me, it's that life has given me very thick skin. And you're smart to be skeptical. I pride myself on my skepticism."

"Okay, good." I smiled. "Well, it was nice talking to you—"

"I heard you take Adderall," he interjected.

I tensed up. This conversation had taken a drastic turn from fun to "this is absolutely none of your business."

"Hey, no judgment from me. I take whatever I need to in order to harness the potential of my brain. They're just tools, right? Tools are neutral, it's how we use them." He looked at me and I nodded slightly. "Good! So do you think Adderall helps you to focus better?"

"Sure."

"And a lot of Adderall helps you focus even more?"

I looked down at my hands.

"Friend, it's about using the tools, both physical and mental, to see through the bullshit of this world and be your true self." He rubbed his hand over the stack of neon-green flyers like it was the holy scriptures. "I don't want you to grieve in your own way, friend. And I sure as hell don't want you to 'be okay with not being okay,' whatever the hell that means." He placed his hand on my shoulder and I shuddered. "I want you to grab grief by the balls and body-slam it. If you don't want grief to be a part of you, you have the power to make that happen. If you want to be even smarter, more outgoing, more creative, then I think you should come hear us out. What do you have to lose?" His speech was impassioned, but somehow sounded reasonable. He was excited but completely in control of himself, his volume, his cadences. He placed a flyer into my hands and stood up. "Has anyone ever told you, you're directionless, aimless, wandering?"

"Uh, yeah, like everyone," I replied. This guy got me.

"Our group, we are pioneers, and pioneers wander with purpose," he said and I felt a lump in my throat. "Thank you for the snack, my friend. I hope we see you tomorrow night."

I looked down at the flyer and smiled.

"The Starlight Pioneer Society," I read aloud. "That's a fucking cool name."

♦ 21 ♦

MEEK AND OBEDIENT

Present

I LOST TRACK OF the days. I think that was the point. I stayed locked in the closet all day and was given water and food twice a day. I mostly slept; I was so very tired. Then Laura let me out once it was dark, and I went to the bathroom and then ate whatever they offered me, knowing full well it was probably laced with who knows what. I wasn't scared anymore. Well, no, I was scared—I was scared of how automatic my behavior had become, how I'd stopped fighting them. I came out, I ate, I sat with them in the living room at midnight and drank the tea they offered. I didn't resist and drained my cup, relieved by the escapism and the visions of warmth and peace that the dreams gave me.

Then I'd wake up in the closet and the whole thing started again. Days went by, but the drugs made it hard to keep track.

I wasn't the only one. Brother Jason was often brought by force to the living room. Did they have him locked up somewhere too? He broke faster than me. And then he came on his own accord and seemed a happy little puppet of Arlon's yet again.

I had a lot of time to think now. I thought about my mom and how Arlon had broken her. It had been different, more subtle. He'd distracted her from her grief. Given her a way to replace it with him, completely. I was beginning to understand. To truly understand. Because the thing was, the more time went by, the more disorientation, the more discomfort I experienced, the less

I thought of Troy. And even though I knew it was wrong, it was also a relief.

I think it was the sixth night that Arlon started talking to me during the midnight ceremony. Specifically me. While everyone else embraced their inner lights, Arlon was at my side, whispering in my ear.

"You are nothing. You are empty. You wander this world purposeless, directionless. No one wants you. No one needs you." I'd swat the air in front of my face to get him to stop, and then he'd grab me and hold me tight, and I'd let him because it was comforting, being held. And then he'd say, "I have you. We have you. We give you purpose. We wander, together, with purpose."

The mornings brought more clarity, and I would work to remind myself that everything he was saying and doing was bullshit. But after so many nights with Arlon sitting right there, both tearing me down and pulling me in, clarity was becoming harder and harder to grasp.

But I couldn't stop. My mom needed me. I was in control. I was in control.

★   ★   ★

"Sister Glinda, did you bring the towels in from the clothesline?"

I looked up at Sister Arianne and blew a piece of hair out of my face.

"Yeah. I took them out to Sister Ann and Sister Laura to fold."

I was currently on my hands and knees, scrubbing the floor of the kitchen with a stiff brush. The foot traffic of thirty people in one house made for some truly unsightly floors. Besides that, everyone was hard at work polishing up the place for the ceremony that evening.

Since I was still not trusted, I was given the lowliest of chores and only permitted in the downstairs of the house. That was fine. Seeing my childhood bedroom turned into some kind of pseudo orgy meditation fest was a little upsetting. So, I was given a pallet in the corner of the living room next to Sister Laura and Sister Arianne. I'd earn a pillow in a week or so. Sister Arianne snored something fierce. I'd almost asked her if her inner light might be interested in a CPAP machine, but thought better of it. As long as they didn't put me in the closet again, I'd endure snoring and uncomfortable pallets.

Thursday morning, we were awoken before the sun was up, to meditate, and then we all went outside to sit in the garden for the sunrise ceremony. That involved a lot of shirtless men prancing around with burning torches and then, of course, Arlon had to stand up and spout off his shit about dreams.

I'd started cheeking my ecstasy pills, but Arlon had figured out my trick and had Brother Jim and Brother Kent hold me down while Sister Arianne forced it down with a glass of water. And then for about thirty minutes, until the drug kicked in, I would contemplate leaving, but each day that seemed like a more and more ridiculous idea. Of course I couldn't leave my mom. And where would I go? To Troy's? To Dorothy's? Ha. Besides, there was a part of me, a part I truly hated, that was anxious for night to fall, for the midnight ceremony when we would drink the tea and then it would all wash away and I would feel that warmth again, that light that ate me up and made me feel whole again. I didn't fight the tea. And I hated myself for that.

We all worked on the house, clearing out furniture Arlon didn't like and putting it in the barn.

It was scary how easily I could compartmentalize, just turn off the part of my emotions that was being absolutely destroyed by the destruction of my family home. Take this box of your dead dad's books to the trash—sure, no prob. Help carry this rocking chair that your mother used to rock you to sleep in and set it in the nasty old barn—of course; it would be my pleasure. I'd like to say that I was mentally treating this like some kind of secret spy mission, where everything I did was for the greater good of the master plan. But truth be told, there was no big, master plan. The plan was this: suck it up, play along, do what I was told, and then maybe, *maybe* I'd get to see my mom again.

I'd lost everyone else. I'd lost my dad. I'd lost both my sisters now. I'd lost the one person who actually defended me. So, as I scrubbed dirt off the tile like a servant in my own house, every-thing just seemed really simple. Scrub the floor, say the chants, listen to Arlon, obey Arlon, and then—then I'd have my person back, my mom.

But then Friday morning arrived. The day of the wedding. And I had run out of time. I'd lost. I'd lost her.

It was a strange feeling, accepting the inevitability of some-thing so horrific. There was a voice I couldn't shut up that screamed at me as I made Arlon's coffee: *What the fuck are you doing? Throw the coffee in his fucking face and run!* But instead I brought him hazel-nut creamer.

"Sister Glinda," Arlon said, looking up from the notes he was scribbling down on a pad of paper that clearly said *Dr. John J. Glass* at the top.

"Yes, Father Arlon?"

"I was telling Mother Julie about your progress. She was very pleased to hear that you are settling in."

"Yes, well, good. I'm glad she's happy." I offered him a spoon. "I'm happy she knows I'm here."

"You know tonight is the ceremony."

"I know, Father Arlon."

"Your mother and I will converge our inner lights." He grabbed my wrist and squeezed it until I dropped the spoon. It clattered down onto the table. He looked up into my face, the corners of his mouth drawn in. "I don't trust you farther than I could throw you. Don't get clever." He released my wrist and I backed away. Then he smiled broadly and chuckled. "You look good in green."

I rubbed my wrist and bowed my head. Swallowing the first ten things I wanted to say to him, I found my pioneer voice: meek and quiet.

"Thank you, Father Arlon. My inner light rejoices."

I turned around, nearly knocking into Brother Jason.

"Sorry," I muttered.

"Hey! Uh, Sister Glinda?" He followed me into the kitchen. I rolled my eyes and turned around, bracing myself for whatever ridiculousness was to come.

"I was wondering if maybe you'd like to meditate with me later?"

"Sorry, I'm all meditated out."

"Oh."

I continued toward the hall, and he followed. I rolled my eyes and faced him. "Can I help you?"

"My wife left me when I joined the Society. I lost full custody of the kids."

I didn't know what to say. So I furrowed my brow and waited for him to continue.

"I knew I wasn't getting her back, not after everything. And so, these people, Arlon, they're all I have."

I wanted to strangle him. Here was an unhappy man who had every freedom to leave and yet remained. "Your family is out there in the real world. They'll take you back."

"You don't understand."

"I understand more than you think."

"I didn't have anybody, and Arlon was there, and he makes me feel worthy again."

"Worthy of what?"

"Of love."

I studied the poor guy. He was probably less than forty, a little gray in his beard, and dark lines under his eyes. This was not a man who had found inner peace. I nodded slowly. "Why are you telling me this?"

"I just—I just felt moved to caution you. I see you battling within yourself, but there is peace to be had, Glinda. There is, but you have to let go of yourself. Let go of yourself."

Let go. I could let go. I could let go of Dorothy and West and Mom . . . and Troy . . . and Dad. I rubbed my face. I had a headache. Jason patted my shoulder and walked off.

A stack of clean towels on the back of the sofa caught my eye. Without being told, I picked them up and headed down the hall to put them away in the bathroom.

The office door was cracked. Arlon was in the dining room. There were two forces, one pulling me away, toward the bathroom, the other nudging me forward. *Go in. Undo this man.*

I set the towels on the ground and looked from side to side. Clear. I slipped into the office.

Maybe it was the smell, the familiar smell of my dad that still lingered, or maybe it was his collection of law books still resting on the top self, untouched, but whatever it was, I had a moment of clarity. I rushed to the desk and started opening drawers, rummaging through papers. I slid the bottom drawer open, and my heart stopped.

Orange prescription bottles were stacked to one side and a hundred baggies full of pills and powders filled the rest of the drawer. I picked up an orange bottle. Beverly McCoy. Jason Waters, Glinda Glass: Valium . . . Xanax . . . Adderall. He was using our names to get his drugs. There was sheet of paper I was pretty sure was LSD. Some of the baggies were labeled in another language, some weren't labeled at all. In the very corner, I noticed a baggie with Sharpie words written across the front: "Caffeine powder."

"Sister Glinda."

The blood in my veins froze, and I turned to face Arlon.

"This is really disappointing, Sister Glinda. Just when I was beginning to think you'd really accepted us."

"No, I have! Please, Father Arlon, I have!" And I meant it. I think I meant it. My brain was so scrambled. Jason stood behind him, a guilty look on his face.

"Do you know how long you've been with us, Sister Glinda?" I didn't know what day it was, let alone how long I'd been there. I shook my head.

"Long enough."

Brother Jim and Brother Kent rushed into the room. Jason shrunk back and scurried away.

"Arlon, please! Please!" I was panicking. I couldn't leave, not without my mom. This was still my home, even with the pioneers crammed into every corner. I sprang forward and grasped onto the bottom of his robe, looking up at him, my whole body shaking.

"Put me back in the closet! Lock me in a week! Just please, don't kick me out!"

Brother Jim marched me out of the office, through the dining room, and opened the back door, pushing me through. I stumbled forward and spun around, ready to fight my way back inside.

Arlon stood on the step, the door closed behind him. We were alone.

It was noon and the sunlight was harsh, shining a white, summertime glow on every surface. Nobody with half a brain was outside at this time of day at this time of year.

"Father—"

"Sister Glinda. I am a loving and forgiving man. But I am not stupid."

"I know—I'm sorry."

"You must prove yourself to me."

"How?"

"Tonight, at the ceremony. You must confess your sins publicly before the pioneers and before your mother."

"I will, I'll confess to going through your things."

"No, not that sin. The original sin."

"The original sin?" I raised an eyebrow.

"James."

"I don't—"

"You tried to kill James."

His words were a knife that momentarily cut through the fog in my brain. "But you—I can't—"

"Glinda, you must do this. And then I will allow you to be with your mother."

I'd get to see Mom. "But I—"

Arlon tilted his head. "Didn't you try to kill James?"

I shook my head, but my thoughts were cloudy again. I needed to sleep. I was hot and stiff from sleeping on the floor so many nights.

"I don't—I mean, it wasn't my fault."

"Of course it's not your fault."

"It's not?" I looked at him. "Then tell me whose it is, because I keep leaving fires burning behind me, and I need to know how it's not my fault." The bridge of my nose burned, signaling tears weren't far behind. I tried to push them back down.

"Someone abandoned you, Glinda." He stepped down and put his hands on my shoulders. I didn't pull away. I should have. But I didn't. "Who left you? Who was it? Who did that?"

"My dad!" I burst out, choking on the words. I was horrified at myself, and even more horrified when I leaned into Arlon's shoulder and cried. He wrapped his arms around me and stroked my hair.

"Yes, yes, your father. He knew you needed him. You needed his help, and he left you to figure it all out by yourself."

"He left me!" I sobbed. "He died, and then how was I supposed to know what to do? He always stepped in when my mom and I were fighting. He always made Dorothy and me make up before bedtime. That was his rule. No fighting after bedtime. And then he died. He died!" I could barely understand myself as I yelled into his robe.

"And everyone told you it was normal to be angry, that it's part of the process. That there's no right way to grieve?" He sounded different. Real. Genuine.

"It's bullshit!" I pulled back and looked up into his face. He seemed concerned. Actually concerned.

"Of course it's bullshit. People say that to make themselves feel better, make them feel like they've helped you. But, Glinda, oh, Glinda, I wish I could take everything I know and just put it in your head. There is a right way to grieve. There is a way not to work through your grief, but to destroy it. Obliterate it. How many people suffer needlessly? Your dad hurt you. But I can fix you. I can take that hurt away."

"How? How could you possibly do that?"

"Stay with me and I'll show you."

I backed up, rubbed my face, and swallowed. He left me. He died and he left me. It hurt. He hurt me. I didn't want to hurt anymore.

"Okay," I heard myself say.

"Okay?"

"Okay, I'll confess tonight."

Arlon clapped his hands and then escorted me back inside to prepare for the ceremony.

• 22 •

RESPONSIBLE AND
GUILT-RIDDEN

I'D KILLED HIM. RIGHT? No, no wait—he wasn't dead. Who was dead? Was James dead? I'd poisoned him. No, wait, I'd hit him with a car. Yes? I shook my head again.

I had ridden in Sister Laura's car to the site of the ceremony. I had no idea where we were going, I'd just gotten in like I was told.

"You look very beautiful." Sister Laura smiled.

"Thank you." I wore a crudely made muslin dress, and we both had our robes on, stifling hot in the summer air.

The car stopped and my heart caught in my throat. I opened the door and took a heavy step out onto the gravel of the May-pole Renaissance Festival's empty parking lot. The castle facade stood like the grand entrance to a ghost town. I swear a tumble-weed rolled across the lot. I took a breath and stepped forward.

Why here?

Our group moved together toward the castle, and then Mark unlocked the gates and we all crowded through. I didn't even think to look for my mother.

The fair was falling apart—I mean worse than usual. Trash cans were overturned, the shops had been boarded up, and the weeds were knee high. Arlon led us so that we were facing the back of the castle. The pioneers got to work building a bonfire.

We arranged ourselves in a circle around the fire. Arlon went to the center, his velvet robe dragging in the dirt. He spun around, a wicked smile plastered across his face.

"My dear pioneers! We gather here, on these grounds that our Brother Mark so generously and selflessly donated to our Society."

This was news to me.

"I know you all have been anxious to hear what I have planned for this piece of terra! Well, I am pleased to tell you that I am finalizing a deal that will turn these acres into a subdivision of houses. A neighborhood. And we, the Society, will finally have the income to sustain ourselves in this world and the next plane of existence! We will expand! We will dominate!"

Cheers erupted around me, but all I could do was imagine Troy, sitting in Bessie's mouth, swinging his legs and looking at me wistfully, like he did.

"But before the construction begins, I wanted to celebrate this achievement by coming here, the place of our success, to marry my bride!"

More cheers. I hadn't seen my mother yet.

"Before we begin, Glinda has something she wants to say." Arlon nodded to me and motioned for me to take the center. I walked forward, my brain desperately trying to keep up. I spun around and faced the crowd. Thirty faces looked up at me. And then Arlon ordered my mother out.

Everyone grew quiet at once. I turned to see my mother walking into the circle, dressed in her white gown, a simple wreath of baby's breath on her head, and her hands clutching a bouquet of black-eyed Susans. She kept her gaze focused right in front of her, directly at Arlon.

For an instant I was tempted to believe that this was a good thing, a moment of happiness for my mother. She looked so beautiful, so serene. But then my eyes traveled to Arlon, stepping forward to take her hand, and I felt dizzy.

He took her by the arm, and they turned to face me. "Whenever you're ready, Sister Glinda."

I surveyed the group again. *Just do it. Get it over with.* Then I could go home and sleep.

"I . . . I just wanted to say that I . . . that I tried to kill my brother-in-law, James."

The look on my mother's face seemed deeply confused. "Brother-in-law?" she said.

That's right. They were married. They got married. And James, there was something about James . . . What was it?

"Keep going," Arlon said, tightening his grip on my mom's arm.

"I wanted him to die, so I poisoned him," I heard myself saying. But then I remembered—just a split-second thing: James, lying in the back of the van, looking up at me, smiling.

"I believe in you, okay?" he'd said. *I believe in you.* He believed me. No, more than that, he believed *in* me.

At that moment, I looked up and there were four new faces standing at the edge of the crowd. Dorothy, James, West, and Troy. All four were staring at me in horror.

They were here. They'd come.

They'd come.

They'd heard my confession.

"Glinda, why would you do this terrible thing?" Arlon prompted me.

I didn't speak. I just stared back at them, my thoughts a giant, tangled mess. I rested my eyes on Troy, but it was too much to see him. I felt like I might actually fall down and die in the dirt.

No. No.

I turned toward the center of the fair and pushed past the crowd. I took off running.

★   ★   ★

Not quite two years ago

"Glinda, I'm not sure about this." My mom glanced warily out the window at the coffee shop. Inside the large, lit-up windows, I could see the group already set up on some couches in a corner, about eight people, including the guy who'd given me the flyer.

I gave my mom's hand a squeeze and killed the engine.

"Mom, I'm really glad you agreed to come with me. Hey, it may be a bunch of baloney, but I think we should at least hear this guy out. This might be the kind of thing you and I need right now." After meeting the man on campus, I had gone back to my room, unable to sleep. I popped a couple pills and wrote some notes for an assignment, and then I found my thoughts drifting back toward the things he had said. I'd gone out to grab a drink, help me relax a little, and that's when I'd ended up at the tattoo shop, getting the words that I decided were my new mantra permanently written on my wrist.

When I'd gotten back to my room in the early morning, I lay on my bed, staring at the ceiling until dawn. By the time my alarm went off, I was convinced that not only was I interested, but the Starlight Pioneer Society might be the exact thing my mom needed as well.

"I just don't know if I can talk about . . ." She trailed off, still watching the shop.

"You don't have to say anything. It's not a stupid support group. That's why I brought you. He said some stuff that really resonated with me." Then, before she could back out, I opened my door, washing us in the orange interior light. She reluctantly followed me across the wet parking lot in the fading daylight. A little bell chimed as we entered.

The man looked up from his place in a large, plush armchair and smiled broadly. He waved us over. I took my mom's hand. It was cold and shaky. With me in the lead, we walked over to the couches and took a seat.

Immediately I realized I was the youngest person there. Several of the members were senior citizens, and the rest were middle-aged. Well, that was okay. I was older than my years, so naturally I'd be more at home with this crowd than with stupid college kids.

"Hello, friends, welcome to the Starlight Pioneer Society!" the man said warmly. The others smiled at us. My mom seemed to relax and unwound her granny square scarf from around her neck, laying it across her lap.

"Hi," I said. "I don't think we actually exchanged names. I'm Glinda Glass, and this is my mom, Julie."

"Glinda and Julie, welcome! My name is Arlon Blight, and my inner light rejoices at your presence." With this, the others nodded eagerly, and each in turn said their name and how rejoiceful their inner lights were. By the eighth inner light, I was a bit on edge. Still, I tried to wrestle down the nagging feeling that I'd made a mistake.

I didn't want to be wrong. If I were wrong about Arlon, then that would be to admit I wasn't as smart as I thought or doing as okay as I asserted I was. Still, there was now a cloud of doubt hanging over my head as the meeting continued.

"Excuse me, Mr. Blight." My mom spoke up in her quiet, considerate tone.

"Please, call me Arlon."

"Okay. Arlon, can you please explain what an inner light is? I have experience with auras. Is it like that?"

I smiled to myself, watching her face light up with a hint of curiosity and excitement.

"Good question!" Arlon said, and the others nodded enthusiastically. "Each of us has an inner light, whether we are aware of it or not. Many different beliefs exist about the inner light—some call it an aura; some call it a soul—but we believe we have boiled away all the nonsense to reveal the true nature and purpose of the inner light. Without boring you, sweet Julie, the inner light is your source of power. It is the trillions of stars, super novas, big bangs, the power of the universe in you. It contains your true essence, and it travels in your physical body, but ultimately it longs to reach the next plane of existence."

I covered a gasp with a cough. I shook my head with a little laugh and looked to Arlon for clarification. "I'm sorry, Arlon, but when you say all this stuff about the inner light and the next plane of existence, you're speaking metaphorically, right?"

"Of course, dear Glinda, of course!"

I sat back, momentarily relieved. Metaphor was fine. I lived and breathed metaphor. My mom's expression was transfixed on Arlon, breathing in every word he was saying.

"The nature of our humanity is pioneering. We are explorers, travelers, yes, but pioneers are wanderers with purpose. We are innovative and resilient. We are journeying together to create and restore." Arlon spoke with such authority, such conviction, that it was hard to disagree. I looked down at my fresh ink, the tiny words delicately scrawled out on my flesh. I smiled. Such a beautiful sentiment. I was a pioneer, and my purpose was to create and restore. I settled back, half listening, mostly daydreaming about my future, free of sadness, free of burden or guilt or any of the things weighing me down.

I needed to pay attention, I needed to learn, but I was getting distracted by my own stupid thoughts. I excused myself and went to the counter to order a coffee, a very sweet latte, which was the only way I could stand to drink the stuff. While I waited, I reached into my purse and popped the lid of the prescription bottle, taking two capsules out. I dry swallowed them and turned back to my mom, paranoid that she'd seen me. The barista handed me a large mug, and I stuffed a couple dollars in the tip jar before rejoining the group.

The woman next to my mom was holding both her hands and telling some long and winding story about her discovery of Arlon's teachings after her husband left her for his secretary. Tears streamed down both their faces. Damn, what had I missed? I sat back down and sipped my coffee.

"And what I got in the settlement, I gave to Arlon. It felt like such a relief, being rid of the weight of the money," the woman said eagerly. I paused and set the mug down.

"Wait. You gave him"—I pointed to Arlon—"*all* your money?" My heart thumped loudly against my ribs.

"My friends," Arlon interjected. "It's time to discuss our dreams. Let's show Julie and Glinda the power of manifestful thinking. Helen, you go first. Tell us your testimony."

A woman sitting across from me perked up, a short woman with cropped gray hair and a vest that looked hand crocheted.

"All right then." She folded her hands in her lap and took a deep breath. "A few years ago I went through a terrible divorce. It was the worst time of my entire life. Thankfully, I retained custody of my sweet Betsy. I turned to shopping to fill a hole in my heart. I'd watch the shopping networks and order things for my Betsy—clothes, shoes. I sent her to a little private school. The more I showered Betsy with things, the more I thought she'd love me."

I sat back and sighed internally. This sounded suspiciously like a support group. I didn't want to sit around and listen to people's sad stories. I had enough sad stories of my own. I drank more coffee and took several deep breaths to try and calm my racing heart.

Helen continued. "But no matter how much I bought for her, Betsy became resentful and cold. She could see through my attempts to buy her love. So one day, she just stood on my bed and urinated directly onto my feet."

I sat up straight, staring at this woman in shock and concern. "How old is she?" I gasped.

"Oh, she was thirty-eight at the time."

"Thirty-eight?" My mouth hung open.

"Well, in human years, yes."

"Maybe we should move on, sweet Helen," Arlon prompted her.

Wait. In *human* years? "I thought Betsy was your daughter?"

"Oh, well, I like to think of her that way, but no, she's my hairless Chinese Crested dog." She pulled a locket out from her sweater and showed me the tiny, faded picture of one of the weirdest looking dogs I'd ever seen—smooth gray skin, a white mane of hair, and crooked little teeth. She'd sent a dog to private school? I was still trying to make sense of this as my mom leaned over and looked at the photo, even holding the locket in her fingers before letting it drop back down to Helen's chest.

"What a sweet doggie," my mom said. Her heart was too kind.

"Arlon is the one who helped me realize that the only way to regain Betsy's love was to break the cycle of my shopping addiction. He helped me get the creditors off my back—"

"Bankruptcy?" I asked.

"Oh no, nothing that crass." Helen laughed, waving her hand dismissively. "No, no, I just transferred my—"

"I think we should hear from Brent now!" Arlon interrupted Helen with a clap of his hands. Helen simply nodded and sat back with a satisfied smile. Brent cleared his throat, but I cut him off.

"I'd like to know how Arlon helped you with your money problems," I said to Helen.

"Oh, dear Glinda," Arlon said. "Hows and whys and what-ifs—these are the traps that lie in our path toward self-actualization."

"Right. But no."

"How I help Helen is going to be different from how I help Brent or Laura or Julie." At the mention of my mother's name, he leaned over and gave my mom's hand a little squeeze.

My stomach lurched upward. My heart was beating faster.

"Two people have now mentioned giving money away. Where is this money going? Is it going to you? Are there dues? Fees? What's the cost of your help?" I looked at him, the scales falling from my eyes. Shit. I'd been taken in. And now that I'd realized it, I couldn't stuff it back in the box.

"No, no, no, you misunderstand, Glinda!" Arlon's ears turned red, as did the top of his forehead.

"Glinda," my mom whispered, and laid her hand on my knee, her sign to me to chill. I lifted the mug and took another swig of my latte.

"This usually isn't something I like to get into with our first-timers, because it's complicated, but I forget how bright you are, and I'm sure your mother is as well." He shot my mom a wide smile.

"Try me," I said returning the smile, disguising my growing disdain.

"Well, first and foremost, we believe that we are held hostage by material things, including the assigned currency of our oppressive governments."

"Rrrright." I held the mug up to my lips to hide my expression.

"Second, as a sign of commitment, we each make contributions for an official meeting hall."

"The owner of this place is tired of us showing up every Friday night," Laura said.

"We're being persecuted," Brent chimed in. "We need our own place."

I glanced around and realized I was the only one in the circle with a drink.

"Well, the owner might like you guys more if you actually bought something while you were here," I quipped. My mother nudged me, her brows knitted. I took another long drink before setting the mug down, ready to undo this little man with reason and logic and—my heart was pounding. I coughed and tensed up.

"Glinda?" Mom peered at me carefully. "What's the matter?"

"N-nothing." My heart was slamming against the walls of my chest. My head was swimming, my vision going blurry at the edges. All the sound, the ambient noise, the clinks of cups on saucers, the hiss of the espresso machine, the chatter of the teens laughing directly behind us—it all faded abruptly to silence. All I could hear was the rapid, inconsistent beating of my pulse in my head. I stumbled up, knocking the mug over, not having the wherewithal to do anything about it, and made it to the restroom. It was a single room, so I clicked the lock. I clutched the sink with both hands to steady myself. Then I turned on the faucet and splashed my face with cold water.

"Glinda?" My mom was at the door, knocking.

"I'm okay!" I called out, taking in deep, shaky breaths and then splashing my face again. The dizziness lessened, and I looked up at the mirror. I looked haggard, dark circles under my eyes. My face was thin, gaunt even. Beads of water stuck to my skin like the dew on a pear.

"Glinda, I'm getting the manager!"

"No!" I pulled the door open and stepped out to greet my frantic mother. "I just, I forgot to eat today, and then the caffeine . . ." I trailed off. She studied me hard and then hooked my elbow in hers.

"Let's get you home," she said. Thank God. She'd had enough too. We were going to escape.

We walked back to the group, who were all watching us in concern.

"Are you all right, dear Glinda?" Arlon asked, standing from his seat in a large armchair.

"I'm sorry, guys," I said, wiping my face with the back of my hand. "Didn't eat enough today—crazy schedule." I placed my hand over my heart, silently pleading with it to slow.

"I'm so sorry to leave early, but I've got to take her home." My mom smiled apologetically as she reached down and grabbed both our purses.

"Oh, wait!" Arlon reached across the coffee table and held out my mom's phone in his hand, which was cuffed with a gold wrist watch. "I hope you don't mind; I took the liberty of putting my number in your phone while you were away."

I was flabbergasted. This guy had just nosedived from eccentric weirdo to full-on creep.

"I hope we'll see you next week—same time and place!" He smiled at us, and my cheeks burned. Fat chance of that.

When we got to the car, where my mother insisted on driving, I was shaking, and I didn't know if it was from my physical symptoms or my anger at this man for tricking me. No, I wasn't mad at him. Con men gonna con. I was mad at myself. I pressed my forehead against the cool windowpane as Mom pulled out onto the freeway.

"Glinda, what's going on?" she asked, glancing at me as she merged into traffic.

"I told you, I didn't eat."

"Are you sure you didn't—I mean, Dorothy has mentioned—"

"What? What has Dorothy mentioned?" I was annoyed now. My heart rate was finally slowing a bit, although I still felt nauseous and my head was killing me.

"Nothing," she said quietly.

"Mom, I forgot to eat, and now I have a migraine. That's it. And listening to that moron talk about inner lights and whatnot just kind of pushed it over the edge." I sighed. "I'm really sorry I dragged you to that. False advertising. And I'm so sorry he took your phone. That was inexcusable. Who does that?"

"Oh, it's fine. I don't mind," she said as though she were excusing someone for speaking out of turn.

"What?" I was shocked. How did that invasion of privacy not bother her?

"I'm glad I went." She smiled the tiniest bit and her shoulders relaxed.

"Seriously?"

"Yeah, I mean I get that it might not be your cup of tea, but I really felt a connection with them. I don't know—it's a gut thing."

I stared at her, skeptical as hell.

I took a breath and tried to think like Dorothy. I mean it wasn't the worst thing in the world that she'd opened up a little, met some new people, even if they all acted like they'd just had a frontal lobotomy. And older people held each other to different standards when it came to phones and privacy. I mean, this was the same woman who had asked everyone for good password suggestions on Facebook.

"If you decide to go again, just promise me you won't give them any of your money."

"Of course not, Glinda." She winked at me. "I'm not completely senile."

We got home and my mom made me recline on the couch while she heated up some kale and potato soup and then brought it out on a little wooden tray. with a glass of orange juice and a stack of crackers made entirely of seeds. I took a bite and thought I'd just broken my front teeth.

"Thanks." I feigned a smile and crunched the shards of cracker fifty times before swallowing. We watched an episode of *The Great British Bake Off*, and by ten, I was feeling like a new person, just snuggling under a quilt on the couch in the dark with my mom. She kissed the top of my head.

"Glinda, you know I only worry about you because I love you."

"Then you must love me an awful lot." I laughed and then went upstairs to brush my teeth. All the things I needed were here at this house: a toothbrush, clothes, my bed. A weekend at home was just what I needed after a crappy start to the semester. I showered, changed into my pajamas, and left the bathroom to cross the hall to my room, when I noticed the light was still on downstairs.

I walked slowly down and found my mom still fully dressed, sitting in a chair, reading a book by lamplight.

"You're not going to bed? It's pretty late?"

"Oh no, I'm waiting on Arlon. I left my scarf at the coffee shop, and he was kind enough to call and offer to bring it by." She was smiling to herself. I hadn't seen the look of happiness on her face in a year.

"He couldn't wait until the morning?" I asked, a sinking feeling overtaking me.

"He insisted, and you know that's my favorite scarf. It took me two months to finish it."

"Oh. Cool," I managed.

I didn't know if my mom had simply forgotten her favorite, handmade scarf or if she'd perhaps left it intentionally. Or there was the darker possibility that Arlon had taken it when she wasn't looking. No matter which, one or both of them wanted the excuse to see each other again, and that gave me the heebie-jeebies.

I was wiped out. The manic state I'd been existing in for the last week had subsided into an extreme exhaustion. I went to bed. I went to fucking bed. Arlon came. He enchanted. He ensnared. And the next thing I knew, my mom was gone, and it was all my goddamn fault.

✦ 23 ✦

DISORIENTED AND DEAD

Present

They'd come. Arlon had lied. Wait—of course Arlon had lied.

I wasn't alone. I had help. I didn't have to save my mom. *We* could save my mom. Because they'd come.

But they'd heard me confess to hurting James. They hadn't come after me when I ran. I wanted to fold up into myself and disappear forever.

I wandered past Bessie, noting the green paint flaking off her wooden scales, the missing fang that Troy had accidently broken when we were climbing her to have our lunch one day.

Pioneers wander with purpose.

I came to the dunking booth and stopped, both transfixed and terrified by the steep ladder, the cloudy, stagnant water, and a horrible, brilliant idea cutting through the fog in my brain.

I looked around and saw no one behind me, so I made a quick dash for the offices, cutting through an alley, and entered a small door that put me in the plywood maze of halls that hid the inner workings of Maypole.

Mike's office was unlocked and dark, and papers littered the floor. Dust hadn't had a chance to settle. The computer sat on the desk, my reflection caught in its dull black screen.

"Please," I whispered, to God, to my dad, to anyone who would listen to me. And then I flipped a switch and held my breath.

★　★　★

Outside, I peered around the corner and spotted two of Arlon's henchmen walking briskly in the opposite direction, heads swiveling in their search for me. I had to get to the dunking booth. I waited until they'd gone around the side of a building, and then I made a dash for it, tripping over my robe, sending a shower of gravel scattering ahead of me on the path.

I stopped, grasping the buttons, ready to tear the cloth from my body, when something stopped me. A feeling, somewhere outside of my own consciousness. Panic. I couldn't take it off. I was a pioneer. The robe was comforting.

I shook my head, trying to clear it. The fatigue, the fog, they were still there, fighting for dominance within my brain. I had to keep it together. I couldn't forget. I couldn't forget the plan.

I dropped the robe in the dirt and took off running in the white linen gown underneath and the worn pair of sandals I'd been wearing since the night I'd left for Broken Bow.

The sun cast long shadows across the fair, which had gone eerily quiet.

The booth was waiting, the seat looming above my head. I imagined Troy standing here, looking up and smiling, giving me the courage to do what I had to do.

So I climbed the ladder. It was all I could do now. At the top, I stood on the familiar platform, holding my arms out for balance, and searched the fair. The entrance was hidden behind buildings, but I could see farther from up here than I could from the ground—and more importantly, I could be seen.

The crunching of gravel pulled my attention back toward the path that led to up to the booth. There was Arlon. He'd left the green robe behind and was dressed in slacks and a button-down shirt with a soft blue tie. It made him look so . . . so normal.

Two of his henchmen appeared behind him, but he waved them away. "Keep everyone back. Make sure we're not disturbed. I need to talk to her alone."

And just for a moment, the urge to crumple with despair was overpowered by a red film of rage. I held onto the shred of clarity I had left and prepared for battle.

They retreated back toward the entrance.

I took a breath and called out to Arlon. "Hey! You found me!"

"Glinda, I've been searching everywhere for you!" he said with feigned relief.

"Why?"

"Come back and finish the ceremony with us."

"I'm good." I laughed. Looking down at him, I felt unreachable; for the first time in days I could see above the smoke.

He raised an eyebrow. "How can I help you, Glinda?" he asked, approaching the tank.

"Ha! No *Sister* Glinda? I guess not, since you're about to marry my mom. That would be weird. So, like, Step-Daughter Glinda?"

"I'm worried about you, Glinda." It was getting easier to see through his bullshit. "Come down and let's continue with the ceremony."

"I can't," I said, preparing myself to provoke him, to bring all his wrath upon myself and hoping that my instincts were right. I was betting everything on it. "You're a criminal, Arlon, and even if I can't prove you killed Matthew Harrigan or Beverly McCoy, there's enough illegal medications and drugs in my dad's office to put you away for a few years."

He coughed and his face betrayed a moment of unease. "You don't know what you're saying."

"Arlon, Arlon, it's like I've said before—you may be a con man, but you're not very good at it." I smiled. "You really think you can run the kind of operation you have been without anybody catching on. But you've left too many loose threads."

Now his face had contorted, and I could see the rage that always lay underneath, just below the surface. "You don't know what you're talking about."

"Like hell I don't." At that moment a wave of nausea washed over me, and I grasped the railing to keep myself from falling forward. I sat down, trying to look calm and collected, while doing my best to stave off the disorienting muddle in my head I'd been fighting to get out of for a week.

Arlon chuckled and scratched his brow. "You need help. Real help, Glinda. Does Troy know how unhinged you are?"

The sound of his name sent a bolt of lightning through me, straight to my heart. "How do you know about Troy?"

He only smirked.

"Mark," I realized aloud. "He spied on us for you."

"So, where is your boyfriend, anyway?"

"He's not my boyfriend," I said under my breath, relieved that Arlon hadn't spotted my family or Troy in the crowd.

Arlon crossed his arms and took another step forward. "You messed that one up too, huh?"

I stayed quiet and bowed my head. Below, the murky water rippled in the orange glow of the setting sun. Maybe he was right. I could climb down, and the pioneers would take me in, and I wouldn't be alone—*stop. No. Focus. He lied. It's all lies. Troy lied. He did. But that's not—no, focus. It's Arlon. Arlon lied. Arlon's here. Troy is somewhere else. Troy is in Oklahoma.* Wasn't he?

I was forgetting something. Damn. The plan. I had to stay lucid. I was so tired. I was starving, and I had no idea what chemicals were still in my system. So tired. The moments of clarity were increasing and lasting longer, but I felt like I was always on the cusp of losing myself again.

"I may be alone, but at least I'm not going to prison," I got out. Immediately, Arlon's face turned a deep shade of scarlet, and his eyes flashed with anger. But just as quickly, he collected himself and smoothed back his hair. Then that disingenuous smile of his spread from ear to ear, and he chuckled.

"You're making a mistake."

"Maybe. But the thing is, Arlon, I've had this hunch for a while, and I've pushed it down because it just seemed so ridiculous. But now—well, that little stash in the office, getting prescriptions in other people's names, the illegal stuff. I just—I got to thinking. Detective Bryant might have a conflict of interest, but Detective Crumble might not. I think Detective Crumble might like to hear from me."

Arlon narrowed his eyes, like he was thinking. He moved his head from side to side. I could hear the bones in his neck pop. And then he looked back up at me. "Tell me, Glinda, how legal is your Adderall prescription? The extra pills, I mean." His eyes flicked down to the water and then back up to me.

"I'm not hiding anything anymore. I take responsibility for my past transgressions," I said, more to the universe than to him.

He burst out laughing, little droplets of spit spraying out. "I feel such pity for you, Glinda," he finally said, and then sighed. "How you shift the blame from yourself to others. I use many tools to help the pioneers reach the higher plane. Whatever you think you saw is perfectly legal—and more than that, it's used for a righteous purpose."

"Brainwashing people is righteous?" I said. "Poisoning them is righteous?"

"So you've made up some fantasy where I murder people?" He sniffed and looked back over his shoulder. We were still alone. "You know, Glinda, you were such a mess when I first saw you that day on campus—you know, the day we met." He paused for a beat. "I instantly knew I could help you if you'd just open yourself up to it. And then you rejected me, again and again. I gave you so many chances."

"So many chances?" I balked. "I'm sorry I wasn't as easily manipulated into your scammy society as you thought I'd be."

"You were the one I wanted." And the look on his face now made my breath catch in my throat. It was like, for the first time, I was seeing the real Arlon. His eyes were clearer, darker, his expression genuine, raw, and cold. It chilled my blood. Without the mask, he was somehow less human than before. The man behind the curtain had turned out to be something worse, something without a soul.

"But you wouldn't have it. Wouldn't have me or my ideas or any of it. I could see that the night at the coffee shop, the night you brought Julie and had taken so many of your little pills you had to leave early."

"What the hell are you talking about?" I watched him, every sense heightened, like my animal brain knew a predator was close.

"You can't say I am not benevolent. When you rejected me that night, I knew I could offer you another chance if I gave your mother a little extra attention. But you're such a little bitch, Glinda. Every chance I gave you to join us, to join me, you walked away. I offered everything, and you spat in my face. Do you know what I do to people who decide to leave me?"

I did. With certainty now.

"You're completely deranged!" I watched him, eyes wide open. "You killed Matthew Harrigan. I know it. But what about Beverly? She didn't want to move to the compound. She wanted out, and she would have taken her money with her. Did you have something to do with that?"

Arlon frowned as I spoke, but then he placed his insincere grin back on his face and resumed his car salesman persona. He looked around again to ensure our privacy.

"Dear Beverly was very old," he said, and I rolled my eyes, ready to take another load of his bullshit. But suddenly, his tone shifted, and he spoke up to me like he was letting me in on the greatest inside joke of all. His eyes glistened, and the corners of his mouth turned up. "She barely moved once the pillow was over her face."

Shit.

"I find it incredibly disrespectful when people betray me, Glinda. Betrayers must be punished. Yet I always give them another chance. I'm too generous."

He wasn't going to let me walk away from this. I wanted to glance at the camera, the little black half orb that sat directly across from the booth, and make sure the red light was still blinking, but he was watching me so closely. I couldn't give him a reason to suspect.

I was in it now. But this was the plan. All that mattered was getting the proof, saving my mom. But that didn't mean I was going to go voluntarily.

"Do you know how happy I was when you returned to us?" Arlon said. "I must admit, I was skeptical at first, but I decided to wait and see, and you seemed so close. So close. But damn."

"The truffles. Arlon, did you try to kill me with the truffles?"

He pursed his lips and chuckled quietly. "Do you know what happens when you mix caffeine powder with an upper like Adderall? I mean, a *lot* of Adderall . . . and a *lot* of caffeine powder? A heart attack. Poor little addict, overdosed. Poof!" He mimicked an explosion with his cupped hands. Then he laughed harder. "But you fucked that up too. You gave them to James and blew up your life for me. It was more than I could have asked for."

A tear fell from my eye and landed in the water below, sending little ripples out from the center. How could I feel such a sense of affirmation and such cold despondency at once?

"You're a sick fuck." My stomach churned, and I shivered. I stole a quick glance at the camera. The red light blinked, and I was washed in relief.

I had everything I needed; he'd said it. I could slide down the ladder and run. I might not get far, but I could try.

He stepped closer. "Now, it's time for you to come down, Glinda. It's time."

"You're done, Arlon." I stood up straighter on the ledge, glancing around, looking for a chance to escape. "And my mother may not believe me at first, but I will not rest until she sees you for who you are." I leaned forward and narrowed my eyes at him.

I could see the raging psychopathy behind his phony expression and his intense concentration trying to hold it back. His eyes darted around quickly, like those of a cornered rodent. Then his eyes planted on the trigger to the tank. He looked around wildly for witnesses, and then, without a word, he reached over and smacked it with the palm of his hand.

The seat creaked and I felt the familiar feeling of the board falling out from under me and the sudden rush down into the cold water.

Suddenly I was in the field of light again, the bright orb in my chest rising. The warmth. But the feeling dissipated, and I was underwater, cold and confused.

My heart was thumping against my ribs as I came up to the surface, spitting water out of my mouth and taking in a deep breath.

Arlon was now perched on the ladder.

"I'm sorry," he said. "I just care for you so, and it hurts me when you reject my teachings." He held out a hand.

I looked up into his face and smiled. His hand, his offer to help me. He could save me. I'd rejected him and he'd forgiven me. Everything was so much simpler when I just trusted him, when I just—

No, this isn't right. This isn't—

I put my hand in his.

But when I saw his eyes, a wave of nausea swept over me. His pupils were dilated, turning his eyes black. He was smiling, his shoulders relaxed, his expression eager. But his eyes . . .

They snapped me back into my right mind, fast and hard, like a slap across the face. This was a man who was about to kill me; I could feel it in my bones. He pulled me to the side and helped me up like Troy the night he dunked me. It was strange that my mind went there, now, in this moment of peril. Troy's eyes, looking into mine, my heart beating faster, my brain fighting against the urge to kiss him.

But now I was face to face with Arlon, and the energy between us was much different, like a current of ice that shot through my chest cavity and wrapped itself around my heart. His lips curled up into a twisted snarl.

"Too many loose threads, you said?" He gripped my hand hard, making me wince in pain. "Time to cut them off."

"What?"

"Your mom is going to have a hard time with this. Her mentally disturbed daughter killing herself the day of her wedding. But you know what she'll do: she'll need me to get through it. So, thank you, Glinda. Thank you for yet again sacrificing yourself to bring your mother and me together."

"Arlon, wait—don't!" I cried out as he released his grip on my hand. I fell back into the water, a thousand thoughts flying through my brain, confusion and certainty swirling together with the drag of the water on my body as I sank down.

When I'd climbed the tank, I known this might happen, and I'd known it was worth it if it meant an end for this evil man. But now that I was face to face with the terror, I didn't want to die. I didn't want to die! I came up gasping—and that's when he wrapped his fingers around my hair and plunged me back down under the water.

I braced my feet against the bottom and pushed up, but he was leaning down over me now, forcing my head under with both hands. My scalp was on fire. My hands broke the surface. I clawed at his arms. The shirt was slick. I couldn't get a grip.

I pulled, trying to go deeper and break free. Something was on my wrists. My hands were tied; I caught a glimpse of the blue silk tie. His hands were on my head, his fingers entangled in my hair. Down. Pressure.

My lungs began to ache. The urge to breathe was fire. My dad wasn't here to pull me out this time, to tell me I was okay, and laugh and cry at the same time with me.

Where were they? They'd left. They'd heard my confession. They'd left. Nobody was going to save me.

Eyes open. Burning. Unbearable. My vision was a series of snapshots in the water, my thrashing legs, the swirl of bubbles all faded to blue. An impenetrable blue haze with black patches floating in and out of view.

I am alone.

Hazy blue and quiet. Water in my mouth, in my nose. Nowhere to go.

So, this was what dying was like.

I was *pissed*.

After everything, after all the miles and tears and epiphanies and near misses, this stupid motherfucker was actually going to kill me.

But the anger faded too. I couldn't stay mad. Not when the visions before my eyes were so lovely. I was sitting across from Troy in the rowboat, the moonlight making his smile light up every part of my body. I looked into his eyes.

"I'm dying, Troy," I whispered.

"It's okay, I'm here." He took my hands and held them tightly, filling me with peace and calm. Quiet and blue. It rushed into my brain, my lungs, and I think I was smiling.

That thought was what played me out.

◆ 24 ◆

RESUSCITATED AND REFOCUSED

I FELT WARM LIPS on mine. I smiled. Blinked. My vision was blurry.

"Kiss me again," I tried to say, but no sound was coming out.

"I think she just said, 'Kiss me again'!" Was that Dorothy? Why was she crying?

I opened my eyes again and directly above my face was West, wearing a revolted expression. "Seriously, Glinda? You almost die and you're still being disgusting?"

My throat was burning and my chest was heavy. I rolled onto my side and coughed. Water sputtered out on the pavement. I groaned and rolled onto my back again, squinting in the greenish light.

"Is she okay?" Troy was kneeling near my feet, looking at me like I was a ghost or something.

I pushed myself up onto my elbows and looked around at their dumb, petrified faces. Even James looked like someone had died.

"What the hell, guys?" I croaked out.

"They held us back, said to give you privacy." Dorothy glanced in the direction of the bonfire, hidden behind several structures. "We couldn't get past them, so finally West distracted them by screaming, and we broke through. We got here as he was pushing you under."

"Your sister is actually the one who pulled him off," James said, rubbing her back. Dorothy looked sick. I glanced at Troy, trying not to be obvious. He was soaking wet. He'd been the one who had jumped in and carried me out.

"Troy and I were going to chase him down because the stupid coward took off running as soon as he realized we were here," James said. "But then Dorothy said you weren't breathing, so we had to let him go."

"You let him get away?" I tried to get onto my feet and failed. Everyone was hovering around me like I was going to break.

"Your life is more important—" Dorothy started, but I cut her off.

"Fuck that! You should have let me die. That bastard still has Mom."

"Well, they're all long gone now," West said quietly as the other three stared at me in horror.

"What are you talking about?" Dorothy had fresh tears in her eyes.

"I'm worthless! You don't need me—you need Mom! You should have saved her and let me die!"

"Stop saying that!" Troy broke in, his voice cracking with frustration. He threw his hands up and stepped back.

Dorothy leaned closer to me, looking into my eyes. "Glinda, listen to me. I don't know what you've been through, but you need to know that I'm sorry. I sent you off and—well, I shouldn't have let you go," she whispered.

"It's fine."

"No, it's not. I realized it almost immediately. The four of us drove back the next day."

I stared at her, not understanding. "You did?"

"Yeah. We've been looking for you for two weeks. Sleeping at Troy's and going to your usual haunts. We checked the house every day, but they said you weren't there, and they wouldn't let us in. We've been staking it out for days, just hoping to catch a glimpse of you."

"I've been there," I said quietly.

"I know. I knew you must be. We waited until everyone headed out tonight, and then we followed, came in during the ceremony."

I put my hands over my face and fell back, groaning. "You heard my confession."

"Hey, Sis," James said. I dropped my hands and looked up at him. He was giving me a gentle smile. "It was your confession that convinced us you were really in trouble."

I sucked in an aching breath. "You didn't believe it, then?"

"Of course not!" James exclaimed. "But that dude has done a number on you."

"You have no idea." I blinked up at the sky. "I think I—I'm trying. I'm really trying, but I don't trust myself."

They were all four silent, watching me trying to figure it out. And all I could do was lie there and try not to cry any more than I already had.

"Hey, West got it on her phone," Troy said finally, not taking his eyes off me. "Let's go turn this son of a bitch into the police."

"That's a little more complicated than you'd think." I grabbed onto West's shoulder and made her help me up. I wobbled a little, but she caught me. "He's got cult members in the force. I don't know how many, and I don't know who. Detective Bryant is one, for sure. Meanwhile, he's got Mom. We have to get to her."

"This is bad," West whimpered.

"If he's smart, he didn't go back to the house," Dorothy muttered.

"Well he's not smart, so—"

"Really, Glinda? Maybe if you'd given him more credit from the start, he wouldn't have tricked us for so long," West said emphatically.

"I—" She had a point. Shit.

"No," Dorothy interrupted. West and I stopped. "Now listen to me, and listen to me carefully—Glinda is *not* responsible for this. We all are. I wasn't paying attention, and I should have been. So, from now on, we're going to work together. We sink or swim as a family."

"Maybe don't use a drowning metaphor right now." I wanted to be sincere. I wanted to throw my arms around her and sob and thank her for coming, but the wall of self-defense was back.

"Glinda, you aren't responsible for all of us." She put her hands on my shoulders and looked right into my face. "You know that, right?" The wall fell. I couldn't say anything.

Troy cleared his throat, and we all turned to him.

"We should get going." Then he looked at me and flicked his eyes up to the security camera. I nodded. He understood.

He and James started walking and talking a few steps ahead of us, while Dorothy and West got on either side of me and walked slowly, as though I might collapse again. It was surreal. I was afraid that I was about to wake up in the closet again. How were my sisters here? The sisters I didn't deserve, not by a long shot.

"Guys, I'm okay."

"You were underwater for a long time," Dorothy said.

"I'm fine, really."

"Were you scared?" West asked.

"West!" Dorothy shot our younger sister a glare across me, but I waved her back.

"It's fine. I'm fine. It's weird . . . I was scared, but then . . . it was strange . . ." The vision of Troy and me in the boat came rushing back all at once. I'd almost forgotten. I stopped walking and looked up to where Troy was walking ahead. He turned back and saw me. Our eyes locked for a moment. He gave me a sad little shrug, and then he turned and said something to James.

Stop it, Glinda. Not now.

Troy then sprinted ahead, toward the offices.

James came back to us. "Said he had to grab something."

I coughed and stumbled, but Dorothy caught my arm.

"Glinda, are you okay?" West was peering into my face, looking for any little sign I was dying.

"I'm just a little woozy. I'm coming off some tea."

"Tea?" West raised an eyebrow.

"Maybe we should take her to the hospital. We could tell them what happened, call the police? Surely the entire force isn't compromised," James suggested. Just then Dorothy's phone started ringing, and she looked down.

"It's Mom! Shh!" Dorothy held the phone up to her ear as we all gathered around, trying to hear. "Mom? Mom?" Her eyes grew wide, and she covered the phone with her hand and whispered, "It's Arlon. He saw West filming him."

"Where's Mom?" I cried.

"Arlon, where is my mother?" She listened and the corners of her mouth drew into a frown. "No, listen, we'll be there, please—dammit!" She lowered the phone and looked at me helplessly. "He hung up."

"If he's heading back to the house, let's go. We've got to get her away from him."

"No, listen to me. He said that he and Mom are going to get married as planned at eight sharp. He said he wants us there, all of us, and we had better bring the phone with the video on it. If we don't, he says he has a very special ending planned for the ceremony. Glinda, he said if we want to see her alive, we had better do what he says." Dorothy was choking on her words, fighting back the inevitable tears.

"That's it! We need to call the fucking police." James put his hand on Dorothy's shoulder. "This has gone way too far."

"No! James, please. He was explicit. He'll hurt her; he might do worse."

"And if we call the police, he'll know," I said. "Brother Bryant will notify him. We've got to get to her. Now."

"*Brother* Bryant?" Dorothy wrinkled her brow.

"I am not giving him my phone." West was indignant.

"West! Seriously!" I cried. "Also, we don't need the phone."

"West, upload your video to the cloud, so if he somehow gets a hold of your phone, the evidence will still be there," James suggested.

"I totally would, but my phone has no internet. Glinda's and my phones got cut off."

"We don't need the phone!" I tried again. They weren't listening. That was fine. Maybe the fewer people who knew my plan, the better.

"Guys, it's 7:43!" Dorothy wailed, holding up her phone.

Troy jogged back over to rejoin our group.

"Arlon said all five of us had to be there." Dorothy started letting out little gasps, leaning against James for support. "What in the world do you think he's going to do to her?"

"I don't know. But Mom is so far gone, he could do just about anything." I looked up at the sun, now an orange ball slipping below the western horizon. There was no time to even think. Every time I thought we had him, that bastard was one step ahead. Maybe he was smarter than me. And he still had control of the one person most important in the world to us. He was insecure and he was a weasel. We had the upper hand, but he was the most dangerous when he was cornered.

"Everybody in the van," I said simply.

"You have a plan?" James looked hopeful.

"No." I shook my head. "My plans usually turn into raging dumpster fires. But Mom needs us. We have to go to her."

Everyone started forward, but I reached out and tapped Troy on the shoulder. He spun around and tilted his head. I waited until everyone was just out of earshot. "You got it?"

"Yep." He patted his pants pocket.

I sighed with relief. "I just—I'm glad you came back for me."

He pursed his lips and glanced around before resting his eyes on me with a stern expression that made me hate myself.

"Of course. Your sisters weren't going to leave you alone with that madman." Then he softened a bit. "I hope you're okay. Are you okay?"

"I . . . I don't know." I swallowed a lump in my throat. "But I need you to know I'm sorry, and I owe you an explanation and a much better apology, but I can't go there right now. I need to focus on helping my mom."

He studied me and then nodded slowly. "Let's do it." And then he did something that broke my heart in half. He gave me what I assumed was supposed to be a supportive smile, but it was fake. The beautiful, genuine radiance that I had grown to love was gone.

I'd lost him.

* * *

Troy jumped in the driver's seat, while James and Dorothy climbed up in the cabin. West and I clambered into the back and shut the door. We sat side by side in the dark, between two crates of MaXouts. As Troy pulled out of the parking lot, West took my hand and gave it a squeeze.

"You really rode back here all the way back to Texas?"

"Yeah, it sucked."

I couldn't help laughing. And then she couldn't help laughing. She laid her head against my shoulder. "Glinda?"

"Yeah?"

"Have you noticed Dorothy's been crying . . . like a lot?"

"Well, her mother is being held captive by an L. Ron Hubbard knock-off who just tried to murder her sister, so yeah, I didn't really think that much of it."

"Yeah, I guess. I mean, she cried the whole drive back to Dallas, and she's cried on and off every day since."

I sat with that a minute. "West?"

"Yeah?"

"Your hair stinks."

She sat up and rolled her eyes. "Stop sitting next to me if you're going to always complain about it."

"Sorry."

After a beat, she muttered, "I ran out of dry shampoo."

I laughed. It felt so strange to laugh.

"Glinda? Mom's going to be okay, right?"

I squeezed her hand and closed my eyes. *I hope so, kid. I hope so.*

"Are you okay?" she murmured. "Really?"

"Yeah, don't worry about me," I lied. *Please worry about me.*

We drove toward the house, and each mile sobered me up and left me with a growing hollowness deep in the pit of my being. For so long, all I'd wanted was to be home—and now, I wanted to be as far from that house and the people and memories in it as possible.

I laughed. It just escaped, like this giddy little burst. West moved her head and looked at me. "What?"

"Nothing. I just—" I rubbed my temples. "I'm so used to saying I'm fine. Without pause. Without question. And I'm not." I laughed again. "Honestly, kid, I think I'm traumatized as hell."

• 25 •

THRILLED AND THREATENED

WHEN WE PULLED OVER a few yards from the entrance to the property, James flipped the interior light on and pulled the curtain aside so we could all talk. He turned to Dorothy, who looked a little pale. "You okay?"

"Yep."

"I don't understand why Troy and I don't just go in there and mess him up. He's a big old coward."

"Because then you could be arrested for assault, dear." Dorothy patted his hand. He bent over and gave her a small peck on the lips. I smiled.

"Well, come on. We can't wait here all night." James looked anxiously toward the drive.

"Wait, let me go look around first, and then we'll figure out how we want to make our entrance." Dorothy was already unbuckling.

"No!" James cried and took her hand.

"It'll be fine."

"No. Not you."

"I'll go." I didn't wait for an argument. I crept to the back doors.

I stepped down onto the asphalt as quietly as I could, and after looking to make sure the coast was clear, I sprinted across the road and to the drive. It was about a five-minute walk from the road to the front of the house. I tried to move without making much noise, but every step resonated. The house was dark and motion-less. But it was not quiet.

They were inside. And Arlon was screaming.

I turned back, jogged along the drive. I could see the van's headlights through the trees. I stepped out onto the road and saw Troy still sitting in the driver's seat. Dorothy was leaning against the passenger door, almost asleep. How could she be fall-ing asleep at a time like this?

Wait. *Wait.*

The crying, the middle-of-the-night pies . . .

I ran back across the street without looking for cars, swung around to the passenger door, and tore it open so fast that it nearly hit me in the face.

Dorothy startled. "What's wrong? What happened?" she exclaimed.

"You're . . . you're not—Wait! You're . . ."

Her eyes grew wide, and she shot a glance over at Troy, who had a super confused look on his face.

"What's going on?" West poked her head through the curtain.

"Nothing—just a minute!" Dorothy pushed me back and climbed out of the cab carefully. She shut the door softly and then grabbed my arm, sinking her nails into my flesh. She pulled me along the side of the van, out of sight of the windows.

"Ouch! Shit!" I pulled my arm away and rubbed the five tiny crescents that were now imprinted in my skin.

"I'm what, Glinda?" Dorothy lowered her voice, watching me carefully.

"You're pregnant?" It sounded surreal coming out of my mouth. Everything seemed delayed as I watched her mouth, waiting for an answer, a reaction, anything.

"Yes. Dammit, Glinda, yes." Her words barreled right past my head, going eighty miles an hour as they left her mouth.

And then everything cleared. The air, the sky, my brain—it all brightened up and came into focus again.

"Oh my God," I gasped.

"You're smiling?" she asked, puzzled.

"I am? Am I?" I put a hand up to my cheek and felt my mouth stretched tight in a broad smile. I giggled.

"What is happening?" Dorothy had her eyebrows raised in surprise as she watched me.

"Are you really?" I whispered.

"Yes."

"Oh my God."

I grabbed her and hugged her tightly. She wasn't hugging me back. In fact, no—she was breathing fast, like she was about to have a panic attack. I pulled away and studied her in concern.

"What's wrong? I'm sorry I guessed. I mean, it's probably the stupid twin thing we have—you know, the telepathy thing."

"Glinda, for the last time, we don't have telepathy." She clenched her jaw tightly, like she was holding back tears.

"Oh, Dor, what's wrong?"

"I'm scared." She sighed.

"That's why you didn't tell me?"

She peeked up at me. "Are you mad?"

What? "Of course not!"

"You were pissed I got married and didn't tell you."

"Well, yeah, but that's different. Gah, Dorothy, you're having a baby!" I balled up my fists and did a little jumping, squealing thing that probably would have embarrassed the shit out of me if I'd been able to see myself, but at that moment I truly did not care. She shushed me and looked around nervously.

"Please don't tell West or Troy. I need to tell Mom first. Oh God, Glinda, I need my mom!" She started wiping away the tears as soon as they escaped her lids, muttering *shit* with every single one. Well, this made some sense. The girl gets herself knocked up two hundred miles from home, and then her crazy sister shows up with a shitload of her own problems, and here I was, wondering why she didn't seem like herself.

"Hey . . . hey, listen to me. I know you do. We all do." I pulled her away so I could look her in the eyes. "And we're going to do everything we can to get her back, Dor. But listen to me: you are going to be okay. You're like waaay better at this whole adult thing than I ever have been. You're going to be a great mom. And if you'll let me, I will be there, to help you."

"Thank you." She wiped her nose with her arm and looked at me, her lip quivering. "I'm sorry, Glinda."

"Nope. No more. We're good."

"Shit!" Dorothy perked up and looked back toward the road. "We've gotta go!"

She was right. With urgency, I rapped on the side of the van and the others hopped out, ready to go.

The five of us moved together; Dorothy found my hand and clamped on hard.

"Be careful," I muttered. "The man tried to murder me."

"We know—we stopped him," James whispered back.

"No, no, I mean before that."

James stopped and spun around. "What?"

"Shh!" Dorothy pressed her hand over his mouth. We were halfway there, standing under the post oaks.

"What are you talking about?" Dorothy breathed.

"The truffles. He poisoned them with Adderall and caffeine powder. They were meant for me. And then I regifted them to James."

I couldn't read their expressions, but no one was arguing with me.

"Okay," James finally whispered. "Okay."

We started moving again.

"Oh, and he told me killed Beverly McCoy."

"What?" West cried, and then slapped a hand over her own mouth.

Dorothy gripped my arm. "Glinda, are you sure about this?"

"I mean, the man locked me in a closet for days and drugged me, so I think he's capable of most anything."

"*What?*" Troy cried out.

"Shh!" I hissed at him.

We stepped out of the trees and beheld the house, looming over us like a mausoleum. And standing in the light of the doorway was Arlon Blight, a big smile on his face.

"Are you coming in or not?"

· 26 ·

TRAPPED AND TORMENTED

"MAKE WAY FOR OUR guests!" Arlon called out and the crowd in the living room parted to let us pass through. The air was stifling hot as thirty bodies pressed against each other. A large fire was roaring in the hearth, adding to the heat. The pioneers opened up a small space in the center of the room for us to stand. I looked at the faces of the members as we walked past. They avoided my eyes. I saw Jason and he gave me a weak smile.

I felt a pang of guilt, which immediately turned to fear. Was Arlon still in my head? How could I trust myself?

Dorothy hung in the back as we entered the circle. As soon as we were inside, the members moved back into place, trapping us in the ring. Arlon was now draped in a white robe with gold thread embroidery along the collar in the shape of stars.

I stepped forward. "Hey, man! It's me, your super alive murder victim!"

"Dear, sweet child, I saved you from drowning yourself this evening. You confessed to the attempted murder of James, here, and then ran when you couldn't face it any longer. I rushed to find you and stop you from this unspeakable decision."

The members oohed and ahhed. Several applauded him.

"Give it up, man." James stepped forward, his face remaining calm, but his eyes betraying an intense anger beneath the surface.

"I have no idea what crazy ideas this delusional girl has put in your head, but I assure you—"

"Don't!" Troy came and stood beside James. "You hate Glinda because she saw through you. You put her down because of how pitiful you are! And you tried to kill her because you're terrified of her!"

"Really? Is that what you think? Tell me, did Glinda tell you how we met? Did Glinda tell you how she begged me save her mother? Or how she joined the Society first?"

"Bullshit!" Troy looked around like he was assessing how he could get to Arlon. Brother Jim and Brother Whoever stepped forward, and each placed a hand on Troy's and James's shoulders. The guys shrugged them off, but the muscle continued to stand directly behind them.

"Oh no, not bullshit. Tell them, Glinda." Arlon smirked at me. "Unless you'd prefer to continue lying to your friends. It is what you do best."

Troy looked at me, nearly wild-eyed.

"It's not—I mean—I—" I stammered. "It's true. I brought Mom to Arlon. Before I knew what he was. I caught on fast, but it was already too late." I hung my head. "It's my fault."

Troy's expression morphed from disdain at Arlon to complete and utter shock. He shrank back; the fight had left him. I couldn't see Dorothy's face, but I expected it looked very similar.

"I believe you have something for me?" Arlon held out his hand to West. She rolled her eyes and reached into his pocket to retrieve her phone.

"Just be careful." She placed it in his palm and stepped back.

Arlon scrolled for a minute and he must have found the video because he watched the screen intently for a moment, before turning the phone off. "I presume you were unable to upload this video to anything?"

"Yes, Arlon. You cut our service," I piped in. I was getting impatient. I needed to see my mom. Where was she?

"And where is the other thing?" Arlon asked, his icy stare boring into me.

I took a slow, deep breath and stared right back. "What are you talking about?"

"Don't play dumb." He squinted his eyes and then motioned toward the crowd. "Brother Mark?"

The skeletal man stepped forward, his green robe hanging off of him like he was the grim reaper himself. He held out his pale hand and uncurled his bony fingers, thrusting his expectant palm toward me.

"You wanted the phone, that's all we have," I said, avoiding looking into Mark's soulless eyes.

"I know you turned the cameras on. I saw you leave the offices," Mark croaked. "Now give it to me."

"I don't have anything!" I shouted. In one fluid motion, Mark shot his clawlike hand out and gripped my throat. I started to pull away, when I felt the cold metal of a boot knife pressing against the flesh beneath my jaw.

Troy and James tried to lurch forward, but the many hands on them kept them firmly in place, their arms restrained behind their backs.

"I swear, I don't have it," I whispered hoarsely. Mark pressed the point of the knife deeper into my jaw, causing a sting of pain.

"I have it!" Troy cried. My heart sank. All heads turned toward him except Mark, who was looking into my face with devilish delight at the horror he must have seen there. His lips curled into a smile, revealing stained, gray teeth.

"Troy, don't!" I tried.

"No, here! Just stop—let her go! It's in my pocket," he continued, nodding down at his left hip. Brother Brent reached in and pulled out a black memory card triumphantly. He brought it over to Mark, who glanced at it and nodded in confirmation.

Brent dropped the memory card into Arlon's waiting hand.

"All right, Brother Mark," he said. Mark kept the knife against my skin. I gasped, trying not to hyperventilate. Drowning was one thing, but the threat of being stabbed was enough to paralyze me.

"Stop! You have everything now! Just stop!" Dorothy was screaming behind me.

"Mark!" Arlon said louder, and Mark sighed and dropped his hand and the knife. I stumbled backward into West, who caught me and hugged me tightly around the waist.

Arlon spread his arms wide again, holding West's phone in one hand and the memory card in the other.

"Brothers and sisters! Today is a great day! Today, Sister Julie officially becomes Mother Julie as she and I are united in matrimony and elevated to a higher plane of existence." Without warning, he flung the phone and the card into the flames. The fire leapt up and hissed wildly as the phone exploded from the heat.

"Nooo!" West wailed, and I held her back. There was no proof now. I had nothing. Yet again, someone had chosen my life over stopping Arlon. A sense of ambivalence overtook me.

"Today, those who would fight against our unity have come here to find that, despite their greatest efforts, they cannot overcome our spirit and our energy. The Society is strong!"

The members all cheered as the five of us looked around wildly.

"Take the two boys out and tie them up in the barn. I'll deal with them after the ceremony," Arlon ordered.

Immediately hands were on Troy and James again. Troy pushed Brother Jim back, while three pioneers grabbed James and held him against the doorframe. There were too many pioneers pressing in on all sides of them.

"Troy!" I cried out as they dragged him out of the room. He grasped onto the doorframe, but Brother Jim struck his knuckles, and Troy and James were gone.

"Stop! Don't hurt them!" Dorothy looked like she was about to jump Arlon. I put my hand on her shoulder to steady her.

"We'll get them," I whispered in her ear as reassuringly as I could.

"Bring out Mother Julie!"

I glanced around the sea of green robes, but I didn't see my mother anywhere.

"You're done, Glinda." Arlon was looking down at me with a sick, smug smile.

"You're insane," I snarled back.

I closed my eyes and waited. The cheering increased until it all just sounded like madness around me, swirling up into screams of torment.

Mom came down the stairs and stood beside Arlon.

"Mom!" I called out.

She turned her head and looked at me, her expression still blank.

"You see, Glinda? Your mother has cast you away, just as we strive to cast all anchors of our past life into the fire." The crackle of the fireplace applauded his words. "Isn't that right, pioneers?"

The multitude agreed loudly.

"I asked you here to witness this, your mother, of her own accord, agreeing to marry me. And then, once and for all, you must accept that she is not yours. She has risen above you." Arlon grinned at me. "Go ahead—say whatever you like to her. You'll see."

"You brainwashed her!" West yelled out.

"Nonsense! No such thing!"

I looked at my mom, saw her white knuckles clutching Arlon's hands, and I stepped forward. "Mom? It's me, Glinda." She looked at me, not betraying a single thing. I lowered my voice slightly. "I know you don't want to do this. I know you're scared, and I know your heart is still broken from losing Dad. So is mine. Please, Mom, come away from this man, and let's heal together."

She opened her mouth to say something, but then closed her lips and looked at me with a hint of sadness.

"You see?" Arlon laughed triumphantly.

Dorothy pushed past me, and Arlon grimaced, but when my mom had no reaction to her either, his face relaxed.

"Mom, it's Dorothy. I'm here. I'm back."

"Yes, the same Dorothy who left home without a word and hasn't seen her mother in almost two years!" Arlon cried. My mother blinked and gazed back up at Arlon. So much for mentally slapping her.

But Dorothy wasn't done. "No! It's the same Dorothy who came back because she needs her mother."

Do it, Dorothy. Tell them.

"Mom, I'm here. Let's get out of here."

"Dorothy the coward! Dorothy who shows up just in time to profit from the amazing things we've built here together!" Arlon cried.

Someone was on the other side of me. West. The three of us stood in a row, face to face with my mother and Arlon, the rest of the cult encircling us all.

"Mom? Do you actually want to marry Arlon?" West looked up at Arlon defiantly, daring him to shut her up.

My mother looked at her, then her eyes shifted to me, and finally to Dorothy. I hadn't seen my mother look at me—I mean really *look* at me—in ages. It sent a shiver down my spine. She was still in there. She really was.

"Answer them!" Arlon bellowed. "Tell them and tell all of us that you are choosing to join with me in a union that will extend beyond the stars!"

But she remained silent, her eyes now on the rug.

Brother Jim returned to the living room and went to Arlon. He handed him something and then nodded. Whatever it was, Arlon slipped it into his pocket and set his jaw. Suddenly, Brother Bryant came racing in. He'd discarded his robe. He stood with his back to us, and they spoke a moment in hushed tones. When he stepped away, Arlon looked more unhinged than ever.

"It seems we have a traitor in our midst." He snarled. "Dammit! I warned you. Fucking hell, I warned you!"

My gaze shifted, and I gasped. Arlon was gripping my mother's arm with one hand and in the other was a small, black handgun. Gasps and cries sounded all around me.

"Brother Bryant has informed me that the police are on their way here. Someone called them, and that someone will pay. Put those two under the stairs!" he barked, waving the gun at Dorothy and me. Then he let go of my mother and grabbed West by the arm. "If you make a single sound, I will blow her head off." Spit sprayed out from his mouth. West whimpered. My mom stood there like a zombie.

"West, it'll be okay!" I cried as two of the pioneers grabbed Dorothy and me. The door to the closet stood wide, like an open tomb. I closed my eyes, grasped my twin sister's hand, and fell forward into the darkness.

Instinctively I ducked and missed the corner of the stairs. I squeezed my eyes shut and tried to breathe, but the air was suffocating. My chest was heavy, and my heart pounded like it might explode.

"Shit. Shit. Shit. I can't be in here, I can't breathe!" I clutched at my throat. Dorothy found my hands in the darkness and pressed them against her chest.

"Slow down and take a deep breath. You're having a panic attack." She sounded so calm. How could she be this calm? Ribbons of light from around the door shone through, broken by the movement of people in front of the closet. I could see her in bits and pieces, but never all of her face at once.

"Dorothy, you gotta call someone. Call the cops!"

"They grabbed my phone, Glin, but it's going to be okay." She sounded so calm, or at least she was pretending to be, to calm me.

"I—I'm going to die in here." I pressed my fingers against my eyes until I saw stars.

"No, you're not. Put your head down and breathe." Dorothy rubbed my back. I took two gasping breaths and tried to relax my shoulders.

"Dor, they put me in here—" I couldn't finish; my throat was closing up again.

"Shh. Hey, you remember when we were little and we'd hide in here with a flashlight and tell each other ghost stories until we scared ourselves, and then run out to find Mom?"

I nodded, trying to catch my breath. "I appreciate—you trying to—distract—me." I was hyperventilating, struggling to get the words out. "But—I can't—I can't be alone—in here again."

"Shh." She kept rubbing my back. "You're not alone. You have me. You have me."

"Do I?" I didn't mean for it to sound as defensive as it came out.

"Glinda, I screwed up."

"What?"

"It's my fault," she said breathlessly. "I've been too scared, and I just don't know how we got like this, but I hate it."

I couldn't say anything. I grasped her hand, my fingers trembling as I clung to hers. My breathing slowed. The panic subsided, replaced with a dull ache. We just sat there, two broken halves, both feeling the pain of being ripped apart and having no idea how to fix it.

After what seemed like forever, she pulled away and used both hands to wipe her eyes and cheeks. We turned to each other, and searched the other's face in the lines of light, like we were just now seeing the other for the first time in years.

"I shouldn't have let you go," she whispered.

"I let you leave Christmas morning and felt like I'd destroyed our family."

"You didn't destroy anything by yourself."

"And now you must hate me even more."

"What?"

"Because of Arlon. Because I never told you I met Arlon first. I fell for his stupid bullshit, Dorothy. I introduced him to Mom. It's all because of me." I pressed my hand over my mouth to suppress a sob.

"Hey, I already knew that."

What? "You did?"

"Yeah, Mom told me when she first started going. I didn't know you were holding onto that guilt."

"Of course I was. It's my fault. It's all my fault—" I couldn't finish. I just pressed my fingers harder against my lips, rocking with each sob as it hit. Quickly, Dorothy wrapped her arms around me and whispered into my ear.

"Glin, I've never blamed you for this. Mom's a grown woman. She's the one who fell for Arlon's crap. She's the one who stayed, and she's the only person who can get herself out of it. Not you, not me. Julie Glass is the only person who can save Julie Glass. We can help, we can try to guide her, but in the end, she's the one who has to realize it."

She held me and we both just sat there, quietly making peace with this newfound sense of clarity that had come too goddamn late.

Who knows how long we would have sat there, but a noise from up the living room caused us both to flinch and pull away.

The voices were muffled, but we could make out a little.

". . . got a call . . ."

". . . wedding! Everything is fine . . ." It was Bryant, assuring the officers that everything was on the up-and-up.

". . . mind if we look around?"

There were officers in the room, officers who weren't cult members. All I had to do was scream. Bang on the door. Dorothy must have been thinking the same thing, because she rose to her knees and moved forward like she was going to pound on the door. She raised a fist in the air, but I grabbed it before it made contact with the wood.

She looked at me and I shook my head, eyes wide, mouth drawn tight.

Don't do it. He's crazy. He'll do it. He'll kill West. He'll kill West and Mom and then himself. He's capable of anything.

And for once our twin telepathy seemed to work, or else she could read the expression on my face. She lowered her hand and sank back on her heels.

"Glinda, I can't take it," she said in a low voice.

"Trust me, Dor, he'll blow everyone away if he has the chance. He's cornered," I whispered back.

There were some thuds, some more voices, and then silence. We waited. Minutes went by. Then there was a change in the air, and they were gone. The murmur of voices picked back up, but it sounded like the anxious chatter of a small crowd.

"We need a plan," Dorothy said.

"I'm out of plans," I muttered in despair . She twisted her lips like she was thinking. I waited, holding my breath, praying she had some brilliant idea that just hadn't occurred to me. But then she frowned and shook her head. We sat in silence again, both knowing that when that door opened, we had no idea what to expect on the other side.

My feet were falling asleep, so I changed positions and then broke the quiet. "Dorothy?"

"Yes?"

"Why didn't you take the bar?"

"This really isn't the time to get into it."

"In case we die, I want to know."

Dorothy turned to me, tears streaming down her face, lips trembling.

"I'm sorry! I shouldn't have asked. Go back to the part where we were making up!" I said frantically, struggling to keep my voice low.

"No. It's okay." She sat up straighter, wiping her eyes with the back of her hand. "I was freaking mad at you that Christmas. That's true enough. But the more I think about it, the more I have to admit to myself that running away was so much easier because I was scared to stay and face the truth."

"What's the truth?"

She twisted her lips to the side. She was quiet for a long time. "The truth is I didn't take the bar because I wasn't sure I wanted to be a lawyer."

"I don't understand."

"Dad was so proud of me and he was such a good prosecutor, and I just—after he died, I couldn't imagine not following through. He would be so disappointed in me." She covered her face with her hands.

I put my hand on her shoulder and thought. "Dorothy, all Dad wanted was for us to be happy."

"I know, but—"

"No, seriously. If he were here, he'd give you a hug and tell you he was still proud of you."

"For what? For running away? For blaming my sister for it?"

"Dorothy?"

"What?"

"I made it pretty easy. I was a little shit."

"No! I love you," she cried, and wrapped her arms around my neck, pressing her face into my shoulder.

"I love you too."

"You fucking bitch!"

The sound of Arlon's cry rang clear through the door, freezing my heart. There was a scream, a thud on the stairs, silence, followed by more screams.

And suddenly the commotion outside was so loud we couldn't make anything out at all.

"No gunshot?" Dorothy was pressing both hands against the door, as though she could will it with her mind to open.

"I didn't hear one." I pressed my ear against the door. It was quieter now, although I could hear a strange rushing sound. A door slammed somewhere overhead.

"West must have done something!" Dorothy said.

"Shit!" I leapt back. White smoke was pouring in from under the door and billowing up in the rays of light that broke through.

Dorothy pressed her ear against the door and then shot back. "The door is hot. Oh my God, I think there's a fire! Glinda, there's a fire!"

We both began banging on the door, hard.

"Let us out! We're still in here!" she screamed, and then turned to me, panic-stricken. "They wouldn't leave us, right? They wouldn't!"

"Of course not!" I lied. I backed up and rammed my shoulder against the door. It bowed slightly but stood firm.

I looked back at Dorothy. Now she was the one who appeared like she was going to hyperventilate.

I backed up and slammed my shoulder against the door again, willing it to give way.

"Please," I whispered to myself. "Just Dorothy, just get Dorothy out of here."

I knew it was no use. I'd spent days in this space trying to get out. We really were going to die in here. The police had left. The fire department would take ten minutes to get here, and that was if someone had actually called the fire in. We wouldn't last ten minutes. I fell back against the opposite wall and hugged my knees.

"What are you doing?" Dorothy gasped, coughing now. "You have to help me get this door open!"

"Dorothy, listen to me—" Just then we were washed in darkness. The power had gone out in the living room. Probably the whole house.

"No, no, no, no!" She pounded on the door. My eyes began to adjust, and then a brilliant orange light shone through the spaces around the door, letting me see her, shaking, one hand on the door, the other over her heart.

"Dorothy?"

"What?"

"Just come sit by me."

"Are you insane? Glinda, this closet is going to fill up with smoke, and we are going to die!" She squinted at me through the hazy rays of light. Slowly the recognition of our predicament showed on her face as the muscles relaxed, and the panic in her eyes dimmed to despair. She sank down next to me and took my hand. She was shaking. Hard.

"I'm sorry, Glinda. I should have believed you from the beginning," she choked out, her voice catching in her throat.

"No, it's my fault you're here. It's my fault that you're going to—I'm sorry, Dor."

She kissed my forehead, and then we pressed our heads together, eyes closed.

"It's only right," she finally sighed. "We came into this world together, and I sure as hell am not going to let you leave it without me."

I gasped back a sob and pulled back slightly so I could see her face.

A thick haze hung between us, but I had never seen her more clearly. There were no more masks, no more fake smiles, no more guards, just two authentic, broken people before each other, ready to face, together, whatever was to come.

And then a key turned in the lock, and the door swung open.

◆ 27 ◆

FREE AND DESTINED

I FOCUSED ON THE face and blinked several times in surprise. It was Jason. He reached in and grabbed us each by an arm, pulling us out into the heat.

The room was on fire. The sofa, the curtains, the wall. Thick black smoke streamed up from the flames and floated along the ceiling.

"Come on!" he shouted, gesturing to the front door.

"No!" I pulled back. "Where's my sister and my mom?"

Jason shot a look up the stairs, then turned back to us with a regretful shrug and ran out of the room.

Dorothy grabbed the railing and started up, but I grabbed her wrist.

"Go get help!" I cried.

"No! I'm coming!"

"We don't have time to argue! You're pregnant and we need help!" I yanked her backward and shoved her toward the dining room. I didn't wait to see if she went. I braced myself on the banister and looked up the stairs. Somehow the power was still on in the second level of the house. The landing was filling with smoke but was not yet on fire. I noticed a robe on the ground next to me. I picked it up, held it to my nose and mouth, and rushed up the stairs.

On the landing, the smoke was thick, but I could see lamplight streaking from underneath my mom's door.

I yanked it open, a cool breeze hitting my face. I jumped inside and closed the door behind me. The air was clear in here, for now.

I didn't know what I had been expecting, but it certainly wasn't the spectacle that greeted me upon entering the room.

My mother was standing with her back to me, holding the gun in shaking hands, pointing it right at Arlon. He was white and sweaty, and he was holding his hands up by his head. West was cowering behind my mom, crying.

"West!"

She looked up at me and her face brightened. "It was Mom! Mom called the cops! They didn't see anything and left, but it was her!"

I was having trouble processing. Mostly because the house was on fucking fire.

"We have to get out, now!" I yelled. "The house is on fire!"

"He did it! He pulled a burning log out of the fireplace and then made us come up here, but Mom grabbed the gun from him!" West hadn't moved. She was in shock. Shit.

"West, take this and cover your face." I held out the robe. She crept forward and took it from me. "Now go downstairs, stay low, and find help." I waved my hand behind me to motion her out.

West hugged me quickly and then raced out of the room without another word, leaving the door open. Smoke poured in. I closed it again, but now smoke was filtering in from under the door. The floor felt hot even through my shoes. We didn't have much time.

Mom kept the gun held up, pointed right at his chest. Arlon took a slow step backward, keeping his hands up, and sat down on the edge of the bed.

"Glinda, get out of here," my mother said, her voice trembling. She was still turned from me.

"Mom, it's okay, but we need to leave."

"Glinda, go!" She cocked the gun.

"Julie, my love! Don't do this! We can still be together!" Arlon sniveled.

"Enough!" My mom narrowed her eyes at him. "You need to shut up!"

And although I was facing death for like the third time in a couple of hours, happiness overtook me as I realized she was there, seeing through Arlon, finally.

"Mom, we need to get out of here."

She didn't move.

"I saw him put something in Brother Matthew's coffee. He said it was a vitamin. I should have known better. It's my fault."

"No! Mom, it is not your fault."

The gun shook in her hand, and her eyes narrowed.

"Mom, he's not worth it. Let's go. The police will come back. They'll arrest him."

"I'm so sorry." Her voice was shaking, and she began to weep softly. She moved her finger to the trigger. "I—I'm so tired."

"I know, Mom. It's okay." I looked at her frail frame, and it broke my heart all over again. She turned to me and gave me a pitiful smile, but one that shone out with authentic love and grief and broken pieces of a shattered soul.

I swallowed the lump in my throat and opened my mouth to tell her how much I loved her, how much I missed her, how much—and that's when Arlon made his move. While my mother's head was turned, he leapt from the bed and snatched the gun right out of her hand. In the same instant, he shoved her to the floor. She went tumbling, and the next thing I knew, I was holding my hands out in front of me as Arlon pointed the gun right at me. I was looking down the barrel, and everything was happening in slow motion.

I know I screamed, or maybe I only thought about screaming, but before I could hear the sound, I saw him pull the trigger and then—a sharp pain in the center of my forehead. I fell backward, crashing against the laundry hamper and then down to the floor. I lay there, not hearing anything, too stunned to move.

And then, like slides from an old projector, I saw feet coming through the doorway in sporadic moments. I heard screaming now, but it was faint and far away. There was Troy, right in my face. He was mouthing something.

I felt a sticky liquid drip from my head down into the palm of my hand. I rubbed my fingers together. There was a lot of it.

Two firefighters were there; one had a tight grip on Arlon's arm and was pushing him forward, through the smoke, into the hallway. The other firefighter had lifted my mom up and was carrying her out of the room.

Mom was safe. Dorothy was safe.

And I'd been fucking shot in the head.

• 28 •

OKAY AND NOT OKAY

"**G**LINDA? ARE YOU OKAY?"

Am I okay? I've been shot in the fucking head. I'm dying . . . again.

"I've been shot," I managed to whimper.

Troy rolled his eyes and then put his arms under me and lifted me up. I wrapped my arms around his neck. He was really sweaty—like, not in a sexy way. He stumbled a few steps and then stopped, lowering my feet to the ground.

"Okay, so apparently I can't actually carry you," he panted, and then started coughing.

"Leave me," I murmured.

"What? Why? Just walk."

"Walk?" I glared up at him, my arms still around his neck. "I've been shot in the head!"

"Glinda, look at your hand."

I glanced down, not wanting to see the blood. I closed my eyes, prepared myself, and then held my hand up to my face.

It was green.

It was neon green.

I put my fingers up to the sore spot on my forehead and rubbed it. No indentation. But now more green on my fingers.

He looked first at my forehead and then my eyes, and then he flashed that stupid, pretty smile of his. I'd missed it so much.

"Come on!" he insisted. He kept his arm around my back, under my arms, and helped support my weight as we staggered out into the hallway. The downstairs glowed orange now, and it was so hot that when I tried to take a breath, it felt like a piece of plastic was over my nose and mouth. We tumbled down the stairs together. At the bottom, an inferno had taken over the living room.

"Come on!" Troy shouted in my ear over the crackling and rushing of the flames. He pulled me into the dining room, and then we both dropped to the floor, where the air was cooler and the smoke was lighter. My knees caught on my stupid gown, and I fumbled forward, unsure of how far we had to go. He stayed behind me, pushing me forward.

The firefighters found us crawling on the floor toward the door. They dragged us out, where we fell in a tangled heap on the grass in the backyard.

One of the firefighters threw off his mask and helmet. "Stay put, I'm going to get the EMTs." He disappeared around the side of the house while the other firefighter stood watch over us.

I tried to stand, but my legs gave out under me, and I sank back down beside Troy.

"Glin, give yourself a minute."

"A minute? I don't need a minute! I need to know how the hell Arlon got a hold of your paintball gun."

"One of those guys took it off me when they grabbed me," I heard him say from far away. "Oh, and here." He held something small to me and dropped into my hand.

"What's this?"

"I'm not an idiot, Glin. I grabbed the memory card with the security footage, and then I found an old card in Mike's desk. The real footage is from the camera that overlooks the booth, camera five. The one I gave Arlon was labeled camera sixty-nine." He pushed his hair out of his face. He smiled and his teeth shone out in contrast with the streaks of ash on his skin. "Arlon just burned Mike's porn collection!"

As I looked down at the small black card with the tiny white label sitting on my green fingers, something in me cracked. I started laughing, a little giggle at first, and then it spun up into hysterics. I was holding my sides and laughing so hard tears were streaming down my face. No wait, was I actually crying? I wasn't sure. What I was sure of was that I'd finally lost it.

I felt arms wrapping around me, and for an instant I thought it was Troy, but then my mother's voice was whispering in my ear. "It's okay, shh." She pressed her forehead to mine.

"I—I—I can't!" I cried. I was hyperventilating. "Mom! Mommy!" She was shaking too.

"Shh," she murmured again.

"No! No! I need you! I'm not okay! I'm not okay!"

She pulled her head from mine and stared straight into my eyes. Her eyes were red and tired, but clear.

When she spoke again, her voice was barely audible. "I'm not okay either."

★ ★ ★

I made my way around the side of the house, like a sleepwalker. People kept saying things to me, their mouths moving, but I couldn't hear any of it. Someone slipped a clear mask over my face. In the front yard, James and Dorothy and about ten other pioneers were filling in a growing number of police officers on what had transpired. The other pioneers had disappeared.

"Ma'am?" an officer said, and I realized he'd been talking to me.

"Y-yes?"

"That's Glinda." James came up beside him. "She's the one I was telling you about."

"Ma'am, we're going to transport you to the hospital," the officer said.

"No. No, my mom. I'm fine. My mom needs help."

"She's coming too."

I was escorted to an ambulance, where an EMT helped me up and started asking me questions I couldn't answer. I looked out of the open doors where a half-dozen police cars were parked in front, lights flashing. Behind them, the firefighters were dousing my house with heavy jets of water as large plumes of white smoke billowed out the windows.

And then I saw Troy standing there, alone, in the center of the drive, and he was staring at me. There were probably twenty feet separating us, but it seemed like an impassable void. The police lights turned his skin blue, then red, then blue, then red, like a psychedelic fever dream.

The doors closed.

◆ 29 ◆

RECOVERING AND
REBUILDING

About three months later

M OM WAS SOUND ASLEEP, and I was drifting in and out, when
West flopped down beside me on our mother's bed. It was
probably afternoon. In the first few days since we'd come back to
live beside the ruins of our house, all my mom and I had done
was sleep. I'd craved sleep like a drug.

Now, three months later, I still enjoyed a long afternoon nap.

"Your hair stinks," I murmured into the pillow.

"Shut up," she mumbled back, and was soon snoring, her arm
draped across me.

When we woke up, it was evening. My stomach was growling and my head was pounding. My mom and West appeared in
much the same state. The three of us rose and stumbled into the
other room of the cramped trailer.

After Arlon was arrested, some of the cult members felt com-
pelled to help us by towing the defunct Starlight Pioneer Meeting
Hall trailer to our property, where they completely gutted it and
helped us refurnish it with things that had been saved from the
fire. It wasn't recognizable as the place where I had first witnessed
the madness that overtook my family. Still, I was all too ready to
be done with this trailer and all that Arlon Blight had touched.

There was light pouring from the open windows. The sofa
bed that James and Dorothy slept on was pulled out but made.
Mom, West, and I shared the bed in the other room. Along the
opposite wall in the main room, where once heavy curtains had

hung, were now rows and rows of framed photos and albums and other assorted personal items that Arlon had ordered be put in the barn or beside the trash, thus unintentionally saving them from the fire.

Dorothy called us outside, where she'd laid a checkered tablecloth over a picnic table in front of the trailer. On it were several pizza boxes, a couple beers, a six-pack of cream soda, and a store bakery cake with Elmo and a big number two.

James and Dorothy were sitting waiting for us.

"Happy belated birthday, West!" Dorothy came around and gave my sister a hug. "Sorry—this was the last cake in the case."

"It's wonderful, thank you! I'm starving." West tore open a pizza box and smiled happily at the vegetarian toppings.

I took a slice and sat down next to my mom.

The police who had initially answered the call hadn't seen anything outright illegal and were pressed by Arlon to leave. But they had remained suspicious after they left, and called for backup. When my mother confessed that she had been the one to call them, Arlon lost it. He took his robe and used it to grab a burning log and hurl it across the room in a fit of rage. Then he'd forced West and my mom up the stairs at gunpoint while the other pioneers evacuated. Well, all except Jason. He'd freed us and then run and untied Troy and James before vanishing into the night.

The house remained standing, though the entire downstairs had to be gutted, and the whole house needed work. Insurance gave us the cost for rebuilding while we waited it out in the trailer. West had decided to push back starting college until the spring semester, so we all five got to know each other again in that sardine can, talking, fighting, crying, laughing, becoming a family—not the same one as before, but stronger.

My mom and I each attended counseling. And I had this bad habit of dreaming that I was locked in the closet again, and the smoke was coming, choking me. Then I'd wake up, gripping West's shoulder. She'd whisper, asking if I was okay. I was okay. I had to be okay, because I'd gotten myself an interview last month and now had a job offer for a really, really good job in Chicago.

So, I was okay. I was okay to be on my own, really and truly on my own for the first time in my life. And I'd be okay to come back home for the trial and face Arlon and make sure he never again hurt anyone the way he'd hurt my mother.

I'd handed over the memory card to Detective Crumble, who, it turned out, was not a cult member. The card contained the complete footage of Arlon attempting to drown me and confessing to suffocating Beverly.

Arlon Blight, aka Donald Lanser, aka Wilfred Wagnor, had been on Crumble's radar in connection to some other items of interest concerning finances and fraud. Crumble seemed almost giddy at the prospect of adding murder, attempted murder, kidnapping, and assault to the list. Bryant and Mark were also going away.

So life had progressed since the night of the fire. I was getting my shit together, my mom was healing, and Arlon was locked up.

And Troy and I hadn't spoken since that night.

I had asked about him several times but was always met with pained looks and shrugs. What the hell was wrong with me? My mom was safe. My sister was back. We were all together, and everything was how I'd dreamed, for so long, it could be. And here I was, sitting with my mind elsewhere.

"You want a beer?" I held out a bottle to Dorothy, trying to get my inner dialogue off the subject of my pathetic little life. She looked at me with wide eyes and shook her head with little twitches, like she was trying to hide it from everyone else. I'd held onto her secret for months now, even as a tiny little bump had started growing under her flowy tops.

"Oh, shit. Sorry."

Her eyes got wider.

"What? What's going on?" West looked up from her new phone.

"Oh my gosh!" My mom covered her mouth with both her hands and gasped. "Are you—?"

Dorothy's cheeks were bright red, and she was nodding at our mom with excitement.

"I knew it!" Mom said.

"Seriously, what's going on?" West was looking around at each of us in confusion.

Mom leapt from her chair and was embracing both Dorothy and James, crying and laughing, and it was so amazing. Every awful thing that had ever happened was forgotten, just for that little moment. It was like old times, when my dad was alive. And I hadn't felt that since. So, it was true. It was possible to be happy again. To be really happy again.

Looking around at my sister and new brother and imagining their child, my very own niece or nephew, and seeing my mom, her face aglow, and my younger sister, still so clueless, made me laugh, I realized my family looked different, but the love, the joy, the life we all shared was the same as it had always been and as it would always be. And somewhere, somehow, my dad was damn proud of us.

And yet. All of this, all of them, it was great, it was wonderful, but it wasn't everything. I was still messed up, feeling like I was only a reflection in the glass of a family portrait. They were mine, forever, but maybe, just maybe, I wasn't theirs . . . not entirely.

I stood up, trying not to scrape the chair legs against the rocky earth. My mom looked up at me.

"What's wrong, Glinda? Where are you going?"

"Nothing's wrong. It's wonderful. I just need some air."

"We're outside already." West rolled her eyes and took another bite of pizza.

"Oh, Glinda . . ." My mother looked so worried now, and I hesitated.

"Let her go. It's okay." Dorothy gave me a knowing look and smiled, her eyes so serene, so warm.

I choked back my tears and fled around the side of the house, the sounds of my happy family floating behind me.

I blinked to keep the tears at bay. My hands gripped the bark of the small trees as I slid my way down the hill. The lights were ablaze above Lothlórien, thankfully untouched by Arlon's path of destruction.

I came to the clearing and practically fell against the rock, catching myself and then heaving several times. I was still trapped. Locked in that closet under the stairs. It didn't matter that it had been burned and boarded up, it was still there, opening its black mouth and swallowing me up.

Up there were people I'd fought for, and all I wanted was to be down here so they wouldn't hear me cry. I sniffed and tossed a stone into the river. It made little ripples that caught the reflection of the string lights.

"No place like home, huh?"

I turned to see Dorothy making her way to me. She sat beside me on the rock.

She seemed lighter somehow, like the whole time we'd been together in Oklahoma, she'd been carrying this heaviness, and she'd left it there.

"What's going on, Glinda?"

"I think I'm broken."

"You're not broken."

I looked back up at the house. The big window in the dining room was still there, and I could imagine it lit, could see my mom and James and Dorothy and West gathered around the table, eating.

Dorothy strung her arm through the crook of my elbow and leaned up against me. Her warmth, her energy, her smell washed over me, and I smiled. I mean, I told my face to smile— whether it cooperated or not, I have no idea.

"So, what's going on with Troy?" Dorothy asked.

As soon as I heard his name, my heart began pounding, hard. I felt hot and cold at the same time.

"I mean, you know as much as I do."

"That's not what I mean. Why haven't you two talked since the fire?"

She hadn't asked that question outright until now. I guess she'd wanted to wait until I was a little better. So at least she saw me as strong enough to talk about it now.

"I said some stuff to him. It's okay . . ." I looked up at the night sky and blinked back stinging tears.

Dorothy was watching me carefully. "You're not okay."

I nodded, not trusting myself to speak without betraying my emotions.

"Kid, I think we both know what's going on here," she said in a low voice.

"Yeah, I was a jackass to a friend, and now he isn't my friend." A stupid tear ran down my cheek. If I never cried again, it would be too soon.

"Okay, so, we might need to peel back some layers. What do you think?"

"What are you getting at?" I knew what she was getting at, but I didn't want to talk about it.

"Troy wants to be more than friends with you."

"He did. I'm pretty sure he's over that." I sighed.

"And you want to be more than friends with him?"

I hesitated. Of course I wanted to be more than friends with him. "No, I don't."

"What's going on with you?" Dorothy narrowed her eyes at me. "We're not in high school anymore, Glinda. You're a grown woman who is attracted to a grown man. What the hell is stopping you?"

What was stopping me? Talk about a loaded question.

"Well, for starters, he despises me and won't speak to me."

"Have you tried to talk to him?"

"No."

"Okay, so maybe he thinks you don't want to talk to him."

"Yeah, so let's pretend that's true. There's the other problem you said."

"What problem did I say?"

"I'm a grown woman and he's a grown man," I croaked. Dorothy just stared at me, a tiny smile just under the surface of her contemplative lips. "See, that's the problem. We are adults. And this would be like a real adult relationship. It'll matter. And I'll hurt him."

"What makes you say that?"

"I hurt everybody I care about. You, Mom, West. Everything I touch turns to shit," I grumbled, keeping my eyes focused straight ahead.

"Bullshit."

I rolled my eyes. "Okay, Dr. Ruth."

"I'm not sure who you're thinking of, but Dr. Ruth is the old sex lady."

"Oh." Dammit, why did she always know more than me?

"Glinda, I'm going to take a stab at psychoanalyzing you, which in itself is a large endeavor, but here we go: I think you're scared to get close to someone because you're afraid of losing them."

"That's not some great insight. That's everybody."

"No. Okay, I'll be more specific. The man you loved most in the world was Dad, and he died. He left you. And ever since then you've clung to me and Mom, afraid to lose us too. So now, you're terrified that if you let your guard down and let yourself feel something for Troy, then he's also going to leave you."

I sighed. "I'm not agreeing with you, but let's say you're right. Wouldn't I have a reason to be wary? Dad died. You left. Mom mentally checked out. West is leaving."

"West is leaving for college; she's not moving to Antarctica. And I came back, didn't I?"

"After a year and a half. And for how long?"

"I don't know yet." She reached over and squeezed my hand. "But I'm not leaving until we're okay again."

I wanted to believe her, but after so long it still felt like some kind of nasty trick. "What about Mom?"

"Counseling is going well for her. It's going well for you too, right?"

I started to say something sarcastic, but instead I bit the inside of my lip and nodded.

She narrowed her eyes. "But back to Troy."

"No."

"Yes. What happened, Glinda?" She paused. "I mean, that night with Patrick." Her voice was soft.

My eyes snapped up to hers. "Why are you bringing that up?"

"Because it occurred to me, that thing you'd said about sometimes the people we think we love are monsters. At the time, I assumed you were referring to Arlon."

"I was."

"And maybe someone else?"

"Maybe." I said it so quietly, I wasn't sure she'd heard me. I put my elbows on my knees and hid my face in my hands.

"You want to talk about it?" she asked, rubbing my back.

"Not really," I whispered.

"Have you talked to your therapist about it?"

I nodded, a couple tears trailing down my cheeks.

Dorothy embraced me and held me for a long time. I pressed my face into her shoulder. "It's okay," she said. "You don't have to tell me."

I pulled away and wiped my cheeks with the back of my hand. "Someday soon, I will want to talk to you about everything. But not yet. I'm still working through it," I said, avoiding her eyes.

She waited and then finally spoke. "You're strong. You know that, right?"

I didn't reply.

"You're strong and you're amazing, and one day, when you're ready, you're going to blaze ahead of all of us. No matter what you choose to do or who you choose to do it with, you're going to light the world on fire."

"Your choice of metaphors is always so inappropriate," I moaned, and Dorothy chuckled.

She looked up into my face; now it was her eyes reflecting the string lights above us. "Glin, there is one thing I need you to do, okay?"

"What's that?"

"I need you to love you."

I laid my head on her shoulder and closed my eyes. She kissed the top of my head and then rested her cheek there.

My heart felt like an origami swan unfolding, growing lighter and freer, even as I grasped at my chest with closed fists and tried not to heave. Strange, unearthly sounds came up from my throat, and I fell down into her lap, clutching at her.

"It's okay, I'm here. I got you now," she said softly, rubbing my back with one hand and cradling my head with the other. "Glinda, I believe in you."

"Okay," I finally breathed.

"Okay?"

"I'll try." I paused and then looked up at her. "Dorothy?"

"Yeah?"

"I thought of another one."

"Go ahead."

"Bushcraft Betty Crocker."

30

HONEST AND DESERVING

WHEN HE WASN'T AT his apartment, I knew exactly where to find him. And sure enough, as I pulled into the parking lot in my sister's car, I saw his van, parked under a light, facing the castle. It was night, but the moon was out, full and bright, lighting up the world. I got out and wandered through the eerily quiet fair grounds, my feet crunching in the gravel. He should have heard me coming. But when I turned the corner, there he was, sitting in Bessie's mouth, swinging his leg back and forth, staring off into the distance, completely unaware of my presence.

"You know what I find odd?"

He started and looked down at me, his eyes wide, his face pale, like he'd seen a ghost. He blinked several times and pushed the shock of seeing me down, resuming his cool demeanor.

I continued. "That you'd come back here—since, you know, it doesn't mean anything to you."

"I just came to get a bag of weed I stashed under Bessie." He patted his pants pocket and continued swinging his leg.

"Troy, you love this stupid place." I took a step closer, and his leg swinging slowed to a stop.

"What did you say about this place?" he said. "Oh yeah. That it was full of man-boys that never stopped playing pretend."

"You remembered that, huh?"

He swung both legs over the edge and then leapt down, landing in front of me and straightening up to look me square in the eye. His eyes had some anger left in them, but mostly, they looked dull and empty. Like someone had just reached inside and ripped out that silly, carefree guy I knew, leaving behind a shell.

I couldn't breathe.

He looked at me as long as he could and then shifted his gaze down, shoved his hands in his pockets, and rocked back on his heels.

Why did this hurt so damn bad? All I wanted to do was throw my stupid arms around him and take back every word I'd said. All I wanted was for him to put his hands in my hair and kiss me hard and then make some stupid joke about how he'd known I wanted him all along. But that wasn't gonna happen. We were past that.

"Shit, I'm sorry, Glinda." He sighed and suddenly his eyes seemed to come back to life and he was familiar again, if not still a little distant. "I had rehearsed what I'd say to you if I saw you—*when* I saw you again—and . . . and then you're here, and here I'm sticking my foot down my throat." He raked his hair with his hand. "Are you okay? I mean, James has been keeping me updated. But, damn, the stuff they did to you . . . God, I'm such an asshole."

"Hey, stop spiraling. I'm the one who spirals." I laughed and he relaxed a little. "I'm good, Troy. I mean, I'm getting better. Counseling is going well for me and my mom." I shrugged. "You know, I've always felt like a screw-up, and I think the thing missing from my life really was a good dose of PTSD." I played it deadpan until a smile cracked, and then he smiled back and wiped his mouth with the back of his hand.

"You seem like your old self," he said.

"Oh God, I hope not!" I laughed.

"How's the house coming?"

"Um, the contractor said it should be move-in ready by Thanksgiving."

"That's great."

"Yeah."

"James said you're leaving." He licked his lips, and I could see a pained look in his eyes.

"Um, yeah. That's part of why I came to find you. Chicago. I got a job."

"That's really great."

"Yeah."

We glanced around for a moment, avoiding each other's eyes. The awkwardness grew. He really was over me. Here I was telling him I was leaving and . . . well, nothing.

I pulled my new phone from my pocket and held up the selfie he'd saved on it that day by the lake. "Thank you, by the way."

"Oh, that." He mumbled, kicking the dirt with his shoe. "It really wasn't that hard. Just had to move every photo—one at a time—from the trash folder, because I couldn't hook it up with the cloud since you had no service. So, actually it was kinda hard. It took forever." I let him ramble while I listened to his voice, the sound of it, the cadences I'd missed more than I knew. He was close enough to reach out and put my arms around him, but I didn't move.

"Thank you. It meant the world to me," I said softly.

"I didn't think you were going to want to see me again," he interjected, like he'd been trying to keep it in and just couldn't anymore.

"I didn't think you'd want to see me!" I burst out. *Oh no, here it comes.* "I said some terrible shit to you. You know I didn't mean a word of it. I wanted to push you away because . . . because I was scared, and I didn't think I was one of those people who . . ." I trailed off.

"I know you didn't mean it. But it still hurt."

I blinked back tears. "I'm sorry."

"It's fine."

"It's not fine. It's not. And I wanted to wait until I'd had some time to process and work on myself before I came and told you." A huge lump was forming in my throat.

"Yeah, well, the thing is . . ." He blew out a long breath, like he was working up his nerve. "I need to tell *you* something."

He took my hands in his. I couldn't tell if his hands were trembling or mine. I started to pull away. This wouldn't work. I was incapable of being that vulnerable with someone. I'd break him, or worse, he'd break me.

"Troy, listen—" I started and stopped. "I'm cold. Are you cold?"

He shook his head. "No."

"My teeth are chattering. I can't seem to—maybe I should go—or—"

"Wait."

I kept talking. "Okay, listen, I've given this a lot of thought, I mean, at least for me and—"

"Wait," he said, so firmly this time I stopped and looked up into his eyes.

There was something different about him. He seemed older, clearer, and steady. The muscles around his mouth were tight as he spoke. His words came out with his usual earnestness, but there was something else about them that sent little shivers down my neck and flushed my cheeks hot.

He squeezed my hands and took a breath. "I need to say something, and I need you not to speak, just for a minute."

"Okay, but—"

"No," he said quietly, and shook his head. "Please." I nodded, trying to swallow the lump in my throat. "And after I've said it, if you walk away, I won't follow, I won't bother you again. Okay?"

I nodded, silent.

"I'm not like you, Glinda. I'm not super smart or quick or whatever. I get it. You are going to go out there and do amazing things with your life, and I'm here, reliving this stupid job in my head before they demolish it. I'm here, broke and stupid, with no plan and no idea what the hell I'm doing." He pulled my right hand up to his chest, right above his heart. I could feel the softness of the shirt and under it, his skin, warm and firm, and under that, the hurriedness of his heartbeat. He was scared.

"I care a lot about you." His eyes darted to the ground and then back up at me, simultaneously pleading and piercing straight through me. "No, no. I think I—I just—I love you."

My heart came to screeching stop. *"What?"* I laughed nervously. "Don't be stupid. I'm not someone people fall in love with. I mean, I—"

"No, no more bullshit, Glinda. Sorry, but stop. You deserve better than me, I know, but you also deserve better than the way you talk about yourself. And I know you've said that this is an unrequited thing, and I can respect that, but I will never forgive myself if I don't tell you exactly how I feel." He rubbed his thumb over the top of my hand and looked into my eyes. "I just wonder if you might love me too, but you're too scared or proud—or maybe too smart—to admit it. So, yeah, that's what I needed to say." The corners of his mouth quivered as he waited for my response. I slipped my hands out of his and bowed my head.

He nodded sadly, dropped his hands to his sides, and shrank back several steps.

"You're not stupid!" I blurted out. "You want me to speak nicely to myself? Well, samesies! You're not stupid, Troy. Not even a little bit."

He gave me a weak smile, one tinged with sadness. That had been easy enough to say, but the next thing I needed to say was now stuck in my throat.

It was weird. I'd never been one to not have anything to say, but suddenly my mind went blank and only one thing was left. And that one thing scared the shit out of me.

I was choking on my own heartbeat.

"You see, the thing is . . ."

He looked up in surprise.

"The thing is, Troy . . . you're my Bigfoot."

"*What?*" He looked down at his feet in confusion.

I laughed. I could breathe again. "No, sorry, that is to say, you're the thing I've been looking for, the person that I believe in, but also the one I've been running from because I'm scared, and I'm pretty sure I'm going to fuck this up. But I *do* believe in you and, I guess, in me. That's weird to say."

He shook his head. "I don't understand."

"I love you too, you idiot!"

I felt weightless all at once, like I had broken through the atmosphere. My stupid face couldn't stop smiling, and I couldn't stop the hot tears rising up in my eyes.

"Really?" He whispered the word so softly I could barely hear him.

I nodded and those dumb tears spilled over my lids. Was this what it felt like to let go? My smile only got bigger, and I laughed. "I love you, Troy. I want to shout it from the rooftops! I love you, and I want to be with you."

He didn't smile back, and for a second my heart dropped, and I thought I'd screwed up. But in two strides he was by side, pulling me close. He cradled my head in his hands and kissed me—not hard like I expected, but with this tenderness that I just melted into.

All the fear, all the self-regulation and rules I'd made up for myself, all the butterflies when he smiled at me, all the stolen kisses and wistful glances, all the moments that should have been but weren't because I was too stuck in my own head—all of it exploded into fireworks in my chest as our lips touched.

He pulled away, his hands still gently cupping my face, and looked at me, his lips slightly apart, his eyes wide in disbelief. "Glin, you have no idea," he whispered, and his eyes were glassy. "You left—I was mad at you, and I let you go, and then I—I'm a fucking idiot—"

"Nope, you're not." I pushed up on my toes and kissed him again. This time, when we came apart, I saw a single tear trailing down his cheek.

"I thought you were dead. I saw him—in the tank—I jumped in and pulled you out, and God, I thought you were dead. You were so pale and you weren't breathing and—the look on your face—"

"Pretty grim?" I guessed.

"No, worse than that. It was *peaceful*, serene even," he continued, his voice ragged and low. "I held you there on the ground, screaming for the others, and I looked into your face and thought, *She's already gone. She's gone, and I let her go. It's my fault.*" He dropped his hands and rubbed his eyes with his thumb and index finger.

"Troy?"

He shook his head and looked at me, a man searching for reprieve.

"First and foremost, I've discovered therapy, and I'm going to put my counselor's number in your phone." I waited for him to crack a tiny smirk. Then I wiped his cheek with the tips of my fingers and continued. "Second, I thought I was dying too. And you know what? It was okay. I mean, it's not something I'd like to repeat, but it was okay because I thought of you. Yes, *you*. In my final moments, you were there, comforting me. And I need you to hear me, okay? Absolutely none of this was your fault . . . except the good parts. Because—"

He pressed his lips against mine before I could finish. They were warm and inviting, and he sucked on my bottom lip ever so slightly when I pulled away. Then he put his hands on my waist and spun us around and lifted me up onto Bessie's scaly, clawed hand, where I wrapped my legs around his waist and my arms around his neck.

We were breathing hard, trading each other's breaths, getting high off our exhales.

"Do you wanna get out of here?" he murmured.

"Nah."

"But I feel like she's watching us." He glanced up toward Bessie's open mouth above our heads.

"Troy, I'm having an emotional breakthrough. Okay?"

"Okay." He smiled.

Then he pressed his forehead against mine, and we both breathed hard, eyes closed, taking in the scent of each other and the night.

"You actually—you actually love me?" he said softly, like he was still in shock.

"Yes. Now shut up and make out with me before I have another existential crisis."

He shrugged, and I shoved my tongue down his throat.

"Wait." He pulled away again. "If they're—is this—I mean like, *my* cousin and *your* sister—so should we be . . .?"

"What are you even talking about?"

"Is this legal?" he asked, his brow furrowed, and gestured between the two of us.

"Oh my lord, Troy. That's not a thing."

"It's not?"

"No."

"Okay, good."

And I kissed him again before he could say anything else. He loved me and I loved him. And I was deserving of it. Of all of it.

31

PEACEFUL AND PURPOSEFUL

I FOLDED A SHIRT and slipped it into my red suitcase.

"I shouldn't go," I said to Dorothy as she came into the room. "The house will be done soon, and y'all are going to have so much work unpacking and—"

"Oh, you're going. I've already bought the paint to turn your old room into the nursery." She was holding a green robe, washed and folded, in her arms.

"What the hell are you doing with that?"

"I thought you might want a memento from this dark chapter of the Glass Family Farm."

"Thanks, I'll pass. Living in this trailer has been enough of a reminder to last me a lifetime."

She shrugged and set the robe on top of the dresser. Then she laid a piece of paper on top of the robe.

"What's that?" I asked.

She grinned. "Confirmation of my registration for the bar exam."

"What?" I yelped, and looked at her in surprise.

"Yeah, I'm going to freaking do it already."

My jaw literally dropped, and I stared at my sister in shock. "But . . . but I thought you didn't want to be a lawyer!"

"I'm scared. I've been scared. What if I spent all these years studying, and I'm terrible? But the thing is, going through this whole thing with Mom, I realized what I really want to do." Her eyes lit up as she spoke. "There's a firm in Dallas that specializes in abuses of power and undue influence. I'm going to stop the next Arlon Blight before more people get hurt."

"Dorothy! That's freaking amazing!"

She was adorably pregnant now, with a large bump under her flowered dress. She was also incredible and strong, and I was so damn proud of her, for everything she'd made her life into. She told me more as I folded clothes, and then eventually I looked down at the open suitcase and sighed. There wasn't anything left to pack.

"I shouldn't go," I said again.

"What are you talking about? You've already leased an apartment."

"So, I lose the deposit."

"Glinda, this isn't just a job—it's a good job. This is the kind of job people don't turn down."

I sighed and knelt down to zip the suitcase closed. "I just think with Mom, and with you doing this amazing thing with your life, and then the baby—"

"Glinda Rainbow Glass, we have spent the last month talking this to death. We're in the final stages of getting the conservatorship, and Mom is in counseling. James and I are living here with her. That's it. She's going to be fine. She's already made so much progress."

"She burned an effigy of Arlon last night. You think that's particularly healthy?"

"Glinda, Mom was eccentric before the cult, and she's going to be eccentric after."

"I think *eccentric* might be downplaying it a bit."

"You think I can't handle it?" Dorothy ran her tongue over her teeth.

"I know you can."

"You'll be back for the trial," Dorothy pointed out.

"Oh, I'll be back before that for this baby person." I looked up at the little bump and smiled.

"I know you will."

"You are going to text me the second you feel contractions," I demanded.

"I will." She rolled her eyes.

"And I already told West that whenever the baby shower gets planned, to let me know immediately so I can book a plane ticket."

"We will. Lord, maybe *you* should have a baby."

"Oh hell no!"

Dorothy smirked. "Ha, didn't think so."

"Okay," I said.

"Okay," she said back. "You want a cup of coffee before you head out?"

I wrinkled my nose. "I don't like coffee, remember?"

And then there really wasn't anything left to say. I was going. After all this time I had been so desperate to put my family back together, and now I was leaving. I wasn't leaving for school with the intention of coming back for the summers. And I wasn't getting an apartment ten minutes away so that my mom wouldn't be in my business all the time but so I could still pop by and do my laundry. This was a new blank page for the family and my childhood home, and I wasn't going to be here to see it off. Nope. I was leaving. End of chapter.

We stepped out of the trailer together and were greeted by our mom, who was just finishing up a phone call.

"Hey, Mom." I set the suitcase down.

"I just got off the phone with the contractor, and he said it was okay to go inside and see the house before you go!" She was so excited that I didn't have the heart to tell her I didn't want to tour the house before I left. So I nodded, and the three of us walked up the drive and pushed open the sheet of plastic that was covering where a front door should be.

The smell of fresh paint and cut wood hit me as I stepped into the living room. The floors were still concrete; the fireplace was just sheetrock; the outlets were just rectangular holes with wires poking out; and the walls were white.

"Bobby said that the upstairs is basically finished," Mom said from behind me. Dorothy and Mom wandered into the kitchen to check out the new cabinets, and I heard her say, "We will have to start burning desert sage in the nursery to get the paint smell out."

"No, Mom, we aren't burning anything in the baby's room."
Their conversation drifted out of earshot.

I stood at the foot of the stairs and looked up. The last
time I'd looked up those stairs I was facing a wall of flames
and smoke and impending death. The stairs were still only plywood, but the new banister had been installed, a sleek, modern iron and dark wood. The whole house was going to look
so different—less homey, more polished and updated, and . . .
empty. I slid my hand along the new banister as I traced up the
steps.

On the landing, I saw my door, freshly painted and ajar. I
timidly pushed it open and stepped into my bedroom. It was
strange, barren, with crisp white walls and hardwood floors
where a mossy-green carpet used to be. This wasn't my room.
This would be a nursery for Dorothy's child. This would be a
great room. But it wasn't mine.

Life was rearranging things, the way it does, and adding and
subtracting until nothing was the same.

Back outside, James was loading things into the back of the
van. He came up and stuffed his hands in his pockets.

"So, hey, um, I just wanted to wish you good luck and stuff."
He cleared his throat and then looked at me. "It's been fun getting to know you better."

"You too." I smiled. "And good luck finding Bigfoot here in
Texas."

"Oh, Texas is a mecca for Sasquatch sightings!" His eyes lit
up, and I couldn't help but grin. I turned to Dorothy, trying to
wipe the stupid smile off my face.

"You made a baby with that man."

"I'm aware." She smirked.

I bent down and whispered at her stomach. "It's okay, little
one. Aunt Glinda is going to be here to make sure you grow up
with some kind of sense of normalcy."

Dorothy swatted me off, laughing. And then James grabbed
me in a bear hug, and Dorothy joined him.

"Just promise me you won't name the poor kid something
weird," I said as he let me go.

"Weird? What's weird about Nessie?" James asked with feigned innocence.

"I thought we'd settled on Cthulhu." Dorothy looked down and rubbed her stomach, fighting back a smile.

"Over my dead body—"

"Glinda!" West cut me off, flying out of the trailer, her phone in her hand and her face red.

"What's the matter?"

"Gah, Glinda! I just got my first college roommate assignment!"

"Okay? What's the problem?"

"Her name is Emily Blakenstone, and she's an English major who plays oboe!"

"And?"

"And she wrote me a five-page email, rambling on and on about life and philosophy and how she tried to teach herself Elvish. Effing Elvish!"

I strained my neck like I was trying to find the issue in my sister's face. She scoffed.

"She's *you*. I'm starting my freshman year a semester late, and now I'm rooming with a Glinda? A big ol', weird, talks-too-much Glinda." West seemed horrified at the notion.

"It builds character," Dorothy said, patting her on the shoulder.

I stepped forward to my mother, who was waiting for me, already crying. "Mom, no. I can't leave you like this."

She put her hands on my shoulders and looked right into my eyes. "I am so very proud of you." She let out a breath. "But it's time for you to stop trying to save me. You're going to start your own life."

"Yes, but—"

"And you can always come home, sweetheart, but my prayer for you is that you won't want to. Not because you don't want to be here, but because your home is someplace else with someone else."

She nodded toward Troy, who was leaning against the door of the van, watching me with wonderment. Our eyes locked, and we both started grinning like idiots. I couldn't stop smiling when I was with him.

I turned back to my mother. "Yeah, well, we'll see, right? We'll see what happens."

She bent forward and gave me a kiss on the cheek. I hugged them all again and again, and then I turned away and climbed up in the van with Troy. James secured the last piece of luggage and slammed the door closed.

We were alone. Like, really alone now.

Troy had already endured several of my panic attacks and night terrors, when I'd wake up screaming, "Let me out!" Each time, he'd held me and brought me back down so I could sleep again. Could he handle that weeks, months, or years out? He said he could. He was so sure of it that he was moving to Chicago with me. I wasn't as confident. But he was here now, and that was enough. I didn't have certainty, but I had hope. And I had my family. The star pendant that my mom used to wear was now dangling from the rearview mirror. Troy took a sip from a thermos of water and then set it down.

"You're not drinking MaXout?"

"Nah. I decided I should probably give up energy drinks for my health."

"Oh wow. I'm proud of you."

"Don't be yet." He laughed. "You're stuck in this van with me for the rest of the day and I am going to have a raging caffeine-withdrawal headache by this afternoon. It's gonna be bad."

"Great." I tried to look annoyed, but when his eye caught mine, I burst out laughing.

It's strange how one part of your life can eclipse everything else. Grief had been a big black cloud, blocking the light and keeping me from seeing anything. Suddenly there were sunrays again, piercing through the cloud and breaking it up into smaller pieces.

I could see now that life was not all sun, and it was not all shadow. Those dark clouds would always be there, casting objects into relief, creating definition, authenticity. I was etched in light and darkness.

Troy took my hand. A giddiness swept through me. He glanced down at my wrist, where a few adjustments to my tattoo had been made a couple nights before:

Why Wander with Purpose?

After all, it's the sidetracks that end up getting you where you want to be. It's the happenchance that gets you home. He squeezed my hand and looked up at me.

"Why do you keep looking at me like that?" I asked as he started the engine.

"Like what?"

"Like you're confused about something."

"Oh, I was just trying to figure out what it is about you that gets me to agree to driving you long distances at the drop of a hat."

"Shut up! You volunteered!" I secured my seat belt and adjusted the sun visor. "Do you know how to get there?"

"No, but as long as I'm with you, it doesn't matter where we end up." He gave me a cheeky wink.

"Actually, it does matter. It matters quite a bit. I'm supposed to start at work on Monday."

"I'll get you there. I promise." And his sudden sincerity hit me so hard that for once I had no comeback.

He pulled out onto the main road.

I'd forgotten to look back.

ACKNOWLEDGMENTS

THIS BOOK WOULD NOT exist without the support and expertise of a great many people. To you all, I am forever indebted.

First, to my family, you are my inspiration and my purpose. Robert, thank you for the years of supporting me and pushing me, and always, always believing in me. Thank you for reading all my rough first drafts, listening to me go on and on about plot holes, and keeping the kids busy while I worked. To my girls, your imaginations are amazing and, frankly, pretty bizarre. I can't wait to read your books someday.

To my mom, Karen, thank you for instilling a love of books and reading in me from a young age. And that goes to all the women in my family, especially my grandma. And mom, I'm sorry I wrote the F word and S word so many times.

Thank you to Jennifer Baxter, my sweet sister, who has been a cheerleader for this book throughout!

Three people have influenced this story more than anyone else: to Laura Mae DuPuy, Arianne Jaco, and Mark Dye, the three of you are so interwoven in the words on these pages that without you, this book would be a hollow shell of itself.

To my agent, Cameron McClure, what can I say? You saw something in my work that other people couldn't see yet, and you brought it to life. You took a chance on me and this weird little story about a cult, and here we are! Thank you, thank you, thank you!

And then there's Jess Verdi, my editor. Your vision and passion for this project is incredible. You made this book sing. Thank you for believing in Starlight and polishing it into something great! And to the whole team at Alcove: Rebecca Nelson, Madeline Rathle, Dulce Botello, Hannah Pierdolla, Jill Pellarin, and others, you've answered my stupid questions, fixed my embarrassing typos, and made this into a book. Thank you!

Appreciation to Mrs. Banner, Dr. Felps, and countless other teachers and friends and family who have always pointed me in this direction. I can't list everyone here, but please know I love you and acknowledge you!

To the incredible family I've made at the Dallas–Fort Worth Writer's Workshop, thank you for always being real with me; tearing me down in the most loving ways; and always, always supporting me. Some of the people I need to thank are John Bartell, Sally Hamilton, A. Lee Martinez, Rosemary Clement, Leslie Lutz, Brooke Fossey, Helen Dent, Sarah Terentiev, Dylan Larkin, Ed Isbell, Maureen Davis, Katie Bernet, and the brilliant Dana Swift. There are too many people to mention, but please know I appreciate you just as much! And to Elise Hanna, thank you for dragging my butt to that first meeting and for being a lifelong friend and creative soul sister.

And finally, to my dumb cats, who walked across my keyboard, knocked over countless glasses of water on my desk, and yowled at me to give them a second breakfast while I was trying to work . . . you know what? Never mind—y'all are both assholes.